Flying Cups and Sauc

FLYING CUPS & SAUCERS

Gender Explorations in Science Fiction & Fantasy

EDITED BY DEBBIE NOTKIN
& THE SECRET FEMINIST CABAL.

EDGEWOOD PRESS ⊞ 1998

Dedication

In gratitude, to Virginia Kidd

in memoriam, to Judith Merril

the real founding mothers

ACKNOWLEDGMENTS

The Secret Feminist Cabal is everywhere, and nothing that the Tiptree Award committee has accomplished could be done without them. We welcome every reader of this anthology to join. More specifically, you wouldn't hold this book without the efforts of:

Tiptree Founding Mothers Karen Joy Fowler and Pat Murphy for tireless energy supporting the award in general and this book in particular.

Freddie Baer, John D. Berry, and Jeanne Gomoll for making the book beautiful.

Scott Custis, for the thankless job of keeping the accounts.

Jim Hudson and Diane Martin, backed by the entire WisCon committee, for sales and record-keeping.

Barb Gilligan, M.L. Konett, Zed Lopez, and Cecelia Tan for essential bits and pieces along the way.

And, of course, James Tiptree, Jr., without whom . . .

MANUFACTURED IN THE UNITED STATES OF AMERICA.
Book design by John D. Berry and Jeanne Gomoll.
Printed by Braun-Brumfield, Inc..

Cover art by Freddie Baer

Edgewood Press
PO Box 380264
Cambridge, MA 02238
booksales@sf3.org
http://www.sf3.org/tiptree/index.htm

Contents

DEBBIE NOTKIN
Why Have a Tiptree Award?

IF YOU WERE BORN BEFORE 1959, you remember where you were when John Kennedy was shot in 1963. If you were any way involved in the fan and professional science fiction communities (and even the littlest bit interested in gender roles in the field), you remember where you were when you learned that James Tiptree, Jr., was a woman.

In fact, I remember where I was when I learned that Tiptree *wasn't* a woman.

But to understand that (in case you weren't involved in this community – or weren't born – in the mid 1970s) you might want a little background.

There have always been women in science fiction. In fact, it's perfectly legitimate to argue that a woman wrote the *first* science fiction novel: what else would you call *Frankenstein*? In this century, we have Leigh Brackett, and C.L. Moore, and Andre Norton, and Marion Zimmer Bradley, and a host of others, whose contributions are legion and should never be underestimated. However, almost none of them wrote under names conclusively identifiable as female, and most of them were consistently lauded for the "fine male qualities" of their writing.

There have also always been gay people, and gender transgressors in science fiction. Their history is chronicled, sometimes directly and sometimes between the lines, in thousands upon thousands of crumbling pages of mimeo ink on Twiltone paper, and no one has yet done a good enough job of telling their story. I'm not even going to try, but here are a few examples:

Forrest J. Ackerman, the grand old man of the horror film community, was an honorary male Daughter of Bilitis (a lesbian club) in the 1930s. Many of the people in that circle, including Marion Zimmer Bradley, were prominent gender radicals. (Bradley wrote lesbian fiction under a pseudonym.)

James Kepner, founder of the International Gay and Lesbian Archives, was an active fan in Los Angeles in the 1940s.

Theodore Sturgeon's pioneering "The World Well Lost," which treats homosexuality very sympathetically, was first published in 1953.

In the 1950s, there was another shift in the gender history of the science fiction community. Women began to change the face of the field *as women,* writing and editing under their own names. Virginia Kidd and Judith Merril, the two women to whom this book is dedicated, stand out in this context. Kidd has been a literary agent for many decades, shepherding the careers of (among others) Ursula Le Guin and Anne McCaffrey. Merril, of course, edited the extraordinary *Best Science Fiction of the Year* series that was among my early introductions to the literature that would become my home. Kidd and Merril were closely followed by a number of women whose careers began in the late 50s and early 60s: Cele Goldsmith Lalli, the editor at *Amazing* who discovered and/or encouraged the fine writers of the 60s: Roger Zelazny, Samuel R. Delany, Thomas Disch, Ursula Le Guin. And the writers themselves, writing under their own gender-visible names: Anne McCaffrey, Kate Wilhelm, Katherine MacLean, and Joanna Russ.

One way to trace the changes in the field in this period is by looking at the awards. The science fiction field has two major awards: the Hugo Award (named for editor Hugo Gernsback and selected by popular vote of the members of each year's World Science Fiction convention) and the Nebula Award (given by the Science Fiction Writers of America). Both are given in several categories, including fiction at varying lengths. The Hugo has been presented since 1953. Anne McCaffrey was the first woman to win in a professional category, in 1968, her award was a tie with a story by Philip José Farmer. Before that time, all women Hugo winners had won in the fannish categories, and had shared the awards with men – generally with their husbands. Also in 1968; McCaffrey and Kate Wilhelm were the first women to win Nebulas, an award that had then been in existence just a few years. Gay (and black) author Samuel R. Delany won three Nebula Awards in the first three years of the award's existence and his unforgettable short story "Aye and Gomorrah," which won in 1967, was the first major work about gender (and sex!) to win an award in the field.

The scales were irrevocably tipping, and the balance changed fast. *The Left Hand of Darkness* by Ursula Le Guin swept the novel awards for 1970 (no woman had ever won the coveted Best Novel award before), and she won again in 1972. In 1973, James Tiptree, Jr. got his first Nebula, and by that time Joanna Russ's incontrovertibly radical "When It Changed" had also been honored.

We return now to our regularly-scheduled discussion of the gender of James Tiptree, Jr.

I bought *Analog* off the stands in a New York subway station in December 1973 (even though I rarely read the magazines), simply because it had a new Tiptree story featured on the cover. After I'd read "The Women Men Don't See," I started announcing flatly to my friends that Tiptree was a woman. No man, I said, could have written that story.

Chelsea Quinn Yarbro told me I was wrong. She was in regular correspondence with "Tip" (as we all called the writer of those fine stories, as well as the ubiquitous letters and postcards that Tip, despite his passion for never meeting people, sent with the slightest encouragement). She pulled out correspondence about being a spook for the CIA, about traveling alone in the Yucatan, about other very male adventures. She convinced me.

And once I thought about it, I was delighted. If a man could write "The Women Men Don't See," the world was a little more complex, and held a little more hope for a meeting of the sexes, than I had previously imagined.

In 1975, in the introduction to the second collection of Tiptree short stories, Robert Silverberg (who would quite reasonably love it if we would all forget this anecdote) stuck his neck out and said:

> Inflamed by Tiptree's obstinate insistence on personal obscurity, science-fictionists have indulged themselves in the wildest sort of speculation about him.... It has been suggested that Tiptree is female, a theory that I find absurd, for there is to me something ineluctably masculine about Tiptree's writing. I don't think the novels of Jane Austen could have been written by a man nor the stories of Ernest Hemingway by a woman, and in the same way I believe the author of the James Tiptree stories is male.

I certainly believed him. Tiptree had, in fact, been thoroughly trounced in the round-robin symposium published in a fanzine called

Khatru (edited by Jeff Smith) for his male pronouncements on subjects women clearly understood better.

And, as I said above, I was actually pretty glad that Tiptree was a man; I liked a world which contained men who were capable of that kind of perception of women.

Not too long after the publication of the Silverberg essay, I got a phone call from one of my best friends, author Elizabeth A. Lynn.

"Debbie," she said, "I have *great* news!"

"Wonderful!" I said. "What?"

"I can't tell you."

We're still friends. When I think about that phone call, I'm not sure why.

"But you'll hear about it in a week or so," she said.

I spent the next week chewing my fingernails and trying to imagine great secret news. Had Liz sold a novel for six figures (at that time, no one in SF ever had) but the deal wasn't signed? Was someone getting married? Or divorced?

No. James Tiptree, Jr., was revealed as Alice Sheldon.

Panic ensued. None of us knew how to react. We had all been convinced by a very convincing story that fit the things we knew about gender. Tip's closest correspondents felt lied to. Some people, like Lizzy Lynn, were simply delighted. I was profoundly disappointed (and a little smug – after all, I'd seen it in the texts; I'd just been convinced not to believe my own ears). Bob Silverberg, of course, was mortified (and issued a *very* gracious apology).

Actually, I think most of us were suffering from a condition that had not been named in 1975: we were encountering genderfuck. We may have been comfortable with homosexuality, but we hadn't done much questioning of gender roles. Transsexuals were a very weird phenomenon only seen on the tabloid edges of the news. Cross-dressers were "sick" and best treated with psychoanalysis, or else they were really closet gays, and just needed to come to terms with their own desire. Intersexuals, of course, did not exist (quite literally, since most of them were – and still are – surgically "altered" for the peace of mind of doctors and parents). And virtually no one had had the experience of having someone who was actively part of their social circle (even if an invisible part) Change Sex.

Overall, we coped. Tiptree wrote a lovely essay called "Only the Signature Was a Lie," simultaneously apologizing and skillfully pointing out that we had all seen what we wanted to see. Everyone took the news in our own different ways and the science fiction world went on about its evermore feminist, gender-exploring business.

John Varley started to publish, so an unmistakable man was writing brilliantly and insightfully about the condition of women. The third Tiptree collection came out with an introduction by Ursula Le Guin explaining about Alice Sheldon. Gay women, as well as men, were writing, and sometimes their characters (and the characters of straight authors) were also gay.

The late Susan Wood, professor of Canadian literature and leading SF fan and critic, began leading feminist panels at conventions, starting in 1976. Then she instituted the "Room of Our Own" feminist spaces at a variety of conventions. Most of them were "men-welcome" space, but they were still different from anywhere we'd been before. We all began talking to one another in new ways, and Tiptree/Sheldon, though she never came to conventions, was frequently one of the topics.

The tables turned again and the 1970s became "the Me decade." Cyberpunk became exciting and some of the new writers/commentators tried to erase Joanna Russ and Ursula Le Guin and Vonda McIntyre and Suzy McKee Charnas and and and... Nonetheless, more and more women writers were entering the field. (Vonda once said, "Science fiction will come of age when mediocre female writers get published as regularly as mediocre male writers do." I don't think anyone would argue that that day has long since come.) It became *de rigueur* for even the most egregiously sexist male authors to include active female characters. Much water flowed under many bridges.

In 1991 my phone rang again. It was Pat Murphy, two-time Nebula winner, fresh from her guest-of-honor stint at WisCon, the "feminist SF convention" held annually in Madison, Wisconsin. "Debbie," she said, "At WisCon Karen and I invented a new science fiction award!" (Karen Joy Fowler is another fine writer and a good friend of Pat's. The two of them are card-carrying troublemakers.)

"Oh, really?"

"Yes. It's an award for works of science fiction that explore and expand gender roles. We're naming it after James Tiptree."

"That's a fine idea."

"Would you chair the first panel of judges and help us figure out how we can make this work?"

And that's why you hold this book in your hands.

Oh, in case you were wondering? Pat and I are still friends too.

Flying Cups and Saucers

KELLEY ESKRIDGE
And Salome Danced

THEY'RE THE BEST PART, AUDITIONS: the last chance to hold in my mind the play as it should be. The uncast actors are easiest to direct; empty stages offer no barriers. Everything is clear, uncomplicated by living people and their inability to be what is needed.

"What I need," I say to my stage manager, "is a woman who can work on her feet."

"Hmmm," says Lucky helpfully. She won't waste words on anything so obvious. Our play is *Salome*, subtitled *Identity and Desire*. Salome has to dance worth killing for.

The sense I have, in those best, sweet moments, is that I do not so much envision the play as experience it in some sort of multidimensional gestalt. I feel Salome's pride and the terrible control of her body's rhythms; Herod's twitchy groin and his guilt and his unspoken love for John; John's relentless patience, and his fear. The words of the script sometimes seize me as if bypassing vision, burrowing from page into skin, pushing blood and nerve to the bursting limit on the journey to my brain. The best theatre lives inside. I'll spend weeks trying to feed the sensation and the bloodsurge into the actors, but... But I can't do their job. But they can't read my mind. And people wonder why we drink.

Lucky snorts at me when I tell her these things: if it isn't a tech cue or a blocking note, it has nothing to do with the real play as far as she's concerned. She doesn't understand that for me the play is best before it is real, when it is still only mine.

"Nine sharp," she says now. "Time to start. Some of them have already been out there long enough to turn green." She smiles; her private joke.

"Let's go," I say, my part of the ritual; and then I have to do it, have to let go. I sit forward over the script in my usual eighth row seat; Lucky takes her clipboard and her favorite red pen, the one she's had

3

since *Cloud Nine*, up the aisle. She pushes open the lobby door and the sound of voices rolls through, cuts off. All of them out there, wanting in. I feel in my gut their tense waiting silence as Lucky calls the first actor's name.

They're hard on everyone, auditions. Actors bare their throats. Directors make instinctive leaps of faith about what an actor could or might or must do in this or that role, with this or that partner. It's kaleidoscopic, religious, it's violent and subjective. It's like soldiers fighting each other just to see who gets to go to war. Everyone gets bloody, right from the start.

Forty minutes before a late lunch break, when my blood sugar is at its lowest point, Lucky comes back with the next resumé and headshot and the first raised eyebrow of the day. The eyebrow, the snort, the flared nostril, the slight nod, are Lucky's only comments on actors. They are minimal and emphatic.

Behind her walks John the Baptist. He calls himself Joe Something-or-other, but he's John straight out of my head. Dark red hair. The kind of body that muscles up long and compact, strong and lean. He moves well, confident but controlled. When he's on stage he even stands like a goddamn prophet. And his eyes are John's eyes: deep blue like deep sea. He wears baggy khaki trousers, a loose, untucked white shirt, high-top sneakers, a Greek fisherman's cap. His voice is clear, a half-tone lighter than many people expect in a man: perfect.

The monologue is good, too. Lucky shifts in her seat next to me. We exchange a look, and I see that her pupils are wide.

"Is he worth dancing for, then?"

She squirms, all the answer I really need. I look at the resumé again. Joe Sand. He stands calmly on stage. Then he moves very slightly, a shifting of weight, a leaning in toward Lucky. While he does it, he looks right at her, watching her eyes for that uncontrollable pupil response. He smiles. Then he tries it with me. *Aha*, I think, *surprise, little actor.*

"Callbacks are Tuesday and Wednesday nights," I say neutrally. "We'll let you know."

He steps off the stage. He is half in shadow when he asks, "Do you have Salome yet?"

"No precasting," Lucky says.

"I know someone you'd like," he says, and even though I can't quite see him I know he is talking to me. Without the visual cue of his face, the voice has become trans-gendered, the body shape ambiguous.

"Any more at home like you, Joe?" *I must really need my lunch.*

"Whatever you need," he says, and moves past me, past Lucky, up the aisle. Suddenly, I'm ravenously hungry. Four more actors between me and the break, and I know already that I won't remember any of them longer than it takes for Lucky to close the doors behind them.

The next day is better. By late afternoon I have seen quite a few good actors, men and women, and Lucky has started a callback list.

"How many left?" I ask, coming back from the bathroom, rubbing the back of my neck with one hand and my waist with the other. I need a good stretch, some sweaty muscle-heating exercise, a hot bath. I need Salome.

Lucky is frowning at a paper in her hand. "Why is Joe Sand on this list?"

"God, Lucky, I want him for callbacks, that's why."

"No, this sheet is today's auditions."

I read over her shoulder. *Jo Sand.* "Dunno. Let's go on to the next one, maybe we can actually get back on schedule."

When I next hear Lucky's voice, after she has been up to the lobby to bring in the next actor, I know that something is terribly wrong.

"Mars... Mars..."

By this time I have stood and turned and I can see for myself what she is not able to tell me.

"Jo Sand," I say.

"Hello again," she says. The voice is the same; *she* is the same, and utterly different. She wears the white shirt tucked into the khaki pants this time, pulled softly across her breasts. Soft black shoes, like slippers, that make no noise when she moves. No cap today, that red hair thick, brilliant above the planes of her face. Her eyes are Salome's eyes: deep blue like deep desire. She is as I imagined her. When she leans slightly toward me, she watches my eyes and then smiles. Her smell goes straight up my nose and punches into some ancient place deep in my brain.

We stand like that for a long moment, the three of us. I don't know what to say. I don't have the right words for conversation with the surreal except when it's inside my head. I don't know what to do when it walks down my aisle and shows me its teeth.

"I want you to see that I can be versatile," Jo says.

The air in our small circle has become warm and sticky. My eyes feel slightly crossed, my mind is slipping gears. *I won't ask, I will not ask*.... It's as if I were trying to bring her into focus through 3-D glasses; trying to make two separate images overlay. It makes me seasick. I wonder if Lucky is having the same trouble, and then I see that she has simply removed herself in some internal way. She doesn't see Jo look at me with those primary eyes.

But I see: and suddenly I feel wild, electric, that direct-brain connection that makes my nerves stand straight under my skin. *Be careful what you ask for, Mars.* "I don't guess you really need to do another monologue," I tell her. Lucky is still slack-jawed with shock.

Jo smiles again.

Someone else is talking with my voice. "Lucky will schedule you for callbacks." Beside me, Lucky jerks at the sound of her name. Jo turns to her. Her focus is complete. Her whole body says, *I am waiting*. I want her on stage. I want to see her like that, waiting for John's head on a platter.

"Mars, what... " Lucky swallows, tries again. She speaks without looking at the woman standing next to her. "Do you want... oh, shit. What part are you reading this person for in callbacks, goddamnit anyway." I haven't seen her this confused since her mother's boyfriend made a pass at her years ago, one Thanksgiving, his hand hidden behind the turkey platter at the buffet. Confusion makes Lucky fragile and brings her close to tears.

Jo looks at me, still waiting. Yesterday I saw John the Baptist: I remember how he made Lucky's eyebrow quirk and I can imagine the rehearsals; how he might sit close to her, bring her coffee, volunteer to help her set props. She'd be a wreck in one week and useless in two. And today how easy it is to see Salome, who waits so well and moves with such purpose. I should send this Jo away, but I won't: I need a predator for Salome; I can't do a play about desire without someone who knows about the taste of blood.

"Wear a skirt," I say to Jo. "I'll need to see you dance." Lucky closes her eyes.

Somehow we manage the rest of the auditions, make the first cut, organize the callback list. There are very few actors I want to see again. When we meet for callbacks, I bring them all in and sit them in a clump at the rear of the house, where I can see them when I want to and ignore them otherwise. But always I am conscious of Jo. I read her with the actors that I think will work best in other roles. She is flexible, adapting herself to their different styles, giving them what they need to make the scene work. She's responsive to direction. She listens well. I can't find anything wrong with her.

Then it is time for the dance. There are three women that I want to see, and I put them all on stage together. "Salome's dance is the most important scene in the play. It's a crisis point for every character. Everyone has something essential invested in it. It has to carry a lot of weight."

"What are you looking for?" one of the women asks. She has long dark hair and good arms.

"Power," I answer, and beside her Jo's head comes up like a pointing dog's, her nostrils flared with some rich scent. I pretend not to see. "Her dance is about power over feelings and lives. There's more, but power's the foundation, and that's what I need to see."

The woman who asked nods her head and looks down, chewing the skin off her upper lip. I turn away to give them a moment for this new information to sink in; looking out into the house, I see the other actors sitting forward in their seats, and I know they are wondering who it will be, and whether they could work with her, and what they would do in her place.

I turn back. "I want you all to dance together up here. Use the space any way you like. Take a minute to warm up and start whenever you're ready."

I can see the moment that they realize, *ohmigod no music, how can we dance without, goddamn all directors anyway*. But I want to see their interpretation of power, not music. If they don't have it in them to dance silent in front of strangers, if they can't compete, if they can't pull all my attention and keep it, then they can't give me what I need. Salome wouldn't hesitate.

The dark-haired woman shrugs, stretches her arms out and down toward her toes. The third woman slowly begins to rock her hips; her arms rise swaying in the cliché of eastern emerald-in-the-navel bellydance. She moves as if embarrassed, and I don't blame her. The dark-haired woman stalls for another moment and then launches into a jerky jazz step with a strangely syncopated beat. I can almost hear her humming her favorite song under her breath; her head tilts up and to the right and she moves in her own world, to her own sound. That's not right, either. I realize that I'm hoping one of them will be what I need, so that I do not have to see Jo dance.

And where is Jo? There, at stage right, watching the other two women, comfortable in her stillness. Then she slides gradually into motion, steps slowly across the stage and stops three feet from the bellydancer, whose stumbling rhythm slows and then breaks as Jo stands, still, watching. Jo looks her straight in the eye, and just as the other woman begins to drop her gaze, Jo suddenly whirls, throwing herself around so quickly that for an instant it's as if her head is facing the opposite direction from her body. It is a nauseating moment, and it's followed by a total body shrug, a shaking off, that is both con-temptuous and intently erotic. Now she is facing the house, facing the other actors, facing Lucky, facing me: now she shows us what she can do. Her dance says *this is what I am, that you can never be; see my body move as it will never move with yours.* She stoops for an imagi-nary platter, and from the triumph in her step I begin to see the bloody prize. The curve of her arm shows me the filmed eye and the lolling tongue; the movement of her breast and belly describe for me the wreckage of the neck, its trailing cords; her feet draw pictures in the splashed gore as she swirls and turns and snaps her arm out like a dis-cus thrower, tossing the invisible trophy straight at me. When I realize that I have raised a hand to catch it, I know that I have to have her, no matter what she is. Have to have her for the play. Have to have her.

When the actors are gone, Lucky and I go over the list. We do not discuss Salome. Lucky has already set the other two women's resumes aside.

Before we leave: "God, she was amazing. She'll be great, Mars. I'm really glad it turned out this way, you know, that she decided to drop that crossdressing stuff."

"Mmm."

"It really gave me a start, seeing her that day. She was so convincing as a man. I thought… well, nothing. It was stupid."

"It wasn't stupid."

"You didn't seem surprised – did you know that first time when he… when she came in that she wasn't…? Why didn't you say?"

"If I'm looking at someone who can play John, I don't really care how they pee or whether they shave under their chins. Gender's not important."

"It is if you think you might want to go to bed with it."

"Mmm," I say again. What I cannot tell Lucky is that all along I have been in some kind of shock; like walking through swamp mud, where the world is warm silkywet but you are afraid to look down for fear of what might be swimming with you in the murk. I know that this is not a game: Joe was a man when he came in and a woman when she came back. I look at our cast list and I know that something impossible and dangerous is trying to happen; but all I really see is that suddenly my play – the one inside me – is possible. She'll blow a hole through every seat in the house. She'll burst their brains.

Three weeks into rehearsal, Lucky has unremembered enough to start sharing coffee and head-together conferences with Jo during breaks. The other actors accept Jo as someone they can't believe they never heard of before, a comrade in the art wars. We are such a happy group; we give great ensemble.

Lance, who plays Herod, regards Jo as some kind of wood sprite, brilliant and fey. He is myopic about her to the point that if she turned into an anaconda, he would stroke her head while she wrapped herself around him. Lance takes a lot of kidding about his name, especially from his boyfriends. During our early rehearsals, he discovered a very effective combination of obsession and revulsion in Herod: as if he would like to eat Salome alive and then throw her up again, a sort of sexual bulimia.

Susan plays Herodias; Salome's mother, Herod's second wife, his brother's widow. She makes complicated seem simple. She works well with Lance, giving him a strong partner who nevertheless dims in comparison to her flaming daughter, a constant reminder to Herod of the destruction that lurks just on the other side of a single *yes* to this step-daughter/niece/demonchild who dances in his fantasies. Susan watches Jo so disinterestedly that it has taken me most of this time to see how she has imitated and matured the arrogance that Jo brings to the stage. She is a tall black woman, soft muscle where Jo is hard: nothing like Jo, but she has become Salome's mother.

And John the Baptist, whose real name is Frank and who is nothing like Joe: I'm not sure I could have cast him if he had come to the audition with red hair, but his is black this season, Irish black for the O'Neill repertory production that he just finished. Lucky says he has "Jesus feet." Frankie's a method actor, disappointed that he doesn't have any sense-memory references for decapitation. "I know it happens offstage," he says earnestly, at least once a week. "But it needs to be there right from the start, I want them to think about it every scene with her." *Them* is always the audience. *Her* is always Jo. Offstage, he looks at her the way a child looks at a harvest moon.

Three weeks is long enough for us all to become comfortable with the process but not with the results: the discoveries the actors made in the first two weeks refuse to gel, refuse to reinvent themselves. It's a frustrating phase. We're all tense but trying not to show it, trying not to undermine anyone else's efforts. It's hard for the actors, who genuinely want to support each other, but don't really want to see someone else break through first. Too scary: no one wants to be left behind.

There's a pseudosexual energy between actors and directors: there's so much deliberate vulnerability, control, desire to please; so much of the stuff that sex is made of. Working with my actors is like handling bolts of cloth: they each have a texture, a tension. Lance is brocade and plush; Susan is smooth velvet, subtle to the touch; Frankie is spun wool, warm and indefinably tough. And Jo: Jo is raw silk and razorblades, so fine that you don't feel the cut.

So we're all tense; except for Jo. Oh, she talks, but she's not worried; she's waiting for something, and I am beginning to turn those audition days over in my memory, sucking the taste from the bones of those encounters and wondering what it was that danced with me in those early rounds, what I have invited in.

And a peculiar thing begins: as I grow more disturbed, Jo's work becomes better and better. In those moments when I suddenly see myself as the trainer with my head in the mouth of the beast, when I slip and show that my hand is sweaty on the leash – in those moments her work is so pungent, so ripe that Jo the world-shaker disappears, and the living Salome looks up from the cut-off t-shirt, flexes her thigh muscles under the carelessly torn jeans. We have more and more of Salome every rehearsal.

On Friday nights I bring a cooler of Corona and a bag of limes for whoever wants to share them. This Friday everyone stays. We sit silent for the first cold green-gold swallows. Lance settles back into Herod's large throne. I straddle a folding chair and rest my arms along the back, bottle loose in one hand. Lucky and the other actors settle on the platforms that break the stage into playing areas.

It starts with the actors talking, as they always do, about work. Lance has played another Herod, years ago, in *Jesus Christ Superstar*, and he wants to tell us how different that was.

"I'd like to do *Superstar*," Jo says. It sounds like an idle remark. She is leaning back with her elbows propped against the rise of a platform, her breasts pushing gently against the fabric of her shirt as she raises her bottle to her mouth. I look away because I do not want to watch her drink, don't want to see her throat work as the liquid goes down.

Lance considers a moment. "I think you'd be great, sweetheart," he says, "But Salome to Mary Magdalene is a pretty big stretch. Acid to apple juice. Wouldn't you at least like to play a semi-normal character in between, work up to it a little?"

Jo snorts. "I'm not interested in Magdalene. I'll play Judas."

Lance whoops, Frankie grins, and even the imperturbable Susan smiles. "Well, why not?" Lance says. "Why shouldn't she play Judas if she wants to?"

"Little question of gender," Frankie says, and shrugs.

Susan sits up. "Why shouldn't she have the part if she can do the work?"

Frankie gulps his beer and wipes his mouth. "Why should any director hire a woman to play a man when they can get a real man to do it?"

"What do you think, Mars?" The voice is Jo's. It startles me. I have been enjoying the conversation so much that I have forgotten the danger in relaxing around Jo or anything that interests her. I look at her now, still sprawled back against the platform with an inch of golden beer in the bottle beside her. She has been enjoying herself, too. I'm not sure where this is going, what the safe answer is. I remember saying to Lucky, *Gender's not important.*

"Gender's not important, isn't that right, Mars?"

Lucky told her about it. But I know Lucky didn't. She didn't have to.

"That's right," I say, and I know from Jo's smile that my voice is not as controlled as it should be. Even so, I'm not prepared for what happens next: a jumble of pictures in my head, images of dancing in a place so dark that I cannot tell if I am moving with men or women, images of streets filled with androgynous people and people whose gender-blurring surpasses androgyny and leaps into the realm of performance. Women dressed as men making love to men; men dressed as women hesitating in front of public bathroom doors; women in high heels and pearls with biceps so large that they split the expensive silk shirts. And the central image, the real point: Jo, naked, obviously female, slick with sweat, moving under me and over me, Jo making love to me until I gasp and then she begins to change, to change, until it is Joe with me, Joe on me – and I open my mouth to shout my absolute, instinctive refusal – and I remember Lucky saying *It is if you think you might want to sleep with it* – and the movie breaks in my head and I am back with the others. No one has noticed that I've been assaulted, turned inside out. They're still talking about it: "Just imagine the difference in all the relationships if Judas were a woman," Susan says earnestly to Frankie. "It would change everything!" Jo smiles at me and swallows the last of her beer.

The next rehearsal I feel fragile, as if I must walk carefully to keep from breaking myself. I have to rest often. I am running a scene with Frankie and Lance when I notice Lucky offstage, talking earnestly to Jo. Jo puts one hand up, interrupts her, smiles, speaks, and they both turn to look at me. Lucky suddenly blushes. She walks quickly away from Jo, swerves to avoid me. Jo's smile is bigger. Her work in the next scene is particularly fine and full.

"What did she say to you, Luck?" I ask her as we are closing the house for the evening.

"Nothing," Lucky mumbles.

"Come on."

"Okay, fine. She wanted to know if you ever slept with your actors, okay?"

I know somehow that it's not entirely true: I can hear Jo's voice very clearly, saying to Lucky *So does Mars ever fuck the leading lady?* while she smiles that catlick smile. Jo has the gift of putting pictures into people's heads, and I believe Lucky got a mindful. That's what really sickens me, the idea that Lucky now has an image behind her eyes of what I'm like... no, of what Jo wants her to think I'm like. God knows. I don't want to look at her.

"Did you get my message?" Jo says to me the next evening, when she finally catches me alone in the wings during a break from rehearsal. She has been watching me all night. Lucky won't talk to her.

"I'm not in the script."

"Everybody's in the script."

"Look, I don't get involved with actors. It's too complicated, it's messy. I don't do it."

"Make an exception."

Lucky comes up behind Jo. Whatever the look is on my face, it gets a scowl from her. "Break's over," she says succinctly, turning away from us even before the words are completely out, halfway across the stage before I think to try to keep her with me.

"Let's get back to work, Jo."

"Make a fucking exception."

I don't like being pushed by actors, and there's something else, too, but I don't want to think about it now, I just want Jo off my back, so I give her the director voice, the vocal whip. "Save it for the stage, princess. You want to impress me, get out there and do your fucking job."

She doesn't answer; her silence makes a cold, high-altitude circle around us. When she moves, it's like a snake uncoiling, and then her hand is around my wrist. She's *strong*. When I look down, I see that her hand is changing: the bones thicken under the flesh, the muscles rearrange themselves subtly, and it's Joe's hand on Jo's arm, Joe's hand on mine. "Don't make me angry, Mars," and the voice is genderless and buzzes like a snake. There is no one here to help me, I can't see Lucky, I'm all alone with this hindbrain thing that wants to come out and play with me. Jo's smile is by now almost too big for her face. *Just another actor*, I think crazily, *they're all monsters anyway.*

"What are you?" I am shaking.

"Whatever you need, Mars. Whatever you need. Every director's dream. At the moment, I'm Salome, right down to the bone. I'm what you asked for."

"I didn't ask for this. I don't want this."

"You wanted Salome, and now you've got her. The power, the sex, the hunger, the need, the wanting, it's all here."

"It's a play. It's just... it's a play, for chrissake."

"It's real for you." That hand is still locked around my wrist; the other hand, the soft small hand, reaches up to the center of my chest where my heart tries to skitter away from her touch. "I saw it, that first audition. I came to play John the Baptist, I saw the way Lucky looked at me, and I was going to give her something to remember... but your wanting was so strong, so complex. It's delicious, Mars. It tastes like spice and wine and sweat. The play in your head is more real to you than anything, isn't it, more real than your days of bright sun, your friends, your office transactions. I'm going to bring it right to you, into your world, into your life. I'll give you Salome. On stage, off stage, there doesn't have to be any difference. Isn't that what making love is, giving someone what they really want?"

She's still smiling that awful smile and I can't tell whether she is talking about love because she really means it or because she knows it makes my stomach turn over. Or maybe both.

"Get out of here. Out of here, right now." I am shaking.

"You don't mean that, sweet. If you did, I'd already be gone."

"I'll cancel the show."

She doesn't answer: she looks at me and then, *phht*, I am seeing the stage from the audience perspective, watching Herod and Herodias quarrel and cry and struggle to protect their love, watching John's patient fear as Herod's resolve slips away: watching Salome dance. When she dances, she brings us all with her, the whole audience living inside her skin for those moments. We all whirl and reach and bend, we all promise, we all twist away. We all tempt. We all rage. We stuff ourselves down Herod's throat until he chokes on us. And then we are all suddenly back in our own bodies and we roar until our throats hurt and our voices rasp. All the things that I have felt about this play, she will make them feel. What I am will be in them. What I have inside me will bring them to their feet and leave them full and aching. Oh god, it makes me weep, and then I am back with her, she still holds me with that monster hand and all I can do is cry with wanting so badly what she can give me.

Her eyes are too wide, too round, too pleased. "Oh," she says, still gently, "It's okay. You'll enjoy most of it, I promise." And she's gone, sauntering onstage, calling out something to Lance, and her upstage hand is still too big, still *wrong*. She lets it caress her thigh once before she turns it back into the Jo hand. I've never seen anything more obscene. I have to take a minute to dry my eyes, cool my face. I feel a small, hollow place somewhere deep, as if Jo reached inside and found something she liked enough to take for herself. She's there now, just onstage, ready to dance, that small piece of me humming in her veins. How much more richness do I have within me? How long will it take to eat me, bit by bit? She raises her arms now and smiles, already tasting. Already well fed.

ELEANOR ARNASON

The Lovers

THERE WAS A WOMAN of the Ahara. She came of a good line within the lineage[1] and grew up to be tall and broad with thick, glossy fur. Her eyes were pale grey, an unusual color in that part of the world. From childhood on, her nickname was Eyes-of-crystal. If she had a fault, it lay in her personality. She was bit too fierce and solitary.

Her home was in the town of Ahara Tsal, which stood on top of the Tsal River bluffs. To the west and south lay the farms and pastures of her lineage: a flat rich land. To the north and east was the river valley, wide and marshy and full of animals. Eyes-of-crystal liked to go down there into the wilderness and ride and hunt. Her mother warned her this was dangerous.

"You'll get strange ideas and possibly meet things and people you don't want to meet."

But Eyes-of-crystal refused to listen.

Don't think this is a story about how she met ghosts or bandits or some horrible great animal like an *ulkuwa* and learned that her mother was right and she ought to have stayed at home. That's another story entirely, and maybe a good one. But the pain that Eyes-of-crystal encountered did not come from disobedience, and it did not come to her when she was away from home.

As mentioned before, she grew up to be large and strong. When she was twenty-five, her relatives decided to breed her.

At this time, the Ahara were the second most powerful lineage in the world, and this young woman came from a line that produced really fine children. The Ahara wanted to breed her with someone important. They looked around, and who did they see? Eh Manhata, who was the greatest warrior of the age. His lineage, the Eh, stood in front of everyone else. They had no equal. Only the Ahara came close.

1. Literally, "of a good thread within the woven cord."

16

So the young woman's relatives entered into negotiations with the senior women of Eh.

Eyes-of-crystal knew about this, but paid as little attention as possible. She had never wanted to be a mother, but she had always known that she had no choice. At times, she wished that she had come from a less excellent line. If only there had been something wrong or unhealthy about her immediate family! Maybe then she would have been left alone.

But her brothers and male first cousins were sturdy fighters. Her sisters and female first cousins were producing babies like furry butter balls. Every relative was co-operative, moral, intelligent, and well-put-together.

What a curse, thought Eyes-of-crystal, and went back down to the river to hunt. There, in the dark forest of the flood plain, she found a kind of peace. Often, she found animals as well and brought them home, dead and bloody, across the back of her well-trained *tsin*. Imagine her as a kind of Diana, a grey-furred virgin huntress, about to lose everything she valued.

After a while, her mother called her in for a conference. One of her uncles was there as well, her mother's full brother, a soldier of middle age with a great scar across his face and one eye missing.

"You know that we have been speaking with the Eh," her mother said. "We wanted Eh Manhata as the father of your child."

"Yes," said Eyes-of-crystal. "I know this."

"He is not available," her mother said. "According to the Eh, they can't afford to take him out of the current war and send him here."

"There may be more going on than we can see," her uncle added. "I have never heard of Eh Manhata fathering any children, even in those periods when the war has slowed down."

Her mother's head tilted in the gesture that can mean either agreement or consideration. "There are men, even great men, who are not able to father children for one reason or another."

Eyes-of-crystal knew the reasons, of course. The People do not enjoy thinking about the unpleasant aspects of life, any more than humans do. But if a thing is unavoidable, then it must be looked at, and they have never misled their children about what was involved in producing the next generation.

Some men were infertile, and others were impotent. These were physical problems and comparatively rare. The most common problem was one that humans would call psychological, and the People would say was moral or spiritual. There were men who simply could not overcome their natural aversion to sex with women. They were fine with other men, but put them in a breeding situation and nothing happened.[2]

"They have offered us Manhata's full brother," her mother said. "He has fathered a number of children, and most of them look good. Your uncle has met him, which is why I asked him to be present at this conference."

"They are twins," her uncle said. "When they came out into the world, Manhata was already bigger and stronger. He has always been quicker and more forceful than his brother. There are people who say he took something from his brother in the womb. I wouldn't be surprised."

"This doesn't sound promising," Eyes-of-crystal said.

"There's nothing wrong with Eh Shawin. He looks very much like Eh Manhata, though he isn't as tall or broad, and something is missing, as I said before. Manhata is like a man in sunlight. No one can overlook him. Shawin is a man at the edge of a forest, in shadow and not entirely visible. But he's a good soldier, and no one has ever questioned his courage or intelligence. And he is Eh Manhata's only full brother."

"No mating can tie us closer to Eh than this one," her mother said. "And no lineage is more important to us. If we're lucky, some of Manhata's qualities will show up in your child or children."

"You want me to do this," Eyes-of-crystal said.

Her mother said, "Yes."

She agreed. A message was sent to Eh. Eyes-of-crystal took her bow and went down along the river to shoot birds.

This happened in the late spring. Eh Shawin did not arrive until mid-summer. He came alone, which was not surprising. The road from Eh to Ahara was usually safe, and his brother was leading a campaign in the north against the Alliance of the Five Less One. All his male relatives would be there. In peaceful times, of course, they would have ridden with him and made rude jokes about heterosexuality. It is always the job of one's own male relatives to demoralize, while the men of the other lineage are required to be friendly and encouraging.

In any case, Shawin appeared alone at the gate of Ahara Tsal. The

2. Literally, "nothing came forward." The *double entendre* is in the original.

guards asked him to wait and sent a messenger ahead. There was time for her family to gather in the courtyard of their great house: her mother, her aunt, the older female cousins, and the two men who were not at war.

Eyes-of-crystal was on a balcony. There were rules and courtesies in a proper mating. One does not meet the man right off. But there was nothing wrong in watching, as she did.

He rode in. His animal was dusty and tired, but had a good shape with powerful haunches and shoulders and a wide head that might indicate intelligence. It was solid brown, a rare and expensive color.

The man was as dusty as the *tsin* and dressed like an ordinary soldier. But he swung down gracefully, and once he was on the ground she could see he was tall, standing eye to eye with her mother and looming over the two old men, as they came forward to welcome him.

All the rituals of greeting were performed. It seemed to her that Shawin moved through them with unusual precision and grace, like the traveling actors she had seen now and then.

They came to Ahara Tsal and set up their stage in the main square. There they danced and told the stories of heroes. It occurred to her as a child that she wanted to be two things: a soldier or an actor. Both were impossible.

One of her sisters was on the balcony with Eyes-of-crystal. She looked down at the man in the courtyard and said, "He isn't much to look at, is he?"

Eyes-of-crystal held her tongue, though there was plenty she could have said. The sister had mated for the first time with a son of Merin, a beautiful man who liked fine clothing and jewelry. His eyes had been blue-green, the color of malachite. His manners had been good enough, especially at first. But it had taken her sister a long time to get pregnant, and the man became obviously restless. He was anxious to get back to the war and to his lover, the men of Ahara said.

When he learned that the sister was finally pregnant, he let out a shout of joy, and he left as soon as he decently could.

Eyes-of-crystal mentioned none of this. For one thing, the sister was still pregnant and with twins, if her size was any indication. Discomfort had ruined the woman's usually good disposition, and it was never a good idea to criticize the father of an unborn child.

Eyes-of-crystal kept her lips firmly closed over the *hwarhath* proverb which means, "handsome is as handsome does."

The next day she was introduced to the man. He'd taken a bath and put on a new kilt, covered with embroidery. The grip of his sword was white bone bound with rings of gold. His fur was brushed and glossy.

That was as much as she learned about him. Their meeting was formal and brief. The words they spoke to each other were set by tradition. When they had finished, her great uncles led Eh Shawin off to meet with other men. She went off with her female relatives.

For the most part, the *hwarhath* would prefer not to think about what their ancestors had to go through, before the development of artificial insemination. But the information is there if you want to look for it, and the author of this story clearly did her research.

Remember that heterosexuality was – and is – frightening to the People. In it lies the power of generation and destruction. They know – and have always known – that the survival of their society depends on keeping men and women apart. But through most of their history, the survival of their society depended on mating.

They did what humans also do, when faced with something frightening and unavoidable: death, for example, birth or marriage. They used ritual to protect the act and limit it and direct its power. They used humor and drugs to diminish their fear.

Eh Shawin spent the day with the men of Ahara, talking and getting a little drunk. Eyes-of-crystal spent the day getting ready for the night, and the author of the story describes every detail: the ritual bath, the ceremonies of protection, the comic skits performed by female cousins, the elaborate mating robe.

Most likely, there is an element of malice in all this description. "Look, look," the author is saying to her readers. "This is what you are trying to forget. This is where we came from. It's as inescapable as shit."

Finally, at nightfall, Eyes-of-crystal was led up to the mating chamber: a large circular room high in a tower. Most of the space was filled by a bed, its wooden frame elaborately carved. Two chairs stood by a window. A lamp burned on the table between them. Eyes-of-crystal sat down. Her robe was stiff with embroidery. There was no way to relax. She had been given a potion, so the bed did not frighten her. Her relatives fussed around, straightening the cover on the bed, trimming the wick on the lamp, offering good advice.

Finally, there was the sound of male voices, mostly drunk, at the bottom of the tower. The women grew silent. Eyes-of-crystal heard footsteps on the stairs: one person only, climbing steadily. The others had stayed behind, as was proper. One fellow kept shouting, "Good luck!"

A couple of the women whispered angrily. This was a serious – a sacred – business, and it ought to be carried forward with gravity. A little bit of something to drink did no harm. But men never knew when to stop. Any excuse for a drinking party!

The door opened, and there Eh Shawin was. A torch shone in back of him, so he was edged with red and yellow light. A moment later, he was in the room and standing in the shadows along the curving wall.

The women left. Several of them touched Eyes-of-crystal as they passed her, but no one spoke. There was only the rustle of clothing, the slap of sandals on the bare stone floor and the breathing of an especially large and solid aunt as she went down the winding stairs. Last to go was Eyes-of-crystal's mother.

Eh Shawin closed the door, came over and sat down in the chair across from Eyes-of-crystal. Now she was frightened, in spite of the potion. He leaned forward and looked at her, frowning. "They have drugged you."

"Yes."

He sighed. "The first night is always like this. I'm going to tell you something, Ahara Pai, though I don't know if you'll be able to understand it at the moment. Still, I believe in acting directly[3] and in saying what's in my mind.

"There are many families who want to interbreed with Eh, and all of them are interested in having my brother as a father. But as you probably know, our lineage cannot let him leave the field of battle.

"Because I'm Eh Manhata's twin, I've been sent on trips like this – " He paused. "More times than I can remember. I know far more about this situation than is usual for a man, and I have formed my own opinions about how to go about producing children." Eyes-of-crystal would have been shocked, if she had been sober. Thanks to the potion, she remained calm.

"These drugs and rituals do nothing good! The woman is frightened, and the man would be, if he wasn't drunk, as he usually is. It's surprising he remembers what it is he has to do.

---

3. Literally, "with *katiad.*" This is the most important male virtue. If a man has it, he is steadfast, forthright, honest, and sincere. He travels like a an arrow that is well-made and well-shot, straight to the target.

"In my opinion, everything goes best if the two people are sober and comfortable with one another. The women seems to get pregnant more quickly, and it's my impression that the child turns out better. And so I have developed my own way of doing this. I try to make it as ordinary as possible."

"Do your female relatives let you have these opinions?" asked Eyes-of-crystal. "It seems odd."

He glanced up and smiled briefly. "Remember that they've known me from childhood. Eh Manhata is fierce. I am stubborn."

He changed the subject then and asked her about hunting. The men of Ahara had told him she liked to hunt. It was an unusual trait in a woman, but not wrong or shameful. His home was on the plain. He knew what it was like to chase game over flat land and along the little rivers of his country. What was the great river like for hunting?

She tried to answer him, but she was frightened, and the drug made it hard for her to think and speak. Her mind kept coming back to the present situation, though with decreasing fear. For one thing, his questions were so ordinary. For another, the drug was making her sleepy. Her thoughts moved more and more slowly, like people wading through a heavy fall of snow.

"Maybe we should have this conversation another time," Eh Shawin said finally. He paused, then continued, his voice quiet and gentle. "There is one thing I have never been able to change. Your relatives and mine have expectations about what will happen tonight. We must meet those expectations.

"I can do the thing slowly and try to find some way to make it pleasant for you, or I can do it quickly and get it over."

"Quickly," said Eyes-of-crystal.

Eh Shawin inclined his head in the motion of agreement, then asked if she wanted light or darkness.

"Darkness," said Eyes-of-crystal.

He licked his fingers and put out the lamp.

The home world of the People has no moon, but the stars are brilliant, and the People have much better night vision than humans. Most likely, the man and woman could see each other as they undressed. Maybe their eyes gleamed occasionally, reflecting starlight. Their dark solid bodies must certainly have been visible, as they moved past the star-filled windows or settled on the bed, which was covered with a mating blanket of bleached fabric as white as snow or bone.

The author of the story does not tell us any of this, though she describes their mating with clinical detail. Most likely, she was working from the old mating manuals, which are still available in libraries, though not (of course) in sections that children can access. There is no reason to believe that she is writing from personal experience.

After they finished, the man went to sleep. Eyes-of-crystal lay next to him, looking out a window at the sky. She could see the Banner of the Goddess, the Milky Way.

What had the Goddess been thinking of, when she devised this method for making people? It was like a great ugly knot in the net of kinship and cooperation and love that held all of them – women and men, adults and children – together. Impossible to understand!

She woke in the morning and found Eh Shawin gone, though she could see the place where he'd lain. Her body hurt. She got up groaning and went down to the women's bathroom. There was hot water ready and a cousin to help her.

Hah! It was good to wash and then to soak in a tub of clean water scented with herbs. The cousin was middle aged, but had never been bred. One of her feet was twisted. It had been that way from birth, and this was not a trait the Ahara wanted continued. She barely spoke to Eyes-of-crystal, either out of envy or embarrassment.

At last, Eyes-of-crystal got out of the tub and rubbed herself dry. The cousin brought a fresh new tunic. She put it on. Her female relatives would be waiting for her in the eating room and the kitchen. She had no wish to see them. Eyes-of-crystal thanked her cousin and went out to the stables.

Light slanted in the little high windows. The air smelled of hay and *tsina*. Most of the stalls were empty, the animals gone to war. But a few remained: the mares and geldings that children rode and her own hunters. She went to look at her favorite, a blue-grey stallion. His legs and hind quarters had white stripes, and his horns were as black as obsidian.

Eh Shawin stood at the end of the stall. "A fine animal," he said. "What do you call him?"

"Direct Action."

"A good name. I talked to your mother this morning and explained that I don't want to inconvenience your male relatives. There are so few home at present, and most are so old! They don't have the energy to be entertaining a guest. And I do best in these situations if I keep regular hours and maintain my ordinary habits. So – " He glanced up briefly and smiled. "Your mother has agreed that it makes better sense for me to go out riding with you. I get the exercise I need, and the old men of Ahara get their rest."

It wasn't like her mother to agree to anything unusual, but Shawin was clever and plausible. There are men who know how to charm women, just as there are men who know how to charm men. These two qualities don't usually come together in one person. Eyes-of-crystal had the impression that Eh Shawin was no exception to this rule. Her male relatives did not dislike the man, but it wasn't likely they'd go out of the way for him.

"My *tsin* hasn't recovered from our journey as yet, but one of your cousins has offered me this animal." He led her to another stall.

She knew the animal there: a large gelding. Its color was solid purple-brown.

"He told me its name is Consistent Behavior, which sounds promising, though I'm curious why an animal this color was gelded."

She knew and told him. The animal had a sullen disposition. This wasn't a problem for riding. "Unless you want to go quickly." But Consistent Behavior was no good for hunting, and the animal would have been dangerous in a war.

Eh Shawin laughed.

"My cousin meant no discourtesy. You see how little we have available." She gestured around at the empty stalls.

"I don't take offense easily. That's my brother."

They saddled and rode out. The author of this story is anonymous, but she almost certainly came from one of the lineages along the river, maybe from Ahara. Her description of the country is detailed and it reads like a real experience, not something she got out of a book.

They went east, along a narrow trail that led past fields of *hwal* and *antim*. The sky was clear, except for a handful of high clouds, and the air smelled of dust and dry vegetation. Small bugs filled the weeds along the trail. The names of the bugs are given: sunfly, hopper, *pirig*, *heln*, and scarlet warrior.

Eh Shawin asked about hunting a second time.

Eyes-of-crystal told him about the many fine animals and birds to be found in the marshes along the river Tsal and in the flood plain forest.

It was obvious that he knew about hunting. The questions he asked were intelligent. But he had never spent much time around water. She told him about the giant fish that lived in the river. They were longer than a man and had teeth like knives. Their dispositions were nasty. Her people hunted them with nets and spears.

"That must be something," Eh Shawin said and then exhaled loudly. They had come to the top of the bluffs. The front of them was the river valley, wide and deep, full of many channels that wound through the forest and marshland, so the entire valley was like a belt made of strips of colored leather woven together: green, blue-green, brown, and pale red.

The two of them dismounted and let their animals graze. They spoke more about hunting. He reached over and stroked her shoulder the way a female lover might. Eyes-of-crystal frowned. After a moment he took his hand away and leaned back till he was lying full-length on the stony ground, his hands forming a resting place for his head.

Now she was made uneasy by his silence. "What is your brother like?" she asked.

He glanced at her. In the bright sunlight, his pupils had contracted to lines she could not see. His eyes were like windows onto an empty blue sky.

"That's a question I've heard before. 'Tell us about Eh Manhata, Eh Shawin.'"

"Does it make you angry to be asked?"

"No. It's always been obvious that he was something special, even when we were children. Everyone knew if he lived to be a man, he would be either a hero or a monster.

"He is fierce and without fear, commanding, strong, clever about war. No one can match him as a leader in battle. So long as he's alive, our lineage will always win.

"He loves our mother and our female relatives, and he never acts without consulting them – except on the battlefield, of course. He is loyal to Eh. He respects the Goddess."

He stopped talking. There was no noise except bugs singing in the vegetation.

"I know all this," said Eyes-of-crystal.

"Then you know Eh Manhata." The man sat up. "Let's ride more."

That day they stayed on the plain above the river. In the afternoon, they returned to Ahara Tsal. At night, they mated again in the tower room. It was as unpleasant as the first time, but she didn't lie awake for as long afterward.

The weather remained hot and dry: good late summer weather. They got in the habit of going out almost every day. Eyes-of-crystal showed the man of Eh her country: the cultivated fields, the marshes and forest. They hunted the animals available in that season, before the fall migrations began. The man was a good companion: patient, observant, respectful of her skill and knowledge, unmoved by violence and death.

She liked him, though she had never expected to like a man who was not a close relative and though he did things that made her uneasy.

One afternoon Eyes-of-crystal shot a *ral*[4] in the marshes along the river. The animal went down, but it wasn't dead. It struggled to rise, making a bleating noise. Eh Shawin was the one who dismounted and cut its throat. As he stuck his knife in, the *ral* jerked and twisted its neck. Blood spurted onto his clothing, and he made the hissing sound that indicates anger or disgust. He finished killing the *ral*, then pulled off his tunic and sank it in a pool of water. Naked, he eviscerated the animal. She had never seen an adult man without clothing. It made her uncomfortable.

She kept herself busy with the *tsina*. Her Direct Action was not troubled by the scent of blood, but the animal that Shawin was riding – a young stallion that she had not finished training yet – was fidgety. He might try to run.

When Shawin had finished, he waded into the water and washed himself, then the tunic.

"Put that on," she said when he came back to shore.

"Wet? No."

"I don't like this."

For a moment he said nothing, but concentrated on wringing out

4. This is a marsh-dwelling quadruped herbivore. Its body is like a small antelope or deer except for the broad three-toed feet. Its head is surprisingly large and looks as if it might belong to a refined warthog. The males have tusks. Both sexes have little piggy eyes and large mobile ears which are striped lavender and pale yellow inside. Their backs are dull red, almost the same color as the dominant vegetation of the marshes. Their rumps are yellow, except around the anus, where there is a circular area that is entirely hairless. The bare skin is bright pink.

the tunic. Then he glanced up briefly. "There's no one here except the two of us, and we have been spending every night in the same bed, neither of us wearing anything. Do you really think we need to be formal?"

"Yes."

"Maybe you ought to go on ahead," Eh Shawin said. "You'll have to take the *ral*. My *tsin* isn't going to be willing to carry it."

She did as he suggested and rode home alone, troubled by the memory of him, his fur slicked down by water and his body evident. He was rangy with large bones and long muscles, narrow everywhere except through the shoulders. Made for speed rather than endurance, Eyes-of-crystal thought. In a way beautiful, though not with the sleek beauty of a woman.[5]

He ought to be more modest. He had not seemed especially bothered by the fact that he was naked. Maybe he had spent too much time fulfilling mating contracts. It had become ordinary for him to be around women who were not relatives and to do things with them that most men did only once or twice in their lives.

That evening, in the tower room, she asked about his behavior.

"If I hadn't washed the tunic right away, the stain would have sunk in, and I like that tunic. It's almost new, and I don't know if you noticed, but the embroidery over the shoulders is really fine. I shouldn't have worn it for hunting. I wasn't expecting to make quite so big a mess."

"Are you this way in battle?" she asked. "Fastidious?"

"No. Of course not. Though I never like it when something good is ruined: a piece of clothing, a weapon. But I don't think about that till later. In battle, there are only two things on my mind: staying alive and following my brother's orders."

There was something in his voice when he spoke about his brother that troubled her. "Do you like him?"

Eh Shawin glanced up. The room was dark except for a single lantern, flickering on the table between them, and his pupils had expanded to wide black bars. "Manhata? What a question to ask." He licked his fingers and put out the light.

5. The build described here is not typical of male *hwarhath*, who tend to be solid with torsos that go straight up and down. The author is giving us a male protagonist who is a bit odd and humanish in appearance.

One of her cousins was home from the war while an injury to his leg healed. By this time, he was starting to hobble around, and he asked Eh Shawin to practice fighting with him. This was something women were not supposed to watch, but Eyes-of-crystal climbed onto a roof that overlooked the fighting ground. The two men used swords, the long heavy kind that had only one purpose. No man even carried a weapon like that, unless he was going to war. Eh Shawin handled his sword with ease. He was obviously a better fighter than her cousin, and this was not due simply to her cousin's injury. He was as quick as she had expected and strong as well. Lovely to watch, the woman thought as she crouched on the roof tiles. If she had a son, this quickness and strength would be useful. If she had a daughter, maybe the child would get Eh Shawin's discipline. With luck, his oddness would not be transmitted.

Her time for bleeding came. So did the blood. She wasn't pregnant. She stayed away from him for several nights, as was customary.

"That tells me I have another forty days here," Eh Shawin said. "I'm not sorry, though I have to say your male relatives are boring. But I like you, and my lineage does not have another breeding contract that requires me. Once you're pregnant, I'll have to rejoin the army."

"You don't like the war."

"It's been going on a long time. After a while, everything seems as if it's happened before. There are only so many ways to kill and die. Even my brother has not managed to find much that is new in those areas."

"You are very peculiar," said Eyes-of-crystal. "I hope it doesn't come out in your children."

He laughed. "No one has complained to my female relatives."

This conversation took place atop a river bluff. They ended in this place often. He shared her love of the wide river valley. The foliage was getting its autumn colors. The river was dark brown like weathered bronze, except where it reflected the forest or the sky. Everything seemed to be shifting and changing. She looked out and thought of traveling like a tree floating in the water or a bird rising on the wind.

Maybe when this over, and she was pregnant, she would go to visit another town. There were several lineages nearby that were closely tied to Ahara. She had relatives, women who had been fathered by men of her lineage. She even had a former lover, a woman of Shulnowa. They had met at a festival and visited back and forth, and then the war grew dangerous for a time, and they exchanged tokens and messages. That ended finally. But maybe she could go to Shulnowa and visit one of her minor cousins. Maybe she would meet the lover. How could she avoid it in a town that size?

Eh Shawin ran a hand down her arm, stroking the fur. "I think I'd like to have sex right now."

"Here? In the sunlight?"

"We aren't getting anywhere by having sex in the dark."

Her bleeding had stopped the day before, so it was possible, though it seemed wrong. She tried to remember some rule that forbade sex outdoors or while the sun was up. Nothing came to mind, and she had done such things with her lover. But that had been at festivals and with a woman. Surely sex for procreation ought to be done in a less carefree manner.

He leaned over and kissed the rim of her ear, then touched his tongue to the bare skin inside.

They had sex on the river bluff in a meadow of dry plants. A group of hunting birds soared overhead. At one point, early on, she looked up and saw them, rising in a wide circle. Later, she found she had become preoccupied. The bright open world seemed to darken and turn in upon itself, and she was not aware of much except her body and Eh Shawin's body.

When they had finished, they lay a while together, listening to bugs sing around them. The birds had gone. Finally, Eh Shawin yawned and sat up. "That's something I haven't done before." He grinned at her. "There's more variety in sex than in war, in my opinion, anyway."

They got up and brushed each other off, then put on their clothing and went to find their *tsina*.

After that, they got in the habit of having sex beyond the town walls. It was the right time of year. The ground was dry, and the biting and burrowing bugs had mostly vanished. Now and then, there was some kind of distraction: a *tsin* would come close while grazing. Once, a fat little *tli* came up to see what they were doing. It stopped just outside reach and reared up on its hind legs, folding its paws against the white fur of its chest.

"Fill your eyes, little trickster," said Eh Shawin.

The animal seemed to listen. It tilted its head and watched them until they were done. Then, as they moved apart, it moved away.

They still slept in the tower room. By now, she had gotten used to sharing a bed with him. His scent was familiar, and it was comforting to lie against his broad back. Every few days her mother would ask how everything was going.

"Fine," she would answer. Finally she said, "I think I'm like my sister."

Her mother frowned. "In that case, we'll have the man with us all winter. I suppose I shouldn't complain. It gives your cousin someone to practice fighting with."

One morning she woke early and heard the cries of birds as they flew over Ahara Tsal. The fall migrations were beginning. There would be good hunting in the marshes along the river. She prodded Eh Shawin. Half awake, he agreed to go into the valley with her. After breakfast, they saddled their *tsina*.

The morning air was cool, and thin banners of mist floated over the surface of the river. The mist would be gone in less than an *ikun*, and the day would be hot by noon. But at the moment she could feel the sharp edge of autumn. She carried her strung bow. Her quiver hung from her saddle. Eh Shawin had brought a pair of throwing spears. He wasn't really in the mood to kill anything, he told her. "But a ride is fine. I can watch you shoot down birds. And if we encounter anything large, I'll be ready."

There were plenty of animals in the valley, but she didn't see the birds she wanted: the ones she had heard as they flew over. She and Eh Shawin kept going, following a road that wasn't much used. Midway through the morning, two men appeared ahead of them, riding *tsina*. They came out of the underbrush and reined their animals, blocking the road. One had a shield on his arm.

Eh Shawin had been riding in back of her. Now he came up along-side. There was a spear in his hand. "Let me take care of this." She reined Direct Action, and he moved past her. He was riding her young stallion, Hope-for-the-Future.

The two men turned their animals so they were facing Shawin, and one drew a sword, a long weapon of war.

Something made a noise in back of her. She glanced around: two more men came riding toward her. They looked like soldiers who had gone to hell: ragged and dirty. One man wore a metal helmet. The other wore a leather cap. They both held battle-swords.

She glanced back at Shawin. He'd thrown his spear, and one of the men in front was falling, shouting as he slid onto the ground. The spear was in his chest.

Shawin pulled the second spear from its holder.

The two ragged soldiers came up on either side of her. One glanced over. "We're sorry that this has to happen in front of you, but – as you can see – we're desperate. It will be over quickly." Then they rode on. Direct Action shook his head. She tightened the reins. There was nothing she could do.

Among the *hwarhath*, warfare is entirely a male activity. The *hwarhath* men direct their violence exclusively toward each other. They do no physical harm to women and children, strange as this may sound to humans. But there is a *quid pro quo*. The *hwarhath* teach their women that they must never fight. Eyes-of-crystal knew that she was almost certainly safe. Unless these men were crazy, they would not touch her. But Eh Shawin was going to die, and all the rules of right behavior told her that she had to look on. This was the way it had always been done.

The man of Eh glanced back. He must have seen the two new soldiers. A moment later, he was charging at the man in front of him, spear in hand. Their *tsina* met. Her young stallion screamed, and a man shouted, she didn't know which one. They were tangled together, their animals turning in a circle. The other bandits reined, as if they were trying to see a good way to attack.

There was no way for Eh Shawin to win. His animal was untried. He didn't have the right kind of weapons. A hunting spear and a sword that was little more than a dagger! As ignorant as she was, she knew this was a bad situation. Finally, he was outnumbered. Her male relatives did not speak much about war, but she had heard them say, "As a general rule, big wins over little and many over few."

Eyes-of-crystal pulled an arrow from her quiver. She fit it into her bow and pulled back the string. Hah! This was easy! They were much larger than a bird and hardly moving at all. She let the arrow go. It went into the neck of the man in the leather cap. He screamed, a noise almost like the one made by her young stallion.

The man in the helmet twisted around, a look of horror on his face. "No!" he shouted.

Her second arrow went into his chest. Her third went into his throat, and he fell. One foot stayed in its stirrup. He ended on the ground with one leg up. His *tsin* was thin and needed a grooming, but evidently it had been well trained. The moment its rider fell, it stopped moving, except to shake its head. Not that it made any difference. The rider was dead. His *tsin* could have dragged him across the valley and done no further harm.

The man she had shot first, the one in the leather cap, was still on his animal, bent over and holding onto the animal's neck. Blood poured down his back.

Beyond these two, Shawin still struggled with the third man. They were on the ground now, though she hadn't seen how this had happened. Their *tsina* danced around them. The men were entangled. Eyes-of-crystal could not risk a shot.

She waited, bow in hand. The struggle ended, and Eh Shawin stood up. His tunic was torn and dirty. He held his little sword. The blade was covered with blood.

"That seems to be it," Eh Shawin said.

Eyes-of-crystal leaned to one side and vomited.

After she finished, Eh Shawin helped her dismount. He was unharmed, except for a few small cuts. "Though I've been beaten like iron on the anvil, and I'll feel it tomorrow. If your relatives think I am going to be good for much of anything the next few days – "

"I killed them," she said.

"Two of the four."

She went on, speaking disjointedly. How could she tell her relatives? What would they do? No woman of the Ahara had ever gotten involved in a battle.

"None that you have been told about," Eh Shawin said. He turned and watched the one man still alive. His *tsin* had become nervous finally and begun to step sideways like a harvest dancer. Then it shook its body, and the man slid off and lay motionless on the dusty road.

"I'll pull out the arrow and drive in my second spear. It's broken, but no one will know when that happened, and you will have killed only one man then."

That was more than enough, said Eyes-of-crystal.

He tilted his head in agreement, then walked over to the man he had killed with his short sword. "I killed this fellow, then captured his sword." He bent and picked it up. "And used it to kill the last man with two blows, one to the neck and one to the chest. If I make cuts that are big enough, no one will notice the arrow wounds. So two men have died from my spears, one from my short sword and one from this." He lifted the battle sword. "What a hero I am! They'll make up poetry about me in Ahara." He looked at her, meeting her gaze. "And you behaved like a decent woman and watched the fight, never moving a hand."

She spoke again. The story was unlikely. She wasn't a good liar. It would be better to tell the truth.

"If you admit to behavior this unusual, your relatives may decide it wasn't a good idea to breed you," Eh Shawin said in answer. "And if you are pregnant already, they might decide to kill the child. Then all my hard work will have been wasted. I'd prefer that my children live, unless they are damaged in some way.

"And I'd prefer that your life be happy. It isn't likely to be, if you admit to violence.

"Lie to the best of your ability. That ought to be sufficient. Remember what you have just seen! If you're upset and don't make a lot of sense, your family will understand.

"And while it's unlikely that I could kill four men, my brother has done as much and more. Maybe I had – for once – his determination and power."

She agreed finally, and he did as he had planned, like a manager setting up the opening of a play. Bloodflies had begun to gather, their bodies shining like sparks of fire in the hazy sunlight. He ignored them, cutting the arrow from the one man with his hunting knife. He worked deftly, making the wound only a little larger, then drove in the broken spear, grunting with the effort. Then he moved on to her second victim and used the borrowed battle sword to slash new wounds. The bloodflies hummed around him and crawled on dead men.

A play would begin with the corpses lying on the stage, looking far more splendid than these fellows. One by one, the corpses would rise, turning into handsome warriors, who would explain to the audience how they came to be in their present situation, acting out the quarrels and moral dilemmas that led to death.

Let nothing like that happen here, said Eyes-of-crystal to the Goddess.

At last Eh Shawin was done preparing the stage. He gathered the men's weapons and loaded them on their *tsina*, then tied the animals to a lead and gave the lead to her. They mounted and rode back toward Ahara Tsal.

They stopped once by a stream. Eh Shawin washed her arrows, which he had kept, then handed them to her.

"I don't want these."

"I don't want them found anywhere close to the place where those fellows died. Someone might wonder. And I can't think of a better place to hide arrows than in a quiver. Get rid of them later."

She put them in her quiver, and they went on.

Hah! It was an event when they arrived at the town, leading four animals, Eh Shawin covered with blood. He did most of the talking, while her relatives comforted her.

Male relatives saddled their *tsina* and rode to find the bodies, led by Shawin. He was fine, he said. A little tired and sore. But he would have no trouble riding back into the valley. The men of Ahara gave him sideways glances that indicated respect.

Her female relatives gave her a bath and put her to bed. After a while, she went to sleep, waking in the middle of the night.

Shawin was settling into bed next to her. She spoke his name.

He said, "We followed their trail back for a distance. There were only the four of them. Bandits, your kinfolk say. Men without a lineage. The world is full of people like that these days. They must have wanted to rob me. The Goddess knows their animals are in bad condition, and they had nothing of value except their battle swords. Hah! To end like that!" Then he went to sleep.

She stayed awake. He had bathed, and he smelled of clean fur and aromatic soap. She found the odor comforting. All at once, she was unwilling to have him leave.

What lay in front of her, after he was gone? Being pregnant and then nursing a child. Then, maybe, if she could convince her relatives that she had no interest in children, she would be free for a while. That happened sometimes. There were women who could not manage to get interested in motherhood. Other women raised the children they bore.

But if the child turned out well, they would breed her again, maybe to someone like the son of Merin who had fathered her sister's just-born child.

And all the while, she would have the secret of her violence in her mind. What if her child was a girl? The trait might be transmitted. She might begin a line of female monsters.

As might be expected, she did not sleep any more that night. In the morning she was queasy and threw up. Not a good sign, the woman thought.

But the next day she was fine, and the day after she and Eh Shawin went riding, though not down into the river valley. Instead they wandered among the fields, now mostly harvested, and went up onto the bluff to their favorite place. They dismounted and sat a while, watching the hunting birds that soared over the valley, circling and chasing one another, not out of anger or from a need to mate, but only (the old women said) for pleasure, from joy in their skill.

Finally Eyes-of-crystal began to speak. She had not been able to shake off her feeling of horror at what she had done, and she did not like to think of living her life with a secret like this one.

"You are not the only person with a secret," Eh Shawin told her gently.

"Not like this," she answered. "And it isn't my secret alone. You know it also."

"I'm not going to tell, dear one."

She glanced at him, surprised. He had used a term that belonged to a lover.

He was lying comfortably full length on the ground, his eyes half closed, his hands folded over his belly. "You are young enough to think that people are the way they appear from the front and that they ought to be so. – What am I? A loyal son of Eh, who carries out an embarrassing obligation as I am told to by the senior women of my lineage?"

"I don't know what to think of you," said Eyes-of-crystal. "I have never been much interested in sex with men. That is one thing I have in common with my brother, though we differ in our attitude toward sex with women. The idea repels him so much that he has always refused to carry out any breeding contract. I like what I do, though my attitude toward the individual women varies. Still, none of them has ever been stupid, and all of them are in good physical condition."

He smiled at her. "Our lineage has been lucky. They have one son who wants to spend his entire life fighting and killing, which has been very useful, and another son – the twin of Eh Manhata – who is willing to put the same kind of effort into mating.

"And I have been lucky. If my brother had been ordinary, I would have spent my life having no sex or sex with men, or I would have become a pervert, sneaking after women. Such men exist, though they are not common, even in this age where everything seems to be unraveling.

"Instead, I am here with you, for which I thank the Goddess and Manhata."

She couldn't think of what to say. They were both monsters, though in different ways. She had acted in a way that no woman ever should, though she had been unwilling and was now remorseful. His actions were proper. He had done as his female relatives had told him. But his thoughts and feelings were perverse.

"What kind of child is going to come from this mating?" she asked finally.

"I don't know," said Eh Shawin. "But the passing on of traits is not a simple process, as we know from breeding animals as well as people, and we both have many good traits. I think it's likely that the child will be fine."

She looked out at the river valley, then up at the birds, still soaring over the bluffs. A crazy idea came into her mind, and she told it to Eh Shawin.

Why couldn't they go off together? The world was full of people who wandered, having lost their homes in the long war. She could disguise herself like a man. Such things were possible. The actors who came to Ahara Tsal played women convincingly. Or else they could claim to be relatives, a brother and sister. She would not have to hide the person she was from the rest of her family. If the child turned out badly, at least it would not be one of the Ahara. He would not have to go back to the war.

He listened to her patiently. When she finished, he said, "How would we earn a living? I have only two skills, fighting and making women pregnant. The second one would be useless, if I didn't belong to a powerful lineage. As for the first skill, I don't want to become a bandit like those men in the valley."

They could hunt, said Eyes-of-crystal.

"And live like animals in the wilderness?"

They could sell whatever they didn't need, meat and fur.

"Most land is held by some lineage or other. Do you think they'll give us permission to hunt? Do you think people will refrain from asking questions, if we bring the hides of animals into a town? I'd be executed as a thief, and you would be sent off to survive as best you could. Most likely, someone would take you in. Even in this age of unraveling, there are people who will not let a woman come to harm. But you would not be the daughter of a famous lineage, and you would not be loved as you are here.

"And if there were more children, what would happen to them? I don't want my children to be beggars."

"Is there nothing we can do?" asked Eyes-of-crystal.

"What we're doing," said Eh Shawin.

After that she was silent, watching the birds.

It was midwinter before her relatives were certain that she was pregnant. The snow was deep by then, and the winter unusually cold. Eh Shawin stayed on till spring, though she no longer spent time with him. She saw him, now and then, at a distance.

When the thaw was over and roads comparatively dry, he rode off with a group of her male relatives who were returning to the war. She was sick that day and did not see him go.

The children were born at harvest time: two boys, large and sturdy. The older became Tsu, which was an old name among the Ahara. The younger became Ehrit, which means 'deriving from Eh.'

She nursed them for a year, as was customary in those days, then turned them over to one of her sisters and went back to her old habits. But hunting interested her less than it had. She missed having company, and she felt less safe than before. What if other bandits came into the river valley? Would she become violent again? Would they become violent?

Gradually, she became more like other women, though she never became entirely ordinary. She remained more solitary than was usual, and she did not lose her fondness for riding. Now she followed the trails that went through cultivated land, and she kept her eye on the fields and pastures. When she took out a weapon, it was usually to deal with some wild animal that was doing harm to her family's herds and crops.

And though she was not especially maternal, she wasn't able to leave her twins entirely in the hands of her female relatives. Maybe if they had been ordinary, she would have been able to ignore them. But they were clever and active and clearly in front of most other children.

When they were two years old, her family bred her again. This time the man came from one of the small lineages that existed at the edges of Ahara.[6] He was solid and handsome with a fine glossy coat, and he

6. The old term for families like this was 'side-clingers,' though the word can also be translated as 'shelf fungus' or even 'barnacle.' They were too small to survive on their own, so became allies of some large and powerful lineage, which chose not to absorb them for various reasons. Most powerful was the need to have a nearby source for breeding and sexual partners. In the area

did what he was asked to do with determination and competence. But he was obviously embarrassed, and it was clear that he preferred to spend his time with her male relatives. Eyes-of-crystal felt disappointed, though this didn't make any sense. The man behaved exactly as he was supposed to, and he was never discourteous. She got pregnant almost at once. The child was a girl who inherited her father's solidity and lovely fur. What about this mating could cause dissatisfaction?

In time, another gift came from this mating: the man's sister, who was as solid and handsome as her brother and who (unlike him) was comfortable around women. Eyes-of-crystal met her at a festival, and they fell in love. This was (the author tells us) no ordinary casual bedfriendship.

It's important, at this point, to realize that the *hwarhath* tend to see women as less romantic and more promiscuous than men. Living on the perimeter, men have time and opportunity for love. But the women live at the center of the family, surrounded by relatives, and their strongest ties are usually with kin. For women sexual love tends to be a matter of brief couplings at festivals or long-term long-distance romances where the two lovers visit back and forth, but are more often apart than together.

Occasionally, female lovers will move in together, and this has happened much more often in modern times. Conservatives see it as yet another example of how society is going to hell in a handbasket. What is going to become of the People, if women languish and hold onto one another like men? Who is going to look out for the family and the children?

In the age of Eh Manhata this kind of female affection-beyond-the-family was unusual, but it did occasionally happen, and the author of this story, who is determined apparently to break all the ordinary rules of romantic fiction, gives her heroine a lover who is willing to move away from home. The woman was maternal and had no children of her own, the author tells us, and she found Ahara Pai's children more interesting than her nephews and nieces.

where this story takes place, the incest taboo forbade – and still forbids – sex of any kind within a lineage. As the lineages grew larger and larger, this began to be a problem, which was solved – at least in part – by the accumulation of clingers.

It's possible that the lover was added to the story to give it a happy ending. The *hwarhath* insist on happy endings in their romances, though their idea of a happy ending is not always the same as ours. Or maybe the author put the lover in to shock and perturb.

Eyes-of-crystal was bred three more times. Each time the man was different and came from a different lineage. The author gives the names of the lineages, but they would mean nothing to a human reader. Two were important. One was another clinger. The children – two more girls and a boy – were healthy enough to keep, and all of them grew to be promising, though none equaled the twins. They really were exceptional boys: quick, well-coordinated, intelligent, forceful, good-humored and charming.

"This is the spirit of Eh Manhata showing," said her female relatives.

No, she thought. The intelligence and good humor came from Eh Shawin. So did the charm, though the boys were able to get what they wanted from both women and men.

Occasionally she heard news about Shawin. Her kinfolk took an interest in him now. His life continued the way he had described it. He was often away from the army, fulfilling contracts his relatives had made. It seemed as if he almost never failed. The children he fathered were strong and healthy. They made it through the dangerous years of childhood with little trouble. His kinsmen began to call him The Progenitor, and this became the nickname that everyone used.

He was less impressive in the war. Not a bad soldier, her male relatives said, but not what they would have expected from Eh Manhata's twin. "Or from the man who killed those four bandits in our valley. Hah! That was an achievement! We still tell people about it! But he has never done anything comparable."

When the twins were fourteen, there was a festival at Taihanin. Eyes-of-crystal went, along with other women and enough men to provide protection, though the war had moved to the east by now, and all of Ahara and Eh lay between them and the nearest enemy. Her younger children stayed at home, as did her lover, but the twins were old enough for traveling, and they joined the party.

One evening they came to a caravanserai. There were people there already: a small group of soldiers from Eh. One of her male cousins went to speak with the soldiers. When he returned, he said, "Eh Shawin is there. I asked him over. He's never met his sons."

Soon the man himself appeared, walking out of the shadows into the light of Ahara's fire. No question that he had gotten older. He was still tall and rangy, but he moved stiffly now. The fur on his shoulders and upper arms had turned pale silver-grey. But when he saw her, he smiled, and his smile was unchanged: brief but affectionate in a way that was not common among men of the People.

She was right, thought Eyes-of-crystal. The boys got their charm from him.

Her cousin stepped forward and introduced the boys. Eh Shawin looked at them. They had shot up in the last year, and it seemed likely that they would be as tall as he was. At the moment, they were thin and as leggy as *tsina* colts. Like colts, they were nervous and shy. They hung back and ducked their heads, unwilling to meet Eh Shawin's gaze, though they gave him many sideways glances. But there is nothing wrong with shyness in young men and boys, and their manners were good. They answered his questions promptly and clearly, Ehrit doing most of the talking, as he always did.

Finally, Shawin ran out of questions. The boys were given leave to go, and he came over to Eyes-of-crystal. It wasn't required that the two of them talk, but it was permissible.

"You've done a good job," he said.

"My sisters more than I," she said. "And my lover, though I taught the boys to hunt, and that was enjoyable."

He asked if she had other children. She named them and their fathers.

"Your relatives have been keeping you busy," he said.

"Not as busy as the Eh have been keeping you, from what I hear."

He laughed and inclined his head.

They spoke some more about the twins. She praised their qualities, while he looked across the fire. The boys were sprawled on the far side. They had gathered stones and drawn lines in the dirt and were playing a game of strategy. Now and then one or the other would glance up and see Shawin watching, then glance back down.

"So everything has turned out well," Shawin said finally. "You have a lover, and six fine children, and I have my life, which has turned out better than I expected. Hah! I was frightened when I first realized where my sexual interests were likely to lead me.

"I thought, our relatives had been wrong. They worried about Manhata becoming a monster. He was always so relentless, and he cared for so few people, and none of them male. But I was the one who was the monster. I thought, they will find out and kill me, or I will kill myself. But none of that has happened."

"Have you never wanted a lover?" asked Eyes-of-crystal.

He glanced at her sideways and smiled. "How could I have one? – I'll do what I can for your boys when they join the war, though they aren't going to need much help, being Ahara and having the qualities you describe. But I find it pleasant to do what I can."

They said goodbye, and he walked back to his campfire, pausing on the way to speak again with his sons.

Eh Shawin lived to be almost eighty, and Eyes-of-crystal reached a hundred, but they never met again, at least so far as the author tells us.

The last part of her story is devoted to the twins, who grew up to be fine soldiers and famous men. When Eh Manhata died at the age of eighty-five, betrayed and murdered by men he trusted, it seemed as if the alliance he had created would be destroyed. It was Ahara Ehrit who held everything together, not through violence, but through negotiation. He was helped (he said) by the fact that the world was full of the children of Eh Shawin. Often, when he met with other lineages, he found that he was talking to a half-brother. And there were certain traits that appeared over and over in Shawin's children. They were reasonable, flexible, good-humored, and willing to make the best of the situation. If they had to, they could fight, but it wasn't their preferred way to solve problems.

Ehrit is known to history as The Negotiator or The Weaver. Eh Manhata began the alliance that finally became the world government, but Ahara Ehrit saved it.

His brother Tsu was better at warfare, and this also was useful to the alliance. He was among the best generals of his generation, though no one in that generation could equal Eh Manhata. Still, Ahara Tsu won most of the battles he fought. His nickname was the Sword of Ahara. In the opinion of Ehrit, his qualities came from their mother. He was more courageous than was typical of the children of Eh Shawin, more relentless, more disciplined, more bloody-minded and more bent on going his own way, though he always listened to Ehrit, and discipline and loyalty kept him from doing anything seriously off to the side.

Neither of them inherited Eh Manhata's great force of character. But the new age did not need this quality. They both had lovers, men who stayed with them for years, and though both of them fathered children, so far as is known they did so without pleasure.

TWO NOTES ON THE TRANSLATION:

In its upper course the river Tsal is confined by high bluffs of sandstone and limestone, but further to the south and east, it runs between low banks across a level plain. In modern times, engineers have built dams and levees to control it, but in the old days, the river changed course often. Its name comes from these changes in course. Tsal means loose, unfastened, unconnected, wandering and homeless. Another meaning has been added in the last few years, since the People encountered humanity and the human concept of freedom, which does not (apparently) exist in any *hwarhath* culture. Tsal is the word they use to translate the English word 'free.' This story, which may be (in part) about freedom, is set by the Loose or Homeless or Untethered or Free River.

In the *hwarhath* main language, there is no way to speak of people without mentioning their gender. The language has singular female, singular male, singular of undetermined gender, female plural, male plural, mixed plural, and undetermined plural. There is no mixed plural form of the word lover. Lovers are always both female or both male. The author of this story could have made up a mixed (i.e. heterosexual) form of the word. It would have been recognizable, and her readers would have been shocked. But for once she played it safe, or maybe she wanted her readers to come to the center of the story – its hearth or meaning – slowly. The title she gave the story, assuming that it was given by her and not by a nervous publisher, is best translated into English as 'The Breeders.' But this title doesn't sound right to humans and distorts the meaning of the story, which is, after all, about love.

Chemistry

"I'M GOING TO FALL IN LOVE TONIGHT," said Marja, "and this time you're coming with me."

Lily had been staring without comprehension at *Screen 8 of 23/ Brain Mechanisms in Mating*. It was too hot for neurobiology; the spex with their heavy displays kept sliding down her nose. When she pushed them back up, *Screen 8* flickered. "I have to study," she said, trying to remember the last time she'd heard a man whisper her name in the dark.

"Face it, Lily, you think too damn much. What your synapses need is a nice warm norepinephrine bath." Marja Zoltowski had snuggled into a nest of pillows and tilted the top of her head backwards against the wall to keep her spex in place. Her Adam's apple bobbed when she spoke.

"You Poles are such romantics." Lily shivered the way she used to when Glenn touched her face. "What is tonight, anyway?"

"I don't know. Monday?"

Lily blinked at the calendar icon and waited a second for the spex to retrieve her tickler from memory. "Okay, tomorrow we have day two of Freddy's virtual autopsy," she said, "and Wednesday is the immunology test. We hardly have time to sleep, much less fall for strangers."

"Listen to yourself." Marja shook her head. "Do you call this a life?"

"Nah," said Lily. *Screen 9 of 12* was a diagram of the septo-hypothalamic-mesencephalic continuum. "I call it med school."

"We could try that new place on Densmore Street. It's supposed to be grade."

"We? These are your urges, not mine. Why don't you just program a window shirt to flash *available* and hang out at Wally's?"

"This isn't about sex, Lily, it's about feelings. Believe me, after they crank your hypothalamus you won't be able tell the difference between neuromance and the real thing."

"Says you."

"Emotions aren't magic, doctor. They are reproducible brain states."

This was something Lily knew to be true, but preferred not to think about – like the correlation between cheesecake and adipose tissue. "Anyway," she said, "we can't afford it."

"Love makes all things possible."

Lily doubted that, but she said nothing.

"I wonder what kind of men go out on a Monday night?" Marja smirked. "Gourmet cooks. Don't fancy restaurants close on Mondays?"

Lily set her spex on the kitchen table, mirror side down, so she wouldn't accidentally catch a glimpse of herself goofing off. "Weekend weathermen," she said. "Priests cutting loose after a long Sunday. I need to study tonight, and so do you." She got up to stretch her legs, but of course there was no room. She and Marja had squeezed into an efficiency apartment off campus and their stuff filled the place to overflowing. Two yard sale dressers, two futons, a MedNet node, a whiny refrigerator, a microwave on the kitchen table, two plastic chairs. They had to wash dishes in the bathroom, which had once been a closet. The closet was a clothesline stretched across the west wall. When the place was picked up she could take four, maybe five steps without bumping into something, but at the moment piles of hardcopy booby-trapped the floor like paper banana peels. There was a word for their lifestyle, she realized. Squalor.

"How long have we known each other?" said Marja. "Almost two years and you haven't even breathed on a man. They're not all Glenns, you know. Look, we can fall in and out of love and still be back in plenty of time to weigh old Freddy's nonexistent spleen."

Lily picked up her spex again and held them at arm's length. From a distance the bright little images on the displays looked like a pair of shirt buttons. Had it really been two years? Maybe it *was* time to unbutton herself.

A private security rover patrolled Densmore Street; the servos of its infrared lenses mewled softly as it wove through the twilight. Most of the stores on the block were just closing: La Parfumerie, Hawkins Fine Wines, a World Food boutique and a couple of art galleries. Next to the Hothouse was the Office Restaurant. Through its windows Lily could see people in gray suits sitting alone at stylized desks, eating absently as they tweaked glowing blue spreadsheets. The neighborhood reeked of money and there was only fifty-three dollars and sixty-seven cents left on her cash card. She wondered how much romance that would buy in the caviar part of town.

At street level the Hothouse was as stolid as a bank: two stories of granite blocks regularly pierced by thin, dark windows. Higher up, it blossomed into a crystalline riot of glass and light. They hesitated in front of the marble threshold.

"I bet they're wearing shoes made of real cow." Lily tucked her purse under her arm as if she expected some rampaging doorman to snatch it from her.

"Don't worry." Marja touched Lily's hand. "You look fine." She had lent Lily a crepe off-the-shoulder dress her grandmother had left her. It was too 90s for Lily's taste, but Marja was the specialist when it came to this sort of thing.

"You too," said Lily, "but that's not what I mean. Look where we are. We can't afford this – unless you don't mind eating Cheerios for supper until finals."

"Come on. How much could it cost?"

"What's the gross national product of Portugal?"

"I'll ask, okay? I'll just poke my head in the door and find out."

"No, I'm coming." Lily rammed her purse deeper into her armpit and clamped it.

Lily had expected flocked wallpaper and leather couches. Instead there were lots of bright plastic surfaces and a rug with all the ambiance of sandpaper. The lobby of the Hothouse was emphatically air-conditioned and illuminated almost to the point of discomfort. Only two of the five ticket booths were open. Beyond them was a bank of sliding doors, textured to look like the trunks of trees.

"Hi." The cashier was a young woman in an extravagant foliage print dress. She had jade highlights in her black hair and an expression as guileless as a pansy. "Are you together?" The button on her collar said *Ju*.

"Yes," said Marja.

"No." Lily nudged her. "We came together, but we're not *together* together."

Ju smiled. "Whatever."

"We're interested," Marja said, "but we're not really sure this place is for us. Can you tell us about it?"

"As in, what does it cost?" Lily said.

Ju slid a brochure across the counter toward them; her fingernails were polished the same green as her hair. "Your basic attraction enhancement is $39.95." She opened it; inside was a map. "Includes admission to all public areas on the third and fifth floors, all gardens, three dance floors, both pools, complimentary swimsuits and towels in the dressing booths. On the fourth floor are stores and services you'll pay extra for. Sit-down and take-out restaurants, bars, gift shops, lingerie boutiques, contraception kiosks, simulators, and personal FX galleries.

It's nothing but a mall, Lily thought. I'm twenty-five years old and still looking for love at the mall.

"We also have fifty-three private encounter rooms," Ju pointed to the map, "on the sixth floor. We're the biggest neuromance palace in the city."

Lily watched a little man in a navy blue jacket and gray slacks approach the other cashier. Her age but not her type; he looked as if he had just finished eating a memo salad at the Office Restaurant. "So how do you make someone fall in love?" she asked.

"Oh, we don't make you fall. We enhance the attraction response. There's a big difference. See, we trick this part of your brain called the hypothalamus into ordering up these special hormones. It's all natural."

"Hormones like LHRH and testosterone?" said Lily.

"Testosterone, right." Ju nodded. "That surprised me when I first heard it. I mean, you'd think you'd grow a mustache – or worse. But it's okay; I've tried it." She gave them a blissful smile. "Don't know about the one with letters, they all sound the same. To tell the truth, they explained this to me once, but it didn't take. All I know is that whatever we do to you is approved by the FDA and licensed by the Board of Health. This card explains…"

"Give me that." Marja snatched it from Lily. "Believe me, the procedure is straight out of Wessinger's neurobiology lab. The less you think about it, the better you'll feel."

"Whatever." Ju dimpled. "But really, one of the best parts is that they tickle something called your vomeronasal organ – don't ask me how. You'll smell stuff you've never noticed before. Unbelievable, how great the food tastes. Try the brownies with brandy sauce." She kissed her fingers to the air and the man waiting at the next booth glanced over at them. Lily thought he might actually be shorter than she was.

"So what if we pay you our forty bucks," she said, "and go upstairs and find there're no human beings left? I don't want to fall for an insurance salesman."

"Oh, that's not a problem, believe me. We offer a money-back guarantee, but only a few people ask. See, when those elevator doors open onto the welcome garden, you're... I don't know... ripe. I can't explain it exactly, but enhancement makes me realize how cute men look, how sweet they can be. At least while they're here. And it's really a grade crowd tonight. Some real hammers, if you know what I mean. I kind of wish I wasn't working myself."

An older man who shouldn't have been wearing red skintights got in line behind them, so they gave Ju their cash cards. While she debited them, she had them press thumbs to a blood drawer. She printed two green buttons that read *Lily* and *Marja* and explained that green was for righties, red for gays. She had them sign liability waivers and told them they'd need to give a urine sample and warned them about side effects. Although enhancement would wear off in four to five hours, they might have trouble falling asleep immediately after leaving the Hothouse; there was a chance their next periods might be a couple of days off schedule. She grinned, reminded them about the brownies and ushered them through the booth.

"We're in this together, right?" Lily whispered as the tree trunk doors opened. "You'll stop me before I do anything stupid?"

Marja laughed and patted her on the back. "Sort of late for that now."

Lily rubbed the button-sized swelling on her wrist where the orderly had poked her with the pressure syringe. Her purse hung loosely by her side.

"Pulse acelerated." Marja was practically vibrating as the elevator climbed to the third floor. "Skin temperature elevated. Apocrine sweat glands – whew!" She peered into Lily's left eye, "Doctor, your pupils are dilated!"

"Stop diagnosing."

"Okay, so how do you feel?"

Lily considered and then giggled. "Like I'm six and it's Christmas Eve. You're losing your corsage."

Marja repinned the orchid which the orderly had laced with phero- mones synthesized from her urine sample. The doors slid open.

Fifteen or twenty faces turned, glowing with expectation. Lily was instantly drawn to them, understanding their conspicuous need be- cause she shared it. They had hauled themselves out of the icy datastream into the warmth of high touch and beautiful feelings. As the enhancement drugs gripped her, she felt the weight of her life drop away. Tomorrow they would all go back to their desks and workshops and counters and she would ligate the arteries of a cybercorpse named Fred. But that was far removed from this bright dream of lush and immediate sensation. She let it fill her lungs and eyes and ears; she wanted to lick it. A band stood poised to play. Leaves like green hands waved at her. She itched to rub her bare feet on the moss rug, shinny up that palm tree, kiss all three of those men by the fountain just to find out how they tasted. No, she wasn't going to ask for her money back. She knew she would find him here. Someone to love, for a little while at least. His identity was a mystery only she could solve: Lily Brewster, girl detective. Maybe he was still lingering at the marble threshhold on Hope Street, ten thousand miles below, or already talk- ing to Ju in the lobby. Most likely he was watching her, one of the happy faces, which she now noticed were arranged in a kind of loose formation. She and Marja stepped down into the welcome garden's central courtyard and smiling people closed around them.

She smiled back, even after she realized she was going to have to square dance.

The bass player had a voice as friendly as a milk commercial.

"All square your sets around the hall,
Four couples to a set, listen to the call."

He chose "The Texas Star," a simple figure dance which featured constant switching of partners.

Her first was the short man from the lobby; his green name badge read *Steve*. She couldn't understand how he had gotten to the welcome garden before her. Just as the dance began, he insisted on shaking her hand. "You're freezing!" Lily said, clasping his cold hand between hers.

He stared as if he were memorizing her face. "I just washed up."

When the fiddles started, he led her into a left-faced turn under his arched right arm. "You know, Lily, your handshake tells a lot about you."

"Meet your partner, pass on by
Pick up your next one on the fly."

Nick, a pale man with a mustache like a caterpillar, said, "I know you! We met at Justin Metaphor's last image launch." He stared at Lily's corsage as if he wanted to eat it. "You came as President Garmezy."

"Not me," she said. "I'm a Neurocrat."

"Smalls back out, bigs go in,
Make that Texas Star again."

"Am I a big or a small?" She crooked her arm into that of a heavy-weight with hair down his neck. Tomasz had feet as wide as shovels.

"You're a small, my kitten, but plenty big enough for me." He had a thick Middle European accent; she decided to leave him for Marja.

"Bigs back out and all circle eight
Circle back to place 'til you get it straight."

The fiddlers stroked their instruments. Was that her roommate, skipping like a girl scout? Lily was determined to initiate the next conversation. "This is probably the silliest damn thing I've ever done," she said to a red badge named Renfred who smelled of cigarettes.

"Never done it before." Sweat beaded across his face like a glass of iced tea. "I'm from Toronto."

"Hand over hand and heel over heel
The more you dance the better you feel."

"I've finally decided who you remind me of." Keith had green eyes and more teeth than a shark. "One of those Vermeer women, standing in front of a window." The fat end of his untied tie dangled in front of his crotch and the skinny end beat against his pocket as he danced. "Vermeer, you know, the painter?"

Not a bad line, she thought, but he ruined it by prompting her. "Keith." She tugged the tie from around his neck and handed it to him. "Is this yours?"

Her next partner ignored her. "Yes, of course I did." He spoke over his shoulder to the Asian woman behind Lily. "She belonged with her parents."

"Tuck in your shirt, pull down your vest
And bow to the one you like the best."

The fiddlers tipped their instruments toward the caller and the dance ended. Lily might have nodded at Keith, the Vermeer fan, if he'd been paying attention, but he was already fawning over an older woman with eyes like targets. Someone tapped her left shoulder; she turned.

"My name is Steve." The guy with cold hands bowed.

"Lily." She glanced down to see that she hadn't lost her name badge. "Obviously."

"Lily, do you know that people rarely change their first impressions?" His eye contact was relentless.

"Is that so?" she said. Steve was as clean-cut as a Marine recruiter. He had stubby fingers and wide shoulders. A thread hung loose from the middle buttonhole of his jacket. "What's yours?" He hadn't gotten any taller.

He held up open palms, as if to show he was unarmed. "That you're gorgeous, lonely, nervous, and still shopping. Will you at least let me shake your hand again?"

"Promise to give it back?" she said. He had a precise and sincere grip that didn't try to prove anything. "You've warmed up." Their hands fit together nicely.

"When my palms get sweaty," he said, "I rinse them under cold water. It's a sales trick: the confident man keeps a cool hand."

She had never understood why men always said such odd things to her.

"Here's another," he continued. "Say we're shaking and you haven't decided whether to trust me. Look where your hand is, Lily. When we started talking, you kept it close to your body. Now that I've drawn it toward me slightly, you've come along with it."

Lily let go of him. She reminded herself that this was a man with a crew cut who practiced sales tricks. "And what are you trying to sell me?"

"I don't know yet." His voice was low. "First I have to find out if I carry what you want."

The elevator doors opened and everyone turned to inspect the new arrivals. It was Old Man Skintights and a thirtyish brunette in a caramel-colored suit. As the dancers moved to welcome them, the fiddlers picked up their bows.

"Never leave a prospect until you schedule your next meeting." Steve grinned. "Shall we say, after this dance?" He strolled away whistling but paused at the edge of the garden and called to her. "I like you, Lily. Obviously." He disappeared behind a hibiscus covered with red flowers.

There's a man who knows exactly what he wants, she thought, and I'm it. She was at once pleased and scared and slightly let down. Where had he gone so abruptly? To rinse in cold water?

The caller tapped the belly of his bass. "*All square your sets...*"

Lily had intended to dance again, but that was what he expected her to do. She thought it better to be unpredictable, make his hands sweat. She spotted some people gathered beneath a statue of a satyr groping a nymph.

"Now you're getting into ideology," a nervous black man said. "Ask Alice about that."

"About what?" said a woman in a poet's blouse and orange tights.

"Keith here claims the female orgasm is vestigial. A leftover, like an appendix."

"Should we kill him now," Betty said to T.J., who had his arm around her waist, "or hear him out first?"

"Hey, I'm not against anyone's orgasm," Keith said quickly. "My point is that in evolutionary terms, female orgasm is irrelevant. Some societies don't even have a word for it."

"We should make one up for them," said Lily. "How about shimmer? Or leap?

"Oh yes, baby, yes, I'm rippling."

Alice shook her head. "Maybe you ripple, honey, but I *surge*."

All the women laughed.

Keith wasn't giving up. "Women reproduce whether they climax or not. With us, orgasm is everything. If we don't come, there's no ball game."

"*Ball* game?" Betty rubbed against T.J. "Why is it that whenever we try to talk about love, men change the subject to sports?"

"It's because we take pleasure differently," said Alice. "A man gets off on objects. He sees tits and an ass and he doesn't care who they're attached to. We need intimacy and tenderness to enjoy ourselves. We don't give a damn how big his cock is; we want to know the size of his feelings."

"All men want is sex." Maya sighed. "We want love."

"Ah, bullshit," said T.J. "I want to dance."

"Look, someone's imprinting."

The band broke into the ceremonial "Only You Tonight" and dancers closed in a circle around a couple, clapping and cheering them on. Lily strained to see who it was. Big Tomasz with the shovel feet – and Marja! "Wait!" As Lily raced across the courtyard, Marja pulled Tomasz down to her. He buried his nose in her corsage. The orderly had explained that once two people imprinted themselves with each others' pheromones, they would be inseparable the rest of the night. When Tomasz came up, his eyes were gleaming.

Lily waved frantically at her but Marja paid no attention. Tomasz offered her the chocolate the Hothouse staff had impregnated with his own musky androstenols. It was wrapped in gold foil; she unpeeled it lasciviously, pressed it between her lips and chewed, her jaws working around a cheek-stretching smile.

The crowd's rhythmic clapping punctuated the impromptu ceremony. "Let's congratulate the new couple," said the caller from behind his bass. Now that they had imprinted, their badges changed to a color which only they shared. It was the purple of venous blood. "Seal it with a kiss!" the caller cried.

The crowd whooped.

"Isn't he grade?" Marja was glowing. "Am I lucky or what? This is Lily, my roommate. Tomasz is a lion tamer, can you believe that?" Lily could smell the chocolate on her breath.

"Mój Boze, Marja, ja Çie kocham."

"Aren't lions extinct?" Lily said.

He didn't hear her; he and Marja were kissing again. By the time they finished, Lily assumed he had forgotten the question, so she asked again.

"In the wild, yes." He kept one massive arm clasped around Marja's shoulder as if she were a trophy he had just won. "I work with the New World cats mostly, cougars and jaguars. We have one leopard." He feinted at her with his free hand and grinned when she recoiled. "All strong enough to kill you."

"I didn't even know the circus was in town."

"They leave Wednesday," said Marja. "Which is why we're going to the fifth floor right now and find a quiet place and tell each other our life stories. Maybe later we can swim."

"I want an olive pizza," said Tomasz, "and a liter of kava."

"Okay, kava and pizza." She nestled up to him. "What else do you want?"

He had a laugh that could worry a cougar.

"So Marja," said Lily, "maybe we should set a time to meet?"

"No, no, I'll get home on my own." She gave Lily a look like a bedroom door closing. "Don't wait up. I'll see you at Freddy's tomorrow."

"Freddy?" said Tomasz.

"He's nobody," she said as she steered her prize away.

Lily filled with doubts as she watched her friend go. They had promised not to let each other do anything stupid. Did falling for a lion tamer qualify? Now that she'd been abandoned, she wished she were home studying. Coming to the Hothouse made sense in the romantic abstract, but the men here were all annoyingly specific. She wasn't attracted to anyone and even if she were, how could she trust her feelings? They'd pumped her so full of hormones she could probably fall for a vacuum cleaner if it smelled right. She decided she didn't much like being enhanced, although she understood that there was no difference between the brain chemistry of neuromance and actually falling in love. Despite her B+ in Wessinger's class, Lily was reluctant to accept a mechanistic view of her inner life. She didn't like being reminded that love, hope, and joy were merely outputs of her limbic system. What she ought to do was march right down for a refund, go home and stare into her spex until she had memorized the immunoglobulins. The idea was oddly comforting: maybe the enhancement was wearing off. Marja had warned her that thinking too much about it might spoil the effect.

"You didn't dance."

She moaned. "Oh, shit." She couldn't help herself. Steve had taken off the navy blue jacket; he was wearing a white shirt and a red striped tie. "I'm sorry. Look, this has nothing to do with you. You seem nice enough. It's just... I'm probably going to leave. Get my money back."

"Why?"

"Because I don't like being programmed. I mean, I realized that's what would happen when I walked in, but I thought somehow it would fool me. Now I know better. This just doesn't feel like love. It's a chemistry experiment."

"You've been in love before, Lily?"

"Of course." He wouldn't take a hint; she'd probably have to be rude.

"What's it like?"

"Oh, come on." She watched him watching her, his pupils like black buttons. "You know."

"No. I've never been in love."

"What, you grew up in a monastery?"

The sarcasm seemed to bounce off him. "I thought I was in love once." He paused, as if deciding how much to tell her. "We worked in the same office. She was older. Married. When her husband found out, she broke it off. She said she didn't love me and that I didn't really love her."

"And you believed her?" Lily didn't know why she was encouraging him.

He nodded. "She was right. The sex was great but it wasn't love. I got all excited because she was beautiful, smart, rich, powerful, what I thought I wanted. But we never talked, except about the business or the weather or what hotel to meet at. The day we broke up she told me she was a Catholic and went to church every Sunday. She said she'd felt really guilty about what we'd been doing. It wasn't a secret, I just never asked."

The elevator doors opened again and a bald Hispanic woman blinked in astonishment at the welcome garden.

"I realized that if I hadn't loved *her*, then I'd never loved anyone."

The musicians were ready. "Hell of a thing to find out about yourself," she said.

"Something I'd like to fix, Lily."

This was her chance; she could escape into the next dance. She wouldn't have to hurt him – not that she cared. Afterward she could sneak away. She didn't need a man with another woman's footprints up his back. But if she left now, who was going to make sure Marja didn't run off with the circus?

"What happened to your jacket?" she said. "Your name badge?"

"I went to find a place where we could be alone. I left them to hold our spot."

The bass player announced a new dance called "Swing or Cheat" and sets began forming around them.

"It's really pretty," Steve said. "There's a stream and a bush with tiny oranges on it and white flowers that smell like honey."

Lily was getting used to the way he made eye contact. Whatever Steve's other faults, she believed he was sincere. Glenn had always looked away when he lied to her.

"You just left your jacket there?" she said. "I hope no one takes it."

He led her down a slate path past the eight-foot wide sheet of falling water which drowned the shrilling of the fiddles. They turned into one of the garden's many little clearings. The bench was wrought iron; it sat low on a lawn of lemon thyme. The stream burbled in front of them and the air hung heavy and sweet. Steve's jacket was folded over the armrest.

"Calamondin oranges." She slid her purse under the bench. "They're sour, just barely edible. They make good marmalade, though."

"How do you know so much about plants?"

"My dad's hobby, actually. He had a greenhouse. I remember in the winter, it was always so bright and warm. Like going on vacation. The pots were all on wheels; when he was away I used to move plants around and build myself a jungle. He was away a lot. He was a doctor too."

"Is he still alive?"

"No, my parents are both dead." She let one of her shoes drop off. "He always said he liked flowers so much he had one for a daughter." She tickled her foot in the thyme. This clearing reminded her of one of her jungles.

"My father is an engineer on an oil tanker," Steve said. "He'd be at sea for three months and then with us for two. I missed him when he was away, but once he got home I couldn't wait for him to ship out again. He was too strict and he yelled at Mom. Since they divorced, I haven't seen him much. Now Mom – she's great. She worked twenty-eight years at Sears, wherever they needed her. She could talk you into a tent or towels or a thinkmate, no problem. I was a shy boy, if you can believe that, but she kept pushing me. She said I had to go out and show the world what a great son she had."

As he spoke, Lily folded and unfolded her hands. She didn't want to hear about Steve's family problems and now she was embarrassed to have shared memories of her father with a stranger. "What are we doing here?"

"I don't know about you, Lily, but I'm enjoying the view." He leaned back and looked her up and down with obvious approval "Pretty flowers, great company – hey, ssh!"

He held a finger to his lips. There were muffled voices, then footsteps on the path. The foliage hid the strollers but as they approached Lily heard a man declaiming with the grandiloquence of a longtime

Shakespeare abuser. "She walks in *beauty*, like the *night* of cloudless climes and *starry skies;* and all that's *best* of dark and bright, meet in her aspect and her *eyes*…"

Lily held in her laughter until they were safely past, then she burst. After a second, Steve roared too, although she suspected that it was only because he was relieved that she was finally unwinding.

"So you can laugh," he said. "What an improvement!"

"It's just… the old Byron trick." She couldn't catch her breath. "The corniest, the lamest…" She started to dissolve again.

"This Byron writes poems?"

"Lord Byron, you dope." It didn't seem to help. "Hey, even I know Byron and I took hackers' English in college."

He leaned forward and reached between his feet for a sprig of thyme. He said nothing.

"I can't believe anyone over eighteen would fall for a line like that."

He started defoliating the thyme. "Maybe she likes poetry."

"But don't you see, that's the whole problem! Tired old poems work, dumb songs work, honesty works, lies work, every trick in the book works. There's no choice involved, we're practically defenseless here."

"You know what the problem is, Lily?" He looked unhappy. "You're too busy thinking to enjoy yourself."

She was surprised at how much his disapproval stung. "Excuse *me*?" He was nobody, a pushy salesman she hardly knew. "Using your head isn't exactly a handicap, you know." She waited for him to apologize, explain himself, make her feel better, but he let the silence stretch. The dumb little bastard. He wasn't going to get away with hurting her; she could retaliate. "So Steve, what was your major in college?" She already knew the answer.

"Didn't have one."

"Oh come on, everyone…"

"Didn't go."

The stream babbled through another long silence. She thought of twelve different things to say, but couldn't speak because she was too ashamed of herself for humiliating him. What a snob she was! If this was neuromance then she could do without it; she'd had more conflicting feelings in the past half hour than she'd had in six months. Steve stood up, put on his jacket, sat down again. She watched him, an emptiness growing within her. Maybe she couldn't fall anymore, maybe the parts of her brain that loved had atrophied.

"You never answered my question, Lily," he said.

"What was it?"

"You were going to tell me what it's like to be in love."

"It stinks, actually." She didn't hesitate. "You lose everything, your friends, your freedom. Your bathroom. He kicks you awake at three in the morning but if he's not there you can't sleep. He never wants the vid you want and he doesn't eat fish and he can't wait to tell you when you're wrong. And when you're fighting, it feels like you're getting an appendectomy without anesthesia."

"You call that a sales pitch?" There was a hint of a smile on his lips. "If it's so horrible, why come here?"

"I don't know why I came here." Another silence that she didn't want loomed. "I'm sorry, Steve."

"Hey, you said my name! That's the first time you said my name."

"I figured it was time, since you've said mine a hundred times already." She gave a dry chuckle. "What is that, anyway, another sales trick?"

"You know studies show only twenty percent of communication is verbal." He slid slowly across the bench toward her. "The other eighty percent depends on nonverbal cues." He kept coming. "Facial expressions, posture, tone of voice." When he stopped, they were six inches apart. "I'm in your personal space now. We're not touching but you can feel me, can't you?"

"Yes." She liked the feeling. It was like coming out of an ice storm and standing next to a crackling fire.

"Sales tricks are based on the way people are, Lily. They connect with real feelings. Sure, some people use them to sell bad products or unnecessary ones, but I don't. I just try to give the prospect what she wants."

Lily watched his mouth as he spoke. For some reason, the way his lips moved fascinated her. She could see his teeth and the tip of his tongue.

"But you don't know what you want, do you?"

"I want to be happy."

"But you don't want to fall in love?" He leaned and brushed his shoulder against her. "Lose your freedom? Everything?"

"Maybe it's too late." She was surprised to hear herself say it aloud, although she had known it for some time. "I wonder what would happen if I sniffed my own corsage?" She touched it absently. "Probably spend the night crouching by the stream, admiring myself."

"I'd like to spend the night admiring you, Lily. Obviously."

She laughed and then she kissed him. When she closed her eyes, he smelled like chocolate. It had to be some kind of trick, she thought before she stopped thinking. When she finished with him, she saw her own smile reflected on his lips.

"I'm hungry." Lily slipped her hand into his pocket. "Do you have anything to eat?" She trapped the candy against his taut abdominal muscles.

He squirmed as if he were ticklish. "Can we do this in private?"

As far as she was concerned, the rest of the Hothouse was nothing but rumors and mist. "We can do whatever we want."

She expected some kind of cortisol and epinephrine boost when she ate the chocolate but all she felt was the lingering warmth of his kiss. It was only when he lowered his head slowly, deliberately, to her corsage, that her blood began to pound. He filled his lungs with her scent. "Nice," he said, "but I prefer the real thing."

"Hey look," she said, "our badges have already changed..."

He covered her mouth with his, filling her world in all directions. He certainly knew how to sell a kiss. She brushed her fingertips across his cheek and he pulled back and rubbed his cheek against hers. "You like to hear me say your name." He nuzzled her ear. "Don't you?" He was whispering. "Lily?"

"Yes," she said. "Oh, yes."

She told him about getting an A– in Professor Graves' Anatomy class where twenty students failed and he told her about the time he'd hit a grand slam off Chico Moran, who was now the number two starter for the Dodgers. She'd done her pre-med at Michigan State and he'd played shortstop for a season and a half with the Red Sox's farm team in New Britain, Connecticut, before blowing out his knee sliding into third. It was the worst moment of his life; hers was when her father died. He was twenty-six, she was twenty-five. She warned him she wouldn't eat artichokes or buffalo or anything with peanut butter in it. He'd never had an artichoke. He bragged about the time his mother sold a watch to Vice President Blaine and made the six o'clock news.

Her mother had never worked, she'd stayed home to take care of Lily and her two sisters and drink blush wine. Lily was the youngest, Steve was an only child. She complained about Marja's shoes. He hardly ever saw his best friend because he caught for the Colorado Rockies. He made her tell him about Glenn who was at Johns Hopkins now studying gerontology because that was where the money was. They'd lived together off-campus their senior year in East Lansing; Glenn had a four handicap in golf and wanted her to wear stupid hats when he was in the mood for sex. He told her a little more about Marsha, how she'd taught him how to sell and how she apologized for her Caesarian scar the first time they'd made love. He said the best times together were when she let him drive her Porsche 717 and Lily laughed and said Glenn had a Mazda Magic which he had never let her drive but that once when he went home for his grandmother's funeral she had swiped his keys and cranked it to 110 on I-96 and had never told anyone until now so they pressed their bodies hard against each other and kissed until their lips were numb and Lily wondered what it cost to rent an encounter room on the sixth floor.

By eleven the clearing was too small for them. It was time to see if their newfound infatuation was portable. They started strolling hand in hand up the slate path before she realized she had left her purse behind.

Almost everybody in the welcome garden had paired up and dispersed; there were only enough dancers to make two sets. Lily thought she detected a note of desperation in the music. As the dancers promenaded, the caller warned them:

"Hurry up strangers, don't be slow,
You'll never fall in love unless you do-si-do."

Maybe the band was ready to pack up. As she watched Old Man Skintights bravely circling the floor, she wondered what it would feel like to get enhanced and then not find anyone to fall for. A refund wouldn't really cover the cost of being iced out at a neuromance palace. She remembered her first glimpse of the welcome garden, when it had bubbled with exotic possibilities. Now it seemed as flat as yesterday's champagne.

"They gave us four or five hours," she said. "At midnight we all turn into pumpkins."

Steve had zero tolerance for melancholy. "This way." He aimed her at the elevators.

"No," she said, "let's walk up."

"Two flights?"

"Oh, we have to peek at shops on the fourth floor," she said. He looked doubtful. "Maybe get something to eat?"

"I'm not hungry."

"Well, what if I am?"

He colored; it was the first time she had seen him embarrassed. "Sorry." He turned reluctantly toward the stairs but when he tugged at her to follow, she let him go.

"Steve, what's the matter?"

"I don't know." He shrugged. "Maybe it's just that I hate being sold things I don't need." She sensed that he wanted to say something else – but he didn't.

"I'll swallow my cash card, okay?" Lily said. He reached out for her and she came to him. "I'll be good. Promise."

Where the third floor had been a hot, dark blur, the fourth was a place to lounge and consume conspicuously. With its open sight lines, it flaunted the true size of the Hothouse. The shops and restaurants ringed an enormous irregularly-shaped pool. Its bays and peninsulas were landscaped with bougainvillea. There were sandy beaches and ten-foot bluffs. They saw couples sprawled on checked tablecloths beside wicker picnic baskets: the picnickers drank wine from bottles with broad shoulders and broke long sticks of French bread.

"We can swim," said Lily. "That's free."

"Sure." When he gave her a forlorn smile, she worried that he was relieved to be getting away from her.

The dressing booths were between the Honey Bun Bakery and the Intimate Moment, a lingerie store. The bakery breathed the yeasty aroma of warm bread onto them. Lily's mouth watered but she said nothing. Instead she kissed Steve and he brightened. They went through separate doors.

Her booth was a four-foot square; its only furnishing was a shelf-like seat. The far wall was a screen on which appeared her image, larger than life. She winked at herself and then giggled because she was certain that she had just discovered Steve's secret character flaw: he was cheap. Somehow that reassured her, perhaps because it was so curable. It wasn't as if he were a womanizer or a drunk or a golfer. Lily believed she understood thrift since she practiced it of necessity herself. Someday, when she was a rich gynecologist, they would come here and she would buy him something from every shop.

Suddenly the little booth seemed very chilly. The enhancement that had helped her fall for Steve would wear off in a couple of hours and then what would be left of her feelings for him? Maybe there wasn't going to be any *someday* with Steve.

"Welcome to the Hothouse." When the booth spoke to her, it was her own image that appeared to be talking. "This is a dressing booth. Occupancy is strictly limited to one. For those couples requiring privacy, may we suggest our encounter rooms on the sixth floor?"

"Oh?" She leered at herself. "And how much would they cost?"

Eight windows opened down the left hand side of the screen. "Encounter rooms range from $20 to $110." Each window showed a differently priced room. Twenty dollars bought a closet with a bed in it; the suite with a chandelier and the flocked wallpaper cost a hundred. "Shall I make a reservation for you now?"

"No, make me a bathing suit."

The rooms disappeared. "Swimdress, tank, two piece, or bikini?"

"Bikini."

She whimpered when saw herself on the screen in a generic black bikini. There had to be some perverse glitch in the booth's software; her skin was the color of cement and her knees looked like doorknobs.

"Would you prefer a bandeau, halter, or athletic top?"

"Bandeau."

"Underwire, sculptex, pump, or natural?"

"Pump?"

She watched in horror as her breasts rose like popovers baking on fast-forward. If they'd been lifted any higher they would have been pointing at the moon.

"No, natural."

They receded. She turned sideways and eyed her figure hopelessly. She experimented with a high-cut brief but the edges of her glutei maximi hung out of it like mocking fleshy grins. The booth could fabricate the suit in any of three thousand prints or 1.2 million solids. With a sigh, she chose something in the mid-cyan range. Letting him see her in a swimsuit on the first date – what *had* she been thinking of? A drawer slid open with the suit and towel in a sealed plastic bag.

"After pressing your thumb to the printreader, deposit your belongings in the drawer for later retrieval." Lily could not help but think of Steve's cool hands as she started unbuttoning the front of her dress.

She came out of the dressing booth and immediately panicked:

Steve wasn't waiting. The door to his booth was open! Her first thought was that he was mad at her and had left. Her skin felt tight. Maybe he'd gone back to the welcome garden to try his luck again, or left the Hothouse altogether. Oh God, what had she been thinking of? They should've taken the damn elevator; she didn't really care about swimming and she couldn't afford to shop. She had to find him, apologize – but should she get dressed first or ransack the Hothouse in her bikini? While she was trying to decide, he came out of the men's room. The sight of him made her eyes burn. This was love, yes, it had already reduced her to a dithering adolescent.

"Lily, are you all right?" he said.

She swooped into his embrace. "Fine now." She didn't know why it had bothered her before that he was short. She put her arms around his compact athlete's body and realized that a larger man wouldn't be quite so huggable. She noticed that he was slightly lopsided, right deltoids and biceps bigger than the left. All those throws to first base. "I just missed you."

"Look at you." He peeled her away from him. "You're beautiful. Fantastic."

They kissed again and she ran her fingertips across his back and felt his skin warming hers. She knew exactly what had happened: the fear of losing him had hit her in the adrenal glands. Hard. Hormones had seeped and messenger chemicals had washed into the deepest parts of her brain but the chemistry didn't matter to her anymore. She wanted him. It wasn't only lust; she wanted to ease his pain over losing baseball, to thank him for listening to her whine about Glenn, to show him what love might be. They would be so good for one another, only she didn't have the $20. She tried to think of a way to get him to split the cost of a room without aggravating him about the money.

"Lily," he murmured. "There's something I have to tell you."

She shuddered – she hated the way men confessed! They didn't know how and besides, whenever they were sorry, it was always for the wrong thing. Lily wasn't interested in what he had to say. She wanted to tell him to shut up. But she didn't have to.

"Lily!" Someone was waving.

"Over here. *Lily.*" Marja stood, hands raised, on a red-checked tablecloth on the beach. Tomasz lolled at her feet like a sleepy tiger.

"Just wave back," said Steve, "we really need to talk."

"She's my best friend. She'll strangle me if I don't introduce you."

Marja was wearing a purple maillot that had a cookie-sized transparency sprite roving across its surface, exposing pale skin. That might have explained why her cheeks were so red, but Lily doubted it. Tomasz sat up as they approached and rubbed his eyes. There was a half-full bottle of kava in the picnic basket. Someone had kicked white sand into an empty pizza carton.

"And who is this?" Marja said.

"Steve." Lily said. "My God, Steve, you haven't told me your last name yet."

"Beauchamp."

"Nice to meet you." They shook hands; Lily watched and wondered what he discovered about her. "I was just about to swim," said Marja. "You two interested in a quick dip?"

"Sure," said Lily. She glanced over at Steve; he was pouting. "Steve?"

He shook his head.

"Good. Let the ladies go." Tomasz rolled toward the kava. "We'll work the bottle."

The two women waded into the tepid water. When it lapped at her waist, Marja sank backwards with a weary moan. "A pretty little one you picked," she said.

"I think so," Lily said. "So, did you do anything stupid yet?"

"I let him talk me into this damn bathing suit. Bad enough people can see my thighs but random nudity..." She snorted in disgust. "My synapses don't snap for Tomasz the way they used to, but it was grade while it lasted."

"How was the sixth floor?"

"What, am I still flushed? For a while I thought my face had caught fire." She ducked underwater and came up spluttering laughter. "He's one of the hammers – isn't that what the receptionist called them? Wasn't much of a talker, but he communicated, wow. Got that from his cats, I guess. Funny to be talking about him in the past tense already." She splashed Lily. "So did you have an encounter?"

"We've talked a lot, that's all. He's very... I don't know... decisive. From the moment we met he seemed so sure that he wanted me. Eventually I started wanting him. A lot." She laughed. "Whatever they gave us must have worked overtime because I... I think really love him,

Marja. I don't want this to be over in an hour." She did a few back-strokes away from the shore, where Steve was gesturing at Tomasz with the bottle of kava. "Is that supposed to happen?"

"Hey, maybe you talked too much, roomie. You're not in the market for a keeper. Besides, where would you put him?"

"He can stay at his place; I just want to borrow him once in awhile. Anyway, right before we spotted you he said he had something important to tell me, which is probably that he's emigrating to Uzbekistan next Wednesday." When Lily waved to him, Steve got up and walked edge of the water. "I should get back," she said.

"Tomasz and I are about done, Lily." Marja looked worried. "Maybe we should both call it a night? Get his number. If you're still hot in the morning, you can call him."

She treaded water, not listening. "Ever hear of a baseball player named Chico Moran?"

Flowers had over-run the fifth floor. They marched down crushed stone paths and spread across parterres and perennial borders. This was a strolling floor, not as private as the third, nor as public as the fourth. The oak benches tucked beside the flower beds were clearly visible from the paths. The only privacy was that afforded by politeness. Lily and Steve passed blindly past two laughing gay men and an elderly couple who had fallen asleep. She, however, could not help but gape at the impossible couple of Alice the feminist and Keith the lizard, entwining passionately

Finally they chanced upon an empty bench which faced a drift of impatiens swarming around the legs of burgundy roses. She leaned over to smell one and then covered a yawn with the back of her hand. It was almost one. Time for him to stop talking and get back to kissing.

Steve waved for her to sit beside him. "Because good salesmen don't lie, Lily." He put his arm around her. "We have to buy before we can sell. First I have to believe that my product is the best for you, otherwise I can't get you interested in it. And I do, Lily. Maybe you still have some doubts, but I know I'd be good for you."

"No, I'm sure too." She was delighted that it was still true. Marja was no doubt already home in bed; Lily's enhancement must have worn off by now. This wasn't neuromance anymore; she was on her own.

"This isn't easy, okay? A salesman never brings up his own negatives. That's anti-selling. If a client has a problem or complaint, I acknowledge it and try to work it out. But if I start telling you what *I* think is wrong with me, not only could I lose you, I might even stop believing in myself."

"I'm sorry; I should've listened before." She leaned her head on his shoulder. "So tell me now."

"Okay, start at the beginning. Ever heard of the new produce?"

"Isn't that the pricey stuff they sell at those food boutiques?"

He nodded. "Here in America we rely on just twenty-four crops for most of what we eat. But there are over 20,000 edible plants. Oca from South America. Arracacha, it's a cross between celery and carrot. Mamey from Cuba. I've spent a lot of time learning the new produce. It's a specialty market now but it has tremendous potential for breakout. I developed contacts all over the country."

"This has something to do with us?"

His voice was tight. "You remember Marsha, the one who taught me about selling? Well, her husband Bill owned the company I worked for. Not only did he fire me, but the son of a bitch is still working overtime to keep me from catching on somewhere else. Like this evening, I stopped by World Food across the street. I used to take the manager there out to the stadium – on my tab. But tonight my good friend informs me that his headquarters says I'm nobody and there's nothing he can do for me." He choked back his outrage. "I'm going to beat these guys, Lily, and soon. Only..."

"You're out of work?" She sat up, giddy with relief. "You poor thing, that's terrible." It was hard to keep from laughing. "How long?"

"Eight months."

"Steve, you're only twenty-six. It's not like you're Willie Loman. You can find something else to sell."

"Willie Loman? Who's he, some fancy marketing professor? What the hell does Willie Loman know about selling glasswort to Piggly Wiggly?"

"Nothing." She slipped her hand onto his knee and squeezed. "Forget it." She didn't want him angry at her, too.

"I gave up my life once, Lily," he said firmly. "What I learned from that is I never want to do it again. But now you know that the real reason I didn't want to go to the fourth floor was that I couldn't afford to. Believe me, if I had money to spend, you'd see all of it. When we were down by the stream, I kept thinking how it would be to take you up-stairs to one of the rooms." He reached into his pocket. "Problem is my cash card flamed out two weeks ago." He pulled a crumpled two-dollar bill taut, smoothed it against his leg and offered it to her. "My life savings."

"You have no money at all? Then why come to a place like this? How'd you even get in?"

"Because the most important sales trick of all has nothing to do with the prospect. See, a salesman has to keep up his own self image. When everyone else is beating him down, he has to treat himself like a winner. Maybe I'm broke, but I'm *not* nobody, damn it! I'm Steve Beauchamp; I go where I want, when I want." He straightened. "Any-way, I talked my way into a discount because I didn't get enhanced. Even so, they took almost everything I had at the door."

"You didn't get enhanced!"

"Didn't need to." He took her hand; his palm was moist. "I know this sounds strange, but when I came out of World Food and saw you with your friend, something happened. I can't explain it, but I thought, there's a woman I need to meet. So I followed you in. Believe me, Lily, I've never done anything like this before. When I saw you again in the lobby, I knew I was right. So what if the cost of admission flattened me? By then I was already falling in love."

"You were not." She pulled away from him. "You didn't even know me."

"I do now." He smiled.

"My God, Steve, this doesn't make any sense." She wasn't sure how she was supposed to react; it was like her recurring nightmare of sit-ting down to a final she hadn't studied for. This man she wanted was either a phony or a pathological romantic. "Just what did you think was going to happen after my enhancement wore off? Most couples leave this place in separate cars, you know."

"Sure, I knew that was a possibility." He shrugged. "But I had con-fidence in myself. And you. The way I figure it, there must be *some-thing* about me you really like because I couldn't afford a treated chocolate." He sifted her hair through his fingers. "Actually, I've been waiting all night for the drugs you took to wear off. I want us to fall in love for real, not because our hormones are boiling over. We need clear heads for something as important as this. That's why you should never close in a bar, unless you're prepared to wake up with a sour head and a sour deal."

"You really think we're in love?"

He paused to consider. "Maybe I don't know enough about love to recognize it, but this is what I hoped it would feel like."

She turned her face toward him and closed her eyes "Sell it to me," she said.

He obliged. Time passed, clothing got rearranged, buttons were unbuttoned. The bench wasn't big enough for them to lie on, but they were approaching horizontality when a rover disguised as a sunflower crunched down the gravel path, aimed its enormous yellow blossom at them and said politely, "For those couples requiring privacy, may we suggest our encounter rooms on the sixth floor?"

"We could leave," Lily said breathlessly. "Go to your place."

"I don't have a place. Actually I've been living out of my car. It's parked about ten blocks from here and it's out of gas and I don't get my unemployment check until..."

"Ssh!" She put a finger to his lips. "Keep bringing up negatives and you'll lose the sale." Lily stood, reached both hands down to him and pulled him up beside her. "My place then." She wasn't sure exactly what she was going to do when they got there. Tack a sheet to the ceiling between her futon and Marja's? Not a simple project at two in the morning – and what if Steve snored?

Lily pushed her doubts away. What had Marja said? Love makes all things possible. She knew she was taking a risk with this intense little man but she'd been smart and lonely for so long. She had to laugh at herself as they stepped into the elevator.

It was time to try something stupid.

URSULA K. LE GUIN

Forgiveness Day

SOLLY HAD BEEN A SPACE BRAT, a Mobile's child, living on this ship and that, this world and that; she'd travelled five hundred lightyears by the time she was ten. At twenty-five she had been through a revolution on Alterra, learned aiji on Terra and farthinking from an old hilfer on Rokanan, breezed through the Schools on Hain, and survived an assignment as Observer in murderous, dying Kheakh, skipping another half-millennium at near lightspeed in the process. She was young, but she'd been around.

She got bored with the Embassy people in Voe Deo telling her to watch out for this, remember that; she was a Mobile herself now, after all. Werel had its quirks – what world didn't? She'd done her homework, she knew when to curtsey and when not to belch, and vice versa. It was a relief to get on her own at last, in this gorgeous little city, on this gorgeous little continent, the first and only Envoy of the Ekumen to the Divine Kingdom of Gatay.

She was high for days on the altitude, the tiny, brilliant sun pouring vertical light into the noisy streets, the peaks soaring up incredibly behind every building, the dark-blue sky where great near stars burned all day, the dazzling nights under six or seven lolloping bits of moon, the tall black people with their black eyes, narrow heads, long, narrow hands and feet, gorgeous people, her people! She loved them all. Even if she saw a little too much of them.

The last time she had had completely to herself was a few hours in the passenger cabin of the airskimmer sent by Gatay to bring her across the ocean from Voe Deo. On the airstrip she was met by a delegation of priests and officials from the King and the Council, magnificent in scarlet and brown and turquoise, and swept off to the Palace, where there was a lot of curtseying and no belching, of course, for hours – an introduction to his little shrunken old majesty, introductions to High Muckamucks and Lord Hooziwhats, speeches, a banquet – all completely predictable, no problems at all, not even the impenetrable giant fried flower on her plate at the banquet. But with her, from that first moment on the airstrip and at every moment therafter, discreetly behind or beside or very near her, were two men: her Guide and her Guard.

The Guide, whose name was San Ubattat, was provided by her hosts in Gatay; of course he was reporting on her to the government, but he was a most obliging spy, endlessly smoothing the way for her, showing her with a bare hint what was expected or what would be a gaffe, and an excellent linguist, ready with a translation when she needed one. San was all right. But the Guard was something else.

He had been attached to her by the Ekumen's hosts on this world, the dominant power on Werel, the big nation of Voe Deo. She had promptly protested to the Embassy back in Voe Deo that she didn't need or want a bodyguard. Nobody in Gatay was out to get her and even if they were she preferred to look after herself. The Embassy sighed. Sorry, they said. You're stuck with him. Voe Deo has a military presence in Gatay, which after all is a client state, economically dependent. It's in Voe Deo's interest to protect the legitimate government of Gatay against the native terrorist factions, and you get protected as one of their interests. We can't argue with that.

She knew better than to argue with the Embassy, but she could not resign herself to the Major. His military title, rega, she translated by the archaic word "Major," from a skit she'd seen on Terra. That Major had been a stuffed uniform, covered with medals and insignia. It puffed and strutted and commanded, and finally blew up into bits of stuffing. If only this Major would blow up! Not that he strutted, exactly, or even commanded, directly. He was stonily polite, woodenly silent, stiff and cold as rigor mortis. She soon gave up any effort to talk to him; whatever she said, he replied Yessum or Nomum with the prompt stupidity of a man who does not and will not actually listen, an officer officially incapable of humanity. And he was with her in every public situation, day and night, on the street, shopping, meeting with businessmen and officials, sightseeing, at court, in the balloon ascent above the mountains – with her everywhere, everywhere but bed.

Even in bed she wasn't quite as alone as she would often have liked; for the Guide and the Guard went home at night, but in the anteroom of her bedroom slept the Maid – a gift from His Majesty, her own private asset.

She remembered her incredulity when she first learned that word, years ago, in a text about slavery. "On Werel, members of the dominant caste are called *owners*; members of the serving class are called *assets*. Only owners are referred to as men or women; assets are called bondsmen, bondswomen."

So here she was, the owner of an asset. You don't turn down a king's gift. Her asset's name was Rewe. Rewe was probably a spy too, but it was hard to believe. She was a dignified, handsome woman some years older than Solly and about the same intensity of skin-color, though Solly was pinkish-brown and Rewe was bluish-brown. The palms of her hands were a delicate azure. Rewe's manners were exquisite and she had tact, astuteness, an infallible sense of when she was wanted and when not. Solly of course treated her as an equal, stating right out at the beginning that she believed no human being had a right to dominate, much less own, another, that she would give Rewe no orders, and that she hoped they might become friends. Rewe accepted this, unfortunately, as a new set of orders. She smiled and said yes. She was infinitely yielding. Whatever Solly said or did sank into that acceptance and was lost, leaving Rewe unchanged: an attentive, obliging, gentle physical presence, just out of reach. She smiled, and said yes, and was untouchable.

And Solly began to think, after the first fizz of the first days in Gatay, that she needed Rewe, really needed her as a woman to talk with. There was no way to meet Owner women, who lived hidden away in their bezas, women's quarters, 'at home,' they called it. All bondswomen but Rewe were somebody else's property, not hers to talk to. All she ever met was men. And eunuchs.

That had been another thing hard to believe, that a man would voluntarily trade his virility for a little social standing; but she met such men all the time in King Hotat's court. Born assets, they earned partial independence by becoming eunuchs, and as such often rose to positions of considerable power and trust among their owners. The eunuch Tayandan, majordomo of the palace, ruled the king, who didn't rule, but figureheaded for the Council. The Council was made up of various kinds of lord but only one kind of priest, Tualites. Only assets worshipped Kamye, and the original religion of Gatay had been suppressed when the monarchy became Tualite a century or so ago. If there was one thing she really disliked about Werel, aside from slavery and gender-dominance, it was the religions. The songs about Lady

Tual were beautiful, and the statues of her and the great temples in Voe Deo were wonderful, and the *Arkamye* seemed to be a good story though long-winded; but the deadly self-righteousness, the intolerance, the stupidity of the priests, the hideous doctrines that justified every cruelty in the name of the faith! As a matter of fact, Solly said to herself, was there anything she *did* like about Werel?

And answered herself instantly: I love it, I love it. I love this weird little bright sun and all the broken bits of moons and the mountains going up like ice walls and the people – the people with their black eyes without whites like animals' eyes, eyes like dark glass, like dark water, mysterious – I want to love them, I want to know them, I want to reach them!

But she had to admit that the pissants at the Embassy had been right about one thing: being a woman was tough on Werel. She fit nowhere. She went about alone, she had a public position, and so was a contradiction in terms: proper women stayed at home, invisible. Only bondswomen went out in the streets, or met strangers, or worked at any public job. She behaved like an asset, not like an owner. Yet she was something very grand, an envoy of the Ekumen, and Gatay very much wanted to join the Ekumen and not to offend its envoys. So the officials and courtiers and businessmen she talked to on the business of the Ekumen did the best they could: they treated her as if she were a man.

The pretense was never complete and often broke right down. The poor old king groped her industriously, under the vague impression that she was one of his bedwarmers. When she contradicted Lord Gatuyo in a discussion, he stared with the blank disbelief of a man who has been talked back to by his shoe. He had been thinking of her as a woman. But in general the disgenderment worked, allowing her to work with them; and she began to fit herself into the game, enlisting Rewe's help in making clothes that resembled what male owners wore in Gatay, avoiding anything that to them would be specifically feminine. Rewe was a quick, intelligent seamstress. The bright, heavy, close-fitted trousers were practical and becoming, the embroidered jackets were splendidly warm. She liked wearing them. But she felt unsexed by these men who could not accept her for what she was. She needed to talk to a woman.

She tried to meet some of the hidden owner women through the owner men, and met a wall of politeness without a door, without a peephole. What a wonderful idea; we will certainly arrange a visit when the weather is better! I should be overwhelmed with the honor if the Envoy were to entertain Lady Mayoyo and my daughters, but my foolish, provincial girls are so unforgivably timid – I'm sure you understand. Oh, surely, surely, a tour of the inner gardens – but not at present, when the vines are not in flower! We must wait until the vines are in flower!

There was nobody to talk to, nobody, until she met Batikam the Makil.

It was an event: a touring troupe from Voe Deo. There wasn't much going on in Gatay's little mountain capital by way of entertainment, except for temple dancers – all men, of course – and the soppy fluff that passed as drama on the Werelian network. Solly had doggedly entered some of these wet pastels, hoping for a glimpse into the life 'at home,' but she couldn't stomach the swooning maidens who died of love while the stiffnecked jackass heroes, who all looked like the Major, died nobly in battle, and Tual the Merciful leaned out of the clouds smiling upon their deaths with her eyes slightly crossed and the whites showing, a sign of divinity. Solly had noticed that Werelian men never entered the network for drama. Now she knew why. But the receptions at the palace and the parties in her honor given by various lords and businessmen were pretty dull stuff: all men, always, because they wouldn't have the slavegirls in while the Envoy was there; and she couldn't flirt even with the nicest men, couldn't remind them that they were men, since that would remind them that she was a woman not behaving like a lady. The fizz had definitely gone flat by the time the makil troupe came.

She asked San, a reliable etiquette advisor, if it would be all right for her to attend the performance. He hemmed and hawed and finally, with more than usually oily delicacy, gave her to understand that it would be all right so long as she went dressed as a man. "Women, you know, don't go in public. But sometimes, they want so much to see the entertainers, you know? Lady Amatay used to go with Lord Amatay, dressed in his clothes, every year; everybody knew, nobody said anything – you know. For you, such a great person, it would be all right. Nobody will say anything. Quite, quite all right. Of course, I come with you, the rega comes with you. Like friends, ha? You know, three good men friends going to the entertainment, ha? Ha?"

Ha, ha, she said obediently. What fun! – But it was worth it, she thought, to see the makils.

They were never on the network. Young girls at home were not to be exposed to their performances, some of which, San gravely informed her, were unseemly. They played only in theaters. Clowns, dancers, prostitutes, actors, musicians, the makils formed a kind of subclass, the only assets not personally owned. A talented slave boy bought by the Entertainment Corporation from his owner was thenceforth the property of the Corporation, which trained and looked after him the rest of his life.

They walked to the theater, six or seven streets away. She had forgotten that the makils were all transvestites, indeed she did not remember it when she first saw them, a troop of tall slender dancers sweeping out onto the stage with the precision and power and grace of great birds wheeling, flocking, soaring. She watched unthinking, enthralled by their beauty, until suddenly the music changed and the clowns came in, black as night, black as owners, wearing fantastic trailing skirts, with fantastic jutting jewelled breasts, singing in tiny, swoony voices, "Oh do not rape me please kind Sir, no no, not now!" They're men, they're men! Solly realized then, already laughing helplessly. By the time Batikam finished his star turn, a marvelous dramatic monologue, she was a fan. "I want to meet him," she said to San at a pause between acts. "The actor – Batikam."

San got the bland expression that signified he was thinking how it could be arranged and how to make a little money out of it. But the Major was on guard, as ever. Stiff as a stick, he barely turned his head to glance at San. And San's expression began to alter.

If her proposal was out of line, San would have signalled or said so. The Stuffed Major was simply controlling her, trying to keep her as tied down as one of "his" women. It was time to challenge him. She turned to him and stared straight at him. "Rega Teyeo," she said, "I quite comprehend that you're under orders to keep me in order. But if you give orders to San or to me, they must be spoken aloud, and they must be justified. I will not be managed by your winks or your whims."

There was a considerable pause, a truly delicious and rewarding pause. It was difficult to see if the Major's expression changed; the dim theater light showed no detail in his blueblack face. But there was something frozen about his stillness that told her she'd stopped him. At last he said, "I'm charged to protect you, Envoy."

"Am I endangered by the makils? Is there impropriety in an Envoy of the Ekumen congratulating a great artist of Werel?"

Again the frozen silence. "No," he said.

"Then I request you to accompany me when I go backstage after the performance to speak to Batikam."

One stiff nod. One stiff, stuffy, defeated nod. Score one! Solly thought, and sat back cheerfully to watch the lightpainters, the erotic dances, and the curiously touching little drama with which the evening ended. It was in archaic poetry, hard to understand, but the actors were so beautiful, their voices so tender that she found tears in her eyes and hardly knew why.

"A pity the makils always draw on the *Arkamye*," said San, with smug, pious disapproval. He was not a very highclass owner, in fact he owned no assets; but he was an owner, and a bigoted Tualite, and liked to remind himself of it. "Scenes from the *Incarnations of Tual* would be more befitting such an audience."

"I'm sure you agree, Rega," she said, enjoying her own irony.

"Not at all," he said, with such toneless politeness that at first she did not realize what he had said; and then forgot the minor puzzle in the bustle of finding their way and gaining admittance to the backstage and to the performers' dressingroom.

When they realized who she was, the managers tried to clear all the other performers out, leaving her alone with Batikam (and San and the Major, of course); but she said no, no, no, these wonderful artists must not be disturbed, just let me talk a moment with Batikam. She stood there in the bustle of doffed costumes, half-naked people, smeared makeup, laughter, dissolving tension after the show, any backstage on any world, talking with the clever, intense man in elaborate archaic woman's costume. They hit it off at once. "Can you come to my house?" she asked. "With pleasure," Batikam said, and his eyes did not flick to San's or the Major's face: the first bondsman she had yet met who did not glance to her Guard or her Guide for permission to say or do anything, anything at all. She glanced at them only to see if they were shocked. San looked collusive, the Major looked rigid. "I'll come in a little while," Batikam said, "I must change."

They exchanged smiles, and she left. The fizz was back in the air. The huge close stars hung clustered like grapes of fire. A moon tumbled over the icy peaks, another jigged like a lopsided lantern above the curlicue pinnacles of the palace. She strode along the dark street, enjoying the freedom of the male robe she wore and its warmth, making San trot to keep up; the Major, long-legged, kept pace with her. A high, trilling voice called, "Envoy!" and she turned with a smile, then swung round, seeing the Major grappling momentarily with someone in the shadow of a portico. He broke free, caught up to her without a word, seized her arm in an iron grip and dragged her into a run. "Let go!" she said, struggling; she did not want to use an aiji break on him, but nothing less was going to get her free.

He pulled her nearly off balance with a sudden dodge into an alley; she ran with him, letting him keep hold on her arm. They came unexpectedly out into her street and to her gate, through it, into the house, which he unlocked with a word – how did he do that? – "What is all this?" she demanded, breaking away easily, holding her arm where his grip had bruised it.

She saw, outraged, the last flicker of an exhilarated smile on his face. Breathing hard, he asked, "Are you hurt?"

"Hurt? Where you yanked me, yes – what do you think you were doing?"

"Keeping the fellow away."

"What fellow?"

He said nothing.

"The one who called out? Maybe he wanted to talk to me!"

After a moment the Major said, "Possibly. He was in the shadow. I thought he might be armed. I must go out and look for San Ubattat. Please keep the door locked until I come back." He was out the door as he gave the order; it never occurred to him that she would not obey, and she did obey, raging. Did he think she couldn't look after herself? that she needed him interfering in her life, kicking slaves around, "protecting" her? Maybe it was time he saw what an aiji fall looked like. He was strong and quick, but had no real training. This kind of amateur interference was intolerable, really intolerable; she must protest to the Embassy again.

As soon she let him back in with a nervous, shamefaced San in tow, she said, "You opened my door with a password. I was not informed that you had right of entrance day and night."

He was back to his military blankness. "Nomum," he said.

"You are not to do so again. You are not to seize hold of me ever again. I must tell you that if you do I will injure you. If something alarms you, tell me what it is and I will respond as I see fit. Now will you please go."

"With pleasure, mum," he said, wheeled, and marched out.

"Oh, Lady – Oh, Envoy," San said, "that was a dangerous person, extremely dangerous people, I am so sorry, disgraceful," and he babbled on. She finally got him to say who he thought it was, a religious dissident, one of the Old Believers who held to the original religion of Gatay and wanted to cast out or kill all foreigners and unbelievers. "A bondsman?" she asked with interest, and he was shocked – "Oh, no, no, a real person, a man – but most misguided, a fanatic, a heathen fanatic! Knifemen, they call themselves. But a man, Lady – Envoy, certainly a man!"

The thought that she might think that an asset might touch her upset him as much as the attempted assault. If such it had been.

As she considered it, she began to wonder if, since she had put the Major in his place at the theater, he had found an excuse to put her in her place by "protecting" her. Well, if he'd tried it again he'd find himself upside down against the opposite wall.

"Rewe!" she called, and the bondswoman appeared instantly as always. "One of the actors is coming. Would you like to make us a little tea, something like that?" Rewe smiled, said, "Yes," and vanished. There was a knock at the door. The Major opened it – he must be standing guard outside – and Batikam came in.

It had not occurred to her that the makil would still be in women's clothing, but it was how he dressed offstage too, not so magnificently, but with elegance, in the delicate, flowing materials and dark, subtle hues that the swoony ladies in the dramas wore. It gave considerable piquancy, she felt, to her own male costume. Batikam was not as handsome as the Major, who was a stunning-looking man till he opened his mouth; but the makil was magnetic, you had to look at him. He was a dark greyish brown, not the blueblack that the owners were so vain of (though there were plenty of black assets too, Solly had noticed: of course, when every bondswoman was her owner's sexual servant). Intense, vivid intelligence and sympathy shone in his face through the makil's stardust-black makeup, as he looked around with a slow, lovely laugh at her, at San, and at the Major standing at the door. He laughed like a woman, a warm ripple, not the ha, ha of a man. He held out his hands to Solly, and she came forward and took them. "Thank you for coming, Batikam!" she said, and he said, "Thank you for asking me, Alien Envoy!"

"San," she said, "I think this is your cue?"

Only indecision about what he ought to do could have slowed San down till she had to speak. He still hesitated a moment, then smiled with unction and said, "Yes, so sorry, a very good night to you, Envoy! Noon hour at the Office of Mines, tomorrow, I believe?" Backing away, he backed right into the Major, who stood like a post in the doorway. She looked at the Major, ready to order him out without ceremony, how dare he shove back in! – and saw the expression on his face. For once his blank mask had cracked, and what was revealed was contempt. Incredulous, sickened contempt. As if he was obliged to watch somone eat a turd.

"Get out," she said. She turned her back on both of them. "Come on, Batikam; the only privacy I have is in here," she said, and led the makil to her bedroom.

He was born where his fathers before him were born, in the old, cold house in the foothills above Noeha. His mother did not cry out as she bore him, since she was a soldier's wife, and a soldier's mother, now. He was named for his greatuncle, killed on duty in the Sosa. He grew up in the stark discipline of a poor household of pure veot lineage. His father, when he was on leave, taught him the arts a soldier must know; when his father was on duty the old Asset-Sergeant Habbakam took over the lessons, which began at five in the morning, summer or winter, with worship, shortsword practise, and a cross-country run. His mother and grandmother taught him the other arts a man must know, beginning with good manners before he was two, and after his second birthday going on to history, poetry, and sitting still without talking.

The child's day was filled with lessons and fenced with disciplines; but a child's day is long. There was room and time for freedom, the freedom of the farmyard and the open hills. There was the companionship of pets, foxdogs, running dogs, spotted cats, hunting cats, and the farm cattle and the greathorses; not much companionship otherwise. The family's assets, other than Habbakam and the two housewomen, were sharecroppers, working the stony foothill land that they and their owners had lived on forever. Their children were light-skinned, shy, already stooped to their lifelong work, ignorant of anything beyond their fields and hills. Sometimes they swam with Teyeo, summers, in the pools of the river. Sometimes he rounded up a couple of them to play soldiers with him. They stood awkward, uncouth, smirking when he shouted "Charge!" and rushed at the invisible enemy. "Follow me!" he cried shrilly, and they lumbered after him, firing their tree-branch guns at random, pow, pow. Mostly he went alone, riding his good mare Tasi or afoot with a hunting cat pacing by his side.

A few times a year visitors came to the estate, relatives or fellow-officers of Teyeo's father, bringing their children and their house-people. Teyeo silently and politely showed the child guests about, introduced them to the animals, took them on rides. Silently and politely, he and his cousin Gemat came to hate each other; at age fourteen they fought for an hour in a glade behind the house, punctiliously following the rules of wrestling, relentlessly hurting each other, getting bloodier and wearier and more desperate, until by unspoken consent they called it off and returned in silence to the house, where everyone was gathering for dinner. Everyone looked at them and said nothing. They washed up hurriedly, hurried to table. Gemat's nose leaked blood all through the meal; Teyeo's jaw was so sore he could not open it to eat. No one commented.

Silently and politely, when they were both fifteen, Teyeo and Rega Toebawe's daughter fell in love. On the last day of her visit they escaped by unspoken collusion and rode out side by side, rode for hours, too shy to talk. He had given her Tasi to ride. They dismounted to water and rest the horses in a wild valley of the hills. They sat near each other, not very near, by the side of the little quiet-running stream. "I love you," Teyeo said. "I love you," Emdu said, bending her shining black face down. They did not touch or look at each other. They rode back over the hills, joyous, silent.

When he was sixteen Teyeo was sent to the Officers' Academy in the capital of his province. There he continued to learn and practice the arts of war and the arts of peace. His province was the most rural in Voe Deo; its ways were conservative, and his training was in some ways anachronistic. He was of course taught the technologies of modern warfare, becoming a first-rate pod pilot and an expert in telereconnaissance; but he was not taught the modern ways of thinking that accompanied the technologies in other schools. He learned the poetry and history of Voe Deo, not the history and politics of the Ekumen. The Alien presence on Werel remained remote, theoretical to him. His reality was the old reality of the veot class, whose men held themselves apart from all men not soldiers and in brotherhood with all soldiers, whether owners, assets, or enemies. As for women, Teyeo considered his rights over them absolute, binding him absolutely to responsible chivalry to women of his own class and protective, merciful treatment of bondswomen. He believed all foreigners to be basically hostile, untrustworthy heathens. He honored the Lady Tual, but worshipped the Lord Kamye. He expected no justice, looked for no reward, and valued above all competence, courage, and self-respect. In some respects he was utterly unsuited to the world he was to enter, in others well prepared for it, since he was to spend seven years on Yeowe fighting a war in which there was no justice, no reward, and never even an illusion of ultimate victory.

Rank among veot officers was hereditary. Teyeo entered active service as a rega, the highest of the three veot ranks. No degree of ineptitude or distinction could lower or raise his status or his pay. Material ambition was no use to a veot. But honor and responsibility were to be earned, and he earned them quickly. He loved service, loved the life, knew he was good at it, intelligently obedient, effective in command; he had come out of the Academy with the highest recommendations, and being posted to the capital, drew notice as a promising officer as well as a likeable young man. At twenty-four he was absolutely fit, his body would do anything he asked of it. His austere upbringing had given him little taste for indulgence but an intense appreciation of pleasure, so the luxuries and entertainments of the capital were a discovery of delight to him. He was reserved and rather shy, but companionable and cheerful. A handsome young man, in with a set of other young men very like him, for a year he knew what it is to live a completely privileged life with complete enjoyment of it. The brilliant intensity of that enjoyment stood against the dark background of the war in Yeowe, the slave revolution on the colony planet, which had gone on all his lifetime, and was now intensifying . Without that background, he could not have been so happy. A whole life of games and diversions had no interest for him; and when his orders came, posted as a pilot and division commander to Yeowe, his happiness was pretty nearly complete.

He went home for his thirty-day leave. Having received his parents' approbation, he rode over the hills to Rega Toebawe's estate and asked for his daughter's hand in marriage. The rega and his wife told their daughter that they approved his offer and asked her, for they were not strict parents, if she would like to marry Teyeo. "Yes," she said. As a grown, unmarried woman, she lived in seclusion in the women's side of the house, but she and Teyeo were allowed to meet and even to walk together, the chaperone remaining at some distance. Teyeo told her it was a three-year posting; would she marry in haste now, or wait three years and have a proper wedding? "Now," she said, bending down her narrow, shining face. Teyeo gave a laugh of delight, and she laughed at him. They were married nine days later – it couldn't be sooner, there had to be some fuss and ceremony, even if it was a soldier's wedding – and for seventeen days Teyeo and Emdu made love, walked together, made love, rode together, made love, came to know each other, came to love each other, quarreled, made up, made love, slept in each other's arms. Then he left for the war on another world, and she moved to the women's side of her husband's house.

His three-year posting was extended year by year, as his value as an officer was recognized and as the war on Yeowe changed from scattered containing actions to an increasingly desperate retreat. In his seventh year of service an order for compassionate leave was sent out to Yeowe Headquarters for Rega Teyeo, whose wife was dying of complications of berlot fever. At that point, there was no headquarters on Yeowe; the Army was retreating from three directions towards the old colonial capital; Teyeo's division was fighting a rear-guard defense in the sea-marshes; communications had collapsed.

Command on Werel continued to find it inconceivable that a mass of ignorant slaves with the crudest kind of weapons could be defeating the Army of Voe Deo, a disciplined, trained body of soldiers with an infallible communications network, skimmers, pods, every armament and device permitted by the Ekumenical Convention Agreement. A strong faction in Voe Deo blamed the setbacks on this submissive adherence to alien rules. The hell with Ekumenical Conventions. Bomb the damned dusties back to the mud they were made of. Use the biobomb, what was it for, anyway? Get our men off the foul planet and wipe it clean. Start fresh. If we don't win the war on Yeowe, the next revolution's going to be right here on Werel, in our own cities, in our own homes! The jittery government held on against this pressure. Werel was on probation, and Voe Deo wanted to lead the planet to Ekumenical status. Defeats were minimized, losses were not made up, skimmers, pods, weapons, men were not replaced. By the end of Teyeo's seventh year, the Army on Yeowe had been essentially written off by its government. Early in the eighth year, when the Ekumen was at last permitted to send its Envoys to Yeowe, Voe Deo and the other countries that had supplied auxiliary troops finally began to bring their soldiers home.

It was not until he got back to Werel that Teyeo learned his wife was dead.

He went home to Noeha. He and his father greeted each other with a silent embrace, but his mother wept as she embraced him. He knelt to her in apology for having brought her more grief than she could bear.

He lay that night in the cold room in the silent house, listening to his heart beat like a slow drum. He was not unhappy, the relief of being at peace and the sweetness of being home were too great for that; but it was a desolate calm, and somewhere in it was anger. Not used to anger, he was not sure what he felt. It was as if a faint, sullen red flare colored every image in his mind, as he lay trying to think through the seven years on Werel, first as a pilot, then the ground war, then the long retreat, the killing and the being killed. Why had they been left there to be hunted down and slaughtered? Why had the government not sent them reinforcements? The questions had not been worth asking then, they were not worth asking now. They had only one answer: We do what they ask us to do, and we don't complain. I fought every step of the way, he thought without pride. The new knowledge sliced keen as a knife through all other knowledge – And while I was fighting, she was dying. All a waste, there on Yeowe. All a waste, here on Werel. He sat up in the dark, the cold, silent, sweet dark of night in the hills. "Lord Kamye," he said aloud, "help me. My mind betrays me."

During the long leave home he sat often with his mother. She wanted to talk about Emdu, and at first he had to force himself to listen. It would be easy to forget the girl he had known for seventeen days seven years ago, if only his mother would let him forget. Gradually he learned to take what she wanted to give him, the knowledge of who his wife had been. His mother wanted to share all she could with him of the joy she had had in Emdu, her beloved child and friend. Even his father, retired now, a quenched, silent man, was able to say, "She was the light of the house." They were thanking him for her. They were telling him that it had not all been a waste.

But what lay ahead of them? Old age, the empty house. They did not complain, of course, and seemed content in their severe, placid round of daily work; but for them the continuity of the past with the future was broken.

"I should remarry," Teyeo said to his mother. "Is there anyone you've noticed...?"

It was raining, a grey light through the wet windows, a soft thrumming on the eaves. His mother's face was indistinct as she bent to her mending.

"No," she said. "Not really." She looked up at him, and after a pause asked, "Where do you think you'll be posted?"

"I don't know."

"There's no war now," she said, in her soft, even voice.

"No," Teyeo said. "There's no war."

"Will there be... ever? do you think?"

He stood up, walked down the room and back, sat down again on the cushioned platform near her; they both sat straightbacked, still except for the slight motion of her hands as she sewed; his hands lay lightly one in the other, as he had been taught when he was two.

"I don't know," he said. "It's strange. It's as if there hadn't been a war. As if we'd never been on Yeowe – the Colony, the Uprising, all of it. They don't talk about it. It didn't happen. We don't fight wars. This is a new age. They say that often in the net. The age of peace, brotherhood across the stars. So, are we brothers with Yeowe, now? Are we brothers with Gatay and Bambur and the Forty States? Are we brothers with our assets? I can't make sense of it. I don't know what they mean. I don't know where I fit in." His voice too was quiet and even.

"Not here, I think," she said. "Not yet."

After a while he said, "I thought... children..."

"Of course. When the time comes." She smiled at him. "You never could sit still for half an hour. Wait. Wait and see."

She was right, of course; and yet what he saw in the net and in town tried his patience and his pride. It seemed that to be a soldier now was a disgrace. Government reports, the news and the analyses, constantly referred to the army and particularly the veot class as fossils, costly and useless, Voe Deo's principal obstacle to full admission to the Ekumen. His own uselessness was made clear to him when his request for a posting was met by an indefinite extension of his leave on half pay. At thirty-two, they appeared to be telling him, he was super-annuated.

Again he suggested to his mother that he should accept the situation, settle down, and look for a wife. "Talk to your father," she said. He did so; his father said, "Of course your help is welcome, but I can run the farm well enough for a while yet. Your mother thinks you should go to the capital, to Command. They can't ignore you if you're there. After all. After seven years' combat – your record – "

Teyeo knew what that was worth, now. But he was certainly not needed here, and probably irritated his father with his ideas of changing this or that way things were done. They were right: he should go to the capital and find out for himself what part he could play in the new world of peace.

His first halfyear there was grim. He knew almost no one at Command or in the barracks; his generation was dead, or invalided out, or home on half pay. The younger officers, who had not been on Yeowe, seemed to him a cold, buttoned-up lot, always talking money and politics. Little businessmen, he privately thought them. He knew they were afraid of him – of his record, of his reputation. Whether he wanted to or not he reminded them that there had been a war that Werel had fought and lost, a civil war, their own race fighting against itself, class against class. They wanted to dismiss it as a meaningless quarrel on another world, nothing to do with them.

Teyeo walked the streets of the capital, watched the thousands of bondsmen and bondswomen hurrying about their owners' business, and wondered what they were waiting for.

"The Ekumen does not interfere with the social, cultural, or economic arrangements and affairs of any people," the Embassy and the government spokesmen repeated. "Full membership for any nation or people that wishes it is contingent only on absence, or renunciation, of certain specific methods and devices of warfare," and there followed the list of terrible weapons, most of them mere names to Teyeo, but a few of them inventions of his own country: the biobomb, as they called it, and the neuronics.

He personally agreed with the Ekumen's judgment on such devices, and respected their patience in waiting for Voe Deo and the rest of Werel to prove not only compliance with the ban, but acceptance of the principle. But he very deeply resented their condescension. They sat in judgment on everything Werelian, viewing from above. The less they said about the division of classes, the clearer their disapproval was. "Slavery is of very rare occurrence in Ekumenical worlds," said their books, "and disappears completely with full participation in the Ekumenical polity." Was that what the Alien Embassy was really waiting for?

"By our Lady!" said one of the young officers – many of them were Tualites, as well as businessmen – "the Aliens are going to admit the dusties before they admit us!" He was sputtering with indignant rage, like an a redfaced old rega faced with an insolent bondsoldier. "Yeowe – a damned planet of savages, tribesmen, regressed into barbarism – preferred over us!"

"They fought well," Teyeo observed, knowing he should not say it as he said it, but not liking to hear the men and women he had fought against called dusties. Assets, rebels, enemies, yes.

The young man stared at him and after a moment said, "I suppose you love 'em, eh? The dusties?"

"I killed as many as I could," Teyeo replied politely, and then changed the conversation. The young man, though nominally Teyeo's superior at Command, was an oga, the lowest rank of veot, and to snub him further would be illbred.

They were stuffy, he was touchy; the old days of cheerful good fellowship were a faint, incredible memory. The bureau chiefs at Command listened to his request to be put back on active service and sent him endlessly on to another department. He could not live in barracks, but had to find an apartment, like a civilian. His half pay did not permit him indulgence in the expensive pleasures of the city. While waiting for appointments to see this or that official, he spent his days in the library net of the Officers Academy. He knew his education had been incomplete and was out of date. If his country was going to join the Ekumen, in order to be useful he must know more about the Alien ways of thinking and the new technologies. Not sure what he needed to know, he floundered about in the network, bewildered by the endless information available, increasingly aware that he was no intellectual and no scholar and would never understand Alien minds, but doggedly driving himself on out of his depth.

A man from the Embassy was offering an introductory course in Ekumenical history in the public net. Teyeo joined it, and sat through eight or ten lecture and discussion periods, straight-backed and still, only his hands moving slightly as he took full and methodical notes. The lecturer, a Hainishman who translated his extremely long Hainish name as Old Music, watched Teyeo, tried to draw him out in discussion, and at last asked him to stay in after session. "I should like to meet you, Rega," he said, when the others had dropped out.

They met at a café. They met again. Teyeo did not like the Alien's manners, which he found effusive; he did not trust his quick, clever mind; he felt Old Music was using him, studying him as a specimen of The Veot, The Soldier, probably The Barbarian. The Alien, secure in his superiority, was indifferent to Teyeo's coldness, ignored his distrust, insisted on helping him with information and guidance, and shamelessly repeated questions Teyeo had avoided answering. One of these was, "Why are you sitting around here on half pay?"

"It's not by my own choice, Mr. Old Music," Teyeo finally answered, the third time it was asked. He was very angry at the man's impudence, and so spoke with particular mildness. He kept his eyes away from Old Music's eyes, bluish, with the whites showing like a scared horse. He could not get used to Aliens' eyes.

"They won't put you back on active service?"

Teyeo assented politely. Could the man, however alien, really be oblivious to the fact that his questions were grossly humiliating?

"Would you be willing to serve in the Embassy Guard?"

That question left Teyeo speechless for a moment; then he committed the extreme rudeness of answering a question with a question. "Why do you ask?"

"I'd like very much to have a man of your capacity in that corps," said Old Music, adding with his appalling candor, "Most of them are spies or blockheads. It would be wonderful to have a man I knew was neither. It's not just sentry-duty, you know. I imagine you'd be asked by your government to give information; that's to be expected. And we would use you, once you had experience and if you were willing, as a liaison officer. Here or in other countries. We would not, however, ask you to give information to us. Am I clear, Teyeo? I want no misunderstanding between us as to what I am and am not asking of you."

"You would be able...?" Teyeo asked cautiously.

Old Music laughed and said, "Yes. I have a string to pull in your Command. A favor owed. Will you think it over?"

Teyeo was silent a minute. He had been nearly a year now in the capital and his requests for posting had met only bureaucratic evasion and, recently, hints that they were considered insubordinate. "I'll accept now, if I may," he said, with a cold deference.

The Hainishman looked at him, his smile changing to a thoughtful, steady gaze. "Thank you," he said. "You should hear from Command in a few days."

So Teyeo put his uniform back on, moved back to the City Barracks, and served for another seven years on alien ground. The Ekumenical Embassy was, by diplomatic agreement, a part not of Werel but of the Ekumen – a piece of the planet that no longer belonged to it. The Guardsmen furnished by Voe Deo were protective and decorative, a highly visible presence on the Embassy grounds in their white and gold dress uniforms. They were also visibly armed, since protest against the Alien presence still broke out erratically in violence.

Rega Teyeo, at first assigned to command a troop of these guards, soon was transferred to a different duty, that of accompanying members of the Embassy staff about the city and on journeys. He served as a bodyguard, in undress uniform. The Embassy much preferred not to use their own people and weapons, but to request and trust Voe Deo to protect them. Often he was also called upon to be a guide and interpreter, and sometimes a companion. He did not like it when visitors from somewhere in space wanted to be chummy and confiding, asked him about himself, invited him to come drinking with them. With perfectly concealed distaste, with perfect civility, he refused such offers. He did his job and kept his distance. He knew that that was precisely what the Embassy valued him for. Their confidence in him gave him a cold satisfaction.

His own government had never approached him to give information, though he certainly learned things that would have interested them. Voe Dean intelligence did not recruit their agents among veots. He knew who the agents in the Embassy Guard were; some of them tried to get information from him, but he had no intention of spying for spies.

Old Music, whom he now surmised to be the head of the Embassy's intelligence system, called him in on his return from a winter leave at home. The Hainishman had learned not to make emotional demands on Teyeo, but could not hide a note of affection in his voice greeting him. "Hullo, Rega! I hope your family's well? Good. I've got a particularly tricky job for you. Kingdom of Gatay. You were there with

Kemehan two years ago, weren't you? Well, now they want us to send an Envoy. They say they want to join. Of course the old king's a puppet of your government; but there's a lot else going on there. A strong religious separatist movement. A Patriotic Cause, kick out all the foreigners, Voe Deans and Aliens alike. But the king and council requested an Envoy, and all we've got to send them is a new arrival. She may give you some problems till she learns the ropes. I judge her a bit headstrong. Excellent material, but young, very young. And she's only been here a few weeks. I requested you, because she needs your experience. Be patient with her, Rega. I think you'll find her likable."

He did not. In seven years he had got accustomed to the Aliens' eyes and their various smells and colors and manners. Protected by his flawless courtesy and his stoical code, he endured or ignored their strange or shocking or troubling behavior, their ignorance and their different knowledge. Serving and protecting the foreigners entrusted to him, he kept himself aloof from them, neither touched nor touching. His charges learned to count on him and not to presume on him. Women were often quicker to see and respond to his Keep Out signs than men; he had an easy, almost friendly relationship with an old Terran Observer whom he had accompanied on several long investigatory tours. "You are as peaceful to be with as a cat, Rega," she told him once, and he valued the compliment. But the Envoy to Gatay was another matter.

She was physically splendid, with clear redbrown skin like that of a baby, glossy swinging hair, a free walk – too free: she flaunted her ripe, slender body at men who had no access to it, thrusting it at him, at everyone, insistent, shameless. She expressed her opinion on everything with coarse self-confidence. She could not hear a hint and refused to take an order. She was an aggressive, spoiled child with the sexuality of an adult, given the responsibility of a diplomat in a dangerously unstable country. Teyeo knew as soon as he met her that this was an impossible assignment. He could not trust her or himself. Her sexual immodesty aroused him as it disgusted him; she was a whore whom he must treat as a princess. Forced to endure and unable to ignore her, he hated her.

He was more familiar with anger than he had used to be, but not used to hating. It troubled him extremely. He had never in his life asked for a reposting, but on the morning after she had taken the makil into her room, he sent a stiff little appeal to the Embassy. Old

Music responded to him with a sealed voice-message through the diplomatic link: "Love of god and country is like fire, a wonderful friend, a terrible enemy; only children play with fire. I don't like the situation. There's nobody here I can replace either of you with. Will you hang on a while longer?"

He did not know how to refuse. A veot did not refuse duty. He was ashamed at having even thought of doing so, and hated her again for causing him that shame.

The first sentence of the message was enigmatic, not in Old Music's usual style but flowery, indirect, like a coded warning. Teyeo of course knew none of the intelligence codes either of his country or of the Ekumen. Old Music would have to use hints and indirection with him. "Love of god and country" could well mean the Old Believers and the Patriots, the two subversive groups in Gatay, both of them fanatically opposed to foreign influence; the Envoy could be the child playing with fire. Was she being approached by one group or the other? He had seen no evidence of it, unless the man in the shadows that night had been not a knifeman but a messenger. She was under his eyes all day, her house watched all night by soldiers under his command. Surely the makil, Batikam, was not acting for either of those groups. He might well be a member of the Hame, the asset liberation underground of Voe Deo, but as such would not endanger the Envoy, since the Hame saw the Ekumen as their ticket to Yeowe and to freedom.

Teyeo puzzled over the words, replaying them over and over, knowing his own stupidity faced with this kind of subtlety, the ins and outs of the political labyrinth. At last he erased the message and yawned, for it was late; bathed, lay down, turned off the light, said under his breath, "Lord Kamye, let me hold with courage to the one noble thing!" and slept like a stone.

The makil came to her house every night after the theater. Teyeo tried to tell himself there was nothing wrong in it. He himself had spent nights with the makils, back in the palmy days before the war. Expert, artistic sex was part of their business. He knew by hearsay that rich city women often hired them to come supply a husband's deficiencies. But even such women did so secretly, discreetly, not in this vulgar, shameless way, utterly careless of decency, flouting the moral code, as if she had some kind of right to do whatever she wanted wherever and whenever she wanted it. Of course Batikam colluded eagerly with her, playing on her infatuation, mocking the Gatayans, mocking Teyeo – and mocking her, though she didn't know it. What a chance for an asset to make fools of all the owners at once!

Watching Batikam, Teyeo felt sure he was a member of the Hame. His mockery was very subtle; he was not trying to disgrace the Envoy. Indeed his discretion was far greater than hers. He was trying to keep her from disgracing herself. The makil returned Teyeo's cold courtesy in kind, but once or twice their eyes met and some brief, involuntary understanding passed between them, fraternal, ironic.

There was to be a public festival, an observation of the Tualite Feast of Forgiveness, to which the Envoy was pressingly invited by the King and Council. She was put on show at many such events. Teyeo thought nothing about it except how to provide security in an excited holiday crowd, until San told him that the festival day was the highest holy day of the old religion of Gatay, and that the Old Believers fiercely resented the imposition of the foreign rites over their own. The little man seemed genuinely worried. Teyeo worried too when next day San was suddenly replaced by an elderly man who spoke little but Gatayan and was quite unable to explain what had become of San Ubattat. "Other duties, other duties call," he said in very bad Voe Dean, smiling and bobbing, "very great relishes time, aha? Relishes duties call."

During the days that preceded the festival tension rose in the city; graffiti appeared, symbols of the old religion smeared across walls; a Tualite temple was desecrated, after which the Royal Guard was much in evidence in the streets. Teyeo went to the palace and requested, on his own authority, that the Envoy not be asked to appear in public during a ceremony that was "likely to be troubled by inappropriate demonstrations." He was called in and treated by a Court official with a mixture of dismissive insolence and conniving nods and winks, which left him really uneasy. He left four men on duty at the Envoy's house that night. Returning to his quarters, a little barracks down the street which had been handed over to the Embassy Guard, he found the window of his room open and a scrap of writing, in his own language, on his table: *Fest F is set up for assasnation.*

He was at the Envoy's house promptly the next morning and asked her asset to tell her he must speak to her. She came out of her bedroom pulling a white wrap around her naked body. Batikam followed her, half-dressed, sleepy, and amused. Teyeo gave him the eye-signal *go*, which he received with a serene, patronizing smile, murmuring to the woman, "I'll go have some breakfast. Rewe? have you got something to feed me?" He followed the bondswoman out of the room. Teyeo faced the Envoy and held out the scrap of paper.

"I received this last night, ma'am," he said. "I must ask you not to attend the festival tomorrow."

She considered the paper, read the writing, and yawned. "Who's it from?"

"I don't know, ma'am."

"What's it mean? *Assasnation?* They can't spell, can they?"

After a moment, he said, "There are a number of other indications – enough that I must ask you – "

"Not to attend the festival of Forgiveness, yes. I heard you." She went to a windowseat and sat down, her robe falling wide to reveal her legs; her bare, brown feet were short and supple, the soles pink, the toes small and orderly. Teyeo looked fixedly at the air beside her head. She twiddled the bit of paper. "If you think it's dangerous, rega, bring a guardsman or two with you," she said, with the faintest tone of scorn. "I really have to be there. The King requested it, you know. And I'm to light the big fire, or something. One of the few things women are allowed to do in public here… I can't back out of it." She held out the paper, and after a moment he came close enough to take it. She looked up at him smiling; when she defeated him she always smiled at him. "Who do you think would want to blow me away, anyhow? The Patriots?"

"Or the Old Believers, ma'am. Tomorrow is one of their holidays."

"And your Tualites have taken it away from them? Well, they can't exactly blame the Ekumen, can they?"

"I think it possible that the government might permit violence in order to excuse retaliation, ma'am."

She started to answer carelessly, realized what he had said, and frowned. "You think the Council's setting me up? What evidence have you?"

After a pause he said, "Very little, ma'am. San Ubattat – "

"San's been ill. The old fellow they sent isn't much use, but he's scarcely dangerous! Is that all?" He said nothing, and she went on, "Until you have real evidence, Rega, don't interfere with my obligations. Your militaristic paranoia isn't acceptable when it spreads to the people I'm dealing with here. Control it, please! I'll expect an extra guardsman or two tomorrow; and that's enough."

"Yes, ma'am," he said, and went out. His head sang with anger. It occurred to him now that her new guide had told him San Ubattat had been kept away by religious duties, not by illness. He did not turn back. What was the use? "Stay on for an hour or so, will you, Seyem?" he said to the guard at her gate, and strode off down the street, trying to walk away from her, from her soft brown thighs and the pink soles of her feet and her stupid, insolent, whorish voice giving him orders. He tried to let the bright icy sunlit air, the stepped streets snapping with banners for the festival, the glitter of the great mountains and the clamor of the markets fill him, dazzle and distract him; but he walked seeing his own shadow fall in front of him like a knife across the stones, knowing the futility of his life.

"The veot looked worried," Batikam said in his velvet voice, and she laughed, spearing a preserved fruit from the dish and popping it, dripping, into his mouth.

"I'm ready for breakfast now, Rewe," she called, and sat down across from Batikam. "I'm starving! He was having one of his phallocratic fits. He hasn't saved me from anything lately. It's his only function, after all. So he has to invent occasions. I wish, I wish he was out of my hair. It's so nice not to have poor little old San crawling around like some kind of pubic infestation. If only I could get rid of the Major now!"

"He's a man of honor," the makil said; his tone did not seem ironical.

"How can an owner of slaves be an honorable man?"

Batikam watched her from his long, dark eyes. She could not read Werelian eyes, beautiful as they were, filling their lids with darkness.

"Male hierarchy members always yatter about their precious honor," she said. "And 'their' women's honor, of course."

"Honor is a great privilege," Batikam said. "I envy it. I envy him."

"Oh, the hell with all that phony dignity, it's just pissing to mark your territory. All you need envy him, Batikam, is his freedom."

He smiled. "You're the only person I've ever known who was neither owned nor owner. That is freedom. *That* is freedom. I wonder if you know it?"

"Of course I do," she said. He smiled, and went on eating his breakfast, but there had been something in his voice she had not heard before. Moved and a little troubled, she said after a while, "You're going away soon."

"Mind-reader. Yes. In ten days, the troupe goes on to tour the Forty States."

"Oh, Batikam, I'll miss you! You're the only man, the only person here I can talk to – let alone the sex – "

"Did we ever?"

"Not often," she said, laughing, but her voice shook a little. He held out his hand; she came to him and sat on his lap, the robe dropping open. "Little pretty Envoy breasts," he said, lipping and stroking, "little soft Envoy belly…" Rewe came in with a tray and softly set it down. "Eat your breakfast, little Envoy," Batikam said, and she disengaged herself and returned to her chair, grinning.

"Because you're free you can be honest," he said, fastidiously peeling a pini-fruit. "Don't be too hard on those of us who aren't and can't." He cut a slice and fed it to her across the table. "It has been a taste of freedom to know you," he said. "A hint, a shadow…"

"In a few years at most, Batikam, you *will* be free. This whole idiotic structure of masters and slaves will collapse completely when Werel comes into the Ekumen."

"If it does."

"Of course it will."

He shrugged. "My home is Yeowe," he said.

She stared, confused. "You come from Yeowe?"

"I've never been there," he said. "I'll probably never go there. What use have they got for makils? But it is my home. Those are my people. That is my freedom. When will you see…" His fist was clenched; he opened it with a soft gesture of letting something go. He smiled and returned to his breakfast. "I've got to get back to the theater," he said, "we're rehearsing an act for the Day of Forgiveness."

She wasted all day at court. She had made persistent attempts to obtain permission to visit the mines and the huge government-run farms on the far side of the mountains, from which Gatay's wealth flowed. She had been as persistently foiled – by the protocol and bureaucracy of the government, she had thought at first, their unwillingness to let a diplomat do anything but run round to meaningless events; but some businessmen had let something slip about conditions in the mines and on the farms that made her think they might be hiding a more brutal kind of slavery than any visible in the capital. Today she got nowhere, waiting for appointments that had not been made. The old fellow who was standing in for San misunderstood most of what she said in Voe Dean, and when she tried to speak Gatayan he misunderstood it all, through stupidity or intent. The Major was blessedly absent most of the morning, replaced by one of his soldiers, but turned up at court, stiff and silent and set-jawed, and attended her until she gave up and went home for an early bath.

Batikam came late that night. In the middle of one of the elaborate fantasy games and role-reversals she had learned from him and found so exciting, his caresses grew slower and slower, soft, dragging across her like feathers, so that she shivered with unappeased desire and, pressing her body against his, realized that he had gone to sleep. "Wake up," she said, laughing and yet chilled, and shook him a little. The dark eyes opened, bewildered, full of fear.

"I'm sorry," she said at once, "go back to sleep, you're tired. No, no, it's all right, it's late." But he went on with what she now, whatever his skill and tenderness, had to see was his job.

In the morning at breakfast she said, "Can you see me as an equal, do you, Batikam?"

He looked tired, older than he usually did. He did not smile. After a while he said, "What do you want me to say?"

"That you do."

"I do," he said quietly.

"You don't trust me," she said, bitter.

After a while he said, "This is Forgiveness Day. The Lady Tual came to the men of Asdok, who had set their hunting cats upon her followers. She came among them riding on a great hunting cat with a fiery tongue, and they fell down in terror, but she blessed them, forgiving them." His voice and hands enacted the story as he told it. "Forgive me," he said.

"You don't need any forgiveness!"

"Oh, we all do. It's why we Kamyites borrow the Lady Tual now and then. When we need her. So, today you'll be the Lady Tual, at the rites?"

"All I have to do is light a fire, they said," she said anxiously, and he laughed. When he left she told him she would come to the theater to see him, tonight, after the festival.

The horse-race course, the only flat area of any size anywhere near the city, was thronged, vendors calling, banners waving; the Royal motorcars drove straight into the crowd, which parted like water and closed behind. Some rickety-looking bleachers had been erected for lords and owners, with a curtained section for ladies. She saw a motorcar drive up to the bleachers; a figure swathed in red cloth was bundled out of it and hurried between the curtains, vanishing. Were there peepholes for them to watch the ceremony through? There were women in the crowds, but bondswomen only, assets. She realized that she, too, would be kept hidden until her moment of the ceremony arrived: a red tent awaited her, alongside the bleachers, not far from the roped enclosure where priests were chanting. She was rushed out of the car and into the tent by obsequious and determined courtiers.

Bondswomen in the tent offered her tea, sweets, mirrors, makeup, and hair-oil, and helped her put on the complex swathing of fine red and yellow cloth, her costume for her brief enactment of Lady Tual. Nobody had told her very clearly what she was to do, and to her questions the women said, "The priests will show you, Lady, you just go with them. You just light the fire. They have it all ready." She had the impression that they knew no more than she did; they were pretty girls, court assets, excited at being part of the show, indifferent to the religion. She knew the symbolism of the fire she was to light: into it faults and transgressions could be cast and burnt up, forgotten. It was a nice idea.

The priests were whooping it up out there; she peeked out – there were indeed peepholes in the tent fabric – and saw the crowd had thickened. Nobody except in the bleachers and right against the enclosure ropes could possibly see anything, but everybody was waving red and yellow banners, munching fried food, and making a day of it, while the priests kept up their deep chanting. In the far right of the little, blurred field of vision through the peephole was a familiar arm: the Major's, of course. They had not let him get into the motorcar with her. He must have been furious. He had got here, though, and stationed himself on guard. "Lady, Lady," the court girls were saying, "here come the priests now," and they buzzed around her making sure her headdress was on straight and the damnable, hobbling skirts fell in the right folds. They were still plucking and patting as she stepped out of the tent, dazzled by the daylight, smiling and trying to hold herself very straight and dignified as a Goddess ought to do. She really didn't want to fuck up their ceremony.

Two men in priestly regalia were waiting for her right outside the tent door. They stepped forward immediately, taking her by the elbows and saying, "This way, this way, Lady." Evidently she really wouldn't have to figure out what to do. No doubt they considered women incapable of it, but in the circumstances it was a relief. The priests hurried her along faster than she could comfortably walk in the tight-drawn skirt. They were behind the bleachers now; wasn't the enclosure in the other direction? A car was coming straight at them, scattering the few people who were in its way. Somebody was shouting; the priests suddenly began yanking her, trying to run; one of them yelled and let go her arm, felled by a flying darkness that had hit him with a jolt – she was in the middle of a melee, unable to break the iron hold on her arm, her legs imprisoned in the skirt, and there was a noise, an enormous noise, that hit her head and bent it down, she couldn't see or hear, blinded, struggling, shoved face first into some dark place with her face pressed into a stifling, scratchy darkness and her arms held locked behind her.

A car, moving. A long time. Men, talking low. They talked in Gatayan. It was very hard to breathe. She did not struggle; it was no use. They had taped her arms and legs, bagged her head. After a long time she was hauled out like a corpse and carried quickly, indoors, down stairs, set down on a bed or couch, not roughly though with the same desperate haste. She lay still. The men talked, still almost in whispers. It made no sense to her. Her head was still hearing that enormous noise, had it been real? had she been struck? She felt deaf, as if inside a wall of cotton. The cloth of the bag kept getting stuck on her mouth, sucked against her nostrils as she tried to breathe.

It was plucked off; a man stooping over her turned her so he could untape her arms, then her legs, murmuring as he did so, "Don't to be scared, Lady, we don't to hurt you," in Voe Dean. He backed away from her quickly. There were four or five of them; it was hard to see, there was very little light. "To wait here," another said, "everything all right. Just to keep happy." She was trying to sit up, and it made her dizzy. When her head stopped spinning, they were all gone. As if by magic. Just to keep happy.

A small very high room. Dark brick walls, earthy air. The light was from a little biolume plaque stuck on the ceiling, a weak, shadowless glow. Probably quite sufficient for Werelian eyes. Just to keep happy. I have been kidnapped. How about that. She inventoried: the thick mattress she was on; a blanket; a door; a small pitcher and a cup; a drainhole, was it, over in the corner? She swung her legs off the mattress and her feet struck something lying on the floor at the foot of it – she coiled up, peered at the dark mass, the body lying there. A man. The uniform, the skin so black she could not see the features, but she knew him. Even here, even here, the Major was with her.

She stood up unsteadily and went to investigate the drainhole, which was simply that, a cement-lined hole in the floor, smelling slightly chemical, slightly foul. Her head hurt, and she sat down on the bed again to massage her arms and ankles, easing the tension and pain and getting herself back into herself by touching and confirming herself, rhythmically, methodically. I have been kidnapped. How about that. Just to keep happy. What about him?

Suddenly knowing that he was dead, she shuddered and held still.

After a while she leaned over slowly, trying to see his face, listening. Again she had the sense of being deaf. She heard no breath. She reached out, sick and shaking, and put the back of her hand against his face. It was cool, cold. But warmth breathed across her fingers, once, again. She crouched on the mattress and studied him. He lay absolutely still, but when she put her hand on his chest she felt the slow heartbeat.

"Teyeo," she said in a whisper. Her voice would not go above a whisper.

She put her hand on his chest again. She wanted to feel that slow, steady beat, the faint warmth; it was reassuring. Just to keep happy.

What else had they said? Just to wait. Yes. That seemed to be the program. Maybe she could sleep. Maybe she could sleep and when she woke up the ransom would have come. Or whatever it was they wanted.

She woke up with the thought that she still had her watch, and after sleepily studying the tiny silver readout for a while decided she had slept three hours; it was still the day of the Festival, too soon for ransom probably, and she wouldn't be able to go to the theater to see the makils tonight. Her eyes had grown accustomed to the low light and when she looked she could see, now, that there was dried blood all over one side of the man's head. Exploring, she found a hot lump like a fist above his temple, and her fingers came away smeared. He had got himself crowned. That must have been him, launching himself at the priest, the fake priest, all she could remember was a flying shadow and a hard thump and an ooof! like an aiji attack, and then there had been the huge noise that confused everything. She clicked her tongue, tapped the wall, to check her hearing. It seemed to be all right; the wall of cotton had disappeared. Maybe she had been crowned herself? She felt her head, but found no lumps. The man must have a concussion, if he was still out after three hours. How bad? When would the men come back?

She got up and nearly fell over, entangled in the damned Goddess skirts. If only she was in her own clothes, not this fancy dress, three pieces of flimsy stuff you had to have servants to put on you! She got out of the skirt piece, and used the scarf piece to make a kind of tied skirt that came to her knees. It wasn't warm in this basement or whatever it was; it was dank and rather cold. She walked up and down, four steps turn, four steps turn, four steps turn, and did some warmups. They had dumped the man onto the floor. How cold was it? Was shock part of concussion? People in shock needed to be kept warm. She dithered a long time, puzzled at her own indecision, at not knowing what to do. Should she try to heave him up onto the mattress? Was it better not to move him? Where the hell were the men? Was he going to die?

She stooped over him and said sharply, "Rega! Teyeo!" and after a moment he caught his breath.

"Wake up!" She remembered now, she thought she remembered, that it was important not to let concussed people lapse into a coma. Except he already had.

He caught his breath again, and his face changed, came out of the rigid immobility, softened; his eyes opened and closed, blinked, unfocused. "Oh Kamye," he said very softly.

She couldn't believe how glad she was to see him. Just to keep happy. He evidently had a blinding headache, and admitted that he was seeing double. She helped him haul himself up onto the mattress and covered him with the blanket. He asked no questions, and lay mute, lapsing back to sleep soon. Once he was settled she went back to her exercises, and did an hour of them. She looked at her watch. It was two hours later, the same day, the Festival day. It wasn't evening yet. When were the men going to come?

They came early in the morning, after the endless night that was the same as the afternoon and the morning. The metal door was unlocked and thrown clanging open, and one of them came in with a tray while two of them stood with raised, aimed guns in the doorway. There was nowhere to put the tray but the floor, so he shoved it at Solly, said, "Sorry, Lady!" and backed out; the door clanged shut, the bolts banged home. She stood holding the tray. "Wait!" she said.

The man had waked up and was looking groggily around. After finding him in this place with her she had somehow lost his nickname, did not think of him as the Major, yet shied away from his name. "Here's breakfast, I guess," she said, and sat down on the edge of the mattress. A cloth was thrown over the wicker tray; under it was a pile of Gatayan grainrolls stuffed with meat and greens, several pieces of fruit, and a capped water-carafe of thin, fancily beaded metal alloy. "Breakfast, lunch, and dinner, maybe," she said. "Shit. Oh well. It looks good. Can you eat? Can you sit up?"

He worked himself up to sit with his back against the wall, and then shut his eyes.

"You're still seeing double?"

He made a small noise of assent.

"Are you thirsty?"

Small noise of assent.

"Here." She passed him the cup. By holding it in both hands he got it to his mouth, and drank the water slowly, a swallow at a time. She meanwhile devoured three grainrolls one after the other, then forced herself to stop, and ate a pinifruit. "Could you eat some fruit?" she asked him, feeling guilty. He did not answer. She thought of Batikam feeding her the slice of pini at breakfast, when, yesterday, a hundred years ago.

The food in her stomach made her feel sick. She took the cup from the man's relaxed hand – he was asleep again – and poured herself water, and drank it slowly, a swallow at a time.

When she felt better she went to the door and explored its hinges, lock, and surface. She felt and peered around the brick walls, the poured concrete floor, seeking she knew not what, something to escape with, something…. She should do exercises. She forced herself to do some, but the queasiness returned, and a lethargy with it. She went back to the mattress and sat down. After a while she found she was crying. After a while she found she had been asleep. She needed to piss.

She squatted over the hole and listened to her urine fall into it. There was nothing to clean herself with. She came back to the bed and sat down on it, stretching out her legs, holding her ankles in her hands. It was utterly silent.

She turned to look at the man; he was watching her. It made her start.

He looked away at once. He still lay half propped up against the wall, uncomfortably, but relaxed.

"Are you thirsty?" she asked.

"Thank you," he said. Here where nothing was familiar and time was broken off from the past, his soft, light voice was welcome in its familiarity. She poured him a cup full and gave it to him. He managed it much more steadily, sitting up to drink. "Thank you," he whispered again, giving her back the cup.

"How's your head?"

He put up his hand to the swelling, winced, and sat back.

"One of them had a stick," she said, seeing it in a flash in the jumble of her memories – "a priest's staff. You jumped the other one."

"They took my gun," he said. "Festival." He kept his eyes closed.

"I got tangled in those damn clothes. I couldn't help you at all. Listen. Was there a noise, an explosion?"

"Yes. Diversion, maybe."

"Who do you think these boys are?"

"Revolutionaries. Or..."

"You said you thought the Gatayan government was in on it."

"I don't know," he murmured.

"You were right, I was wrong, I'm sorry," she said with a sense of virtue at remembering to make amends.

He moved his hand very slightly in an it-doesn't-matter gesture.

"Are you still seeing double?"

He did not answer; he was phasing out again.

She was standing, trying to remember Selish breathing exercises, when the door crashed and clanged, and the same three men were there, two with guns, all young, black-skinned, short-haired, very nervous. The lead one stooped to set a tray down on the floor, and without the least premeditation Solly stepped on his hand and brought her weight down on it. "You wait!" she said. She was staring straight into the faces and gun-muzzles of the other two. "Just wait a moment, listen! He has a head injury, we need a doctor, we need more water, I can't even clean his wound, there's no toilet paper, who the hell are you people anyway?"

The one she had stomped was shouting, "Get off! Lady to get off my hand!" but the others heard her. She lifted her foot and got out of his way as he came up fast, backing into his buddies with the guns. "All right, lady, we are sorry to have trouble," he said, tears in his eyes, cradling his hand. "We are Patriots. You send messish to this Pretender, like our messish. Nobody is to hurt. All right?" He kept backing up, and one of the gunmen swung the door to. Crash, rattle.

She drew a deep breath and turned. Teyeo was watching her. "That was dangerous," he said, smiling very slightly.

"I know it was," she said, breathing hard. "It was stupid. I can't get hold of myself. I feel like pieces of me. But they shove stuff in and run, damn it! We have to have some water!" She was in tears, the way she always was for a moment after violence or a quarrel. "Let's see, what have they brought this time." She lifted the tray up onto the mattress; like the other, in a ridiculous semblance of service in a hotel or a house with slaves, it was covered with a cloth. "All the comforts," she murmured. Under the cloth was a heap of sweet pastries, a little plastic handmirror, a comb, a tiny pot of something that smelled like decayed flowers, and a box of what she identified after a while as Gatayan tampons.

"It's things for the lady," she said, "God damn them, the stupid God-damn pricks! A mirror!" She flung the thing across the room. "Of course I can't last a day without looking in the mirror! God *damn* them!" She flung everything else but the pastries after the mirror, knowing as she did so that she would pick up the tampons and keep them under the mattress and, oh, God forbid, use them if she had to, if they had to stay here, how long would it be? ten days or more – "Oh, God," she said again. She got up and picked everything up, put the mirror and the little pot, the empty water jug and the fruit-skins from the last meal, onto one of the trays and set it beside the door. "Garbage," she said in Voe Dean. Her outburst, she realized, had been in another language; Alterran, probably. "Have you any idea," she said, sitting down on the mattress again, "how hard you people make it to be a woman? You could turn a woman against being one!"

"I think they meant well," Teyeo said. She realized that there was not the faintest shade of mockery, even of amusement in his voice. If he was enjoying her shame, he was ashamed to show her that he was. "I think they're amateurs," he said.

After a while she said, "That could be bad."

"It might." He had sat up and was gingerly feeling the knot on his head. His coarse, heavy hair was bloodcaked all around it. "Kidnapping," he said. "Ransom demands. Not assassins. They didn't have guns. Couldn't have got in with guns. I had to give up mine."

"You mean these aren't the ones you were warned about?"

"I don't know." His explorations caused him a shiver of pain, and he desisted. "Are we very short of water?"

She brought him another cup full. "Too short for washing. A stupid God-damn mirror when what we need is water!"

He thanked her and drank and sat back, nursing the last swallows in the cup. "They didn't plan to take me," he said.

She thought about it and nodded. "Afraid you'd identify them?"

"If they had a place for me they wouldn't put me in with a lady." He spoke without irony. "They had this ready for you. It must be somewhere in the city."

She nodded. "The car ride was half an hour or less. My head was in a bag, though."

"They've sent a message to the Palace. They got no reply, or an unsatisfactory one. They want a message from you."

"To convince the government they really have me? Why do they need convincing?"

They were both silent.

"I'm sorry," he said, "I can't think." He lay back. Feeling tired, low, edgy after her adrenaline rush, she lay down alongside him. She had rolled up the Goddess' skirt to make a pillow; he had none. The blanket lay across their legs.

"Pillow," she said. "More blankets. Soap. What else?"

"Key," he murmured.

They lay side by side in the silence and the faint unvarying light.

Next morning about eight, according to Solly's watch, the Patriots came into the room, four of them. Two stood on guard at the door with their guns ready; the other two stood uncomfortably in what floor space was left, looking down at their captives, both of whom sat crosslegged on the mattress. The new spokesman spoke better Voe

Dean than the others. He said they were very sorry to cause the lady discomfort and would do what they could to make it comfortable for her, and she must be patient and write a message by hand to the Pretender King, explaining that she would be set free unharmed as soon as the King commanded the Council to rescind their treaty with Voe Deo.

"He won't," she said. "They won't let him."

"Please do not discuss," the man said with frantic harshness. "This is writing materials. This is the message." He set the papers and a stylo down on the mattress, nervously, as if afraid to get close to her.

She was aware of how Teyeo effaced himself, sitting without a motion, his head lowered, his eyes lowered; the men ignored him.

"If I write this for you I want water, a lot of water, and soap and blankets and toilet paper and pillows and a doctor, and I want somebody to come when I knock on that door, and I want some decent clothes. Warm clothes. Men's clothes."

"No doctor!" the man said. "Write it! Please! Now!" He was jumpy, twitchy, she dared push him no further. She read their statement, copied it out in her large, childish scrawl – she seldom handwrote anything – and handed both to the spokesman. He glanced over it and without a word hurried the other men out. Clash went the door.

"Should I have refused?"

"I don't think so," Teyeo said. He stood up and stretched, but sat down again looking dizzy. "You bargain well," he said.

"We'll see what we get. Oh, God. What is going *on*?"

"Maybe," he said slowly, "Gatay is unwilling to yield to these demands. But when Voe Deo – and your Ekumen – get word of it, they'll put pressure on Gatay."

"I wish they'd get moving. I suppose Gatay is horribly embarrassed, saving face by trying to conceal the whole thing – is that likely? How long can they keep it up? What about your people? Won't they be hunting for you?"

"No doubt," he said, in his polite way.

It was curious how his stiff manner, his manners, which had always shunted her aside, cut her out, here had quite another effect: his restraint and formality reassured her that she was still part of the world outside this room, from which they came and to which they would return, a world where people lived long lives.

What did long life matter? she asked herself, and didn't know. It was nothing she had ever thought about before. But these young Patriots lived in a world of short lives. Demands, violence, immediacy, and death, for what? for a bigotry, a hatred, a rush of power.

"Whenever they leave," she said in a low voice, "I get really frightened."

Teyeo cleared his throat and said, "So do I."

Exercises.

"Take hold – no, take *hold*, I'm not made of glass! – Now – "

"Ha!" he said, with his flashing grin of excitement, as she showed him the break, and he in turn repeated it, breaking from her.

"All right, now you'd be waiting – here" – thump – "see?"

"Ai!"

"I'm sorry – I'm sorry, Teyeo – I didn't think about your head – Are you all right? I'm really sorry – "

"Oh, Kamye," he said, sitting up and holding his black, narrow head between his hands. He drew several deep breaths. She knelt penitent and anxious.

"That's," he said, and breathed some more, "that's not, not fair play."

"No of course it's not, it's aiji – all's fair in love and war, they say that on Terra – Really, I'm sorry, I'm terribly sorry, that was so stupid of me!"

He laughed, a kind of broken and desperate laugh, shook his head, shook it again. "Show me," he said. "I don't know what you did."

Exercises.

"What do you do with your mind?"

"Nothing."

"You just let it wander?"

"No. Am I and my mind different beings?"

"So... you don't focus on something? You just wander with it?"

"No."

"So you *don't* let it wander."

"Who?" he said, rather testily.

A pause.

"Do you think about – "

"No," he said. "Be still."

A very long pause, maybe a quarter hour.

"Teyeo, I can't. I itch. My mind itches. How long have you been doing this?"

A pause, a reluctant answer: "Since I was two."

He broke his utterly relaxed motionless pose, bent his head to stretch his neck and shoulder muscles. She watched him.

"I keep thinking about long life, about living long," she said. "I don't mean just being alive a long time, hell, I've been alive about eleven hundred years, what does that mean, nothing. I mean…. Something about thinking of life as long makes a difference. Like having kids does. Even thinking about having kids. It's like it changes some balance. It's funny I keep thinking about that now, when my chances for a long life have kind of taken a steep fall…."

He said nothing. He was able to say nothing in a way that allowed her to go on talking. He was one of the least talkative men she had ever known. Most men were so wordy. She was fairly wordy herself. He was quiet. She wished she knew how to be quiet.

"It's just practice, isn't it?" she asked. "Just sitting there."

He nodded.

"Years and years and years of practice… Oh, God. Maybe…"

"No, no," he said, taking her thought immediately.

"But why don't they *do* something? What are they *waiting* for? It's been nine *days!*"

From the beginning, by unplanned, unspoken agreement, the room had been divided in two: the line ran down the middle of the mattress and across to the facing wall. The door was on her side, the left; the shit-hole was on his side, the right. Any invasion of the other's space was requested by some almost invisible cue and permitted the same way. When one of them used the shit-hole the other unobtrusively faced away. When they had enough water to take cat-baths, which was seldom, the same arrangement held. The line down the middle of the mattress was absolute. Their voices crossed it, and the sounds and smells of their bodies. Sometimes she felt his warmth; Werelian body temperature was somewhat higher than hers, and in the dank, still air she felt that faint radiance as he slept. But they never crossed the line, not by a finger, not in the deepest sleep.

Solly thought about this, finding it, in some moments, quite funny. At other moments it seemed stupid and perverse. Couldn't they both use some human comfort? The only time she had touched him was the first day, when she had helped him get onto the mattress, and then when they had enough water she had cleaned his scalp-wound and little by little washed the clotted, stinking blood out of his hair, using the comb, which had after all been a good thing to have, and pieces of the Goddess's skirt, an invaluable source of washcloths and bandages. Then once his head healed, they practiced aiji daily; but aiji had an impersonal, ritual purity to its clasps and grips that was a long way from creature comfort. The rest of the time his bodily presence was clearly, invariably uninvasive and untouchable.

He was only maintaining, under incredibly difficult circumstances, the rigid restraint he had always shown. Not just he, but Rewe, too; all of them, all of them but Batikam; and yet was Batikam's instant yielding to her whim and desire the true contact she had thought it? She thought of the fear in his eyes, that last night. Not restraint, but constraint.

It was the mentality of a slave society: slaves and masters caught in the same trap of radical distrust and self-protection.

"Teyeo," she said, "I don't understand slavery. Let me say what I mean," though he had shown no sign of interruption or protest, merely civil attention. "I mean, I do understand how a social institution comes about and how an individual is simply part of it – I'm not saying why don't you agree with me in seeing it as wicked and unprofitable, I'm not asking you to defend it or renounce it. I'm trying to understand what it feels like to believe that two-thirds of the human beings in your world are actually, rightfully your property. Five-sixths, in fact, including women of your caste."

After a while he said, "My family owns about twenty-five assets."

"Don't quibble."

He accepted the reproof.

"It seems to me that you cut off human contact. You don't touch slaves and slaves don't touch you, in the way human beings ought to touch, in mutuality. You have to keep yourselves separate, always working to maintain that boundary. Because it isn't a natural boundary – it's totally artificial, manmade. I can't tell owners and assets apart physically. Can you?"

"Mostly."

"By cultural, behavioral clues – right?"

After thinking a while, he nodded.

"You are the same species, race, people, exactly the same in every way, with a slight selection towards color. If you brought up an asset child as an owner it would *be* an owner in every respect, and vice versa. So you spend your lives keeping up this tremendous division that doesn't exist. What I don't understand how you can fail to see is how appallingly wasteful it is. I don't mean economically!"

"In the war," he said, and then there was a very long pause; though Solly had a lot more to say, she waited, curious. "I was on Yeowe," he said, "you know, in the civil war."

That's where you got all those scars and dents, she thought; for however scrupulously she averted her eyes, it was impossible not to be familiar with his spare, onyx body by now, and she knew that in aiji he had to favor his left arm, which had a considerable chunk out of it just above the bicep.

"The slaves of the Colonies revolted, you know, some of them at first, then all of them. Nearly all. So we Army men there were all owners. We couldn't send asset soldiers, they might defect. We were all veots and volunteers. Owners fighting assets. I was fighting my equals. I learned that pretty soon. Later on I learned I was fighting my superiors. They defeated us."

"But that – " Solly said, and stopped; she did not know what to say.

"They defeated us from beginning to end," he said. "Partly because my government didn't understand that they could. That they fought better and harder and more intelligently and more bravely than we did."

"Because they were fighting for their freedom!"

"Maybe so," he said in his polite way.

"So..."

"I wanted to tell you that I respect the people I fought."

"I know so little about war, about fighting," she said, with a mixture of contrition and irritation. "Nothing, really. I was on Kheakh, but that wasn't war, it was racial suicide, mass slaughter of a biosphere. I guess there's a difference.... That was when the Ekumen finally decided on the Arms Convention, you know. Because of Orint and then Kheakh destroying themselves. The Terrans had been pushing for the Convention for ages. Having nearly committed suicide themselves a while back. I'm half Terran. My ancestors rushed around their planet slaughtering each other. For millennia. They were masters and slaves, too, some of them, a lot of them.... But I don't know if the Arms Convention was a good idea. If it's right. Who are we to tell anybody what to do and not to do? The idea of the Ekumen was to offer a way. To open it. Not to bar it to anybody."

He listened intently, but said nothing until after some while. "We learn to... close ranks. Always. You're right, I think, it wastes... energy, the spirit. You are open."

His words cost him so much, she thought, not like hers that just came dancing out of the air and went back into it. He spoke from his marrow. It made what he said a solemn compliment, which she accepted gratefully, for as the days went on she realized occasionally how much confidence she had lost and kept losing: selfconfidence, confidence that they would be ransomed, rescued, that they would get out of this room, that they would get out of it alive.

"Was the war very brutal?"

"Yes," he said. "I can't... I've never been able to – to see it – Only something comes like a flash – " He held his hands up as if to shield his eyes. Then he glanced at her, wary. His apparently cast-iron self-respect was, she knew now, vulnerable in many places.

"Things from Kheakh that I didn't even know I saw, they come that way, " she said. "At night." And after a while, "How long were you there?"

"A little over seven years."

She winced. "Were you lucky?"

It was a queer question, not coming out the way she meant, but he took it at value. "Yes," he said. "Always. The men I went there with were killed. Most of them in the first few years. We lost three hundred thousand men on Yeowe. They never talk about it. Two-thirds of the veot men in Voe Deo were killed. If it was lucky to live, I was lucky." He looked down at his clasped hands, locked into himself.

After a while she said softly, "I hope you still are."

He said nothing.

"How long has it been?" he asked, and she said, clearing her throat, after an automatic glance at her watch, "Sixty hours."

Their captors had not come yesterday at what had become a regular time, about eight in the morning. Nor had they come this morning.

With nothing left to eat and now no water left, they had grown increasingly silent and inert. It was hours since either had said anything. He had put off asking the time as long as he could prevent himself.

"This is horrible," she said, "this is so horrible. I keep thinking…"

"They won't abandon you," he said. "They feel a responsibility."

"Because I'm a woman?"

"Partly."

"Shit."

He remembered that in the other life her coarseness had offended him.

"They've been taken, shot. Nobody bothered to find out where they were keeping us," she said.

Having thought the same thing several hundred times, he had nothing to say.

"It's just such a horrible *place* to die," she said. "It's sordid. I stink. I've stunk for twenty days. Now I have diarrhea because I'm scared. But I can't shit anything. I'm thirsty and I can't drink."

"Solly," he said sharply. It was the first time he had spoken her name. "Be still. Hold fast."

She stared at him.

"Hold fast to what?"

He did not answer at once and she said, "You won't let me touch you!"

"Not to me – "

"Then to what? There isn't anything!" He thought she was going to cry, but she stood up, took the empty tray, and beat it against the door till it smashed into fragments of wicker and dust. "Come! God damn you! Come, you bastards!" she shouted. "Let us out of here!"

After that she sat down again on the mattress. "Well," she said.

"Listen," he said.

They had heard it before: no city sounds came down to this cellar, wherever it was, but this was something bigger, explosions, they both thought.

The door rattled.

They were both afoot when it opened: not with the usual clash and clang, but slowly. A man waited outside; two men came in. One, armed, they had never seen; the other, the tough-faced young man they called the spokesman, looked as if he had been running or fighting, dusty, worn out, a little dazed. He closed the door. He had some papers in his hand. The four of them stared at one other in silence for a minute.

"Water," Solly said. "You bastards!"

"Lady," the spokesman said, "I'm sorry." He was not listening to her. His eyes were not on her. He was looking at Teyeo, for the first time. "There is a lot of fighting," he said.

"Who's fighting?" Teyeo asked, hearing himself drop into the even tone of authority, and the young man respond to it as automatically: "Voe Deo. They sent troops. After the funeral, they said they would send troops unless we surrendered. They came yesterday. They go through the city killing. They know all the Old Believer centers. Some of ours." He had a bewildered, accusing note in his voice.

"What funeral?" Solly said.

When he did not answer, Teyeo repeated it: "What funeral?"

"The lady's funeral, yours. Here – I brought netprints – A state funeral. They said you died in the explosion."

"What God-damned explosion?" Solly said in her hoarse, parched voice, and this time he answered her: "At the Festival. The Old Believers. The fire, Tual's fire, there were explosives in it. Only it went off too soon. We knew their plan. We rescued you from that, lady," he said, suddenly turning to her with that same accusatory tone.

"Rescued me, you asshole!" she shouted, and Teyeo's dry lips split in a startled laugh, which he repressed at once.

"Give me those," he said, and the young man handed him the papers.

"Get us water!" Solly said.

"Stay here, please. We need to talk," Teyeo said, instinctively holding on to his ascendancy. He sat down on the mattress with the netprints. Within a few minutes he and Solly had scanned the reports of the shocking disruption of the Festival of Forgiveness, the lamentable death of the Envoy of the Ekumen in a terrorist act executed by the cult of Old Believers, the brief mention of the death of a Voe Dean Embassy guard in the explosion, which had killed over seventy priests and onlookers, the long descriptions of the state funeral, reports of unrest, terrorism, reprisals, then reports of the Palace gratefully accepting offers of assistance from Voe Deo in cleaning out the cancer of terrorism....

"So," he said finally. "You never heard from the Palace. Why did you keep us alive?"

Solly looked as if she thought the question lacked tact, but the spokesman answered with equal bluntness, "We thought your country would ransom you."

"They will," Teyeo said. "Only you have to keep your government from knowing we're alive. If you – "

"Wait," Solly said, touching his hand. "Hold on. I want to think about this stuff. You'd better not leave the Ekumen out of the discussion. But getting in touch with them is the tricky bit."

"If there are Voe Dean troops here, all I need is to get a message to anyone in my command, or the Embassy Guards."

Her hand was still on his, with a warning pressure. She shook the other one at the spokesman, finger outstretched: "You kidnapped an Envoy of the Ekumen, you asshole! Now you have to do the thinking you didn't do ahead of time. And I do too, because I don't want to get blown away by your God-damned little government for turning up alive and embarrassing them. Where are you hiding, anyhow? Is there any chance of us getting out of this room, at least?"

The man, with that edgy, frantic look, shook his head. "We are all down here now," he said. "Most of the time. You stay here safe."

"Yes, you'd better keep your passports safe!" Solly said. "Bring us some water, damn it! Let us talk a while. Come back in an hour."

The young man leaned towards her suddenly, his face contorted. "What the hell kind of lady you are," he said. "You foreign filthy stinking cunt."

Teyeo was on his feet, but her grip on his hand had tightened: after a moment of silence, the spokesman and the other man turned to the door, rattled the lock, and were let out.

"Ouf," she said, looking dazed.

"Don't," he said, "don't – " He did not know how to say it. "They don't understand," he said. "It's better if I talk."

"Of course. Women don't give orders. Women don't talk. Shitheads! I thought you said they felt so responsible for me!"

"They do," he said. "But they're young men. Fanatics. Very frightened." And you talk to them as if they were assets, he thought, but did not say.

"Well so am I frightened!" she said, with a little spurt of tears. She wiped her eyes and sat down again among the papers. "God," she said. "We've been dead for twenty days. Buried for fifteen. Who do you think they buried?"

Her grip was powerful; his wrist and hand hurt. He massaged the place gently, watching her.

"Thank you," he said. "I would have hit him."

"Oh, I know. God-damn chivalry. And the one with the gun would have blown your head off. Listen, Teyeo. Are you sure all you have to do is get word to somebody in the Army or the Guard?"

"Yes, of course."

"You're sure your country isn't playing the same game as Gatay?"

He stared at her. As he understood her, slowly the anger he had stifled and denied, all these interminable days of imprisonment with her, rose in him, a fiery flood of resentment, hatred, and contempt.

He was unable to speak, afraid he would speak to her as the young Patriot had done.

He went around to his side of the room and sat on his side of the mattress, somewhat turned from her. He sat cross-legged, one hand lying lightly in the other.

She said some other things. He did not listen or reply.

After a while she said, "We're supposed to be talking, Teyeo. We've only got an hour. I think those kids might do what we tell them, if we tell them something plausible – something that'll work."

He would not answer. He bit his lip and held still.

"Teyeo, what did I say? I said something wrong. I don't know what it was. I'm sorry."

"They would – " He struggled to control his lips and voice. "They would not betray us."

"Who? The Patriots?"

He did not answer.

"Voe Deo, you mean? Wouldn't betray us?"

In the pause that followed her gentle, incredulous question, he knew that she was right; that it was all collusion among the powers of the world; that his loyalty to his country and service was wasted, as futile as the rest of his life. She went on talking, palliating, saying he might very well be right. He put his head into his hands, longing for tears, dry as stone.

She crossed the line. He felt her hand on his shoulder.

"Teyeo, I am very sorry," she said. "I didn't mean to insult you! I honor you. You've been all my hope and help."

"It doesn't matter," he said. "If I – If we had some water."

She leapt up and battered on the door with her fists and a sandal. "Bastards, bastards," she shouted.

Teyeo got up and walked, three steps and turn, three steps and turn, and halted on his side of the room. "If you're right," he said, speaking slowly and formally, "we and our captors are in danger not only from Gatay but from my own people, who may... who have been furthering these anti-Government factions, in order to make an excuse to bring troops here... to *pacify* Gatay. That's why they know where to find the factionalists. We are... we're lucky our group were... were genuine."

She watched him with a tenderness that he found irrelevant.

"What we don't know," he said, "is what side the Ekumen will take. That is... There really is only one side."

"No, there's ours, too. The underdogs. If the Embassy sees Voe Deo pulling a takeover of Gatay, they won't interfere, but they won't approve. Especially if it involves as much repression as it seems to."

"The violence is only against the anti-Ekumen factions."

"They still won't approve. And if they find out I'm alive they're going to be quite pissed at the people who claimed I went up in a bonfire. Our problem is how to get word to them. I was the only person representing the Ekumen in Gatay. Who'd be a safe channel?"

"Any of my men. But... "

"They'll have been sent back; why keep Embassy Guards here when the Envoy's dead and buried? I suppose we could try. Ask the boys to try, that is." Presently she said wistfully, "I don't suppose they'd just let us go – in disguise? It would be the safest for them."

"There is an ocean," Teyeo said.

She beat her head. "Oh, why don't they bring some *water*...." Her voice was like paper sliding on paper. He was ashamed of his anger, his grief, himself. He wanted to tell her that she had been a help and hope to him too, that he honored her, that she was brave beyond belief; but none of the words would come. He felt empty, worn out. He felt old. If only they would bring water!

Water was given them at last; some food, not much and not fresh. Clearly their captors were in hiding and under duress. The spokesman – he gave them his war-name, Kergat, Gatayan for Liberty – told them that whole neighborhoods had been cleared out, set afire, that Voe Dean troops were in control of most of the city including the palace, and that almost none of this was being reported in the net. "When this is over Voe Deo will own my country," he said with disbelieving fury.

"Not for long," Teyeo said.

"Who can defeat them?" the young man said.

"Yeowe. The idea of Yeowe."

Both Kergat and Solly stared at him.

"Revolution," he said. "How long before Werel becomes New Yeowe?"

"The assets?" Kergat said, as if Teyeo had suggested a revolt of cattle or of flies. "They'll never organize."

"Look out when they do," Teyeo said mildly.

"You don't have any assets in your group?" Solly asked Kergat, amazed. He did not bother to answer. He had classed her as an asset, Teyeo saw. He understood why; he had done so himself, in the other life, when such distinctions made sense.

"Your bondswoman, Rewe," he asked Solly – "was she a friend?"

"Yes," Solly said, then, "No. I wanted her to be."

"The makil?"

After a pause she said, "I think so."

"Is he still here?"

She shook her head. "The troupe was going on with their tour, a few days after the Festival."

"Travel has been restricted since the Festival," Kergat said. "Only government and troops."

"He's Voe Dean. If he's still here, they'll probably send him and his troupe home. Try and contact him, Kergat."

"A makil?" the young man said, with that same distaste and incredulity. "One of your Voe Dean homosexual clowns?"

Teyeo shot a glance at Solly: Patience, patience.

"Bisexual actors," Solly said, disregarding him, but fortunately Kergat was determined to disregard her.

"A clever man," Teyeo said, "with connections. He could help us. You and us. It could be worth it. If he's still here. We must make haste."

"Why would he help us? He is Voe Dean."

"An asset, not a citizen," Teyeo said. "And a member of Hame, the asset underground, which works against the government of Voe Deo. The Ekumen admits the legitimacy of Hame. He'll report to the Embassy that a Patriot group has rescued the Envoy and is holding her safe, in hiding, in extreme danger. The Ekumen, I think, will act promptly and decisively. Correct, Envoy?"

Suddenly reinstated, Solly gave a short, dignified nod. "But discreetly," she said. "They'll avoid violence, if they can use political coercion."

The young man was trying to get it all into his mind and work it through. Sympathetic to his weariness, distrust, and confusion, Teyeo sat quietly waiting. He noticed that Solly was sitting equally quietly, one hand lying in the other. She was thin and dirty and her unwashed, greasy hair was in a lank braid. She was brave, like a brave mare, all nerve. She would break her heart before she quit.

Kergat asked questions; Teyeo answered them, reasoning and reassuring. Occasionally Solly spoke, and Kergat was now listening to her again, uneasily, not wanting to, not after what he had called her. At last he left, not saying what he intended to do; but he had Batikam's name and an identifying message from Teyeo to the Embassy: "Half-pay veots learn to sing old songs quickly."

"What on earth!" Solly said when Kergat was gone.

"Did you know a man named Old Music, in the Embassy?"

"Ah! Is he a friend of yours?"

"He has been kind."

"He's been here on Werel from the start. A First Observer. Rather a powerful man. – Yes, and 'quickly,' all right... My mind really isn't working at all. I wish I could lie down beside a little stream, in a meadow, you know, and drink. All day. Every time I wanted to, just stretch my neck out and slup, slup, slup... Running water... In the sunshine... Oh God, oh God, sunshine. Teyeo, this is very difficult. This is harder than ever. Thinking that there maybe is really a way out of here. Only not knowing. Trying not to hope and not to not hope. Oh, I am so tired of sitting here!"

"What time is it?"

"Half-past twenty. Night. Dark out. Oh God, darkness! Just to be in the darkness... Is there any way we could cover up that damned biolume? Partly? To pretend we had night, so we could pretend we had day?"

"If you stood on my shoulders, you could reach it. But how could we fasten a cloth?"

They pondered, staring at the plaque.

"I don't know. Did you notice there's a little patch of it that looks like it's dying? Maybe we don't have to worry about making darkness. If we stay here long enough. Oh, God!"

"Well," he said after a while, curiously self-conscious, "I'm tired."

He stood up, stretched, glanced for permission to enter her territory, got a drink of water, returned to his territory, took off his jacket and shoes, by which time her back was turned, took off his trousers, lay down, pulled up the blanket, and said in his mind, "Lord Kamye, let me hold fast to the one noble thing." But he did not sleep.

He heard her slight movements; she pissed, poured a little water, took off her sandals, lay down.

A long time passed.

"Teyeo."

"Yes."

"Do you think...that it would be a mistake...under the circumstances... to make love?"

A pause.

"Not under the circumstances," he said, almost inaudibly. "But – in the other life – "

A pause.

"Short life versus long life," she murmured.

"Yes."

A pause.

"No," he said, and turned to her. "No, that's wrong." They reached out to each other. They clasped each other, cleaved together, in blind haste, greed, need, crying out together the name of God in their different languages and then like animals in the wordless voice. They huddled together, spent, sticky, sweaty, exhausted, reviving, rejoined, reborn in the body's tenderness, in the endless exploration, the ancient discovery, the long flight to the new world.

He woke slowly, in ease and luxury. They were entangled, his face was against her arm and breast; she was stroking his hair, sometimes his neck and shoulder. He lay for a long time aware only of that lazy rhythm and the cool of her skin against his face, under his hand, against his leg.

"Now I know," she said, her half-whisper deep in her chest, near his ear, "that I don't know you. Now I need to know you." She bent forward to touch his face with her lips and cheek.

"What do you want to know?"

"Everything. Tell me who Teyeo is..."

"I don't know," he said. "A man who holds you dear."

"Oh, God," she said, hiding her face for a moment in the rough, smelly blanket.

"Who is God?" he asked sleepily. They spoke Voe Dean, but she usually swore in Terran or Alterran; in this case it had been Alterran, *seyt*, so he asked, "Who is Seyt?"

"Oh – Tual – Kamye – what have you. I just say it. It's just bad language. Do you believe in one of them? I'm sorry! I feel like such an oaf with you, Teyeo. Blundering into your soul, invading you – We *are* invaders, no matter how pacificist and priggish we are – "

"Must I love the whole Ekumen?" he asked, beginning to stroke her breasts, feeling her tremor of desire and his own.

"Yes," she said, "yes, yes."

It was curious, Teyeo thought, how little sex changed anything. Everything was the same, a little easier, less embarrassment and inhibition; and there was a certain and lovely source of pleasure for them, when they had enough water and food to have enough vitality to make love. But the only thing that was truly different was something he had no word for. Sex, comfort, tenderness, love, trust, no word was the right word, the whole word. It was utterly intimate, hidden in the mutuality of their bodies, and it changed nothing in their circumstances, nothing in the world, even the tiny wretched world of their imprisonment. They were still trapped. They were getting very tired and were hungry most of the time. They were increasingly afraid of their increasingly desperate captors.

"I will be a lady," Solly said. "A good girl. Tell me how, Teyeo."

"I don't want you to give in," he said, so fiercely, with tears in his eyes, that she went to him and held him in her arms.

"Hold fast," he said.

"I will," she said. But when Kergat or the others came in she was sedate and modest, letting the men talk, keeping her eyes down. He could not bear to see her so, and knew she was right to do so.

The doorlock rattled, the door clashed, bringing him up out of a wretched, thirsty sleep. It was night or very early morning. He and Solly had been sleeping close entangled for the warmth and comfort of it; and seeing Kergat's face now he was deeply afraid. This was what he had feared, to show, to prove her sexual vulnerability. She was still only half awake, clinging to him.

Another man had come in. Kergat said nothing. It took Teyeo some time to recognize the second man as Batikam.

When he did, his mind remained quite blank. He managed to say the makil's name. Nothing else.

"Batikam?" Solly croaked. "Oh, my God!"

"This is an interesting moment," Batikam said in his warm actor's voice. He was not transvestite, Teyeo saw, but wore Gatayan men's clothing. "I meant to rescue you, not to embarrass you, Envoy, Rega. Shall we get on with it?"

Teyeo had scrambled up and was pulling on his filthy trousers. Solly had slept in the ragged pants their captors had given her. They both had kept on their shirts for warmth.

"Did you contact the Embassy, Batikam?" she was asking, her voice shaking, as she pulled on her sandals.

"Oh, yes. I've been there and come back, indeed. Sorry it took so long. I don't think I quite realized your situation here."

"Kergat has done his best for us," Teyeo said at once, stiffly.

"I can see that. At considerable risk. I think the risk from now on is low. That is..." He looked straight at Teyeo. "Rega, how do you feel about putting yourself in the hands of Hame?" he said. "Any problems with that?"

"Don't, Batikam," Solly said. "Trust him!"

Teyeo tied his shoe, straightened up, and said, "We are all in the hands of the Lord Kamye."

Batikam laughed, the beautiful full laugh they remembered.

"In the Lord's hands, then," he said, and led them out of the room.

In the *Arkamye* it is said, "To live simply is most complicated."

Solly requested to stay on Werel, and after a recuperative leave at the seashore was sent as Observer to South Voe Deo. Teyeo went straight home, being informed that his father was very ill. After his father's death, he asked for indefinite leave from the Embassy Guard, and stayed on the farm with his mother until her death two years later. He and Solly, a continent apart, met only occasionally during those years.

When his mother died, Teyeo freed his family's assets by act of irrevocable manumission, deeded over their farms to them, sold his now almost valueless property at auction, and went to the capital. He knew Solly was temporarily staying at the Embassy. Old Music told him

where to find her. He found her in a small office of the palatial building. She looked older, very elegant. She looked at him with a stricken
and yet wary face. She did not come forward to greet or touch him.
She said, "Teyeo, I've been asked to be the first Ambassador of the
Ekumen to Yeowe."

He stood still.

"Just now – I just came from talking on the ansible with Hain – "
She put her face in her hands. "Oh, my God!" she said.

He said, "My congratulations, truly, Solly."

She suddenly ran at him, threw her arms around him, and cried,
"Oh, Teyeo, and your mother died, I never thought, I'm so sorry, I
never, I never do – I thought we could – What are you going to do? Are
you going to stay there?"

"I sold it," he said. He was enduring rather than returning her embrace. "I thought I might return to the service."

"You sold your *farm*? But I never saw it!"

"I never saw where you were born," he said.

There was a pause. She stood away from him, and they looked at
each other.

"You would come?" she said.

"I would," he said.

Several years after Yeowe entered the Ekumen, Mobile Solly Agat
Terwa was sent as an Ekumenical liaison to Terra; later she went from
there to Hain, where she served with great distinction as a Stabile. In
all her travels and posts she was accompanied by her husband, a
Werelian army officer, a very handsome man, as reserved as she was
outgoing. People who knew them knew their passionate pride and
trust in each other. Solly was perhaps the happier person, rewarded
and fulfilled in her work; but Teyeo had no regrets. He had lost his
world, but he had held fast to the one noble thing

IAN MCDONALD
Some Strange Desire

19 NOVEMBER, 10:30 P.M.

The *hru-tesh* is a beautiful piece of craftsmanship. Mother says he can remember Grandmother taking him, while still very small, to watch Josias Cunningham, Gunsmith by Appointment, of Fleet Street at work on it. In that small shop, in those small hours when the city slept, Josias Cunningham worked away while the spires and domes of Wren's dream of London rose from the ashes of the Great Fire, chasing and filing and boring and inlaying. It was a work of love, I suppose. A masterpiece he could never disclose to another living soul, for it was the work of demons. On the bone-handled stock is a filigreed silver plate on a pivot-pin. Underneath, an inscription: Diabolus me Fecit. The Devil Made Me.

He was *ul-goi* of course, Josias Cunningham, Gunsmith by Appointment, of Fleet Street.

After three hundred years, the firing mechanism is still strong and precise. It gives a definite, elegant click as I draw back the bolt and lock it.

Lights are burning in the apartment across the street. The white BMW sits rain-spattered under its private cone of yellow light. Have you ever known anyone who drives a white BMW to do anything or be anyone of any significance? I cannot say that I have, either. I blow on my fingers. I cannot let them become chilled. I cannot let their grip on the *hru-tesh* slacken and weaken. Hurry up and go about your business, *goi*, so I can go about mine and get back into the dry and the warm. Cold rain finds me in my bolt-hole on the roof, penetrates my quilted jacket like needles. None so cold as the needle I have waiting for you, *goi*. I touch the thermos flask beside me, for luck, for reassurance, for the blessing of the *hahndahvi*.

Come on, *goi*, when are you going to finish what you are doing and go out to collect the day's takings from your boys? Voices are raised in the lighted apartment across the yellow-lit cobbled street. Male voices. I cannot make out the words, only the voices.

Even on my rooftop across the street, the blow is almost palpable. And then the weeping. A door slams. I uncap the thermos, shake a tiny sliver of ice into the breech of the *hru-tesh*. The street door opens. He is dressed in expensive leather sports gear. In the dark I cannot read the labels. He turns to swear one last time at the youth at the top of the stairs. I let a drop of saliva fall from my tongue onto the needle of ice resting in the chamber. Slide the breech shut. Move from my cover. Take aim, double-handed, over the fire-escape rail.

Coptic crosses and peace medallions catch the yellow street light as he bends to unlock the car door. The silver filigree-work of the *hru-tesh* crafted by the three-hundred-year-dead hand of Josias Cunningham, Gunsmith by Appointment, glitters in that same light. I squeeze the trigger.

There is only the faintest *tok*.

He starts, stands up, clasps hand to neck. Puzzlement on his meatlike face. Puzzlement under that so-cool baseball cap at that ideologically correct angle. And it hits him. He keels straight over against the car. His head rests at a quizzical angle on the rain-wet metal. Complete motor paralysis.

I am already halfway down the fire escape. Flat shoes. No heels. I have it all planned. As I had thought, bundling him into the passenger seat is the hardest part of the operation. I think I may have broken a finger wresting the keys from him. It will be academic, soon enough. As I drive up through Bethnal Green and Hackney to Epping Forest I pass at least twenty other white BMWs. I sample his CD selection, then scan across the AM wavebands until I find some anonymous Benelux station playing hits from the forties. Childhood tunes stay with you all your life. I chat to him as we drive along. It is a rather one-sided conversation. But I do not think he would have been much of a conversationalist anyway. It is really coming down, the wipers are on high speed by the time we arrive at the car park. I shall get very wet. Another crime against you, *goi*.

It is wonderful how much can be expressed by eyes alone. Anger, incomprehension, helplessness. And, as I pull the syringe out of my belt-pouch, *terror*. I tap the cylinder a couple of times. I can tell from his eyes he has never seen so much in one needle before. He may consider himself honored. We have our own discreet sources, but we, like you, pay a price. I squat over him. He will take the image of who I am into the dark with him. Such is my intention.

"Hear these words: you do not touch us, you do not harass us, you do not try to recruit us or bully us into your stable. We are *tesh*, we are older and more powerful than you could possibly imagine. We have been surviving for centuries. Centuries."

He cannot even flinch from the needle.

I find a sheltered spot among the bushes and crushed flat lager cans, away from the steamed-up hatchbacks, and go into *tletchen*. I strip. I dress in the denims and shell-suit top I brought in my backpack. I stuff the rainsoaked clothes in around the *hru-tesh*. I go to the cardphone half a mile down the road and call a minicab to pick me up at the pub nearby and take me back to Shantallow Mews. The driver is pleased at the generosity of the tip. It is easy to be generous with the money of people who have no further use for it.

The *hru-tesh* goes back to its place under the hall floor-boards. Rest there for a long time, beautiful device. The unused needles go into the kitchen sink to melt and run and lose themselves in the sewers of London town. The soaked clothes go into the machine, the jacket will need dry cleaning. I make tea for my sister, bring it to him on the Harrods tray with the shelduck on it.

The only light in the room is from the portable television at the foot of the bed. The remote control has slipped from his hand. His fingers rest near the "mute" button. Late-night/early morning horror. Vampires, werewolves, Freddies. A little saliva has leaked from his lips onto the pillow. So peaceful. On the pale blue screen, blood is drunk, limbs dismembered, bodies chain-sawn apart. I want that peace to last a little longer before I wake him. By the light of the screen I move around the room setting the watches and wards, the little shrines and votaries to the Five Lords of the *tesh* that keep spiritual watch around my sister. Pere Teakbois the Balancer, Tulashwayo Who Discriminates, Filé Legbé Prince of the Changing Ways, Jean Tombibié with his bulging eyes and hands crossed over replete belly, Saint Semillia of the Mercies: the five *hahndahvi*. I trim wicks, tap ash from long curls of burned incense, pour small libations of beer and urine. I may not believe that *hahndahvi* are the literal embodiments of the character of the Universe, I have lived long enough among the *goi* to know the Universe is characterless, faceless. But I do believe power resides in symbol and ritual.

He is awake. The brightness in his eyes is only the reflection of the television screen. Awake now, he seems a thing of horror himself. Shrunken, shriveled, transparent skin drawn taut over bird bones, fingers quivering spastically as they grip the edge of the duvet. Trapped in that final *tletchen*, too weak to complete the transformation. His breasts are slack and withered like the dugs of old bitches.

"I've made tea, but it's probably cold now." I pour a cup, milk and sugar it, hold it steady as he lifts it to his lips. The tea is cold, but he seems glad of it.

"You were out." His voice is a grotesque whisper.

"Business." He understands. Our clients, both *ul-goi* and *goi*, are never *business*.

"That pimp?"

"He won't trouble you again. I can promise that."

"This isn't forty years ago. They've got computers, genetic fingerprinting."

"The people in the car park, if any of them even noticed, will tell them it was a woman got out of the car. The taxi driver will swear he drove a man."

"Still…"

I take his hand in mine, modulate my pheromone patterns to convey calm, assurance, necessity. It was more than just a pimp harassing us to join his stable, more than him breaking into this apartment, terrorizing my sick sister, overturning the furniture, desecrating the shrines of the *hahndahvi*. It was *security*, *tesh* security, which is more powerful and paranoid than any *goi* conception of the word, for it has its roots in ten thousand years of secrecy.

I offer him a Penguin biscuit. He shakes his head. Too weak. Too tired. I pull the stand from its position behind the headboard close by the side of the mattress. From the fridge in the kitchen I take the next-to-last bag of blood. As I run a line in, he says,

"There was a call for you. I couldn't get to it. Sorry. It's on the answering machine."

I am back in the kitchen, filling a basin with water. I test the temperature with my elbow.

"Vinyl Lionel?"

I fetch the natural sponge I bought from the almost-all-night chemist around the corner, whip the water to froth with Johnson's baby-bath.

"A new one," my sister Cassiopia says.

I pull back the duvet. The smell of the sickroom, the terrible smell of prolonged, ingrained sickness, is overpowering. As the blood, my blood that I pumped out of myself into plastic bags yesterday, runs into him, drip by drip, I wash my sister's body. Gently. Lovingly. With the soft natural sponge and the gentle baby-bath; neck and arms and sagging, flat breasts, the small triangle of pubic hair and the tiny, wrinkled penis and testicles, smaller even than a child's, and the shriveled labia.

15–16 NOVEMBER

Only four days. It seems like a small forever, since the afternoon Cassiopia came back from the pitch at Somerville Road with twenty pounds in his pocket.

"He insisted on paying. One of the lace-G-string-and-stocking brigade. Took me back to his place. Why do they always have posters of racing cyclists on their walls?"

Though we do not do it for money – genetic material is the price we ask for our services – cash in hand is never refused. I had taken the twenty down to the off-license for a bottle of Californian Chardonnay and a sweet-and-sour pork while Cassiopia changed for the evening client, an *ul-goi* who liked to tie our wrists to the ceiling hooks while he slipped rubber bands around our breasts, more and more and more of them, tighter and tighter and tighter. Thank God once every six weeks seemed to satisfy him. Vinyl Lionel had Word he was Something in the Foreign Office. Whatever, he had taste in tailoring. We made sure he paid for his game with the rubber bands.

When I returned Cassiopia had *tletched*. He is very beautiful as a woman. When he *tletches*, it is like a flower blossoming. Yet there was a subtle change in the atmosphere, something in his personal aroma that smelled not right.

"It hurts," he said. "Here. Here. Here. And here." He touched breasts, loins, neck and, on the final *here*, pressed fingers into belly in the way that says *deep within, everywhere*.

Of course, you never think it can be you. Your lover. Your partner. Your sibling. I gave him two paracetamol and a cup of corner-store Chardonnay to wash them down with.

He scratched all night. I could not sleep for his scratching, scratching, scratching. In the shower he was covered in yellow crusted spots. The sting of hot water made him wince. Even then I pretended not to know. I convinced myself he had picked up some venereal bug from one of the *goi*. Despite the fact that our immune systems make us almost invulnerable to *goi* infections. Such was my self-deception, I even bought some under-the-counter antibiotics from the Almost-All-Night Pharmacy.

You can imagine the smell of sickness. It is not hard, even for your limited senses. Imagine, then, a whole street, a whole town, terminally sick, dying at once. That is what I smelled when I came home after an afternoon with a first-timer who had passed furtive notes: *what are you into, I'm into, I got a place.* under the partitions of the cubicles in the gents' toilets.

I found him lying on the carpet, hands opening and closing spastically into tight, futile fists. He had failed halfway in *tletchen*, caught between like something half-melted and twisted by flame. I cleaned thin, sour, vomited-up coffee and slimmer's soup from his clothes. Over and over and over and over and over and over, he whispered, *Oh my God oh my God oh my God oh my God.* I got him into bed and a fistful of Valium down him, then sat by his side in the room that was filling with the perfume of poisoned earth, looking at everything and seeing only the shadow my thoughts cast as they circled beneath my skull.

We have a word for it in our language. *Jhash.* There is no direct translation into your languages. But you know it. You know it very well. It haunts your pubs and clubs and Saturday night scores. It is the unspoken sermon behind every mint-scented condom machine on the toilet wall. Like ours, yours is a little word too. When I was small and ran in gray flannel shorts wild and heedless over the bomb-sites of Hackney Marshes, my grandmother, who was keeper of the mysteries, taught me that *jhash* was the price Pere Teakbois the Balancer with his plumb-bob in his hand demanded of the *tesh* in return for their talents. I think that was the point at which my long, slow slide from faith began: Grandmother had been a gifted spinner of tales and his graphic descriptions of the terrible, enduring agony of *jhash* left me nightmar-

ish and seriously doubting the goodness of a god who would deliberately balance the good gifts he had given us with such dreadfulness.

The bomb-sites have given way to the tower-blocks of the post-war
dream and those in turn to the dereliction and disillusionment of mon-
etarist dogma and I no longer need faith for now I have biology. It is
not the will of Pere Teakbois, Pere Teakbois himself is no more than
the product of ten thousand years of institutionalized paranoia: *jhash*
is a catastrophic failure of the endocrinal, hormonal, and immune systems brought on by the biological mayhem of *tletchen*.

It can take you down into the dark in a single night. It can endure
for weeks. None are immune.

Let me tell you the true test of caring. We may be different species,
you and I, but we both understand the cold panic that overcomes us
when we first realize that we are going to die. We understand that
there is an end, an absolute end, when this selfness will stop and never
be again. And it terrifies us. Horrifies us. Paralyzes us, in the warmth
of our beds, in the dark of the night with our loved ones beside us. The
end. No appeal, no repeal, no exceptions.

You are *goi* and I am *tesh* and both love and life are different things
between us but this we both understand, that when we contemplate
the death of the one we love and it strikes that same paralyzing, cold
panic into us as if it were we ourselves, that is caring. That is love. Isn't
it?

20 NOVEMBER, 9:15 P.M.
Vinyl Lionel's Law: Everyone is either someone's pimp or someone's
prostitute.

By that definition, Vinyl Lionel is our pimp, though he would be
quite scandalized to think that the word could be applied to himself.

Vinyl Lionel subscribes to the roller-and-tray school of cosmetics
and wears a studded leather collar. Studs, in one form or another,
characterize Vinyl Lionel's personal style. Studded wristbands, studded peak to his black leather ss cap, studded motorbike boots pulled
up over his zip-up PVC one-piece with studded thighs and shoulders.

I remember PVC from the Swinging Sixties. You sweated like shit in
those boots and raincoats. Vinyl Lionel maintains they are trying to
remix the Sixties for the Nineties. Vinyl Lionel should know about the
Sixties. He has an old-age pensioner 5 free bus pass, but he won't
show it to anyone. If the Nineties are anything like the Sixties, it will

be that whatever is happening is always happening somewhere else. My memory of the Swinging Sixties is that they may have been swinging in the next street or the party next door, but never swinging in your street, at your party.

Strangefella's is the kind of place where advertising copywriters and the editors of those instantly disposable street-culture magazines like to convince people they party all night when in fact they are at home, in bed, exhausted by their workloads, every night by ten-thirty. If the Nineties are swinging, it is somewhere else than Strangefella's. Vinyl Lionel has a customary pitch as far as the architecture will permit from the AV show and the white boys with the deeply serious haircuts doing things to record decks. He is always pleased to see me. The pleasure is mutual. When he has a couple of gin slings down him he can be a delightfully effervescent conversationalist.

"Darling heart, you're looking especially radiant to-night!" He kisses me, on the cheek, not the mouth-to-mouth soul kiss of *tesh* meeting. He calls for cocktails. "Your mother is well, dismal suburbia notwithstanding?"

I reply that business is booming, and tell him about the pimp.

"I heard about that on *News at Ten*. That was you? A gangland killing, they said, made to look like an overdose." He takes a Turkish from his silver cigarette case, taps it once, twice, three times. "That was bit of a bloody risk, wasn't it, dear heart?"

"He'd broken in. Credit him with some intelligence, he could have worked out something was going on."

"Still, Orion darling, you could have left him to us. It's our job to look after you, and yours to provide us with what we want. You people have a vicious streak a mile wide. One of your less endearing traits. Smoke?" I take the proffered cheroot.

"So, this new client."

Vinyl Lionel examines his chrome-polished nails. "Well, there's not a lot to say about him. Nice enough boy. You wouldn't think to look at him, but then you never do, do you? Fat Willy recruited him, you know, the usual way." He moistens a finger in his Singapore sling, draws a yin-yang symbol on the marble table top.

"How much does he know?"

"The bare minimum. He'll talk the leg off you, dear heart. One of those confessional types. Well, fiddle-dee-dee, if that isn't him now…" Vinyl Lionel waves flamboyantly, trying to attract the attention of the lost boy by the door, fidgeting and conspicuous in a chain-store gent's-ready-made suit. "Oh God, I told him don't dress up, Strangefella's isn't that kind of place, and what does he do? Well, don't blame me if the gorillas bounce him."

"Nerves, Lionel," I say. "You were as bad the first time.

"Bitch," says Vinyl Lionel. He resents any overt reminder of his fall from youth and beauty while we remain changeless, ageless, ever-young. He beckons the young man between the tables and the smokes and the back-beat and the bass. "I'll bet you fifty he drives a Ford."

One bet I won't be taking, Lionel. A Ford Sierra, metallic gray, F-registration, the odd rust spot. Something to do with metallic finishes, I always think. Garfield crucified upside-down on the back window. Open the glove compartment and cassettes fall out. Home bootlegs, all of them, apart from the mandatory copy of *Graceland*. Nothing more recent than three years ago.

He is nervous. I can smell it over his Heathrow Duty-Free after-shave. Nerves, and something I cannot quite place, but seems familiar. I do not much like being driven by someone who is so nervous. Gaily lit buses swing past headed down across the river South London way; girls in smogmasks, denim cut-offs over cycling shorts and ski-goggles weave past on clunking ATBs like the outriders of some totalitarian, body-fascist invasion. I light up a cheroot Vinyl Lionel gave me as a keepsake as we surge and stop, surge and stop along Shaftesbury Avenue. Lionel, the outrageous old *ul-goi*, was right. This one seems to want to talk but is afraid of me. I weave pheromones, draw him into a chemical web of confidence. On New Oxford Street, he opens.

"I cannot believe this happening," he says. "It's in-credible; that something so, so, *huge*, could have been secret for so long."

"It has several thousand years of pedigree as a working relation-ship," I say. "As long there have been *tesh*, there have been *ul-goi*. And our mutual need for secrecy from the *goi*."

"*Goi?*"

"Humans." I wave a lace-gloved hand at the rain-wet people hud-dling along Holborn. "Those. The ignorant mass."

"And *tesh?*"

I draw a circle on the misted-up quarter-light, bisect it with a curv-ing s-shape. Yin and yang. Male and female in one. From time before time the symbol of the *tesh*.

"And *ul-goi?*"

"Those who can only achieve sexual satisfaction with a *tesh*."

The word seems to release him. He closes his eyes for a reckless moment, sighs. "It's funny. No, it's not funny, it's tragic, it's frightening. It's only recently I've found where it started. When I was a kid I read this comic, the *Eagle* or the *Lion* or the *Victor*. There was one story, one scene, where this skindiver is trying to find out who's been sabotaging North Sea drilling rigs and the bad guys catch him and tie him to the leg of the rig until his air runs out. That was where it started for me, with the guy in the rubber suit tied and helpless, with death inevitable. It was such an anti-climax when he got rescued in the next issue. I used to fantasize about wetsuits. I must have been Jacques Cousteau's number one fan." He laughs. Beneath folding umbrellas, girls in Sixties-revival PVC raincoats and Gerry-Anderson-puppet hairdos dart between the slowly grinding cars, giggling and swearing at the drivers.

"You don't know what it is at that age. But it was a major motivation in my childhood: tight clothing. Superheroes, of course, were a real turn-on. I remember one, where the Mighty Thor was being turned into a tree. Jesus! I nearly creamed myself. I was addicted to downhill skiing. If there was ever anything in the Sunday color supplements about downhill skiing, or ballet, I would cut it out, sneak it up to my room and stare at it under the sheets by the light from my electric blanket switch.

"Jane Fonda was, like, the answer to my prayers. I used to borrow my sister's leotard and tights and dress up, just to feel that head-to-toeness. Sometimes... sometimes, when the evenings were dark, I'd pass on late-night shopping with the family so I could dress up, nip over the back fence onto our local sports field and walk about. Just walk about. It was good, but it wasn't enough. There was something in there, in my head, that wanted something more but couldn't tell me what it was.

"When I was about seventeen I discovered sex shops. The number of times I would just walk past because I never had the nerve to push that door and go in. Then one day I decided it couldn't be any harder going in than just walking past. It was like Wonderland. I spent the fifty pounds I'd been saving in one pig-out. There was one magazine, *Mr. S.M....* I'd never seen anything like it before, I didn't know people could do that sort of thing to each other. Then, after I'd read them all twenty, fifty, a hundred times, I realized it wasn't doing it anymore. I bought new mags, but they were the same: there were things going on in my head that were far, far more exciting than what was going on in those photographs. In my best fantasies, there were things like no one had ever thought of before."

"This happens," I say. They all think they are the only ones. They start so differently, men and women, back among the sand castles and Dinky toys and Cindy dolls of childhood; they think there cannot be anyone else like them. But already they are being drawn toward us, and each other. They realize that what excites frenzies of passion in others leaves them cold and uncomprehending, and everything falls apart: friends, lovers, jobs, careers, hopes, dreams, everything except the search for that something that will fulfill the fantasy in their heads. Can anyone be as tormented, as depraved, as they? I do not disillusion them: fantasies and confessions, and the small absolutions and justifications I can offer; these are treasures held close to the heart. Tell me your story, then, *ul-goi* boy in your best suit, and I will listen, for, though it is a story I have heard ten thousand times before, it is a story that deserves to be heard. You have had the courage that so many lack, the courage to reach for what you truly want.

For the homosexual, it is the image in the mirror.

For the transvestite, it is the flight from ugliness to imagined true beauty.

For the sado-masochist, it is the two-edged embrace of guilt.

For the bondage enthusiast, it is the relieved plummet from the burden of being adult into the helplessness of childhood.

For the rubber fetishist, it is the return to the total comforting enclosure of the womb.

For the *ul-goi*, it is the frustration of desiring to be what they *are* and what they *are not* simultaneously.

Where have all the fluorescent re-spray Volkswagen Beetles started to come from?

What is he saying now? About some 0898 Sexline he used to dial called "Cycle Club Lust" ; how he sat hanging on the line running up obscene bills waiting for the payoff that never came. How Telecom regulations compel them to use words like "penis" and "buttocks" and "breasts." How can you get off on words like that? he says.

And I sense it again. A scent... Almost totally masked by my own pheromone patterns; that certain uncertainty. I know it. I know it... Tower cranes decked out with aircraft warning lights like Christmas decorations move through the upper air. Towers of London. Close to home now. I show him a place to park the car where it will be fairly safe. In this area, you do not buy car stereos, you merely rent them from the local pub. On the street, with his coat collar turned up against the drizzle, he looks desperately vulnerable and uncertain. The merest waft of pheromones is enough to firm that wavering resolution. Gentle musks carry him through the front door, past the rooms where we cater for the particular tastes of our *goi* clients, up the stairs and along the landing past Cassiopia's room, up another flight of stairs to the room at the top. The room where the *ul-goi* go.

18 NOVEMBER
On the third day of the *jhash*, I went to see Mother, a forty-five-minute train journey past red-brick palazzo-style hypermarkets under Heathrow's sound-footprint.

When the great wave of early-Fifties slum clearance swept the old East End out into the satellite New Towns, it swept Mother and his little empire with it. Three years after the bombing stopped, the Blitz really began, he says. After three hundred years of metropolis, he felt a change of environment would do him good. He is quite the born-again suburbanite; he cannot imagine why we choose to remain in the city. With his two sisters, our aunts, he runs a discreet and lucrative brothel from a detached house on a large estate. The deviations of suburbia differ from, but are no less deviations than, the deviations of the city, and are equally exploitable.

As Mother opened the door to me an elderly man in a saggy black latex suit wandered down from upstairs, saw me, apologized and vanished into the back bedroom.

"It's all right dear, he's part of the family," Mother shouted up. "Really, you know, I should stop charging him. He's been coming twenty years, boy and man. Every Tuesday, same thing. Dresses up in the rubber suit and has your Aunt Ursa sit on his face. Happily married; he's invited us to his silver wedding anniversary party; it's a nice thought but I don't think it's really us, do you?"

To the eye they were three fortysomething slightly-but-not-too-tarty women, the kind you see pushing shopping trolleys around palazzo-style hypermarkets, or in hatchbacks arriving at yoga classes in the local leisure center rather than the kind that congregate at the farthest table in bars to drink vodka and laugh boorishly.

My mother was born the same year that Charles II was restored to the monarchy.

We kissed on the mouth, exchanging chemical identifications, tongue to tongue. I made no attempt to mask my feelings; anxiety has a flavor that cannot be concealed.

"Love, what is it? Is it that pimp again? Is he giving bother?" He sniffed deeply. "No. It's Cassiopia, isn't it? Something's happened to him. The Law? Darling, we've High Court judges in our pockets. No, something else. Worse. Oh no. Oh dear God no."

Chemical communication is surer and less ambiguous than verbal. Within minutes my aunts, smelling the alarm on the air, had cut short their appointments with their clients and congregated in the back room where no non-*tesh* was ever permitted. In the deep wing-chair drawn close to the gas heater sat my grandmother, seven hundred years old and almost totally submerged into the dark, mind wandering interminably and with death the only hope of release from the labyrinth of his vast rememberings. His fingers moved in his lap like the legs of stricken spiders. We spoke in our own language, sharp-edged whispers beneath the eyes of the *hahndahvi* in their five Cardinal Points up on the picture rail.

Jhash. It was made to be whispered, that word. I suggested medical assistance. There were prominent doctors among the *ul-goi*. Sexual inclinations do not discriminate. What with the advances *goi* medicine had made, and the finest doctors in the country, surely something...

"It must be concern for your sister has temporarily clouded your judgment," whispered Aunt Lyra, "otherwise I cannot imagine you could be so stupid as to consider delivering one of us into the hands of the *goi*."

My mother hushed him with a touch to his arm.

"He could have put it a bit more subtly, love, but he's right. It would be no problem to recruit an *ul-goi* doctor, but doctors don't work in isolation. They rely upon a massive edifice of researchers, technicians, laboratories, consultants: how long do you think it would be before some *goi* discovered the truth about Cassiopia?"

"You would let my sister, your daughter die, rather than compromise security?"

"Do not ask me to answer questions like that. Listen up. One of our regulars here is an *ul-goi* lawyer. Just to make conversation I asked him once what our legal position was. This is what he told me: we may think and talk and look like humans, but we are not human. And, as non-humans, we are therefore the same as animals – less than animals; most animals enjoy some protection under the law, but not us. They could do what they liked to us, they could strip us of all our possessions, jail us indefinitely, use us to experiment on, gas us, hunt us down one by one for sport, burn us in the street, and in the eyes of the law it would be no different from killing rats. We are not human, we are not under the protection of the law. To compromise our secrecy is to threaten us all."

"He is dying and I want to know what to do."

"You know what to do." The voice startled me. It was like the voice of an old, corroded mechanism returning to life after long inactivity. "You know what to do," repeated my grandmother, stepping through a moment of lucidity into this last decade of the millennium. "Can I have taught you so badly, or is it you were such poor pupils? Pere Teakbois the Balancer demanded *jhash* of us in return for our enormously long lives, but Saint Semillia of the Mercies bargained a ransom price. Blood. The life is in the blood; that life may buy back a life."

Of course I knew the story. I even understood the biological principle behind the spurious theology. A massive blood transfusion might stimulate the disrupted immune system into regenerating itself, in a similar sense to the way our bodies rebuild themselves by using *goi* sex cells as a template. I had known the answer to *jhash* for as long as I had known of *jhash* itself: why had I refused to accept it and looked instead for, yes, ludicrous, yes, dangerous alternatives that could not possibly work?

Because Saint Semillia of the Mercies sells his dispensations dear.

Mother had given me a shoeboxful of equipment, most of it obsolete stuff from the last century when the last case of *jhash* had occurred. She did not tell me the outcome. Either way, I was not certain I wanted to know. In the house on Shantallow Mews I ran a line into my arm and watched the *Six o'clock News* while I pumped out two plastic bags. Internecine warfare in the Tory party. Some of the faces I knew, intimately. The blood seemed to revive Cassiopia but I knew it could only be temporary. I could never supply enough: after only two pints I was weak and trembling. All I could do was hold the sickness at bay. I took the icon of Saint Semillia of the Mercies down from the wall, asked it what I should do. His silence told me nothing I did not already know myself. *Out there. They are few, they are not perfect, but they exist, and you must find them.* I *tletched*, dressed in black leotard, black tights, black mini, black heels, wrapped it all under a duster coat and went down to the Cardboard Cities.

What is it your philosophers teach? That we live in the best of all possible worlds? Tell that to the damned souls of the cardboard cities in the tunnels under your railway stations and underpasses. *Tesh* have no such illusions. It has never been a tenet of our faith that the world should be a good place. Merely survivable.

Cloaked in a nimbus of hormonal *awe*, I went down. You would smell the piss and the beer and the smoke and the dampness and something faint and semi-perceived you cannot quite recognize. To me that thing you cannot recognize is what is communicated most strongly to me. It is despair. Derelicts, burned out like the hulls of Falklands' warships, waved hallucinatory greetings to me as I swirled past, coat billowing in the warm wet wind that blew across the wastelands. Eyes moved in cardboard shelters, cardboard coffins, heads turned, angered by the violation of their degradation by one who manifestly did not share it. When it is all you possess, you treasure even degradation. Figures gathered around smudge fires, red-eyed from the smoke, handing round hand-rolled cigarettes. Where someone had scraped enough money for batteries there was dance music from boom boxes. They would not trouble me. My pheromones made me a shadowy, godlike figure moving on the edge of the darkness.

Where should I go? I had asked.

Where no one will be missed, my mother had replied.

I went to the viaduct arches, the motorway flyovers, the shop doorways, the all-nite burger-shops, the parking lots and playgrounds. I went down into the tunnels under the stations.

Trains ground overhead, carrying the double-breasted suitmen and cellphone women back to suburbs ending in "ng" or "wich," to executive ghettos with names like Elmwood Grove and Manor Grange. The tunnels boomed and rang, drops of condensation fell sparkling in the electric light from stalactites seeping from the expansion joints in the roof. I paused at the junction of two tunnels. Something in the air, a few vagrant lipid molecules carried in the air currents beneath the station.

How will I know them? I had asked.

You will know them, my mother had said.

The trail of pheromones was fickle, more absent than present. It required the utmost exercise of my senses to follow it. It led me down clattering concrete stairways and ramps, under striplights and dead incandescent bulbs, down, underground. As I was drawn deeper, I dissolved my aura of *awe* and wove a new spell: *allure*. Certain now. Certain. The lost children in their cribs barely acknowledged my presence, the air smelled of shit and *ganja*.

She had found a sheltered corner under a vent that carried warmth and the smell of frying food from some far distant point of the concourse. An outsize Aran sweater – much grimed and stretched – was pulled down over her hunched-up knees. She had swaddled herself in plastic refuse sacks, pulled flattened cardboard boxes that had held washing machines and CD midi-systems in around her.

I enveloped her in a shroud of pheromones. I tried to imagine what she might see, the tall woman in the long coat, more vision than reality, demon, angel, standing over her like judgment. How could she know it was my pheromones, and not her own free will, that made her suddenly want more than anything, anything she had ever wanted in her life, to bury her face between my nylon-smooth thighs? I knelt down, took her chin in my hand. She looked into my eyes, tried to lick my fingers. Her face was filthy. I bent toward her and she opened her mouth to me. She ran her tongue around the inside of my lips; whimpering, she tried to ram it down my throat.

And I was certain. Truth is in the molecules. I had tasted it.

I extended a hand and she took it with luminous glee. She would have done anything, anything for me, anything, if I would only take her away from these tunnels and the stink of piss and desperation, back to my apartment: I could do whatever I wanted, anything.

The corridors shook to the iron tread of a train.

She loved me. Loved me.

With a cry, I snatched my hand from the touch of her fingers, turned, walked away, coat flapping behind me, heels ringing like shots. Faster. Faster. I broke into a run. Her calls pursued me through the tunnels, *come back come back, I love you, why did you go, I love you....*

I rode the underground into the take-away-curry-and-tins-of-lager hours. *We are not human,* my mother told me from every poster and advertisement, *we cannot afford the luxuries of human morality.* Saint Semillia of the Mercies smiled upon me. I rode the trains until the lights went out, one by one, in the stations behind me, and came home at last to Shantallow Mews.

The house looked and smelled normal. There was nothing to see. From the outside. He had broken in through a rear window and trashed a path through the rooms where we entertained the *goi*. Finding the locked door, he had kicked his way into Cassiopia's room.

The pimp had done a thorough and professional job of terror. Empty glasses and cups of cold tea shattered, a half-completed jigsaw of the Royal Family a thousand die-cut pieces scattered across the floor, magazines torn in two, the radio-cassette smashed in by a heel. Shredded cassette tape hung in swaths from the lights and stirred in the draft from the open door where I stood. The metal stand by the bedside was overturned; the blood, my blood, was splashed and daubed across the walls.

Cassiopia was in the corner by the window, shivering and dangerously pale from shock. Under the duvet he clutched the icons of the five *hahndahvi* and a kitchen knife. Bruises purpled down the side of his face, he flinched from my gentlest touch.

"He said he'd be back," my sister whispered. "He said unless we worked for him, he'd be back again. And again. And again. Until we got wise."

I made him comfortable on the sofa, cleaned the blood from the walls, made good the damage. Then I went to the never-quite-forgotten place under the floorboards and un-earthed the *hru-tesh*.

Saint Semillia, the price of your mercies!

20 NOVEMBER, 10:30 P.M.

But for the insistence of my perfumes urging him through the door at the top of the stairs, I think he would run in terror from what he is about to do. Often they do. But they are always drawn back to this door, by the sign of the yin-yang drawn in spilled vodka on a table top, by addresses on matchbooks or slipped under toilet partitions. They come back because nothing else can satisfy them.

The *hahndahvi* placed at their five cardinal points about the room fascinate him. He turns the icon of Filé Legbé over and over in his hands.

"This is old," he says.

"Early medieval," I say, offering him a drink from the cocktail bar. He takes a tequila in one nervous swallow. "The *hahndahvi*. The Five

Lords of the *tesh*. We have our own private religion; a kind of urban witchcraft, you could call it. Our own gods and demons and magics. They've taken a bit of a theological bashing with the advent of molecular biology, when we realized that we weren't the demonic lovers, the incubi and succubi of medieval legend. Just a variant of humanity. A subspecies. Two chromosomes separate me from you." As I am talking, he is undressing. He looks for a wardrobe where he can hang his smart suit and shirt and jazz-colored silk tie. I slide open one of the mirror-robes at the end of the room. His fastidiousness is cute. I pour him another tequila so that he will not be self-conscious in his nakedness and guide him to the Lloyd-loom chair at the opposite side of the room. As I seat him I smell it again, that uncertain something, masked and musked in a cocktail of his own sweat, after-shave and José Cuervo. Familiar.

He sips his drink, small, tight, fearful sips, as I strip down to my underwear. I slowly peel off panties, stockings, suspenders, kick them away. His penis comes up hard, sudden, taking him by surprise. The glass falls to the floor. The tequila spreads across the carpet. He begins to masturbate slowly, ecstatically. Standing naked before him, I slip into *tletchen*. I feel the familiar warmth behind my eyes as waves of endocrines and hormones surge out through my body. I will them into every part of me, every empty space, every cell, every molecule of me. I am on fire, burning up from inside with chemical fire.

"Do you know anything about mitosis and meiosis?" I ask him as the hormones burn through me, changing me. *Moses supposes mitosis are roses. Moses supposes erroneously.* "The old legend was that incubi and succubi visited humans to steal sexual fluids. Sperm, eggs. It's true, insofar as we need haploid cells to self-impregnate every cell in our bodies and, in a sense, continually give birth to ourselves. That's how we live five, six, seven hundred years, world events permitting. Though, of course, our reproductive rate is very very low." I have found over the years that many of them find the talking as exciting as the physical act. It is the thrill of abandoning themselves to the implacably alien. As I speak my breasts, so full and beautiful, dwindle and contract to flat nipples; the pads of flesh on my hips and ass are redistributed to shoulders and belly; muscles contract my pelvis; my entire body profile changes from wide-hipped narrow-shouldered hourglass femininity to broad-shouldered, flat-chested narrow-waisted triangular masculinity. My genitals swell and contract and jut and fold themselves into new configurations. It excited me enormously, that first time when Mother guided me into *tletchen*, the ebb and swell of my genitals. Now what I sense is an incompleteness, a loss, when I change from female to male. But I can see what a shock of excitement it is to my client. I come to him, let him savor my new masculinity. He runs his fingers over my flat chest, twists my flat nipples between thumb and finger, caresses my buttocks, thighs, genitals. As he thrills to me, I continue, my voice an octave lower.

"We're essentially an urban phenomenon. We were there in the cities of the Nile and Indus, of Mesopotamia, of Classical Greece and Rome – some lesser members of their respective pantheons are *tesh* in disguise. We need a large population to draw genetic material from without becoming too obvious – in rural communities we have rather too high a profile for our liking. Hence the medieval legends, when the country was almost entirely rural, which died out with urbanization when we could become anonymous in the cities. My particular family came with the Norman invasion; but we're comparative new kids on the block; the branch we bred into one hundred and fifty years back up in Edinburgh has been here since the end of the Ice Age."

There are tears in his eyes. Pressed close within his embrace, I smell it again. Intimate. Familiar. Too familiar.

I know what it is, and where I have smelled it before. But I am not finished with him yet. I step backward, out of the reach of his imploring fingers and summon up the *tletchen* energy again. Contours, profiles, genders melt and run in the heat of my hormonal fire. My body, my identity, my *tesh*ness, my Orion-ness dissolve into a multiplicity of possible genders. I blossom out of genderlessness into full hermaphroditism. Male and female, yin and yang in one. He is sobbing now, milking his penis in long, slow, joyous strokes. He is close now to complete sexual satisfaction for the first time in his life. I let him touch me, explore the mystery of my two-in-oneness. He stands, presses his body to mine, shuddering, moaning; long keening, dying moans. Exposed. Truly naked. From every pore of his body, every gland and mucous membrane and erogenous tissue, it pours out. The room whirls with his giddy perfume, the storm of chemicals is overpowering. *Yes! Yes! Yes!*

I look into his eyes.

"Do you know how we get our names?" I tell him. "We have public, *goi*, names, but among ourselves we use our *tesh* names. We are named after whatever constellation is in the ascendant on the night of our birth. My name is Orion. My sister is Cassiopia." I tell him, because I want him to know. I owe him at least a name. I open my mouth to kiss him, he opens to receive me. Thin ropes of drool stretch and break. I taste him. And he is right. It is the work of moment for my saliva glands to work the chemical changes. A drop of toxin falls from my tongue onto his. It runs like chain lighting from neuron to neuron. Even as the thought to react, the awareness that he may have been betrayed, is upon him, it locks him into rigidity.

He is easy to lift. In hermaphrodite gender we have the benefit of the musculature of both sexes, and the hormonal violence of *tletchen* gives us a supernatural strength. I carry him down the stairs and along the little landing into Cassiopia's room. I can feel his heart beating against my shoulder. He fits comfortably into the bedside chair.

Cassiopia is suspended in a fever dream between sleep and waking; muttering, crying out, twitching, eyeballs rolled up in his head, crazy with hallucinations. I fetch the equipment from the Reebok box under the bed, run a line into Cassiopia's right arm, and let the blue, burned poison drip from his arm into a basin on the floor.

Only his eyes can move. He sees the needle I have for him. Have I said elsewhere it is remarkable how much can be expressed by the eyes alone? Say a thing once, and you are sure to have to say it again, soon. He does not flinch as I run a line into his right arm and connect him to Cassiopia. As I pump his blood along the old rubber tubes, I tell him the tale my grandmother told me, of Pere Teakbois's bargain and the price of St. Semillia's mercy. At the very end, he deserves to know. And at the very end, I think he does begin to understand. Vinyl Lionel's Law. Everyone is someone's pimp, someone's prostitute. Everyone is user or used. Down in the tunnels, she had loved me. You had desired me. She had not loved me of her own free will. You did. I made her love me. I did not make you desire me. Understand, *goi*, why I could kill the pimp without a moment's moral uncertainty, why now it is your blood pulsing down the rubber tube. We were both the used, she and I. You and he, the users. Believe me, *goi* boy, I bear you no malice. I do what I do because an older, harder mercy demands it.

When the last drop is gone, I close the tubes. Cassiopia has lapsed into a quiet and tranquil sleep. Already the *jhash* pallor is gone from his skin, he is warm to my kiss.

I look at the boy, the rigor of my neurotoxins glazed over now with the serenity of death. When you went to those clubs and bars and made those contacts, did they never tell you the unwritten law of the user?

Every prostitute has his price.

In *tesh*, the words for *love* and *passion* are antonyms. It is not so different, I think, with you.

CAROL EMSHWILLER

Venus Rising

YOU ARE OF US and you remember it in your dreams. Your night-mares are of sharks (our sharks – the ones we also fear) sharks that look up at you from below with cruel little eyes, or you dream great waves (the waves we also fear) coming closer. At first it seems so slowly that you almost think you might have time to run up the beach to higher ground, but that's not true and you wake up screaming (like we used to scream) not knowing what it is you are afraid of, just knowing this nameless thing that keeps coming and coming, having turned into a wave of fear rather than fear of a wave, and so it is with us, also, a wordless fear, for we have no word for it, only cries and whistles that mean danger. But you have your good dreams, too, as we do, of floating as though you fly. Also you like to make love in the water.

When your children, as our children, have water, they need no other plaything. Your lakes are ringed with houses, your beaches are always full at the seasons for it. Ask yourself could any ape dive like you dive and like our People dive? There are places where we, and you, dive down naked, down and down, and not a single lesson except from our big brothers and sisters. We do it sometimes just for the fun of it. This is something to remember, and you do remember it, though not completely.

I say that if those others are your ancestors, then you would go on vacation to the trees because those others never cared about the water. And then your children would be climbing up and hanging in the highest branches by one arm and swinging around, and even the old people would get a kick out of getting up on some high limb instead of standing in the shallows or sitting on the beach. When it was smart and cool enough to hang around in the trees, we did do that, and when the future was on the beach, we found out about it and we went there and did that and all that went with it. Those others that stayed in the trees (what trees were left) the trees made them what they have become just as the beaches changed us, made us and made you as you are, crying seal tears as we do, but those others never do.

So (and including That One, then) we are the ones that are your ancestors, and (except for That One, then) we are as hairless as you are, no more, no less. You might be surprised. Sisters and brothers to the hippopotamus and not ashamed of it.

In those days, before That One came, we would never tease a manatee. We called them friends and swam with them as well as with seals and walruses.

Those were good days. Every family had its bay and some People slept where the rocks hung over. They had a good spot. It was so cool there sometimes they even came out of the water to play on the beach before the sun went down.

But usually our children come on into the water with us in the morning and don't leave again until dusk. The littlest ones float around grasping our long, long hair, and, if the older ones come out of the sea in the day time, it's most often so as to jump into it again from some high rock. So everybody has a lot of fun and stays cool. If one of us waits long enough to snatch at a fish, it's only because we are tired of easier things to eat like clams and mussels and periwinkles.

Some of you may think we have no names, but we do though for a while I didn't have one, but everybody knew who I was even so, and I knew who they were whether they had a name or not. And when we saw That One, we knew who he was, though at first we didn't. Some of us have swum far and been told tales of others not like we are and wondered how such people could be and laughed about them that they had hair on their bodies as, at first, we laughed at That One for the same reason and for other reasons, too.

There's a place where we go and steal berries from the Berry People. They have one over there with big feet with six toes and big hands with six fingers. (Those people are always the fastest swimmers. We have People like that over on our shore and we always call them Toes. We like that funny name. We have two Toes now, Old Toes and Little Toes.) The one over there is called Deep Diver for two reasons. Sometimes he's just called with a gesture that means sex so his name is also Middle Finger even though he doesn't have a middle finger. That's another good funny thing. They say he wanted to mate with me, but this was before That One came and changed everything.

But I was thinking maybe Deep Diver will be glad to see me this year because I'm much, much fatter than I was at berry time last year. I have come, now, into my good fat and I will – but this is what I think before That One comes – Yes, I will go into the water with him. His eyes are as blue as the many, many eyes of the blue-eyed clam and as beautiful. We'll be like two big fish together, and I think about a child hanging on to my hair.

Ma says, In the beginning this is how it always was, ma and child, ma and child, and this is how it always will be, though if a storm lasts a long time, then let the child be swept off the beach back into the sea that gave it, for children come from water. They creep inside while you're making love, so, if a big storm that's the sign that you should let the child be taken back.

The land away from the beach is not good. Nothing to eat there but a few small things. Here the sea takes care of us and washes up to us all that we ask for. He was a land man, That One, but even he didn't like the land. He was glad to get where we are and chew on our conchs.

There are a lot more places and times in the world than this one, Old Man Lost Egg says, and not just once or twice, that once we were the very best of the best of the best of the tree people, and, in that other time, we came to the water because our trees died. Once, he says, we liked the sun. That was a strange season, nodding to her, then, instead of towards the water, but the sun changed and then the sea took us in and made us happy, and gave us all our friends and relatives and all the little soft things to eat and shells to put things in and to blow into. It's the sea, Old Man Lost Egg says, that goes on almost forever even as we stand here on the edge of it. This is also true of the land, so there will be many more times and places and a time also for you. Old Man Lost Egg has heard all this by listening into conch shells.

He got his name from first being Old Man Lost Leg, but Lost Egg is a lot funnier, so we call him that. He only lost a little bit of his leg. On land he moves like a seal, but in the water he's just like everybody else.

Other men do not grow old except for Old Man Lost Egg and Old Oyster. We used to call Old Oyster The-Man-With-Seal-Lady, because he had a seal for a friend but That One killed Seal Lady so we call Old Oyster Old Oyster now. It's a good joke, as though he had an oyster for a friend.

Those days lots of us had seals for brothers and sisters and swam with them or lay with them, on cooler days, out on the rocks.

That One killed Seal Lady. Old Man Lost Egg says it comes from living too much on the land which is full of emptiness. That One killed one of us, too, but before that he killed Seal Lady and ate her.

We had not seen anything like That One so we watched and thought how thin and hairy, and how hot he must be, out on the land. We were not surprised that such a creature would do strange things and would kill Seal Lady. It was hard to keep from laughing even so because he moved so much like People move, yet not, and because he had so many things hanging about him and his penis was almost as small as one of the tree people's, though we've not seen that, only heard tell of it. That made us laugh, and his feet like hands.

He's not happy in his fur, shaking himself and dripping and even sitting in the sun to dry himself after he washed. His hands are almost just like ours, only a little hair on the backs but smooth in front though ours have more skin between the fingers.

He calls that hot stuff, fie. I was the one he told first. But he calls everything by its wrong name, and, anyway, we don't need that stuff because we already have water. By the time he told me, fie, he had a few of the right words for things.

He killed Uncle in just one second, so fast nobody was sure how he did it.

That One would rather stay over there with the Rocks-Hanging-Over People because of the shade, but they throw stones at him every time he comes near so he has to stay with us. Those Rock People know something about him we don't know, but they won't tell us because what he did was too bad to talk about.

We were wondering how he has any fun if he kills Seal Lady people or Uncle, but maybe he didn't mean to do it, maybe something strange happened, but, to come upon him then made us feel like watching from a distance and we wondered what would happen to him after he had eaten some of Seal Lady, but he only went down to the damp, cool sand and dug a little sleeping pit and went to sleep almost the same way we always do. It was in the morning that Uncle was dead, and those who saw it said it was a flash from the eye. They said That One has an eye to watch out for... that no one should look him in the eye, but others said it was a flash from the finger or the penis, and others said it was a rock, like we do sometimes, though we always miss.

"I come from the only place there really is," he said. (This was after he began to talk with us.) But I could see that the place now was this place because he and I were both here in it and the other place could only be told about, and I said so, and I asked him which of the four corners of the world it was and which of the twelve times that have been and are to be, but he only laughed. I was glad I had made him laugh. That's a hard thing to do.

Sometimes he says he comes from beyond the sun but Old Man Lost Egg says that nothing is beyond the sun except that one woman, Sun Ma, who hides behind it peeking out at us. Old Man Lost Egg has seen her.

Like a baby, That One learns to speak and to swim at the same time.

I keep thinking that I'll go out and see if Deep Diver will be with me, except I'm busy teaching That One. I'm the one to do it because the other women won't go near him. They say he has walked on the land too much and the sun has looked at him in a bad way. I know they're right about that, but I feel for him as if he's my little brother. I have no little brother so who do I have to be it? But perhaps I feel this because I'm the only one who heard him cry.

We cried. We cried like young seals, first for Seal Lady and then when the other uncles took Uncle out to where the rip-tide runs between the islands so he could be carried away to another time and place. Everybody had a turn holding Uncle in their arms to take him out there. Everybody had a chance to swim with him one last time. And later, That One cried to himself in the night. Perhaps about Uncle. I heard the crying in spite of the waves. We didn't let That One sleep near us, but I was on the edge and heard and I came and put my hand on him like we do to a young seal that's lost its mother. No one, whether of the land or not, should have to cry in the night without a touch from some other creature. Strange, though, he didn't have any tears. I thought to lick them away, but there were none.

That One says he has a name, and that the name says that he's coming and to move out of his sky. And he says that he is the head man's son of the head man's son of the head man's son, as if Old Man Lost Egg had many sons of sons of sons which isn't possible because Old Man Lost Egg's son was taken away by a shark and his other son also something of the sort. Besides, we are not so sure of sons except for the six-toed ones who swim so fast. Most of our sons, anyway, belong to the brothers of their mothers. After he heard that, he said he was the head uncle's son of the head uncle's son, and so on and on, but I said I wouldn't call him by any such name and I have already forgotten it.

It was that same day one of my big brothers began to walk crab-wise along the beach and we began to laugh and do it, too. And then the men began to shout and to dare the land and they ran into it until you couldn't see them anymore even from the highest place. And we women worried, but we laughed anyway, because what else was there to do? And we tried to guess who would come home last, and pretty soon everybody came back. Nobody got lost out there that time. And they jumped into the water from the highest place like they were children and then we all did that. That was also the day that That One said pretty soon he would dare the land and the sea both, but he didn't even dare to jump into deep water from the high place. We hid our smiles behind our hands like we do so as not to hurt the feelings of young seals or children. I have come to know him as if he were my own child, I, holding his chin up as he learns to swim. He holds my hair and I swim him out and in, up and down. I run my hand over the coarse fur of his back. It feels funny. He's such a strange "child": keeps his strings and stones and things in a hole in the rocks while he learns to swim, is always frightened. I see it in his eyes – strange eyes, the color of the sky at night, while ours are the color of the sky in the day-time. His are always frightened, as though every day was a stormy day and every night was a waiting for the big wave, the one that comes suddenly with no warning. I laugh to myself to think he said he would dare the land and the sea both.

Then one of those biggest things of all the living things comes out to die on the beach like they always do, out on Berry Island. Deep Diver came over and told us and said that we could go over and have some of that fat. The People of the overhanging rock place come, too, and so does That One. By that time he can swim well enough to go. I said there was no need, but he said there was a need, and he puts on all his strings and things and comes.

It is just as Deep Diver said, a dead largest-one-of-all is on their beach. We were sad for the big, playful thing. What a lot of playful-ness, all gone now. Such a big thing needs a lot of crying even though it wasn't a special friend, so we do that first.

The Berry People use some sharpened shells and some of that shiny-black rock and begin to make holes so as to give each of us our share, but That One stops them. He tells them he wants to do this his way, that he has a special reason and, since he is the son of the son of the son of many head uncles, we should let him, and, even though here is someone who can just barely swim and can't catch a fish at all no matter how hard he tries, and who still doesn't know all the words for things, they let him because he has a knife almost as sharp as the black stone blades and larger and stronger. That's the stick he keeps tied to him that's usually covered up and that we thought he had – before we knew it opened to a knife – we thought he had because his penis was too small. "Let him do the work, then." Everybody says it, and most of us go out to pick berries which are beginning to get ripe. But the Berry People sit on the beach and watch him cut into the big happy thing to make sure everybody gets a nice share.

I go with Deep Diver. (We usually mate with the People of the beach of the big stone, but there isn't anybody over there for me, and, anyway, I like Deep Diver best of all.) He says how nice and fat I've grown. He wants to be with me in the water. I say it isn't the time yet, though I say that's what I want to do, and soon, too.

When the tide creeps into me as we mate, I know that if I do it with Deep Diver I might have one like him with six toes, because the tides come into the ma by way of the male so that something of the male is let into a ma along with the tide that washes the child in. (Sometimes you can see the babies waiting in the bubbles of the foam.) I want big children like he is so that my sons can be big uncles and the sons of my daughters also. I tell Deep Diver I will keep a little-finger shell, or even two, near me the whole time I'm with child so as to make sure it will come out like him, but, of course, none of this will happen and instead my child will be almost as thin as That One, though not as hairy.

This is the time when That One made the thing he called his bowawa. We don't need things like that. He made it out of that big skin. He stays out there in the berry land and cuts and cuts for many days, and gives away all the good parts. What he eats himself he won't eat unless it has been changed by that stuff he calls "fie." We make a song and dance about it: the "fie, fie, fie, fee, fup, fup," dance and we sing it almost every night out there. The Berry People have six good conchs to blow into so they do that while we sing and clap.

Out there visitors have to sleep in the pools on the rocks. They only have one small beach and they keep that for themselves. That One doesn't like it because he wakes up choking in the water sometimes. I have to sleep in the same pool with him and help him up in the middle of the night as though he's still tiny. In some ways he hasn't grown up at all from the very beginning and yet he always wants to tell everybody what to do. The others wonder why I stay near him and help him. They say he should be let die by his own clumsiness but I like his strangeness and the funny things he tells about. I like to wonder about him and who he is and where he comes from. I know it's not from beyond the sun, but I know it's not from around here either.

That One thinks the dance and song we made is all about him because he's so great and brought us fie which we don't even use and don't even want to. It's too hot. We don't say he's wrong about that song and dance, but we put in some new words he doesn't know and that we'll not tell him, about how it's worth sand. We sing, "fie, fie, fie, and all worth sand and you, too, worth sand," and we come onto the beach and throw sand up like we do sometimes, and People get it in their eyes and have to go back into the water to wash it out even though we're all crying at how funny it is. The first time we sing that song, That One stands up and swings his arms around, and the second time we do it he stands on a high place and says that this is right for us to do for him, but that we shouldn't laugh so much. Well, why do it if not to laugh?

I brought him berries. That made him smile. He's so hard to make smile sometimes I think that's another reason why I stay around with him, just to see if I can do such a hard thing. He said he didn't know we had berries, and I said, "You're glad we do." He looked happy while he was eating them. That was the first time I thought he had a nice face even though it looks so funny.

I'm becoming a talker (which is what I do become). It all starts with That One telling things to me and me telling things to him. So, in the future, I will be telling everybody all about it so it will be known that all that happened is happening.

He puts together that big skin and bones of the biggest thing of all in a different way than they were before, and when he's done he tells me I'm part of the plan and that I have to do it with him.

"You'll be Zuesa's woman. You'll be above all the other mas. There's no word in your language for what I'll make you. There'll even be stars named after you."

I say, no. No is a word not to say, but I say it. (If ma is the first word, then no is the last, or so we always say.) I'm glad none of the others hear me say it.

Then he says (and it isn't the first time) that I and we all should call him Zuesa and not call him That One anymore. This is his real name which is the name of one so big that we don't have a word for it yet because we're not that far advanced, but we change Zuesa to Zand for sand and to Zat One and to Zeaweed, and we're glad we have so many new things to laugh about. Then he says this berry place will be called Zuesa's beginning because this will be where he starts from, bringing fie and bowawa and many other good things to the whole world. So we mustn't call it Berry Place anymore. But we decide that we'll just point to it and laugh. We'll not call it anything, and everybody will know exactly where we mean,

Now he stands on the hill and tells us things we already know. The world is round – as round as the moon, but that can be seen by any child who has gone from swim to walk and can stand on a high place and look out from it. It's a very large circle. We all know that. We don't talk about it, we just know it – that we live here on a round place like on the moon, just as he says.

I tell him to stop talking. (This is after all that talk.) I brush his funny belly hair with my hand. As I do it, I see Zat One's little penis come out and up. I'm just playing with his belly hair and not thinking about going into the water with him or with anybody and he turns and, almost before I know what he's doing, it's done already. I had not given him my cowery, and there it is, done, and so fast. My first time and no laughing. Done from behind, too, like lizards do, like bugs, no looking eye to eye, no swimming around no laughing – not even smiling.

But Zat One is very happy. "You'll be the first mother of the men of fie," he tells me. "There'll be lots, but you'll be the first and you'll be above all the others." Then he turns to do the thing again and from the back again, but I go off into the water, too far for him to follow.

This is the beginning of all the bad things.

Out there with the Berry People there are three women that are not pregnant yet. Like me, they have come into their full fat. And there are two girls that are just beginning to get into their fat time though they have their moons at the full of the moon like the rest of us. One dawn, when the bowawa is already finished and sits on the sand with some shells full of berries in it, I hear a great noise of brothers and uncles and Deep Diver is with them. They come to me to say it's all my fault, that I let Zat One be here and then this happened, and I say, What? And they say every one of their women that were ready for it. He has been with them and not even in the water and not even laughing and not even just one, but all, and in that single night, and he did it in such a way that they hardly even knew it had happened. Then they throw stones at me and at Zat One. "Don't be here anymore," they tell me. "You and Zat One also. You both go."

Zat One says that now I *have* to come with him or they'll hurt me but he has done a very, very bad thing, and I'm thinking it's true the land is a bad place to have made him like he is. I say, no, and, no, again, but all the time I'm running with him because I don't know what else to do. I know my People don't mean for me to go away forever, but I know I should go for a while so they have a chance to forget some of this. Zat One and I push the bowawa off the sand and jump into it and they don't swim out after us. They just begin to laugh a lot. They watch us go off this funny, slow way, wobbling in the waves. I have to laugh, too, in spite of what's been happening. And that's not the only funny thing about it. Zat One has made two things of skin, two little moons he stuck on each end of a big bone. He waves these around and makes them be the arms of the bowawa so it can go along. I lie there in it laughing and laughing and I can hear the people on the beach laughing, too, even though they're angry, and I think what Old Man Lost Egg says sometimes that, well, it's done so it's done, so if you can laugh, might as well do it, so I do it, and I hear those others doing it too.

We go right on past my beach. I feel like getting out and swimming back home to be there when they all get back from Berry Island. I think maybe when they come with that nice fat and those berries mixed into it, they will have forgotten all this a little bit but Zat One says to wait and I'll be glad I did, but I doubt it. He says not to forget I'll be the mother of the men of fie, but I don't even like fie and I tell him so. I know how to make it now. It's no big thing, and I can't think of a time I would ever want to do it. Besides, it used up that good stuff that the sea washes up to us. I do stay there with him, though, but for a different reason. The water is humping up and I can smell the wind coming. He can't see that or smell it. He goes on talking and pushing the bowawa along in that funny way. I stay because I don't think this bowawa will be very good when the waves get big, and I know, if I'm not there with him, Zat One will surely die. He's not a good Person, if Person at all, but is he so bad I shouldn't help him? So I let us pass my home beach, but I think I'll swim back to it as soon as they will be glad to see me there. I think Zat One can't last very long anyway even with me staying. Nobody likes him. I'm the only one that wonders about him and helps him. All he knows is what I taught him and there hasn't been time to tell everything. So I go on, watching after him like he is my little one, and he *is* my little one.

ZUESA

Where I come from, giants rule... generations of princes, lords, barons, sitting in the royal setting on tree limbs that represent ten thousand warriors, all the leaders having swung down via private chutes or air bridges of their own suspending, having entered through the sky gates of the messengers of good tidings, all, feathered like sun birds, swinging princely arms as far as is allowed and sometimes even farther, and I, one of them, my arms raised, I, permitted to take my place at the topmost royal hearth when the fires burn brightest. Now all gone, my master hat tossed from my head, my strings – except for these colorless copies – slashed; even access to any tree, whether figurative or real, impossible to me. Except there are trees. That, the captains surely didn't know. They thought the land too hot and dry. Uninhabitable, they said, and left me here because it was uninhabitable. A little circle of green around the edges of the poles, and, on purpose, they didn't drop me off at either one. I'm to suffer. And I have suffered: eaten disgusting fish-things, chewed seaweed, sucked at things I couldn't chew or swallowed them whole – I can't get that sea-taste out of my mouth. Even the eggs taste of the sea – thought many times I'd not be able to take one more breath of this hot air, nor another step across the desert, but I've seen a giant, dried-up trunk on one of the beaches – a trunk almost large enough to be one of our own. It would have taken five men with outstretched arms to gird it. I've eaten steaks bigger than they ever knew existed... sea mammal steaks. I've had berries sweet as tree-top blossoms. Out of this world I'll build a new one, half me, half these things that swim. The best revenge will be to bring it about. I'll call the planet Zuesa so, if they ever come back they'll know this all came from me.

It's clear these once were land creatures. As far as I can tell, all the mammals here were also, at one time, of the land, but they've gone back to the beaches and into the oceans. The land got too hot. Under these circumstances it'll be hard to make a decent civilization.

Can there be such a thing as a civilization without trees?

That's always been the question and I've heard those captains debating it, crouched under their crowns. After all, the trees made us what we are. There was a time when we had shelters of slabs of bark tied about our nests of leaves. There was a time when we counted nuts and fruits and packaged them in tree pods and made strings of fibers in order to make the knots which we used to count the packages, so the stuff of the trees was the beginning of everything. "From the gods of the forest," as they used to say, but no trees here that I've seen except for that one old log washed ashore from gods know where. Only that one, as though a sign of hope to me, and I do hope. It pleases me to think that somewhere, far north or far south, there is a forest of giants almost as big as the giants of home and that, one day, I might be able to stretch my arms again and swing and leap and sleep to the rocking of the wind instead of the rocking of the waves.

I will go north and create a new civilization. It won't be easy with these creatures. You'd think life was all play the way they go about giggling. She, too, laughs too much. Even so, I think of her as my sister-wife. I call her that because, in times to come, my sons will have to marry their sisters, otherwise my genes would get lost. My ideal is for a much thinner People, certainly with fur, but as tall as these creatures are, and with great, showy penises continually exposed, as theirs are, so that when my captains come back, *if* they come back – I must keep in mind they may never see any of this – but if they do, they'll get the same shock I did. Here will be Zuesa's men of fire, all with my face, all with the hats and crowns of their status and all with enviable penises.

Ah, but *she*... I'll call her sister, but I'll also call her by my mother's name just to be able to say that word again and to remind me how a woman can really be. I mustn't get used to these soft gigglers. I want to remember how a woman can be thin and stringy, with tiny, woodland breasts, black tipped. Had she been a man, my mother would have been a warrior. She was a flier from branch to branch. Lived in the upper reaches. Our house was at the top. Mother hardly ever came down. She liked the sway of things up there. She slept in the highest hammock. Her fur was orange-red. She was like fire herself. That's how I'd like my sons to be, all like her, thin and fiery, phosphorescent eyes glowing out in the night, not like the pale eyes of these creatures, all the color of the water that they spend their days floating around in.

I taught them... I never wanted to be of the teaching caste, but I taught all her group fire. They didn't like it. How can one like or not like a thing like that? I showed them boat, and they said they didn't need that either, though these are all part of progress. Yet I they did sing about me (if you can call that waa waa boo baa singing). They threw up sand and blew into shells. They know my worth even though she's the only one who shows it. The rest are afraid. Though they have no castes, they sense a higher rank in me.

But I do realize how much I need her – just as she is, actually – to help me. If it hadn't been for her, I'd have died for sure in the storm. We lost the boat. At first I thought for good, but she found it. I don't even remember how we got to that beach. I came to myself afterwards when we were already up on the cliff where only the spray from the waves could reach us. More of those creatures were up there, too, waiting out the storm. They don't seem to care how wet they get. None of them, she included, bothered to go up where the spray couldn't reach. I suppose it's that layer of fat that does it. They did huddle together, but it seemed more for friendliness than for warmth. Zoe (she doesn't know yet I've named her that) Zoe did keep me warm, though; held me to her all night long. I was throwing up and shaking. I think I was in shock. Gods, she's big! Like a feathered nest. I sank right in, stopped shaking and slept through it as though I was one of theirs.

In the morning, when those creatures of hers got a good look at me, they didn't much like what they saw, that was clear. Zoe told them we'd go as soon as she found the boat, and she left me there alone with them and went out swimming. (I can't see how they do that – swim off with all kinds of weird fish out there. I got stung when a poison tail whipped me and I saw fish with needle teeth.) The creatures turned their backs to me. I wasn't afraid they'd do anything. I know they throw stones, but they always miss. It got hot as usual. I went part way in to cool off and even then – as usual – I felt so hot I couldn't breathe. The young ones came swimming up to me to feel my fur and laugh. They have less fear of me when I'm in the water. That was true with the other pods, too. Those young ones really laughed to see me learning to swim. Even the young are fat and hairless except on their heads.

Zoe said the storm felt like taking me, but changed its mind at the last minute. (I'll not let her say things like that to my children.) She said she would go to see if the storm had decided to take the boat or not. She said she could do it faster by herself. My mother never spoiled me by doing anything of that kind. Mother would say, "Climb up and see for yourself to your kites and gliders or any hot air toy." (I had all those toys that ride over the tree tops. Mother thought they were good for me, and that was true because I became a great pilot though what good is that now?) But I'll write it all down for my sons – for the princes and lords of lightning. Though the first priority is seeding them. Zoe's son will be above them all. It's what these creatures need most, gods and emperors. I, the god, having dropped from the sky, which is true. I really am their gift from the stars. I was thinking all this when the young ones splashed around laughing at me and the adults turned away and covered their smiles, and I thought, go ahead and laugh. You'll soon see.

Then I thought it would be a good idea, when Zoe came back with the boat, if I should try to plant some more sons, two or even three if I could be fast about it. (It's a good thing I'm young and quick and have practiced the "single thrust" method our highest leaders prefer in order to conserve energy for more important tasks and also to conserve energy in order to impregnate as many as possible in the shortest amount of time.) I must pick out the ones not yet pregnant, those with their shells still near them. Zoe could wait for me with the boat all ready to get out of there fast. It always takes those big uncles a while to find out what happened. Even the women don't react that quickly, almost as though they're not sure it happened at all. They're confused when it happens on land, which makes it all the better for my plans.

VENUS
We have to go away again as fast as we can, though not much stone throwing. Those cliff People don't know what to do about us, but I know we should go before they decide something. The bowawa needs to be fixed. We have to find a good stopping place, but first we have to get away. Zat One has me cup the water out as we go. My hands, he says, are made for it. We go along, but not as fast as we could if we were swimming except Zat One can't swim even this fast.

He's smiling at me when he says my hands are good. That's another one of his smiles. I'm counting up maybe one hand's worth in all, but I'm not sure this one belongs with the others. It's not a good smile, so I'm not smiling back at him. "What are you doing," I say, "using up cowery-shell women?" Already I'm not talking any longer like my People talk. I'm talking like he would talk if he could talk as well as we can. I'm asking questions about things that shouldn't be asked about, except things like this didn't happen before Zat One came. "This is a thing to say, no, about." I say. "It should be learned without having to say anything about it," and I say, "I won't let this happen."

"I have a plan," he says, but I know all those furry children he plans on will be left out for the waves to take. I don't say it, but I think it. Those thin, hairy things won't like the ocean. They will have gotten inside the mas by the way of the air instead of by the way of water as they should get in. The mas won't know what to do with them. They will be given up to the storms and swept away like they should be. But then I think again, and this time I think maybe they should be left out for the land... for the sun to take, or lizards, or anything of the land.

"North," he says, and asks me if I know what that is. Then he tells me, and I see by what he's telling that I *do* know what north is. It's the second corner of the earth. I tell him that, but he says there are no corners to the earth, but I know that also. Old Man Lost Egg, when he was young, did as the young ones do sometimes. He swam out and around and only came back much later and much older, saying that the world is, in truth, a series of circles, and that it went on and on, and that there were People on good beaches and good rocky places and on islands of stones which they shared with the seals.

Zat One tells me, "We go north," and I say, "I'm not going." I say, "I'll go as far as where you can stop and fix this bowawa but not farther." Then I turn my back and keep on scooping up the water and he jumps on me, again from the back. It's over in the time it takes to scoop a fish. I don't know what to do. I stop scooping out the water so that the bowawa fills up and we have to land in a place that's not a Food place, but we manage it. He climbs half way up the cliff and begins to try to fix the bowawa there on a little ledge. I stay in the water, thinking. I see he watches me. I let myself drift out with the pull of the tide. He calls. I thinks he's thinking I'm not coming back. I'm thinking the same thing, and thinking he'll die soon without me, but then I think maybe he won't die as easily as I want him to. Maybe he'll go on doing that bad thing and live a long time going on doing it, I think I'll have to be the one to kill him if the sea doesn't do it soon. But then I have a good idea. I swim back. "Come." I say, "we'll find a better place to fix the bowawa."

This time I swim while he paddles the bowawa along. He's so little and light that the bowawa doesn't fill up so fast as it does when I'm in it since I'm so fine and big. We stay just beyond the surf and I find a tiny beach only big enough for us. Nobody lives there, not even a seal. I'm thinking that here, I'll teach him about life. He'll know a whole new thing. He'll be a real Person and smile a lot and then I'll be able to love him and let myself have this child of the air and land.

He thinks to sit and dry himself, but I tell him to lie down. I tell him it's time for something different and that the land has made him forget himself. "I've heard," I say, "of an uncle who stayed out on the land too long and when he came back the sun was stuck in his eyes so he could hardly see, and stuck inside his thoughts, too."

I start by stroking his belly fur as I did before, but when his penis comes out, I say, "Not yet." I stroke him all over and lick and hold him to my big, round breasts. He plays with the nipples a little and hugs me, but he doesn't do much more than that. He lets me do the playing of it and I gladly do, only he keeps trying to come in from the back all the time. I laugh and stop him and make him follow me into the water. I hold him up and float around with him on top because I know he can't do it as we would do it. I make him come to me face to face, looking into my eyes. I play until he's tired, but I know he likes it. He doesn't laugh like we do, but he likes it. Afterwards he falls asleep with a little half-smile on his face, and I know he never thought things could be like this. I know he's surprised. He didn't know we were as smart as this, but we are, and we also know many other things. Now I'll be able to love him. We can go to the second corner of the world where he'll be cooler and I'll go gladly and help him get there.

In the morning he tells me about wree. He says wree is a very good land thing and there are some up in the second corner. He said we had part of one that had washed up to us. He says wree makes shady places where he can be in it and live there and stretch his arms there like they like to stretch. He tells me about fruwa and kinds of land-leaves that you can eat like we chew on sea lettuces. He says there are places where the land is the best of all possible places. He says when I see wree I will believe him.

After he fixes the bowawa he chips at a stone. He chips until the stone begins to look like me. "This is you," he says. "You are the ma of all the mas, and I like you like I've not liked any other creature here. Don't forget that," he says, "no matter what happens," and I'm thinking he's cured of all the bad things. He's cured because of love. He doesn't know that word, but he has the feeling.

I tell him I love him. I'm not sure about that, but there is a need to say it and it's always better to say it than not because later might be too late, so I do say it.

ZUESA

I should have been working on the boat, but I worked on the stone instead. I needed the rest... the first real rest since they dropped me off here. And this turned out to be a good time to teach her a few things. I told her about civilization, what it is and how important it is. I told her what she means to me. I confessed that, without her, nothing will come of me at all. I told her how I need to become the big head uncle of all of them, and that I want her to be Big Ma with me. She just laughed, but she really listened when I told her about trees and the climbing stairs and the vines and the kites we ride. I explained about writing and how the trees had given us smooth barks to write on before we invented paper. I told her the trees had given us the ideas for almost everything. This time wasn't wasted because she began to understand things and I saw, also, that she's beginning to love me. She said so. I need her to feel this way. When she almost ran off I realized how lost I'd be.

After spending this sex time on the beach with her, I realized why I'd been able to succeed with the seeding as well as I have. With them, when it comes to sex, they take their time about it. They even consider that a virtue, and I admit they have a point, but one hasn't very often got a whole afternoon, not if one is in charge of several others of lower ranks. Even then I had things I should have been doing, yet I let myself rest. I thought maybe one more day of it while I finished the statue, which is part of my plans.

So I sat and carved, and later I began to tell her about my mother. I told her Mother could fight almost as well as a man, though I had to use their words "scuffle" and "tussle." They aren't advanced enough to have a word for war or fight that I can tell. I told her I'd never seen Mother cry, even when my brother was brought in so mangled he'd never swing in the trees again, having been beaten in battle (I had, of course, to use their word scuffle) by the men of the lesser trees. Those little trees, I told her, grow in the mountains, which are cliffs like she's never imagined could exist. The trees and we men of the valley are larger. All the valleys have larger men. If one of those mountain men had been left off here, they'd really have had something to laugh about and then she'd have seen how big I am compared to them. I told her I was one of the seventy-two, and that there had been thirteen symbols on my head-dress. I told her how red Mother is and how I wanted red sons that were like her so they could be my men of fire. She said they would be beautiful and that sometimes their people also have red hair on their heads, though it's rare. But I said beautiful was not what I wanted my sons to be. I wanted to say, impressive and grand, but I couldn't find the words in their language except uncle or ma of the moon or of the sun. (I thought it ironic that one so huge and so hairless... that one with buttocks like buttocks I'd never seen before, could speak about beauty. And yet I must admit she was looking pretty good to me. I can see a kind of beauty in her odd, sea-colored eyes and in her long hair, also like the sea in the way it hangs down her back in waves.)

I've begun to write all this out for my sons. I'm using the back of my number codes list. I'll not have any use for that again. First I made an alphabet for them and then addressed them as "conquerors" as well as "your excellences." Also I've put some writing (the simple, humble form) along the sides of the boat so as to teach my new Zoe. I want the first words she learns to read to be "your excellency."

Tomorrow I'll get back to work. I've rested too long and wasted too much seed and the energy to spend it. I'll sleep turned away.

VENUS

We go, then, in the bowawa, and I sit with him so we can be together in it though I'd rather be swimming. I touch his feet that are there in front of me. I tickle his toes. He looks at me like he cares about me, though he doesn't smile. I'm thinking, his eyes are the color of the bottom of the sea as well as the sky at night, while our eyes are like the sky in the day time. Then he asks me to say that I'll keep his baby son and not let him get swept away.

"Why would I let that happen," I say, "when I love you now?"

"Say anyway," he says. "Cross your arms over your breasts like this and say." And I do it though I don't know why I need to when I already said I wouldn't do it.

This is one of those strange, cloudy days. I can remember the last time I saw a day like this. It was before I became a woman. I'm hoping there might even be a sprinkling like there was that time, and maybe some flowers might come out and we could go into the land and cover our heads with all the yellow we'd want and we'd dance and bugs would come out and dance with us. I tell Zat One about it. I tell him I want him to see such a thing as those flowers which I've only seen twice before and that even Old Man Lost Egg has only seen six times in all his long life. And I tell Zat One about the little bugs that come to hop with us. He says if such a thing happens, maybe he'll go see it, but that he doesn't have time and so maybe he won't. Time, he says, is the most important thing of all and we mustn't waste it, but I think going into the land to see the flowers would be using time well and I remember how Old Man Lost Egg says he would like to see those flowers once or twice more before being taken with the tide, so I hope it will happen again now for him.

We go on and the sky water doesn't come. The clouds go away overhead, but hang a long ways off on the edge of the world circle, out where the sky and sea roll into one thing so it's easy to see that the sea is the low part of the sky and the sky the high part of the sea. I've seen Berry Island, and other islands, too, float on the sky some mornings and some evenings, too, so that if Zat One comes from the stars, as he says, that isn't so strange, it's just a long way around. It's wree that surprises me – that such a thing like a giant sea weed could grow also on the land.

After a while we come to another nice beach full of People. Maybe as many as I would count up on hands and feet if I had six toes and six fingers like Deep Diver. We land there. Everybody pretends not to look, but they do anyway, and laugh behind their hands at Zat One, but they look at me, not laughing, for I'm a fine big woman. I'm just what all the People like best, which is why one like Deep Diver wants me and I want him for the same reasons. I never wanted a little furry one like Zat One.

He calls out to them, but they only stare at the clouds that hang in the elbow where the sky rises from the sea. Then Zat One holds up the little ma stone, and they do come,

They've never seen such a thing as a ma to fit in the hand like this one does. Zat One is saying, "This is great ma of the moon and of the sun and I'm her greatest uncle. I'm here to bring you many new things." Then he makes fie and shows them how to do it, but they're like us, they don't care about fie. They like the little ma stone. And then they call me ma, though no one ever called me that except as a joke when I was thin and little and couldn't have been a ma at all.

I tell them that I'm The One with Zat One, and no more than just what they see. Zat One gets angry when I say that, but I think he can't say, no, in front of all these People. But then he does say, no, and not just once. "No, no, no," he says, and in a voice more like a sea gull than a Person. The People turn their faces to the elbow of the sky again, and I see – and I'm sorry for it – that he's counting up the women who are just coming into their fat, and I say, "No," to him, then, so we're two strange People (if Zat One really is a Person) that say, no, to each other.

"I must," he says.

"I will keep you from it," I say.

"This is important. This is what I've been dropped from the sky for."

"This is not a loving nor a playful thing."

"Love has nothing to do with it. I need fie People, and you need them, too."

He's yelling this. The People haven't heard such a thing before except if it's a game. They want to make it into something funny. They begin to dance and throw sand and splash and make an imitation of his yelling and everything gets confused and full of sand so that everybody gets sand in their eyes. During this time I see already he has gone to two young ones just coming into fat. It's as if the anger and confusion make him even faster and better at it than if things are calm and happy.

Then I'm the one yelling and sounding like a sea gull. I say he's a shark that steals women and right then he's in the middle of having another one. The People don't understand because it's from the back and on land, but then they do see it's true. "Swim him off." I keep yelling it, and I pull at him and he's hitting me. These are real hits. I didn't think he would do such a thing. Then I give the whistle that means shark, which should never, ever be given except when there *is* a shark. When I do that, one big uncle comes with a stone and hits Zat One on the head as though to open a clam. I've not seen this done to a Person before, nor to any seal or any such thing. Zat One takes that thing, like his finger that he wears on those strings he has. He kills that big uncle in one of those flashes. All the People step away, then, except for me. I'm still trying to pull Zat One away from there. Another big uncle comes, but I can see he doesn't know what to do. Before he can think of something, there's another flash and he's down, too. After that Zat

One is running to the bowawa, pushing off and going on as fast as he can make it go. They're telling me to get away from their beach, too, so I go. I follow him but not near. He calls but I don't come. He's calling, "Zoe, Zoe," which he's been calling me now, but I don't want to be reminded of that land ma he was telling about. I don't care about her.

Pretty soon I see him do a strange thing. He passes by an island and there's an otter lady lying on her back in the water near it. She has her little white, fuzzy baby resting on her chest. Zat One floats over there slowly as if he thought she would swim away, but she's not afraid. Why should she be? She probably plays with those People from that last beach. She might even trade babies with those mas sometimes, putting one of theirs on her stomach while they hold hers. My People do that sometimes, too, just for the fun of it. Zat One comes closer and then reaches over suddenly and takes the baby. He grabs it by the back flippers and swings it up and around and down against a hard part of the bowawa. The otter lady dives away and makes a sad sound that I make, too, and I know, even more than I knew before, that I must kill Zat One. A Person without time should go where there isn't any time and let the tides take him.

He goes on until he comes to a place too small for anybody to live there except maybe one or two, but nobody lives like that so there's nobody there. He makes fie out of dried sea weed and dead grasses. Then he cuts up the baby otter and puts its parts on stones in fie. After that he sits and dries himself in the setting sun. I don't go close because I don't want to see him eat the baby. I sleep resting on the waves out from the shore in the seaweed. It's a nice calm night for it. I eat a few clams. I open them with a stone on my chest like the otters do. Then I lie on my back and doze. In the morning I see he's already making another ma stone to take the place of the one that got left back there. This one's bigger. I come in close to get a better look, because this ma doesn't have any feet or hands, which is funny. I laugh out loud and he turns and sees me there. "I know you'll not leave me." he says. "You said you loved me and you don't know how not to say what you mean. You don't even have a word for that."

I stop laughing and I don't answer.

He carves and chips all that day and eats the baby which makes me not hungry. The next morning I see he sits sad, maybe because he sees how I am, but maybe not. He used to sit sad all the time, though not so much lately. He sits sad, but he goes on carving that bigger ma stone. It's the size of two, maybe even three hands. Maybe even three hands as big as Deep Diver's. Having three hands makes me smile, but I don't laugh out loud. I don't want him to hear me. He's eaten more of the baby and he's stretched the little white fur on bones. I think how my People wouldn't do such a thing. They'd gathered around the otter baby and its mother and say what a wonderful baby it is. Tears come to me as I think this. I miss my brothers and sisters and all the mas and uncles. I miss laughing together and hugging. I miss my cousin's baby which I'm thinking of as though she was that baby otter. I'm wondering if Zat One would do such a thing to that baby. And I'm missing Old Man Lost Egg's talk about how the world is, and I think I'll have things to tell, too. Maybe pretty soon I'll be able to understand what the conch whisper. I can say already how round and round again the world is and I have lots to say that nobody else has had to say. They'll hardly recognize me. I even wonder at myself that I have this thing I have to do because the waves won't do it for me. Even when they had the chance they didn't do it. Why must it be that I must become like a wave and suck away Zat One all by myself?

The next day Zat One puts what's left of the baby in the bowawa and the big ma stone, and goes off again. I follow but well behind. He lands on the next big beach with People on it. I see him holding up the big ma stone. I can't hear him, but I can guess what he's saying. He's waving his arms around in that funny way he does and pointing at the sun. This time it looks as if he's making the sun the most important one of all, though we all know water is what we can't do without. I know he's looking them over, too. There are three red-headed ones here. I know this is important to him so I come in. The People see me coming, but he doesn't. I pick up a stone almost as big as the ma stone he's holding and I wait behind him while he talks. This time he says that the ma of the sun is the most powerful because it's the sun that kills. That's the proof of it's power. "Water gives and the sun kills," he says, "and this is why the sun is above everything else." This is a new thing. I wait because I don't want to be mistaken about him. I want to make sure he's going to do what I think he's going to do. All those People have moved out of the water on to the beach and are looking at the ma stone. Even though I'm behind him, I know his little penis is peeping out because I can see that the People are looking at it and covering their mouths with their hands, and I also see that he has somebody picked out. She's sitting close to him and she's beautiful even though she's not into her full fat. She's one of the red-haired ones.

I'm holding the rock ready to do something I've never done before, but now he's being different again. He's saying he'll leave the ma stone in exchange for the red woman. He says he's been looking for just this one for a long time. Then he asks her to come and be the greatest ma of the killing sun and I can see that she doesn't know how to answer or what to do. I think she wants to say, no, but not in front of her own People.

"You have the hair of fie," he says and then makes fie for them.

These People are a little different about that fie. They seem to like it no matter that it's much too hot to be of any use. Maybe that's because there are those three red-haired ones here. Zat One is telling them that those red People are fie People and that they're like the sun, but they keep saying they're just like everybody else and that if he knew them better he would know that. Then he tells them he'll take the red-haired Person out in the bowawa. He says just for the time it takes to snatch a fish, and she does get up, then, to see what that bowawa is like, and he leads her to where it is, but then I see that she sees what's left of the otter baby in it. Most of the baby is touched with fie and doesn't look like anything at all anymore, but Zat One has kept the white fur of it stretched out on those bones. You can see in it what it used to be. You can also see, when you're close to the bowawa, who the bowawa is made of. You can see it's one of the biggest playful ones of all. She sees that, too, but he pushes her in. I'm behind them and I see he takes her from the back right then, as though that act is some way to push her in with and a way to push her down into the bowawa, and I know she isn't even sure that it happened to her. I'm thinking that I'm not surprised he never feels the fun of anything. I can tell by now that those who don't feel fun are dangerous to everybody. I'm wondering if his babies will be strange and terrible. I'm thinking I'll kill mine right away before I get to know it. I'll kill it even if it looks like a real Person so that the future won't come about. Only the present will go on and on. I remember I crossed my arms and said I wouldn't kill it, but I'm thinking it might be right to change what I said to a better saying.

But now I'm whistling shark again and Zat One is pushing the bowawa off with her in it. One big uncle is coming out to them. That uncle goes right to the bowawa and tries to tip it over and I start to help him. I'm thinking what a good idea that is, but that it'll take two of us, at least, to do it. But then, quick, Zat One takes that finger thing and flashes it, and the big uncle is rolling around in the water like a fish on land and then he's dead. By the time I turn around from that uncle, Zat One and the red-haired one are beyond the surf.

I'm angry even at myself because I had the stone in my hand but I just watched and waited to see if he would be like he usually is, and then he was, and now here's this beautiful, red, young Person which he's trying to make the ma of some thin, hairy baby that won't be able to feel fun either. That young Person should be having her nice, fat, red-haired child, and she should have a good chance to laugh and play around in the water with somebody she likes.

Then I see Zat One is doing another thing I haven't seen before. He's taking some of that string stuff he has and he's tying the red Person's wrists together and then he ties her to the edge of the bowawa. I'm surprised, and I think to myself that this isn't some other strange and much later time, this is now, and just as strange as if it were some place else entirely.

They go along, and I follow, wondering where is the fun in all this and why do it? Then I remember how land-touched and sun-touched he is. Zat One may be half lizard. I've seen a lizard look in his eyes. I feel very, very, very, very sorry for that red-headed Person who maybe only just picked out her cowery.

She sees me coming and I see her seeing me. I stay back, but I wave the wavy-wave that means I'll follow wherever she goes. She can't wave back, tied up like that, but she shakes her red hair at me and I know what she means.

I smell sky water. Though I've only smelled it twice before I remember it. There's not only the smell of water from the sky, but the smell of storm, too, and the waves are swelling up. I think maybe Zat One will be swept away if I'm not going to help him, but then I think I have to help the red one. I must find something to cut her free with. Zat One has a nice sharp thing.

I smell wet storm more and more and I know the red one smells it too because I see her raise her head and sniff. I'm also seeing the red hair hanging down her back and I think, no wonder Zat One has taken her to be his Zoe instead of me, but I worry that she's stuck to the bowawa and that the storm will come and she won't be able to save herself, so I move closer. "Go on in to shore." I say, for we're far out, but he says, no. Then the red one say, "Go in," too. He looks up into the wind and it seems he can tell what we can see and smell. Those clouds are still over at the elbow where they've been floating all these days, but I think now they'll come. "Go in while there's still time to do it," I say, and he does.

I want him swept away for the good of all of us. I don't think about you and the future that might be. I want him gone, but not this red one. I think of her like a little sister and I don't think that her hair's like fie, but that her hair is like the sweetest berries, or like when the land gets wet, which may begin to happen now. Mostly it's yellow flowers, but there are a few red ones, too. I think I'll call her Red Flower Person. No one would wonder who was being called, so she'll know.

There's no good place to come ashore, but we do it anyway because by that time we have to. Zat One won't untie Red Flower Person even now, though I ask him to, and more than just once. I come, then, and help, so we do all get there, first to a flat rock and then to a split place and up that to a long, steep slope. It's not easy with Red Flower Person stuck to the bowawa and his hands tied together, but Zat One makes her stay that way. He says, "Life isn't always just picking up clams as you creatures seem to think it is," but we know that.

The higher we go, the higher the waves come. I think they want somebody and I'll see to it the one they get will be Zat One. I'll give him to the storm so that nobody's baby will have to be swept away.

Then suddenly we see it's not spray anymore, and Red Flower Person and I look at each other because it's sky water and even though things aren't so good for us right now I see a good kind of look in her eyes and I see that she can see a good look in mine. In a day the land will flower. Everything will change then. Maybe even Zat One will feel the fun and be changed by it. How could it not be?

That night Zat One turns the bowawa upside down on himself and sleeps inside it with Red Flower Person still tied to it, inside with him. Later the bowawa blows off and almost takes Red Flower Person down the slope to the cliffs to be swept away, except I hear her whistle and go to help and we pull the bowawa to a better spot and put some rocks on top of it.

I don't sleep. I keep wondering what to do and I wonder even more after that because I should have pushed Zat One off right then but I didn't, partly because of his sharp thing that I think to use to cut Red Flower Person free and partly because I would have to push him down all the long sloping place before we'd get to the cliffs and by that time he would have killed me with that other thing and then who would help Red Flower Person get free?

I have this place a little away from them, and I sit and sing storm songs to myself. Sometimes Red Flower Person sings along with me when the storm isn't so loud we can't hear each other. Her words are a little different from mine. I play a one, two, six, six game. I lick the good sky water off myself. I catch some in my hands and drink. This sky water is the sweetest water of all. The sea of the sky is *all* made of this good stuff. I sleep a little finally, but I worry about what Zat One is doing to Red Flower Person in there under the bowawa.

It's the next night before the storm stops, and there's a good lot of sky water. After it stops, I really do sleep and when I wake up, everything is as bright as it usually is, and calm.

When Sweet Red Person comes out from under the bowawa, as best she can still tied up to it, I see that good look in her eyes again. We tell Zat One it's a thing full of fun and we must see it, but he says, no. We tell him we have to and that he should untie Sweet Red Person and that all three of us should go out into the land and drink sweet water and dance and watch the thing happening which has already begun, but he says no, again. Then I think I'll cut Sweet Red Person free right then. I'll get his sharp thing and do everything now. Why have I been waiting? I pick up a stone and come to him, but he takes out that thing that flashes and points it at me. I see the lizard look in his eyes, and yet I think I see that he doesn't want to do this, but I also see that he will if he needs to. I put the rock down. I turn my back to him and sit. So let him do it, then, except I worry that he will and it isn't me who needs to die, but if me, who will help Sweet Red Person?

"There's no time for the land," he says and puts that thing away. "Time! I've told you how important it is. We have to get this thing started."

But I wonder why we can't wait a few days until the color comes out. This is what People always do. You will do it. You'll go off to where the land blooms best for no other reason than to see it. You'll be like us in that.

I think that maybe I could leave Zap and Sweet Red Person and go into the land by myself, but I know I won't even though I want to, because Sweet Red needs me. I need to stay also, to help all the People get rid of Zap. I'm even thinking that we should not let you all come into being. I'll be the one to stop it in spite of what Old Man Lost Egg has said about an entirely different time and place than this one. But this isn't another time. This is right now. This isn't even back when Old Man Lost Egg spoke about it.

Then I remember that I had a dream of wrees during the storm. The water came down from them all the time and they blew back and forth like seaweed and splashed the land with sky water. Under the wrees the flowers grew so that everything was yellow and the ground looked like the sun and we lived on the land as if we were sun People. It was shaded and wet and we lived there as if it were the bottom of the sea, but we missed swimming around. I was sad in my dream, and then I was frightened because land sharks came... a great school of land sharks and I had no place to go because I was up on the land already so there was no place to escape to.

The water is calm now. We take the bowawa down and we go on as we did go, me in the water and he, pushing the bowawa along with those funny things, and Sweet Red Person in it, still tied to it. Sometimes she splashes herself with water so as to feel cooler. Sometimes I do it for her. We laugh. Splashing always makes us laugh, maybe because we feel like children.

This time Zap has some of those stones in the bowawa and sometimes he stops to rest and when he does, he chips at a stone again. Other times he stops and makes marks in that thing he says is for his son. The ma stones are all still me, not Sweet Red Person. They're all a woman who has come into her full fat just like I am.

We stay far from shore. We pass beaches sometimes with People, but we don't stop, and then, almost by mistake, we do get to see the land flowers. We come to a place where the banks of the sea roll down smooth like I've never seen before, and there are tips of green there already. As we go along we begin to see more and more yellow and then a lot of it and some little patches of red. Then, after all, Zap brings the bowawa in closer to take a look and everything is like it is on the sun. Zap stands up in the bowawa and Sweet Red Person does, and I wish I could stand up and see better, too. We go closer, but he doesn't come in to be in it and feel it and dance. He just sits down again and we go on. When he lands, it's on a beach where he chases out some seals, though it's their beach.

This beach is full of stones and will be uncomfortable and it's a place where we can't see the yellow, though there are some small patches of it back where it's not so stony. It's almost as if Zap picked it because of not many flowers. It's as if he wants the opposite of fun. Could such a person be?

I'm getting more and more worried about Sweet Red Person being stuck like that to the bowawa. I tell Zap again that this isn't safe for her. I tell him she won't run away. "Let her come on back into the land with me," I say, "so as to be, for a little bit, as if standing on the sun." But Zap won't let that happen. He pulls the bowawa up where it's not quite so rocky, turns it upside down, and they sleep there. I sleep just out beyond the surf. It's a good night for it. Zap sits, the next day, making more one-hand-sized ma stones. He's getting good at it and faster. He makes as many as two hands worth.

All the while, I bring food to Sweet Red Person because it's impossible for her to go out and find something to eat. (Zap eats clams, but I don't get them for him.) I give Sweet Red Person the best of what I find. I call her Sister Sweet Red and she calls me Sister Sweet Ma though I tell her I'm not a ma yet. "But I'll watch over you, anyway." I say, "as if I was a ma of your own home people."

We talk, but not about what we really want to talk about. Zap sits too near. (I'm sorry now I taught him all those words.) After a while I go back a little ways into the land beyond the rocks and bring Sweet Red all the flowers I can carry. I tie them to themselves in little bunches and put them all around Sweet Red and we laugh and I see I'm making Sweet Red happy even though she's worried about being tied up. We hug, and laugh and play almost as if we were in the water, though you can't play very well on land. I see Zap watch us, but I can't tell what he's thinking. It's always some land kind of thought. Even if I knew what it was, I wouldn't even know it.

Then Sweet Red tells me sad things. She says that the big uncle that was killed was her mother's oldest brother, and she cries. She says he was called Old Bird because once he had helped one of those big, black birds. Old Bird fed it fish, and it would sit on Old Bird's head when he was standing about in the water or even when he was swimming. And then Sweet Red smiles because that's a good memory. "It stayed with Old Bird until it died, but it had a good death. Right after that the land bloomed."

We're in the shade of the bowawa or else we would have to be in the water because of the heat. Even Zap is down where the waves wash over him. He moves up with the tide, but Sister Sweet Red is stuck above where the water comes. Then I think to cup up water in a big shell and cool Sweet Red. After I make her good and wet and the pebbles and sand around her good and wet, we sit and watch the sun go down.

In the morning I see one of those stingers that maybe I slept close to all night and didn't know it. I'm always thinking what to do about Zap, so I think about that stinger. It's washing in slowly. Maybe Zap doesn't know about those things. Maybe I can use it.

ZUESA

This has been coming out better than I ever thought it could. I've found my real Zoe. I hadn't thought I'd be so lucky as to find a red-haired one. There's a current flowing north and I felt it had grown a little cooler though that might be because of the rain. Maybe the flowers have a coolings effect. I thought, before I left that beach, I'd make each of them a hat out of seaweed and brush. Some of that seaweed is good and strong. They'll not have had hats before. Even the big one may like it. I worry about that one, though, and I wondered how jealous they get? It's a powerful emotion and I only had one shot left. I was saving it for her, just in case. She had been looking around for some way to get me even before, but they're all so childlike I can read everything they're about to do on their faces. They always hesitate. They never just do something. I saw her look and think about a jellied mass floating just beyond the surf and stopped that before she got started with it.

I'm glad I didn't let them go out to see the desert blooming. I hope it taught them something. That kind of thing goes with that all-day sex they do and I've no time for it. I want to see this world begin before I'm too old to keep control. I want to be in my prime when my sons are grown so I can help them learn. Rapid seeding is my first priority.

However I stayed on at that beach all the next day. The little goddesses were finished but I thought to make not only the hats, but a sun shade for the boat. I wondered that I'd not thought of it before. Poor Zoe. She was always splashing water on herself.

I was busy with the sun shade when she (what should I call her now?) she went out to get that jelly thing, holding out a shell and a piece of drifted up bush. I thought to teach her another lesson. I took out the zapper and told her to come on back and quickly. I said that even though I was about to make her a gift I knew she'd like, I'd not hesitate to kill her. I said she was no more than a seal or an otter to me, which wasn't true. I even told her I'd eat her, and that if I ate her, I'd know everything she knew. Of course I'd do no such thing. I said it even though I knew it would just add to her superstitions. I don't want to kill her. As much as I can say I like any of these creatures, these two I like, but it may come down to a matter of me or her.

The way she looks at me... I've had that kind of look many times before. I've captured those small men from the mountain trees, and I've had four at once looking at me like that. And not so long ago, I've had my own captains looking, at me in the same how-to-get-rid-of-him manner. But these creatures will never be fast enough to do it.

VENUS

I like the thing he calls hauwa. That's a real thing. It has a nice wideness to it. It balances. It makes me feel like laughing. It's the very first land kind of thing that's a good thing. I'm surprised we haven't thought of it ourselves. And then, when he makes the hauwa for the bowawa I'm surprised we didn't go around making things like that, too. After he gives me my hauwa, I put some of those flowers on it. I don't have to go far. There are clumps near our beach. I do that for Sweet Red's hauwa, too, even more than on mine. Then, when he finishes the hauwa for the bowawa, we go off again, me swimming not far behind. It's good they go slowly because I'm doing a lot of thinking, and I'm still worrying about Sweet Red being stuck to the bowawa all the time and what will happen to her if something happens?

But now he's landing at another beach full of People. I stay out in the water and wonder what to do. This beach has a lot of big clumps of rock out from the shore. Zap leaves the bowawa in the water and hooks it to one. I hide behind the rocks, but I come in closer when those People come out of the water to see what's happening with Zap on the beach. I don't hide on purpose exactly. I just wonder what to do and when and if. Things are going all wrong and I'm not fixing them. My mind isn't enough like a lizard. That's what I think. I never know what to do. I just wait.

Zap lines up all the new little ma stones in a half circle and then he begins to say everything all over again and then he's building fie like he always does, but these People have a lot more stuff on their beach to do it with, not only dry seaweed, but a lot of washed up land stuff, too. Zap takes all the stuff they have and makes a big circle of fie near the little ma stones he stuck into the sand. It's the biggest fie I ever saw and I think maybe this fie really is something even though it has no usefulness and is even hotter than I thought.

Sweet Red is still sitting stuck to the bowawa. She's in the shade of the hauwa that's on the bowawa, so she isn't wearing her own hauwa. Those hauwas are down in the bottom of the bowawa. By now all the People are gathered around Zap and are looking at the ma stones and at the fie. I swim over behind the bowawa and I take Sweet Red's hauwa out. I take that one because it has more flowers on it than my own. I go out away and put it on and then come ashore straight into them, standing up at the end and walking through the surf.

I am beautiful. Sweet Red is not yet as beautiful as I am though she will be even more so, but now I'm the most beautiful one that I know of. My hair hangs down and, it is whitened by the sun and I know it all shines. I walk in a way I've not seen anybody walk before. I don't know why I thought of it. I keep my arms up and out as wide as the hauwa, which is very wide. It comes out to beyond my shoulders. I walk slowly and I come to the edge of the half circle of fie and the half circle of ma stones. I'm the big one of all these little mas. I see I've surprised even Zap. He's backing up. I see he's not sure if this is a good thing or a bad thing, and, even though he saw the hauwa before and knew it was covered with yellow and some red, too, his eyes get as if he never saw such a thing as me in my hauwa coming up out of the sea, walking in this special way. And those People... they don't know what to do either. They back up a little, like Zap does. Fie didn't make them do it, and not the little ma stones, but I, with this hauwa, did it. I know what they think, too, with all this yellow and this big round thing on my head. They think I'm the ma that peeks out from behind the sun.

I don't know what to do. I still haven't thought about any of it, but I already know that water can stop fie and I'm wet and so is the hauwa. This is a big fie, so I'm not sure, but I walk into it and don't think about if it hurts or not. I stand on one part of it and I drip there and make that part go away. This is right, I think. This is water over land things and even over the cruel sun.

"I am big water ma," I say. Then, again, I don't know what to do next, but I know I have to keep on doing something. I begin a song and dance which isn't like any song and dance I've ever seen or heard of before. I pick up some of the little ma stones and I dance on more fie and put that out, too. I sing "I big water ma. Big water." It sounds so good I slap my thighs, but nobody dances with me. I'm too much for them. Then I say, "Here is Sweet Sweet Red," and Sweet Red stands up in the bowawa for them to see her and puts on my hauwa which is only a little less yellow than her hauwa that I'm wearing. Then I say how another beautiful one came blowing in with the sky water – that she was washed up to them by the good sea. And I say that the strange uncle is going to take her off the bowawa so she can dance with them. I really think that he will have to do that, but he says, no, so loud that everybody looks at him in a funny way.

Then I do know what to say and do. I say, "Those who say, no, to water ma are all worth sand. Throw sand at him. Do him the sand dance." So they do, everybody laughing and crying together, except I know Zap can't do that. He has no tears.

By now the sand has put out all the fie and I see that *all* our things can put cut that thing of Zap's, so I think I can get him, too. I whistle, "Shark, shark," thinking, the People will come and help me, but they think I mean real shark and they run up the beach away from us. Zap is running to the water and I know he wants to get away, in the bowawa with Sweet Red. I can get to him fast when he's in the water. I hold his head under as much as I can. He tries to get the zap thing. I know that if he does, he'll zap me and not even stop to think about it, so I don't stop to think either. I do everything, fast, too. I pull out his sharp thing. I should have cut away the zap thing and thrown it away right then, but I'm only thinking to get Sweet Red free, which I do while Zap is sputtering in the water and half blind with sand. Then Sweet Red jumps out of the bowawa and we push Zap into it. I tie his hands together and then tie him to the bowawa just like he did to Sweet Red. She helps me. How she helps is she sits on him. Even though she's not into her full fat, she can keep him down that way. Then we push him away from there in the bowawa, and I tell Sweet Red, as we push him along, that she should go home, but she doesn't. I'm thinking we are becoming stranger and stranger, and that even I don't know I'll do next because here I am, going on to the second corner of the world instead of back home, too, even though Zap is tied up and can't make me do it.

A funny thing is going on with me. I want to see. I want to watch the shores change, and maybe even see those things Zap always talks about, those wrees. And I'm thinking the bowawa isn't such a bad thing upside down on the shore or to use to carry things along as you swim or to carry a person.

Sweet Red and I talk and talk. I keep telling her she should go back to her people, but she thinks she should stay with me and that we can help look after each other. She says it isn't good to be alone, that there's nobody to laugh with, and that's true. At first I don't tell her what I have in mind to do, which is to kill Zap before he zaps me or any more big uncles. But then I change my mind. I do tell her. And I tell her why, and the whole story about you – coming or not coming into being. I also tell her that, whether he's dead or alive, I'll be going on to see wree in a place I think is maybe full of flowers all the time.

We come into shore late. We just have time to turn the bowawa over on Zap. Then we go and make ourselves a nice sleeping place. We like each other so much we make just one pit. We sing a little night song.

In the morning we see that the flowers are beginning to wilt, and not just on our hauwas, but all over. We've missed the best part of the flowering land, and yet we still feel like singing.

ZUESA

"Gods," I'd shouted, "come leer at me and laugh. Gods trick the devils like the devils trick the Gods. Gods must, and must know all the tricks and how to use them since the devils are tricky ones." So spoke the Sarshina, though he, also, was an unbeliever. I tried to trick these creatures by telling a true story. They said there was a thing they call a shark out there so we stayed where we were. They gave me stones so I could carve. It wasn't easy with my hands tied. We stayed where the waves could wash over us, the boat part way in the water and us in it's shade. They lay for a change not even playing. Well, perhaps playing for they twined their fingers together and, now and then, counted strange combinations of numbers. You'd think they were giving their military codes, though they never went over twelve. I thought, in this quiet mood of theirs perhaps I could convince them to let me go so I told the truth. And I decided I wouldn't scale down my thoughts for them anymore. I used words from my own language when I didn't find any in theirs. I hoped that, if they only half understood, that would impress them all the more.

"There is a place where everything is known," I said. "This is the place called Tree of the Valley of Lightning. All bow down to the thunder of its name and to its men of fire, that's where I come from. I want to tell you the truth for the sake of time and forward motion, not for myself. There'll be a new kind of people, red and brown and silver. Each will have a particular place both in the trees and on the ground. The red people will have the highest places because they're the finest. I say that though I, myself, as you can see, am not one of them. And you'll be living changed lives, too, with boats and hats and robes and fire and beautiful containers that shine like the sun and some that can be seen through as though they were made of water and yet they can contain it. I can promise you such things will be of great advantage to your children and your children's children. I'm nothing but a worker for the sake of the future. You think this sex and seeding is fun for me. You should be able to see that it isn't. It's a duty more important to me than my own life or than any fun I might have. Surely you can see there is no fun in any of this for me."

For the first time since I was dropped here, I spoke as if to my own kind and with some of the gestures befitting my station, though I was tethered to my boat, even so I had a happy moment. Not as happy as if I swung on my own lanyards in the tops of towers or trees, but happy as a representative of my lineage, and, though but a lower prince among the princes, yet a prince, and speaking like a prince. And I saw that they heard and stopped their finger play in wonder at it.

Venus

The land makes for strange ways of talking. Zap is saying a lot of funny things, and I don't know why he would think we wouldn't believe him, but he says, over and over again, that what he says is true. Why would it not be? Sweet Red and I laugh behind our hands at that.

I have a different idea of the future than the one Zap talks about. I have the one Old Man Lost Egg hears when he listens to the biggest of the conch shells. I think I'll look around to find a good conch and see if it will talk to me. I need to hear more about our kind of future. I'm not one that would listen in on anything that belongs to Old Man Lost Egg except that I'm so far away and I'm not the same person I used to be and I need to know things.

I do find one. The inside is like Sweet Red's hair and the outside is full of spikes. I go far from them and sit and stare out to sea like I've seen Old Man Lost Egg do, and then, when I feel ready, I put the conch to my ear.

For a long time I hear nothing but the waves and the wind. This place in my ear is the spot where the past and future both come from, all swirled around in the conch, gettings smaller and smaller and farther and farther away until there's nothing but a tiny dot of the memory of it left on either side of time. I wait and listen and then I seem to hear Old Man Lost Egg's voice, but he's whispering so I can't tell what he's trying to tell me. Then I hear that the voice is whispering that he isn't Old Man Lost Egg, but a different old man. His name is Last Verse for he sang, a long time ago, the last verse of the last song of all.

"I've been waiting for you," he tells me. "I've been whistling out of every conch. I've been on the wind to you. I tell you you must go on a long ways to the second corner of the world which is full of wrees. You must be wise about them and do the things to be done in wrees and eat the strange eggs of wree birds. You'll have to stand away from the wind because of the cold."

"But what about Zap?" I say, because this is the reason I was listening, into the shell.

"Never once will he be called uncle or be worthy of it. You, however, will be ma, and not only ma, but great ma, not of the cruel sun nor of any such land kind of thing, but ma of the weeds of the sea, so you'll be called Weed. You'll be the egg for out of you will come the new time, so you'll be called Egg. You'll hear things in the conchs, so you'll be called Conch. You'll feel things by the wind on your cheeks, so you'll be called Wind. You'll lean against the banks of the beaches, so you'll be called The Leaning Ma of the Banks of the Beaches. There is nothing you won't be called because everyone will be calling you."

His voice is fading, but he's going on and on though not about anything I need to know. "Zap," I say, "Zap. How or when shall he be killed and if?"

"Watch out!" he says.

I look up and see that Sweet Red is playing by the water but Zap is looking at me through the finger eye of the zapper even with his hands tied. I get behind a rock though I don't know if that thing can go around and find me there or not, but he doesn't do it. Then I think how silly I was not to take that zap thing away in all this time that he's been tied up. I see that I'm not a good thinker about this kind of thing and I name myself Silly Old Do Nothing When It Should Be Done. I laugh at such a funny name and I know that Zap hears me laughing, here behind my stone and I wonder if he's naming me, The One Who Laughs When She Should Be Afraid, and I wonder if he thinks I'm even sillier than he was thinking I was when I left that zap thing with him. Then I laugh again to think of all the funny names he could be calling me. Sweet Red comes over to me and I tell her about it and we laugh together, but we keep watching Zap because now we know we have to all the time.

Sweet Red says we should, just the two of us, go off and leave him right now and here – that the shark wouldn't bother us. "You and I," she says, "he can have his zap thing for a friend." That makes us laugh again. I haven't had a time like this since I left my brothers and sisters back at my home beach. We needed to laugh. It makes us feel like, no matter what harpens to us, we had a good time right now.

I tell Sweet Red how we have to get the zap thing, but that we should play we've forgotten about it like we really did. I tell her to keep on laughing, and go on out to him as though to sit in the shade of the bowawa with him, except she should sit on him like she did before and I would come and take the zap thing away. I tell her we'll have to be strong and fast as if to snatch a fish.

But that's not how it comes out. No wonder Last Verse didn't tell me what to do about Zap because it isn't something I wanted to know about or I'd not have had so much fun laughing with Sweet Red, which I'm glad I did.

Zap on land is different from Zap in the water even with his hands tied. He's like a lizard. He saw that Sweet Red was going to sit on him before she began to do it. We both tussled with him but he got his zap thing out and was trying to get it turned towards me. Sweet Red kept getting in his way on purpose so he couldn't point it at me. Then it seemed he thought he could zap me, she was moving fast and it was Sweet Red, and not me, that got zapped – that rolled on the beach and tried to hold herself together but didn't. And Zap said, "Oh no," a lot of times, and, "Gods, come leer." Then Sweet Red is really dead I get angry like I've never been or knew I could be. I get on top of him while he's still saying all that and holding Sweet Red. I take one of the biggest of the ma stones and I hit and hit. I hit until he stops. Then I take him out for the shark to have so it won't want Sweet Red when I will take her for the tide. When we get in the water, he wakes up and struggles but then he says, "All right. Go ahead and drown me," and I say that I will do that, and he sees that I will. Then he says, "You said you'd not leave my son out for the storms to take." But I'm thinking he's already a dead man. Why should I answer? There's a lot of blood on his head, so the shark will come in the time it takes to snatch a fish and I want to get back to the beach.

Five new ma stones sit where The Killer Of Sweet Red sat in the shade of the bowawa. They're all me as they always are. I wish there was one like Sweet Red so I'd have a thing to remember her by, but things are just things, and I'll always remember her anyway.

I pick one stone ma up. I like it. Mostly there were bad things about The Killer Of Sweet Red, but there were one or two good things, like the funny things he told about. Flying around in and under land things is a thought I never had before. And wree, though I'd seen their bones. I have to wait before I can take Sweet Red out. So I take one of the mas that's not finished and I take one of his other stones and start to do as he did. It's not easy. My ma stone doesn't look like much except maybe a blow fish. But I get better fast and see that I could make a lot of these, too. I can make fie and sing a song about it. I can make a bowawa. I can walk like big water ma and sing that, too, and I, myself, can make a Sweet Red stone if I want to, and I do want to. I'll go see wree and the second corner of the world. Killer Of Sweet Red is right, I am going to have a baby. I'm not sure what I'll do about it, but I'll see who it turns out to be before I decide.

I pick up the conch shell then, wanting to hear Last Verse again, more for company than for advice, I already know what I'll do. But he does tell me some things I did want to know. He says my baby is going to be a girl. We both have a good laugh about that. She's going to have red hair just like Sweet Red even though she isn't Sweet Red's child. Last Verse says that I'll call her Sweet Red and not just ten or twelve times, but I'll call her that all the times I call her, which will be many, many times.

GRAHAM JOYCE AND PETER F. HAMILTON
Eat Reecebread

BURROUGHS WAS MUNCHING on a reeceburger, a disallowed act in the Charles Street ops center. Too much highly-prized Command and Coordination computer hardware lined up on our desks. Amazing what a stray crumb could engender in the network terminals, still electronic, unlike the crystal processing core in the police station custom-built basement – a top-of-the-range Packard-Bell optronics model. Leicestershire's regional taxpayers are still whining about the finance.

I should have growled at him, but I'd never been good at pulling rank. Besides, Burroughs-watching had become a macabre fascination for me over the last few weeks. His appearance was ordinary enough: a 28-year-old with a rounded, pink, and permanently sweaty face. His thick, pointed ginger beard was a carefully cultivated emblem of masculinity – a lot of men sported beards nowadays. There was an irritating certainty in his carriage, in the way he liked to swing his arms and trumpet his androcentric prejudices. Just to let you know whose side he was on.

That confidence had been crumbling before my eyes recently. Burroughs had been accosted by a sudden insecurity that even led to physical tremblings. I knew disguised panic when I saw it. Today his odd malaise was bad. His worst yet.

He was sweating profusely when I stopped behind him, his shirt collar undone, tie hanging loose, skin blotched and red. His appearance wasn't enhanced by the cold blue neon flashing from across the street, exhorting us to EAT REECEBREAD. I had little sympathy. Despite his discomfort he was excited by the morning's gossip which flashed through the building faster than optical fibre could carry it.

"Hear the news, Mark?" he asked, an indecent thrill raising his voice an octave. That "Mark" was new. It should have been "sir" but I let it go.

"What news?"

"There was one of them working here. A shagging Hermie on the force! Fifteen years operating in the same building as the rest of us. Just shows you don't know who you're working with half the time." His undercooked reeceburger dripped white juice into his beard.

"That's right, Burroughs. You never know."

"Did you know who it was?"

"Nope."

"Come on, you must have! Time you've been here? You know everyone!"

Of course I knew the poor creature, but I wasn't going to give Burroughs the satisfaction of probing me with more stupid questions. I stared at the amber script on his monitor as if I was actually doing my job and searching for errors.

Burroughs continued to speak with his mouth full. "It lived in one of the Nu-Cell adapted flat complexes. Sod was intercepted while it waited for the bus into work this morning. Usual thing. Clothes torn off by the mob and ten bells kicked out of it before the panda car arrived. Uniform boys said it looked like a monkey's miscarriage in a reeceblender. Yuk! Hoo hoo hoo!"

That was indeed the usual pattern. An anonymous call informs the Charles Street duty officers, who duly load the information into the nearest panda car's situation bulletin display. In theory the constables should be at the location within two minutes to pick up the offender. But somehow there is nearly always a delay, combined with a tip-off to some thug well placed to lead a lynch gang. Well, it saves the expense and the mess of hauling them before the judiciary. The moral mess, that is.

What really galled me was that the problem obviously originated in the police ops room. It was one of my people, corrupting my routines and my communication networks.

The reason I went in for technical specialization after coming off the beat was to be above all the grey behavior endemic to the side of the force interfacing with the public. Reality, I suppose, that's what I couldn't handle. The sheer emotional clutter of dealing with people – turning a blind eye to this, giving that the nod. Computers and programs don't have fuzzy edges. They're also a valuable new tool in fighting modern crime since the Federal Parliament in Brussels passed the Civil Authority Unlimited Data Access act. I thought I'd found myself a comfortable little niche. Ironic it should turn out to be the heart from which the new global war of persecution was waged.

A scarlet priority symbol started flashing on Burroughs's monitor. He sat up with a lurch, the reeceburger dumped into his bin with an accurate, lazy lob. Script rolled down the monitor as he muttered into his throat-mike.

"Christ look at that. We've got another fish. Two in one morning."

The priority request came from another duty officer taking a phone call. Somewhere out on Leicester's streets a good citizen was informing on a Hermie. The duty officer would be tracking down the call, though most people were smart enough to use a coin box to avoid detection. Brussek are already phasing 'em out: soon it will be credit cards for everything, traceable, incriminating.

"This time I don't want any mistakes," I told Burroughs sharply. "Make damn sure a panda car gets there within the allocated response period. Alert two or three if you have to. But get the uniform boys there in time!"

He wiped the back of his hand across his feverish brow, giving me a sullen glance. "Why bother?" he murmured.

"I'll pretend I didn't hear that, Burroughs."

I walked away before he had the chance to show how little respect he had for my authority. Safe back in my glass-walled supervisor's office at the rear of the ops room, I sat at my own desk and hurriedly asked my terminal to display the data on the Hermie.

Morton Leverett, the monitor printed, a middle manager working in an insurance company office. Personal details followed as I accessed his citizen's file. No family, thankfully. That could have been tricky.

I summoned up my private alert program and fed in Leverett's number. His netcom unit would be bleeping, displaying the simple warning message. With luck, he would get clear in time.

There would be no record of the call – one of the benefits of being the city's chief data control officer. My program would wipe all memory of it from British Telecom's processor core.

I was still working on improving the program in the evenings. When it was complete it would snatch the data on Hermies as soon as it was entered into the station's network, warning the impending victim even as they were being informed on, increasing their odds for getting away.

I wrote that program with pain-soaked memory driving me. You see, I knew what it was like to be on the receiving end of an informer. I'd turned a Hermie in myself once. It's not something I can ever forget, let alone forgive. But I do what I can to work off my penance. And I wait for the world to stabilize.

Her name was Laura, and she was quite beautiful. I say "her" and "she" because when I first met her, I didn't realize what she was. You might laugh and call me a slow starter, but it was three months before I found out. The year we spent together was a hiatus of halcyon bliss until she demanded too much of me, and that's when I tried to turn her over to the police. How do I sleep at night? You may well ask.

Yes, Laura was a Hermie, as different and as ordinary as all the others. At that time the Hermies had enjoyed nearly forty years of tolerance and acceptance. When I met her, everything was just starting to go crazy. There was no single trigger, no one fateful incident which turns rational people into a screaming mob. It was more of a growing fear of them, their potential, that ultimately spilled over into hysteria. In part that fear was due to the first wave of Hermies who had now matured, and who were beginning to exert a slightly disproportionate influence in their respective fields.

The first Hermies had appeared in what used to be called Third World countries. A blizzard of theories blew up to explain the phenomenon. One suggested they were the product of genetic mutation after careless biological weapons-testing in Africa. It seemed plausible at the time, and most people went for it. This theory fell apart faster than the second Iraqi spaceplane flight, when numerous cases came to light in the West. Scandalized Western parents were just more inclined to make a dark secret out of the thing than their African counterparts; especially since the obvious physical signs hadn't fully developed until a child was in its seventh year.

Because of superstitious fears and the dread of stigma, it was at first impossible to collect reliable statistics. Eventually it became plain to everyone that the spread of hermaphrodite births was evenly distributed around the globe.

"Hi!" Laura had said when I first met her, two years ago now. God, the ordinariness of it! It was in a book-shop.

I wasn't actually looking for something to read. Leicester in those days was a spectacular place to live, an exciting city on the cutting edge; I enjoyed wandering round watching the changes Nu-Cell was making to arguably one of the most mundane urban sprawls in England. The company was an adjunct of the university, formed to produce and market the products of Dr Desmond Reece's biotechnology research. As far as the public was concerned he would forever be known as the genetic-engineering pioneer who'd solved the immediate world food crisis with his vat-grown reecebread. It was a protein-rich algal which came in several varieties; textures and taste varying from meat to vegetables to fruit. Even the most undeveloped countries could build the kind of fermentation vat needed to breed it in. Nu-Cell licensed the process to anyone who wanted it, charging a pittance of a royalty. Reece wasn't really interested in the money; he was a genuine philanthrope, happy to see the specter of famine ending.

But his other projects at the university were equally important in metamorphosizing our world. Landcoral revolutionized buildings; the way we designed them, the way we thought of them. Not just new constructions, but the old, tired, ugly structures which blighted our cities too.

Property owners bought the seeds and planted them eagerly. It was like watching broad slabs of marble growing up out of the ground, enveloping the existing brickwork and concrete. A marble that was colored like a solidified rainbow, dappled with gold, black, and silver.

I walked down Rutland Street, where the topaz and turquoise encrustations had already reached the ledges of the second-floor windows of the dreary brick buildings. The landcoral had been pruned from doors and first-floor windows, a process that had to be carried out continually until the building was completely covered, then the polyp could be stabilized by an enzyme Nu-Cell sold along with the seeds. After that it would simply renew itself, maintaining its shape for centuries. The new resplendent growths made such a wonderful change from the grime-coated streets I grew up in. How could you not have hope in your heart, living in an environment so vividly alive? It lifted the human spirit.

So maybe I was a little giddy with optimism when I saw her through the bookshop window. That first sight of her cut me like a laser. A 25-year-old in a university sweatshirt and indecently tight jeans. I was nearly fifteen years her senior, but she was so magnetic I just had to go and stand next to her. I hadn't got a clever line, I'd no plan of how to talk to her, but I had to approach her. At least I wasn't in uniform. I can imagine the effect that would have had.

"I'm looking for *The Last Written Word*," she said. "Have you seen it anywhere?"

It was by Franz Gluck, perhaps the second most famous "public" Hermie in the world at that time after Desmond Reece himself. Everybody was reading it. Very intellectual stuff, which was why I'd given it a wide berth. I remember going puce in the face. "They must have sold out again. I'll lend you mine if you want. If you promise to let me have it back." I hadn't got a copy, but I knew some theoretically intelligent people who had.

That was it. We started meeting regularly, even though I was a bag of nerves whenever I sat next to her. I might have been older, but I'd generally avoided sexual experience. Something about Laura made all the muscles in my body lock, and my mouth would go dry. She had a searching way of looking at you when you spoke, as if everything you said counted.

It was a wonderful summer, one of those long, dry, wearingly hot periods which always turn conversations to the greenhouse effect. We alternated our time between my three-room flat overlooking Victoria Park and her landcoral dome on a new estate in Humberstone. That place really opened my eyes to the promise of the future. Laura worked for Nu-Cell in their gene-therapy lab; as an employee she got the dome for a peppercorn rent because it was experimental: lit by bioluminescent cells; its water siphoned up by a giant tap root; power supplied by an external layer of jet black electrophotonic cells. I hadn't realized how advanced Nu-Cell's technology was before then.

"Every city is going to change the way we're changing Leicester," she said. "Think how much of our materialistic attitude will be eradicated when you can just plant a landcoral seed and grow your own home. Ninety percent of your working life is spent paying off your mortgage, what a difference it'll make freeing yourself from that burden!"

Her optimism had a ferocity far exceeding mine. She believed in Desmond Reece and Nu-Cell with an almost religious fervor. The newest of the new world orders to be promulgated since the end of last century's Cold War. Most of the hours we had together would be spent with her talking, explaining her visions of tomorrow. I just listened for the sheer joy of having her invest her time in me.

Her impassioned arguments and stubborn convictions might have frightened away some males. Fiery intellectual women are still frightening things, especially to a simple cop. But Laura was also intoxicatingly feminine. I can still see her that first night we spent together: wearing a sea-green cotton dress with slender straps and a ruff-edged skirt. Gold-tinted hair brushing her bare shoulders, eyes sparkling and teasing from the wine we'd drunk.

It was her dome, her bedroom, with its wan blue light and sunken sponge-mattress bed. I simply wanted to kiss her. And she smiled and beckoned me, because she knew me so well although I always said so little. It was a surprise for me when I finally found what she'd got under her clothes.

Summer faded into autumn, even though the strange symmetrical trees Nu-Cell had planted in Victoria Park kept their scarlet dinner-plate-sized flowers long after the first morning frosts turned the grass to a hoary silver plain. I walked down the avenues they formed on my way to work; Laura wrapped up snug and warm in her coat and ridiculously long scarf, hanging on to my arm until we reached the pavilion and parted, me to the station, her to the university. With the cold came the grey stabbing rains. But something more sinister began to stir right across the continent.

The boys in the tabloid press had stayed sober for long enough to make a few simple demographic calculations based on the most recent, and more comprehensive, surveys of hermaphrodites. Once the stories started they developed a momentum of their own; "interest items" became center-page features. From there they progressed to front-page articles and finally graduated to concerned editorials.

Since hermaphrodites all came perfectly equipped with both a vagina and a penis, they could of course enjoy the usual sexual relationships with either sex. Whether they grew up appearing – on the face of it at least – male or female was more or less accidental and irrelevant; the only major give-away was the difficulty male-aligned Hermies had in growing beards. Once the superficial gender-stamp had stabilized (again at about the age of seven) it usually stayed that way as a matter of social convention. That wasn't what bothered people – after they had recovered from the initial shock, you understand. The problem was this: hermaphrodites, in contrast to mythology, were very fertile. If an hermaphrodite bred with a non-hermaphrodite, the possibility of them producing an hermaphrodite child stood in a positive ratio of seven-to-ten. If an hermaphrodite bred with another hermaphrodite, the result was always an hermaphrodite.

The future of the human race was certain.

Those boys in the tabloid press may be slow, but when this statistic finally penetrated the alcohol fog of the long lunchbreak, they sharpened their knives. They were vicious. Before long, stories began to appear in the papers about "the hermaphrodite conspiracy." Unsubstantiated allegations were reported as hard facts. Hermaphrodites everywhere stood accused of crimes ranging from deliberately littering the pavements to global sabotage.

I raged impotently while Laura looked on in sad silence. "Conspiracy, God! Hermies can't even spot each other in the street, never mind get together to organize megalomaniac plots. You should answer back! Demand airtime!" I waved at the inarticulate Euro MP smirking on the TV news as he hedged his bets for the interviewer.

"Who should answer back, Mark? Hermies don't have an organization to speak for them. That's what makes this all so stupid."

"God!" I stood at the window, kneading my hands. Out in the park the trees had finally shed their leaves; the bark had turned chrome blue. "Take a news crew to film round your department. Show how you're helping ordinary humans, that you've dedicated your life to it. It sounds brutal, but sick kids always get to people. Maybe the public will realize Hermies aren't ogres like the press makes out."

Laura massaged her temple. "A lone documentary isn't going to change public opinion, especially not the kind of public that's turning against us. In any case, we still haven't made enough progress on viral vectoring or transcription factors to cure children who suffer from the really severe genetic disorders.

She had explained viral vectors to me: organisms which integrate plasmids (small loops of DNA) into a cell's DNA so that defective chromosome sequences can be corrected. It's how cystic fibrosis and hemophilia were eradicated early in the new century, literally replacing the old genes which caused the illness with new ones.

It was also the same basic method which Reece had used to convert useless pond scum into reecebread, and aquatic coral into landcoral: inserting modifications and improvements, distorting the original DNA out of all recognition. But constructing transgenic plants was an order of magnitude easier than human gene therapy.

Laura and her team had been working on the more difficult hereditary cancers. They didn't have organisms which could be junked and burnt when a modification failed or mutated into teratoid abominations. Reaching perfection was a long laborious business.

But it was good work. Important, caring work. People should be made to see that.

"There must be something you can show them," I said in desperation. "What about the university hospital clinic? Nu-Cell funds have been going there for years."

"Not everyone that works for Nu-Cell is a Hermie, you know. We're not even a majority in the company, nowhere near. Besides, showing Hermies conducting experiments on bedridden children? Not a good idea, Mark. Nu-Cell has already given the world reecebread and landcoral and petrocellum beet. What more can we give?"

I put my arms round her, trying to stroke away the tensions I found knotting up her muscles. "I don't know. I really don't."

The comments and conspiracy accusations continued to fly unabated as Christmas drew near. It took on an almost ritual quality. The tabloids had found another scare image to rank alongside illegal African migration into Mediterranean Europe, Russian nuclear power-station meltdowns, Japan's re-emergence as a military superpower, and the Islamic Bomb. But even they couldn't have predicted the full horror, the tidal wave of violence and hysteria which swept the planet.

The physical attacks started in public places as the New Year broke. It only seemed to make things worse that a disproportionate number of hermaphrodites had made a significant contribution to the world of arts, medicine, science, and engineering. So much for my idea of a Public Relations coup.

It was the week before Easter when the first trouble hit Leicester. We were out shopping in the city center, buying chocolate eggs for nephews and nieces. It was a fine spring day, we strolled idly. The clock tower pedestrian precinct had been completely converted by landcoral, with only the old white stone tower itself left free as a centerpiece. It looked handsome; the unprepossessing clash of concrete and brick, architecture from the mid-1950s to the early 2010s, all eclipsed by seamless sheets of iridescent sapphire, emerald, and amber marble; buttressed by colonnades of braided gold and bronze cords. Speckled rooftop domes reflected a harlequin gleam under the cold bright sun.

We heard the noise as we walked out of the Shires mall. The crowds were growing denser up ahead, people flocking to the edges like iron filings caught in a magnetic field.

"What is it?" Laura asked.

A column of blue smoke rose in the distance. Cheers rang above the background babble. We steered our way through knots of people, anxious and curious at the same time. I wondered where my colleagues were.

Someone had broken the windows of W. H. Smith's. Books were being flung out onto the pavement through the gaping holes. People scooped them up and slung them onto a flattish bonfire blazing on top of one of the flower troughs.

"What the hell's going on?" I tried to sound authoritative.

"Hermie books," a woman crowed. She grinned wildly. "Clearing 'em off the shelves. Not before time."

Laura's hand covered her mouth, eyes staring helplessly at the blackening pages. I grabbed her arm and began to tug her away. Se was in tears when we finally left the crowd behind.

"How can they do that?" she wailed. "What does it matter who wrote them? It's the words themselves which count."

I pulled out my netcom unit and called Charles Street to report the event. It took another twenty minutes for the first panda car to arrive. By then all was ash.

Some days after the bookburnings, Dr. Desmond Reece made a powerful public plea for the attacks on hermaphrodites to stop. The morning after his speech he was kicked to death on the steps of Nu-Cell's botanical research laboratory.

I spent the next three days helping to orchestrate the police reinforcements brought in to protect Nu-Cell's buildings and the University campus. The county commissioner was badly worried the mobs would wipe out the region's premier economic asset. Reece's murderers were never caught. The commissioner didn't consider the matter a priority. Right across Europe, the Americas, and the far East citizens were burning Hermie books and cutting up Hermie doctors with scalpels; but their mouths were still red from munching on their reeceburgers. The hypocrisy of it all was driving me insane.

Nobody was really safe walking the streets. There were plenty of cases of non-hermaphrodites caught in the hysterical onslaught. Laura said very little, but she would lie awake at nights wondering when they would find out. In the dead of night she would just look at me with her moist, frightened eyes, but say nothing. She never dreamed I'd be her Judas.

The Brussels parliament was under pressure to act to halt the slaughter. But with Federal elections looming, you knew the mob was going to win either way. Under The (Hermaphrodites) Public Order and Disenfranchisement Enactment of that year, the following restrictions were ordered:

1. All hermaphrodites are required to register with their regional authority.
2. All hermaphrodites shall resign from holding public or civil office.
3. Hermaphrodites will be disenfranchised forthwith from all municipal, regional, state and federal elections.
4. An enquiry to be launched into the origins of hermaphrodism and into allegations of hermaphrodite conspiracy

There were a lot of other clauses in the statutes, about publishing and other things with which I won't bore you. The point was that it didn't satisfy anyone. No-one gave two hoots whether a Hermie was allowed to put a cross on a ballot paper once every five years. What they wanted, as the tabloids pointed out on a daily basis, was to stop the filthy Hermies from breeding.

I got home late from work one evening towards the end of spring.

"I'm pregnant," said Laura.

"Jesus!" I said.

"Hermes," she said. "Aphrodite." It was sort of a joke. We went and lay down and, I'll admit it, I cried like a baby.

The wave of attacks subsided for a while. Burro and a few other people at work were visibly disappointed, but I began to feel less anxious about Laura's safety. Meanwhile the official enquiry went into labor. A surprising number of prominent people spoke up for the Hermies, risking careers and tabloid derision, not to mention public assault. But a lot of people had been sickened by the street attacks.

Meanwhile the tabloids characterized the debate as two basically opposed theories. One they called Millennium Fever. The other was known as Martian Theory.

It seems that at the turn of every century a number of people get taken with Millennium Fever. The symptoms of Millennium Fever are a certain itchy credulity in the belief system and a nervous suggestibility, all brought on by the conviction that the turn of the century will signal some major development in the course of human history. The Next Big Step. The Giant Leap. The MF people argued that the arrival of the hermaphrodites semaphored that this had already happened. They pointed out that the first birth cluster of hermaphrodites, born around the end of the 20th century, were already making disproportionate contributions to the culture and progress of the species. Hermaphrodites, it was true, were characterized by their resourcefulness, their meekness and their fertility. It was the assertion of old gods, the MF people argued. Hermes the messenger. Aphrodite the goddess of love. The presence of the hermaphrodites was Messianic. To a planet in dire need, it was a message of love.

The tabloid louts just adored that. They staggered back from their reeceburger-and-beer lunchbreaks and wrote up the Martian Theory. Which gives you an idea of the kind of level this was pitched at.

The Martian Theory assumed some cosmic plot on the part of another species somewhere in the galaxy. This alien species had littered the planet with spores – and how they loved that word spores – to reproduce their race. At the same time the overthrow and extinction of the human race was guaranteed. Message of love? No, trumpeted the Martian Theorists, it was a message of war.

To me, both arguments sounded about as rational as a jar of ether at a teenage psych-out party. But given the choice, and the intelligent level of debate conducted through the media, most people plumped for the Martian Theory.

So did the board of enquiry. Under their proposed (Hermaphrodites) Public Order and Disenfranchisement Enactment Amendment, several new clauses were to be added. It was never going to be anything else than major trouble.

Predicting the results of the enquiry, most hermaphrodites had failed to register as previously directed. Chief among the Amendment clauses was one which made it law that anyone knowing of an unregistered hermaphrodite should report their presence to the authorities.

Laura was well into her pregnancy when the findings were published. "This is it. We've got to take some kind of a stand." Suddenly that soulful, searching look of hers had taken on a blade edge. "No bloody way am I registering."

I could hardly argue. You see, there was another, rather more sinister clause included: a blanket prohibition on any hermaphrodite breeding, either with another hermaphrodite or with a non-hermaphrodite. Enforced contraception was the solution offered. But contraception has never been one hundred per cent successful. It would take only a few accidental pregnancies and sterility would become the only publicly acceptable answer.

The enquiry board made no mention of what was to happen to unborn children.

Unfortunately, the new law not only directed people to inform on their neighbors and colleagues. It also introduced retrospective interpretation of the law. Anyone who had previously consorted with an hermaphrodite was obliged to inform. Failure to do so was a Category A offense. If Laura and I were ever to part company and her secret was to be discovered at some future date, I too would face certain prosecution.

As a further complication, that week had seen the delivery of a set of highly classified Recordable CDs to Charles Street. They contained a program written by the experts of the Federal Detective Agency in Paris. It was a specialist monitor which would track an individual's movements on a 24-hour basis. Not physically, not optically; we're not that close to Orwell's nightmare, not yet. But the trail any one person leaves through the civil datanets is comprehensive enough to build up an accurate identikit of their movements – traffic control routing your car guidance processor, timed purchases through credit card, phone calls from home, netcom units, or office, mail, faxes. From that can be worked out who was in the pub with you, who shared your bus, your taxi, whose home you visited. And how often, that was the key. It looked for patterns. Patterns betrayed friendships and interests, contacts with criminals, even drug habits and bizarre sexual preferences.

It couldn't be done for the entire population; not enough processing power available. But the Packard-Bell sitting so princely in the Charles Street basement could quite easily track a troublesome minority clean across Leicestershire.

I had already been instructed to load the program. The county commissioner was simply waiting for the Amendment to be passed by Brussels before entering the names of all known hermaphrodites in the county.

No question, Laura would be found. She had a lot of hermaphrodite friends, some registered, others not. They would meet, talk on the phone, have meals together. Her name would be slotted into a pattern of seemingly random binary digits that flowed and swirled along the city's streets in the wake of its human occupants. And my name was linked with hers, irrevocably.

I didn't know what to do.

I watched the duty officers at their terminals, busy keen-eyed youngsters, analyzing requests and assigning priorities. Oblivious to each other and to their immediate environment. Three rows of desks, with a big situation screen on the far wall. All of it geared up to maintain the rule of law. It was all so bleakly efficient.

My own heart was slowing to its normal rate. The ops room, focused on the gritty problems that the streets dumped on our overstretched uniform boys and girls, wasn't my main concern. No, it was the detectives upstairs who worried me. We had a new division at Charles Street, the Registration and Identification Bureau, formed six months ago, with the sole task of spotting Hermies. They might begin to wonder why so few Hermies were being brought in after tip-offs, or even why the precious monitor program was producing so few names. And I wasn't the only computer expert in the building.

But it looked as if Morton Leverett was going to get clean away. I asked the terminal for a display of panda-car routings. When the street map with its flashing symbols flipped up I saw Burroughs had assigned Leverett only a blue coding, about level with shoplifting.

It would mean he had more than enough time to get away. Delight warred with anger inside my skull. I'd given Burroughs a deliberate and very pointed order to get officers there fast.

I looked up to see Burroughs talking into his throat-mike. His agitation had reached new heights. His blotchy skin betrayed him.

I used my supervisor's authority code to check his desk's communications network. He was using an outside line. Mistake, Burroughs, big mistake.

I patched the call into my own headset.

"...about twelve minutes," Burroughs's whined. "That sector's panda car is dealing with a mugging right now. I'll see if I can find another amber call to hold 'em up when they're finished. But I can't promise."

"We'll be there," a low voice replied.

The next minute was a blank. I sat there staring at nothing.

Burroughs! Burroughs was the one feeding the Hermies to the organized lynch gangs! He was responsible for men, women, and children being torn to pieces, several hundred of them over the last eighteen months.

But then, I think I was always ready for that. My dislike for Burroughs went deeper than his slob personality and vile bigotry. A lot deeper. Perhaps it was a psychic thing, some basic animal instinct.

On the other side of the glass he was standing up, clutching his arms to his chest. His shoulders were quaking inside his baggy shirt. Face wearing the desperately grim expression of someone holding back vomit.

I stuck my head round the door. "Burroughs, where the hell do you think you're going?"

"Toilet," he gasped.

"You're off shift in half an hour. Can't it wait?"

He stopped halfway to the door. "No it can't wait!" he screamed. "I want to go! And I'm shagging well going! All shagging right?" A bead of spittle dribbled from anaemic lips.

The entire ops room had come to a halt at the outburst.

"All right?" he yelled shrilly.

"Why, Burroughs, something's put you in a terrible mood today..."

He snarled something incoherent, then turned and ran for the gents.

I smiled evilly at his sweat-soaked back.

For the start of summer it had been a chill night. I'd walked along paths lined by surreal purple and black ferns, taller than myself, which made up the garden hedges in the Nu-Cell housing estate. Out in the city I imagined the pubs hosting raging debates on the approaching ice age.

Laura had sounded odd when she phoned, timorous but insistent.

Policeman's instinct, maybe, but I wasn't looking forward to the meeting. I thought I could guess the reason.

The mobs had started attacking Hermies again. Encouraged by the findings of the enquiry they'd returned with a vengeance. I'd never seen such naked hysteria before. When they got hold of someone, it was like watching a storm.

When I arrived at the dome there were five other people with her. All Hermies, and all working at the University or Nu-Cell. It confirmed my worst fears. The police had suspected the existence of Hermie cabals for some time. But the fact that Laura was a member was horrifying.

"We can't just sit by and do nothing," she said. "Not any more. It's gone too far now. They're killing us! We have to resist."

"And do what?" I asked.

"Stop the police collusion with the lynch gangs for a start."

"What the hell can I do? You don't seem to realize the position I'm in."

"You've got the power! You're there! You've got access to information. You know when the calls come in from informers. You can warn people. If you can't help us, who can?"

"And put my head on the block?"

One of the others cleared his throat, a male-aligned 30-year-old Gerald, or at least that was the name he gave when introduced. Laura said he worked at NuCell.

"Assisting our fellow Hermies here in Leicester would only be a very small part of our overall stratagem," he said.

"Stratagem?" I exclaimed. "Keep on using that kind of language, and people really will begin to believe in the Hermie conspiracy."

"When events force a minority into collusion to survive, then the term conspiracy is wholly appropriate."

"Jesus!"

"Will you listen," Laura hissed.

"We have to buy ourselves time," Gerald said. "That's all. After that the inevitable sweep of history will protect us. But the intervening years will be extraordinarily difficult for us as a race."

"What?"

He gave me a small contrite smile and held up a thin sheet of some transparent plastic. It was printed with rows of black lines, like a bar code. "I've been mapping the genome of various hermaphrodites working at Nu-Cell," he said. "I've identified the genes which produce both our dual sexual characteristics and enhanced neuron structure as well as other physiological improvements. Do you remember the so-called Martian Theory?"

"Yes," I said wearily.

"It is completely inaccurate."

"Astonishing," I said dryly.

Laura shot me a vicious glare.

"We have not resulted from artificial interference," he continued. "And that means that even if every hermaphrodite alive were to be sterilized, ordinary humans would still continue to give birth to more hermaphrodites. Within five generations every human born will be a hermaphrodite. So what we need is an interval in which people are forced to face reality and come to terms with our racial future."

"How do you know this?" I asked.

"Over 95 per cent of human DNA is inactive spacing, literally garbage. The active genes, those which make us what we are, account for a tiny three or four percent. Until now geneticists have considered those inactive genes to be part of our heritage; primitive genes that have been switched off as we evolved out of our remote ancestry through simian stages until we arrived at what we are today. That theory is incorrect. Once I identified the hermaphrodite genes, I went back and examined the genomes of ordinary humans. They too contained the hermaphrodite genes. But they were inactive; for the moment, part of the spacing. Hermaphroditism is part of humanity's on-going evolution."

"What switches the genes on?"

He shrugged lamely. "It is their time to be switched on. Our time. God, if you prefer, Mr Anderson, God has decided to bring us forth. Just think, in a hundred generations another sequence of genes will activate themselves. Who knows what our descendants will look like."

"And in the meantime, we get slaughtered," Laura said.

"Registration dodging isn't the answer," I said. "It criminalizes Hermies in everyone's eyes."

"Neither is registration," Philippa said. She was about the same age as Laura, with auburn hair and a small compact body. Aggression simmered, barely contained, below her calm surface persona. "Not when all that does is bring the lynch gangs down on you."

"It's not our fault," I shouted. "When the police arrive it's always too late."

"That's because someone inside your precious ops room is tipping off the lynch gangs," Laura said. "And you're just standing by and letting it happen."

I knew she was right. At the time I just didn't know who was doing it. I sank down into one of her scoop chairs. "I don't know where the leak is coming from," I said. "Believe me, I've looked."

"This may help," Philippa said with deceptive calm. She was holding out an RCD.

"What's this?"

"See for yourself." She indicated Laura's desktop terminal.

I slotted the silver disc. The program it contained was simple enough, designed for the Packard-Bell core, a number of subroutines that would work inside the original operator shell. Once loaded, any file that was started on a Hermie would be switched with another citizen file selected at random. That meant a duty officer sending a panda car to pick up a suspected Hermie would target the wrong person. Some innocent non-hermaphrodite would be cut up on the streets instead.

"No chance," I said.

"It would not have to be in effect for very long," Gerald said. "I intend to confront my non-hermaphrodite colleagues with my discovery. They are rational people, they will accept it. Then the intellectuals and leaders of the world will be made to understand what is really occurring. Hermaphroditism is inevitable."

Philippa snorted. She didn't believe in Gerald's wishful-thinking solution any more than I did. She didn't like the idea of being civil to a policeman, either. I could virtually see her mind working out ways to blackmail me into loading her program.

"Please, Mark," Laura said. "What kind of world will the baby come into if we don't try to bridge the gulf? This gives us the time to do it."

"I'll think about it," I lied.

She sat beside me and twined her arms round my neck. "Thank you."

I knew it was disastrous for Laura to get involved with these people. It was only a matter of time before they were rounded up; if they weren't informed on the monitor program would track them down anyway. I loved Laura, and I would have done anything to protect her and our baby. She had taught me so many incredible things, things I would never have understood on my own. But I also believed in the system, believed that the system would protect us. I decided to take action before we were bath up on a charge of insurrection.

The simplest thing to do was have her picked up. Crazy? Not really: once registered, her name would be entered in the monitor program. If she contacted her cabal members the monitor would spot them. She would never knowingly betray them, so she would steer clear of them.

And me? Well, I was prepared to face the consequences. As I said, I ultimately believed in the protection of the system. Remember, this was before I'd found out about Burroughs. What's more, I would be there to prevent anything from happening.

The day after the meeting I told Laura to meet me at Guys & Dolls restaurant for lunch. Then I bypassed the normal log-in procedure and loaded an informer's report of a Hermie into the ops room network, giving Laura's name and profile, telling them where she would be. One of the duty officers would pick it up, and assign a panda car to collect us both from Guys & Dolls.

I hurried towards the restaurant hoping Laura wouldn't be late. When the uniform boys picking her up found they had a senior officer as a witness they would have to act strictly according to the book. She would be perfectly safe in my presence. After that I would inform the Chief Constable of my relationship with her, but only after she'd been correctly processed.

On the way over to Guys & Dolls I got caught up in the lunchtime traffic snarl. I sat under my perspex bubble sweating for half an hour. In the end I jumped out and walked.

I turned the corner of the street and made for the restaurant with a growing sense of anxiety. When I saw the crowd outside the restaurant I felt a strange taste in my mouth. Fingering the buttons on my uniform, I had to fight down a rising panic. Then I found myself sprinting towards the crowd.

The lynch gang had already done its work. Their victim lay naked and bloody in the gutter. One of them turned the lifeless body over with the toe of his boot. They had hacked off the penis. And as I looked, I saw that their victim had been expecting a child, and that they had sliced open her belly. The bloody foetus was almost indistinguishable from the rest of the carcass. I looked around for Laura, as if somehow just by looking I could make that figure on the ground not be her. A neon sign flashing above the crowd exhorted us all to EAT REECEBREAD.

Philippa found me, hours later. I was sitting on the New Walk bridge over the carriageway running through the heart of the city. Down below, the fuel-cell driven cars formed a silent steady stream of colorful metallic beetles, scurrying home from work. Rushing towards their loved ones.

"What good will that do?" Philippa asked gently.

I didn't even look up. "It will stop the pain."

"Only for you. There are soon going to be others in your position. Millions of us. Do you want them to endure it as well?"

"I don't care."

"Yes you do. Laura taught you to care."

I started sobbing. Philippa led me away from the parapet.

Behind me the ops room was abuzz with duty officers gossiping over Burroughs's hypertantrum; calls for assistance and reports of crime were going unanswered. It was my job to marshal them back to work. Not today. I pushed the door of the gents open, and walked in.

There were five stalls along one wall, stainless steel urinals at the far end. White tiles gleamed soullessly under harsh tubelight. The stall at the end of the line was occupied.

Gerald, quiet intellectual Gerald, had been quite right; oppress a minority enough and no matter how meek, how mild, eventually they begin to fight back. He even led the fight.

The whole world would be Hermies in time, he said. But time was the one thing the first generation didn't have. Our father Hermes and our mother Aphrodite might be bringing hermaphrodites into the world, but they were doing it too slowly. Even gods need a helping hand occasionally.

I tested the stall door with my hand. Burroughs had slipped the tiny bolt. A fragile whimpering sound was coming from inside. I was going to have to break down the door. I was already four months pregnant with Philippa's child, and exertion like that wouldn't be good for the baby, but I kicked at the lock anyway. The bolt flew off and I was able to push open the door.

After identifying the Hermie genes, Gerald had fed the sequence into a DNA synthesizer. Plasmids came out of the other end, the essence of Hermaphroditism, all that we are. Philippa and her more militant colleagues incorporated them into the new improved varieties of reecebread that Nu-Cell was giving to the world. And the people of the world ate. Both the meek and the greedy, eating their reeceburgers. The plasmid-carrying viruses slithered into their digestive tract, into their bloodstream, into their cells, into their nuclei. And, finally, began raping their DNA.

But we're not heartless. Manipulating human genes is a tricky business. So much can go wrong. The plasmids needed to be tested first. I once said you can't experiment with gene therapy on living humans. I was wrong. There are certain individuals who can be exempt from such moral posturing.

Our test subject, myself, showed no ill-effects after a solid month of eating the modified reecebread. It was enough for us to release it for general consumption. That was six months ago.

Burroughs was sitting crammed into a corner of the stall, his trousers and pants crumpled round his knees. His wretched face jerked up as I looked in, his mouth open in a silent plea.

No wonder he'd been in such a rotten temper all week.

The chicken-flesh at the base of his scrotum had split open. A mucus plug had voided from the raw open slit, followed by a dribble of blood.

Burroughs was having his first period.

L. TIMMEL DUCHAMP

Motherhood, Etc.

THE ROOM HAS a long, glass-topped conference table. The room's windows look out on the ocean, but the chair to which they direct her puts her back to the view. The man wearing a black and white polka-dotted tie identifies himself as "Wagner." He introduces the bald man facing her across the table as "Dr. Johns." Wagner asks most of the questions. The other man stares moodily over her shoulder, at the ocean.

"He called himself Joshua," she answers the first question. And: "I liked him because he was different," she answers the second.

The man across from her jerks his eyes off the ocean to stare at her. She blushes. Already she has made a mistake.

"Different, I mean, from all the other guys I'd ever gone out with," she amends. "He liked to talk about real things. And he listened, too. A lot. He had a cute laugh." She looks down at her hands, folded tightly and whitely together. "And the most wonderful brown eyes."

She gets stuck there, does not want to go on. Her eyes skim the walls, looking for the video camera. They are clever about these things, but she thinks she has found it, embedded in a metal sculpture. The bead of red light gives it away.

An "interview," is how they'd billed this ordeal. No one used the word *interrogation*. And no, they said, she was not under arrest. Though she cannot of course go home. If she were reasonable, she would understand why.

They kept telling her to be reasonable. To consider "the implications." They said that the interview… would help. Would help them, the "authorities." Who would know best what to do, much better than she. Who was only an inexperienced, nineteen-year-old… female. Who was in no position to judge the danger, to understand the stakes. She must trust them.

Right.

Wagner prompts her. He has moved to her side of the table. He perches on it, uncomfortably close to her. One of his feet rests on the chair to her right. The cuff of his somber black pant-leg is rucked up. The black sock underneath looks as though it could be silk. Probably, she guesses, it goes all the way up to his knee. Certainly it covers his calf. She's sure that the skin of his leg is dead white. And crawling with coarse red hair. The hair on the backs of his hands and knuckles, certainly, is coarse red. And plentiful. Probably it covers his body.

"We saw one another just about every other night for a month before I first stayed over with him," she replies to the next question. She swallows, and looks away from Wagner's looming bulk, and wishes she could get away from him.

He wants all the details, "Everything," he says. Like the prurient evangelist con-artist who corners the timid into "confess[ing] all sin, all filth, all wickedness in your heart." So, she elaborates, "Yes, we slept together when I stayed over. In pajamas. Both of us. And wearing underpants."

God, Ulrike, he's so weird. I mean, he said I couldn't sleep with him unless I'd keep my underpants on and wear at least the bottoms of the pajamas. He says he doesn't want to spoil our emotional relationship, which is what he says will happen if we rush ahead with the sexual side of things. He says he knows from past experience. And that I have to trust him.

Telling it to Ulrike had (at the beginning, at least) made it seem all quite wonderful, an exemplar for what "normal" *should* be. But it hadn't *felt* "normal." It would be middle-of-the-night dark when Joshua's lips and fingers woke her. She'd hear his breathing, and her own, and other noises she knew involved her (or his?) genitals – *sexual* noises she couldn't identify. And little sounds coming from her own throat, that she couldn't mute, because of the explosive sensations rippling in wild, lingering streams of movement through her body. All the while a small observing part of her tried to visualize – as though to watch – what was happening, tried to fit it all into the fictional and theoretical ragbag that constituted her "knowledge" of Sex. His hands are now *there*, doing *this*, the detached observer would note. His right thigh is *there*. And his genitals are...

But little of it fit. And his genitals...

"Are you saying," the bald man grates, impatiently tapping the closed manila folder on the table before him, "that you never saw his genitals? Even once? That you never felt them with your hands? And that you didn't think it abnormal that after five months' sleeping together you still had not had intercourse with him?"

He sounds incredulous.

There is no way she's going to tell these men that only now and then had she managed to cop a feel, a vague fleeting touch to his genitals before Joshua had maneuvered them out of her reach. Joshua had claimed that her touching him there would turn him on too much. Timidly, she had suggested that since he used his fingers (et cetera) to bring her to orgasm, that she should do the same for him. How can she explain? In the night, she did think it weird. But she couldn't know for sure, because she'd never slept with a man before. And besides, Joshua always made her feel, well, weird for wanting more. Isn't it enough? he'd ask her. How can you miss what you've never known? Don't you enjoy what we do?

Sometimes they spent half the night coming. She recalls that one night he got up three times to change his underpants. (It is unreal remembering, with Wagner looming over her and Dr. Johns looking cold and dissatisfied and writing in a small thin script on the yellow pad to one side of the manila folder. They keep saying they want her to tell them everything. Imagine having them write *that* down. *Three pairs of underpants.* They'd probably ask her what his come smelled like. And whether it left stains.)

He had made her feel that wanting to touch his genitals was... immodest. Or at the least premature. Which was totally weird, considering all their discussions about freedom and Being and the need to find Meaning in the face of an utterly random Universe...

These men, she thinks, would feel comfortable with the archaic terminology she and Ulrike had used to discuss it. "Virginity," "hymen," and an "unnaturally prolonged state of innocence." And "clitoral versus vaginal orgasm..." They giggled when they used such language. But it was the only way she had known how to talk about it with Ulrike.

Now Wagner presses Dr. Johns' incredulity. She knows he must have figured out he's found one of her most vulnerable spots.

"Look," she says, "I'm nineteen. I'd never been with a man before. Sure, maybe I thought something might be a little strange. But hey, when you're new at it, *all* sex is weird."

Wagner lays his freckled hairy paw on her neatly (but tensely) folded hands. The touch of it, even the *sight* of it, makes her want to throw up. Talking about sex in general and about her and Joshua in particular with these creeps is obscene. "You're making me feel like an old goat, young lady," he says with one of those man-style chuckles (utterly unlike Joshua's frank crackups).

"But intercourse, you must have known that vaginal intercourse is the normal point of sexual relations," Dr. Johns lectures her. He raps his knuckles on the manila folder. "It says on your transcript that you've had three psychology courses. You can't expect us to believe you didn't know something was wrong!"

She is blushing again. And not only can she not stand a second longer of Wagner's touch, but her hands have started trembling. Chagrined, she snatches them away and buries them in her lap. Then she scoots her chair back from the table and glares up at him, though he's definitely too close for comfortable eye contact. (But what distance would be comfortable? A thousand yards?)

"What are you accusing me of?" she demands. "I've never heard that people have a legal obligation to report men who don't take every available opportunity to fuck a willing woman! I have a right to know what you think I've done wrong," she adds, though without faith that they're going to be willing to grant her any "rights" whatsoever, however de rigueur they were supposed to be.

"Now, Patty," Wagner remonstrates. "You know we're not accusing you of anything. We're talking public health, public safety here. We're talking *viruses*, Patty, *communicable* viruses. We're talking a virus that this guy whose name you won't tell us passed to you." He leans forward, so that his thickly freckled face is right up in hers. "Now I thought your doctor explained all that to you. Am I right?"

Patty. On top of everything else, their calling her that just about made her want to scream. But no way was she going to tell *them*. They'd probably just go on calling her that to bug her. And besides, as she'd long ago figured out, if adults you didn't know called you something you didn't ordinarily answer to, a name that was basically alien to you, it meant you were just that much more private from them, and that every time they used the hated name it reminded you of what jerks they were to call you something without first finding out what it is you wanted to be called.

Now the bald man in the navy silk suit opens the manila folder he's been persistently fingering. *Dr. Johns,* she sneers to herself. *Wagner.* Prurient jerks extraordinaire. Much, much worse than the doctor at the hospital. Whether they are as bad as the federal official who'd coerced her into submitting to the exam and photography remains to be seen. The vibes she is getting off Wagner, though, make her feel, in her gut, that they might be worse.

"I told you," she insists. "He said to call him Joshua. If he mentioned his last name to me, I don't remember."

Wagner shakes his head and sighs. "I can't believe a bright young lady like you could be so careless. You know you can't tell these days what you might be getting into, don't you? There's some pretty nasty STDS out there, raging out of control. Besides AIDS. You do know that, Patty, don't you?"

The doctor, now standing, leans over the table and arranges half-a-dozen or so photos – all 8$\frac{1}{2}$" × 11" – down the center of the table. Pat stares at the little tuft of gray, like feathers, gracing the top of his shiny pink dome. He sits down and glares at her. "You've got a problem with denial," he announces. "But you can't deny *these.*" He takes a stapled sheaf of pages from the folder and waves them at her. "Your DNA has mutated. Your blood doesn't match any known type, even though your medical records say you are type O. And your sex chromosomes now have three Xs and one Y. Which is to say, strictly speaking you're not a woman." He points at the photo nearest her. "And take a look at the eruptions of tissue, there." His words are coming through his teeth, as though he's almost too furious to talk.

Face aflame, she jumps out of her chair and grabs wildly at the photos. "How *dare* you," she seethes as she gets a look at her own pubic hair in larger-than-lifesize glossy black and white. "How dare you *slimeballs* turn my body into sleaze!" She wants to rip the photos to shreds and burn them. *Her* genitals, on public display. For creeps like these!

The doctor goes for the photos, to protect them, and Wagner for her – to slam her back into her chair and keep her pinned there by the shoulders. "Now, Patty, I want you to calm yourself," he says.

"Take your filthy hands off me!" she spits, struggling to twist out of his hold.

"You're not going to get hysterical on us, are you?" he says.

The cold spot of fear inside her – that first appeared yesterday – spreads. When she refused to let them examine her, the federal guy also warned her against "getting hysterical," saying that if she did they'd have to give her something to calm her down. Totally cowed, she went along with everything, the crowd of masked witnesses, the cameras, *everything*.

"These photographs are the property of the federal government, young lady," the doctor scolds. "Perhaps you weren't aware of it, but intentional destruction of government property is a very, very serious offense. One you could go to prison for."

She folds her arms across her chest. "Government property," she sneers. "Of sleaze. I can just imagine."

"Important scientific evidence," the doctor snaps.

"Sleaze," she repeats. "Made and distributed without my permission, and definitely against my will."

The doctor looks over her head at Wagner. "People used to say that about Sigmund Freud, you know. But then there have always been people with minds too small and narrow to accept Science."

"And maybe Freud really was just a dirty old man," Pat mutters. She glares at the doctor, who looks as though he'd like to slap her – and ignores (as best she can) the increase of pressure on her shoulders. "Consider, after all, whose side he took in rape and incest cases."

The doctor's eyes lift, presumably to exchange knowing looks with Wagner. "This is intolerable," he says. "We have about two dozen important questions it is essential she answer. And she hasn't answered even one of them yet."

The room is suddenly so quiet that Pat can hear the surf of the ocean through the double panes of glass behind her. The doctor's eyes are still focused over her head, so she guesses the men are involved in some sort of silent communication.

"It's really, you know, that Patty here doesn't yet understand just how serious this situation is," Wagner finally says. His hands lift from her shoulders. For a few seconds she hears him moving around behind her. "And, you know, girls her age are sometimes painfully embarrassed about anything to do with sex." His manly chuckle rumbles briefly. "Especially with men our age." His face is suddenly right next to Pat's. "Am I right, Patty?"

Embarrassed, right. You stupid boob.

But fear is gaining on anger. She feels too exhausted to shove his face away, or scratch it, or do any of the other things popping into her head every second he's bent over her. "Yeah," she says, "that must be it." She coughs delicately and scoots her chair to the right. "No offense, but I think I must be allergic to your cologne." And she puts her hand to her mouth and hacks loudly, to disguise the giggles suddenly shaking her.

Wagner's breathing gets considerably heavier, but he moves out of her face. She wonders how he's going to get back at her. (There's no doubt in her mind that he will: he's just that kind of guy.) A scenario involving drugs starts playing through her mind. Is there, she wonders, really something called *truth serum?* Can they shoot her up with a drug that will make her babble indiscriminately?

She just can't stand the idea of reviewing her sexual relations with Joshua for creeps like these. And she doesn't believe they have valid reasons for prying inside her head. What she does with another person is none of their business. It's her body. Which is sacred ground. Off-limits. And no one's concern but her own.

The walls and window resonate with a fast rapping on the door.

"The CDC has arrived," Wagner mutters (presumably to Dr. Johns).

The door swings open and a blond giant fills the threshold. The thought flicks through Pat's head that the blond has been imbibing a Wonderland cocktail labeled DRINK ME. "Elliott Hardwick, CDC," he booms. "Apologies. My plane was late."

Though blonds are not Pat's type, she has to admit the man is a knockout. ("A pretty boy," Ulrike would call him.) He exudes energy and good health. You can see it rippling beneath his soft loose Pima cotton shirt, shining out of his purest of thick-lashed blue eyes, bursting out from his smile. She watches him shake hands, first with Baldie, then – leaning across the table – Wagner. She loves his salmon pink suspenders, she thinks they're perfect for the black jeans and pearl gray shirt. She only wishes he wore at least one gold ring in his ears.

"And *this*," the knockout says, crinkling his eyes in a major heat-storm of a smile, "must be Patricia Morrow." He thrusts his hand at her. "How do you do. I'm Elliott Hardwick. Everyone calls me Sam, I hope you will, too."

He's overwhelming her. On purpose, she thinks. But she gives him her hand to shake.

"And what do you go by?" he wonders. "Patricia, Pat, Patty, or something entirely different?"

The blue eyes are like something out of a book, of the trashy romance sort. *Amused, knowing, powerful...* Also, he's still holding her hand after shaking it. She blushes, and clears her throat. "Pat," she says. "I go by the name Pat."

He nods, squeezes her hand and lets it go. It's almost a relief when he takes his eyes off her to swing his attache case onto the table and open it.

Wagner walks to the end of the table, rounds it and walks back up the other side to the center. "If I could have a word with you outside, Sam," he says, jerking his head towards the door.

Elliott "Sam" Hardwick flashes his smile all around. "Sure, Bill," he says in such an easy way that Pat wonders if he has a West Coast background. "But you know, before we settle down to the hard work of eking out the story, what say we take a little break. My working style is just a lit-tle bit different." He *winks* at Pat. "I'd like, for one thing, if it's okay by her, to stretch my legs for a bit on the beach." He beams at Pat. "I bet *you're* up for a walk, Pat, am I right?"

Baldie makes a nasty sound in his throat. Pat shoots a quick glance at him. He looks as though he's swallowed something disagreeable, but though he tamps together the sheaf of photos with undue violence, he says nothing.

Pat shoves back her chair, grabs her bag and stands up. "Damned straight I'm up for it," she tells Sam.

He nods at her bag. "You don't need *that.*"

Pat looks at Wagner, then back at Sam. She slings the strap of the bag over her shoulder and quickly rounds the table. Somebody ransacked her house last week. Her doctor was indignant when she suggested he might know who had done it. They're all sleaze, even Gorgeous Sam. And she knows she'd be a fool to forget it.

While Sam "snatches a quick briefing" from the Dynamic Duo, Pat waits outside. Scanning the beach, she wonders if there's any point in trying to run. Her guess is that most of the homes (if that's what they are) overlooking this beach are encased in heavy-duty security fences. But supposing she did get up to the street. She doesn't know the terrain in this La Jolla neighborhood. Buses aren't frequent. And taxis simply don't cruise residential areas looking for fares at ten A.M.

A sudden gust of wind makes her full skirt balloon up. *Surely you must have noticed,* her doctor had chided her for not having come in "at once." And now she's afraid to wear pants or any close-fitting skirts, except with a long loose shirt or sweater that could be counted on to keep the line of her crotch well-disguised. As for what is *there*... it makes her queasy every morning when she wakes and finds all of it there, between her legs, crowding and sweat-making, scary because if you move or touch yourself the wrong way it can hurt, and making it so damned involved to pee, every morning its presence inexorable, something to be gotten used to all over again, like a bad dream about losing a body part that on waking turns out to be true....

It can all be removed, quite easily, they say. Only they want to wait, to see just how far "it" develops....

Every morning she's nauseated with revulsion, yes.... But sometimes, especially in the evening, after a day of having accepted it, a perverse excitement breaks out of her, and she knows that though she wants it removed so that she can at least *look* normal (even if her blood and DNA will never again be), there's something powerful about the experience, too. And sometimes a secret voice in her head says there's something neat about being a freak. (If only she hadn't gone to the doctor in the first place.) And sometimes that voice whispers to her that there's a reason, there's a *meaning* in it all, that it's not just an accident of nature but a special event, fated to her in particular....

And of course Joshua hadn't thought the changes in her genitals in the least bit odd. (Though of course he'd only seen the early stages.) And so she had in turn thought that maybe so much stimulation and excitement just naturally caused certain (small) changes, which she thought of as swellings. (But that was before everything had gotten out of hand.) It had made a weird kind of sense to her when she thought of all that blood suffusing those tissues for hours and hours and hours.

Such matters had always been mysterious to her. And so she had told herself that just because people didn't talk about the enlargement of the urethra and swelling just below it didn't mean such things weren't commonplace. It's not as though she had ever read any sex manuals or descriptive pornography that could be counted on to reveal such mature-audience side-effects. And ever since she had been a little girl, she has been discovering that where sex and reproduction are concerned, the weirdest most unthinkable things often turn out to be true.

There still lurks in the back of Pat's mind the weird superstitious thought that the cause of the virus is to be found in the hours and hours of "messing around." A book that Ulrike had shown her, warning about such perversity, claimed that sexually stimulated women suffer "congestion" when they fail to achieve "deep vaginal orgasm," which (it claimed) can come only from "proper heterosexual inter- course." Ulrike's concern had been so embarrassing. It had gotten so that Pat hated to come home mornings and face the question *Well, did you finally do it? Have you lost the Big Vee?* And so she had mostly let Ulrike think they didn't do much besides, well, cuddle and *sleep.*

After about fifteen minutes Sam opens the door above and comes out onto the top deck. He waves at her, then starts down the stairs, past the middle deck and the hot-tub, to the deck set on stilts into the sand. There he stops to remove his Birkenstocks and the beautiful salmon socks that match his suspenders. When he straightens up he gestures her to join him. Pat sighs, but heaves the bag back onto her shoulder and trudges over the bit of beach between them and up the bottom flight of stairs to the deck.

"Gotta say that after twenty days of Atlanta's temperature inver- sion, this is purely fantastic," he says, tossing a tube of sun-block at her.

She catches it, looks at the label, then up at the sky. "The sun isn't hitting the water yet," she points out. "I really think this is overkill."

"If you knew the stats that I know," he remarks, "you'd never be caught out in U.V. rays without it."

She nods at his golden-tanned face. "But you go in for *tanning sa-lons?*"

His eyebrows shoot up, and then he laughs. "Oh, you're referring to my face. Believe me, it only goes down as far as my neck. From the slopes. Got this great package deal, for weekend skiing this winter."

Pat sighs and rubs some of the #12 cream into her face. She will humor him. But she wishes she weren't so attracted to him. On top of Joshua, it makes her feel like a nymphomaniac. Sam may be a dish, but pretty boys aren't ordinarily her type.

They walk for a while along the water line, then pause to look out at the lusciously turquoise water. They may not have as long a stretch to walk as they would at Torrey Pines, but this beach is certainly a lot more private. "I gather," Sam begins, "you've gotten into a pretty adversarial relation, shall we say, with my colleagues." When Pat snorts, Sam grins at her. "Right. You don't have to say anything. But what *I* want to say about that is that all that's just a problem of com- munication. We're basically on the same side, Pat. Now I'm not saying it's *all* their fault, but my guess is that your, well, negative reactions are probably due to their not leveling with you, not explaining what we do and don't know, and what you know and can tell us that we need to know – and, maybe most important, *why* we need to know."

Pat's heart starts racing. "Look, I just don't think any of this is anybody's business but my own!" she exclaims. "Okay, my body's fucking up. I understand that. But I'm not a danger to anyone. I haven't done anything wrong. Whatever my relationship with Joshua is is my own damned business!"

Sam puts his back to the surf. The sun that pours onto his face makes his eyes sparkle the same lush blue of the water. "Pat, can I ask you to do something for me?"

He gazes intensely down into her eyes, and Pat has to swallow several times. Even in the throes of so much magnetism she's practically squirming at her own reaction. She's convinced she's so transparent he's deliberately manipulating her. She wishes she could say *Fuck you!* and stomp off down the beach. But she can't. She's too interested in milking every second out of him she can. Instead, she says, "Will I be allowed to go back to classes when the new quarter starts next week?"

It makes her mad to hear the childish pleading anxiety in her voice. How could her voice so betray her, when she was feeling snarlingly surly at the very second the words came out? And it doesn't help when Sam lightly touches her shoulder and says: "I wish I knew the answer to that, because if I did I would tell you. But for one thing, I've just been brought in on this, so I can't begin to guess how things are going to go. Certainly we'll do everything we can to keep from disrupting your life any more than necessary. But I also have to add, Pat, that the answer depends a great deal on you. On how quickly we can get the most important questions answered...."

Blackmail, Pat thinks. Covert, but intended. The bastard.

Pat drops her bag to the sand and shoves her hands into her skirt pockets. She wonders if all this would have been avoided if she'd gone home over break. But she and Joshua had planned to have an entire week together, and she hadn't been able to bring herself to tell her parents he'd (apparently) canceled....

Better yet if she hadn't gone to the doctor to get an IUD in the first place. Then it would be just her – and Joshua's – little secret.

"No, Pat, please," Sam says quickly, seemingly reading her face if not her mind. "It's not going to help if you get pissed at me for telling you the truth. As I said before, what we have here is a mystery. A very frustrating and serious mystery. And though some of the answers will be hard to find, others of them, of almost equal consequence, are there, inside your head, if only you would give them to us."

Pat's hands, still in her pockets, ball into fists. "You *say* they're important. But what I *know* is that everybody wants me to surrender my privacy, just like that." Her face burns as she remembers the photos and Wagner's questions and sly innuendo. "Because to you people, it's nothing. Like I have no rights. Like I'm this pornographic *object* you're all screwing over!"

Her outburst both embarrasses her and further fuels her rage. She can't remember ever talking to an adult this way before, except of course her parents and their co-members in the collective. Close to tears, she picks up her bag and taking big rapid strides resumes her progress up the beach. If the water weren't so cold she'd walk straight out into the surf, to hide.

"Pat, wait, please!" The wind whips Sam's words at her. "Please, if you would just stop for a minute and let me tell you what we need to know and why." He's caught up with her, and has her by the arm. "I know it would put a whole different spin on what you've been perceiving as a reckless invasion of your privacy."

Pat stops. Her breath is coming fast. She stares down at the sand. The man talks like the baby-boomer he is. "Right," she gasps. "I've heard it all already, from those goons up there." She jerks her head back up the beach. "They're grossed out. And they think I might be contagious!"

"Listen, I've seen your transcript. There's not a doubt in my mind that you can understand the specifics."

She looks at him, and twists her mouth into a derisory smile. *He* probably thinks he's being flattering. All her A's, and Advanced Placement and a double major in biology and English. Adults are always pretending that sort of thing is "impressive." Right. But she's still just a nineteen-year-old *female*. Which is to say, she's somebody to be browbeaten and manipulated and sidetracked from everything important.

His eyes scan the beach fronts, and he lifts his hand to his brow to shield his eyes from the sun. Pat wonders whether he sacrificed wearing shades on the walk – protection from the wicked UV rays bombarding them – so as to seem more accessible. He points to a concrete bench at the foot of some stairs not far from them. "Shall we sit for a bit?" he proposes.

Pat is glad for the chance to get the bag off her shoulder, so she shrugs and follows him into dry, loose sand. When they are settled, well above the high-tide mark (towards which the dirty-foamed water line is inexorably creeping), Sam, staring out at the water, begins: "I'm not sure how much you've been told. So what I'm going to do is tell you the story as it unfolded in the file they faxed me last night." Pat thinks of the photos, and her throat closes painfully. The very existence of such a file, and its being faxed who knows how many times to who knows how many people...

Sam draws a deep breath. "That there was a problem first became apparent during your office visit to your gynecologist, to be fitted with an IUD." He looks at her. "It occurs to me from the things you've been saying that you might feel more comfortable talking with a woman, Pat. But I have to say that I assumed you wouldn't mind my being a man for the simple reason that you chose a male gynecologist."

Pat snorts. "Do you have any idea how hard it is to get a woman? Everybody wants them. And there aren't that many of them. So if you're in a hurry you don't have much choice. You know?"

Sam nods. "I see. Well, the problem is, we're in something of a hurry here, too, and all the principal investigators in this case are men. And like women gynecologists, women epidemiologists are hard to come by in a hurry, too."

Pat crosses her arms over her chest. She has to bite her lip to keep from flinging at him her own intention to become a medical researcher.

"But to continue." Again Sam gazes out at the water; and Pat does the same. "It seems your doctor initially diagnosed you as having a case of what is known as androgen-dihydrostestosterone deficiency. Which, in plain English, is a genetic condition that often does not become apparent until adolescence, in which the male sex organs make a late appearance in an individual that had previously been mistaken for female."

"That's interesting," Pat remarks. Some of the waves are coming in crooked. It amuses her to see them crash into one another from odd angles. "And I have to say it's the first time I've heard it." She smiles bitterly. "You see, my doctor never bothered to *share* his diagnosis with me."

"Well there were tests he was having done," Sam says quickly. "I'm sure he was just waiting for confirmation. But then when both the chromosomal analysis and blood chemistry reports came in, everything got much more complicated. Because, you see, the first startling thing was the discovery that your sex chromosome was polyploid." Sam looks at her. "To be specific, instead of having an ordinary diploid chromosomal pair, you've somehow got a quadriploid, a double pair. Given all the biology you've had, I assume you understand what I mean by *that*."

Pat frowns. "Except that it sounds like gibberish. I mean, how could I possibly have four sex chromosomes?"

"That's one of our mystery questions," Sam says drily. "Of course polyploidism is not completely unknown – in nonhuman species. Mostly in plants. Often engineered. And in such cases the mechanisms of reproduction are asexual. But that's neither here nor there."

"So I can think of myself as becoming like a plant?" Pat retorts.

Sam clears his throat. "I'm going to assume you mean that as a joke." His folded hands tug isometrically against his right black jean-clad knee, which he's raised a little above his left. "To continue. Your doctor had good reason to doubt his diagnosis, even before seeing the first batch of lab reports. For one thing, he knew from his examination that your female sexual and reproductive organs were all fully developed and morphologically normal. For another, because you were being fitted with an IUD, you were menstruating at the time of the examination. So right from the start there were reasons to doubt the diagnosis." Sam glances at her. "But one can hardly blame him for the mistake. Intersexes are usually discovered at birth, and forced into one sex or the other. An OB/GYN would be understandably fuzzy about the possibilities. So. Your test results start trickling in. The tissue sampled is indeed discovered to be male genital cells. Which seems to confirm the diagnosis. But your blood chemistry shows something else. First, that your sex chromosomal pair is not a pair, but one pair of each sex. Second, that your blood is no longer type O, as it had been when you donated blood in a drive at UCSD last fall. So, given all these mysteries, your doctor takes more blood from you, orders more tests, and seeks consults from colleagues in three different fields of specialization. And the new tests show estrogen in your blood." Sam grins at her. "And you know what that means, don't you?"

Pat snatches a quick look at him, then concentrates again on the water. "Sure. It means that my ovaries are working. Because estrogen is produced primarily in the ovaries, just as testosterone is produced in the testes."

"Right. So your doctor sees there's a problem, but a rather intriguing one. He – and one of the three specialists he's consulting – decides that you have two separate problems, unrelated. His idea is that you're an odd, hitherto-unobserved case of intersex, a *true* hermaphrodite, manifesting organs of both sexes that are not only morphologically correct, but – as we now think will be the case – *functionally* correct. Which would be quite an interesting phenomenon, since intersexes on the whole tend to be sterile."

"But there's the problem of other cellular changes," Pat says when he pauses.

"A coincidence, your doctor believes." Sam chuckles. He has a pleasant, not unduly "manly" chuckle, Pat decides, though it doesn't compare with any of Joshua's so-infectious giggles, chortles and belly-laughs. "But, needless to say, not what the hematologist thinks."

Pat crosses her legs, and catches herself mentally bracing for the squashing of her balls. She has half-a-dozen times in the last two weeks, on moving incautiously, been afflicted with horrible abdominal cramps. This time, though, the shift goes off safely, and the sensation of that extra bit of flesh pressing against sexually sensitive places is strictly pleasurable.

"The endocrinologist is also not so certain. And the oncologist is positive it's not."

"Oncologist!" Pat exclaims. "Are you saying this growth is cancerous?" The thought has not before occurred to her, for no one has said anything about changes other than in her blood type, her chromosomes and her genitals. But she sees now that she should have been worried about such a possibility all along.

Sam lays his hand over hers. "The indications are good that this is a controlled, directed growth, Pat. We can't be sure, of course. But the theory everyone's going with now is that the new genetic material is directing the growth." He sighs. "But that leaves open the question as to whether there have been other chromosomal changes. And, most important, what caused the change in your DNA to start with."

Pat snatches her hand away. "Well it just burns me up that that damned bastard never mentioned any specialists, any doubts, any problems. Until yesterday I thought it was some kind of freak endocrine problem. That's what he led me to believe! And that once the so-called 'new tissue' had 'fully developed' it would be removed, and everything would be hunky-dory!" Her hands clench into fists. She'd like to pummel him. He's one of *them*, even if he is finally telling her *some* of the truth. (To manipulate her!) And it only makes matters worse that she's feeling *excessively* attracted to him – and in spite of the resentment. (And so what that he knows how to dress? That proves nothing. Her parents' generation's mania about judging people by hair and dress attest to that!)

Sam raises his legs; and staring at his bare toes, wriggles them. Even his feet are strong and shapely (though white white). "He's older, isn't he," Sam says. "Well his generation was taught that women especially want doctors to be God. That you don't tell patients more than you have to, especially when you're not 100% certain of what you think you know." He sighs, and lowers his legs. "You want to get your blood pressure up sometime, you should read through the OB/GYN journals of the 1950s and 60s." He sweeps the air with his hand. "But to continue. On-going, intensive work is being done on your blood. The leading theory currently is that there's a virus operating." He shrugs. "The big breakthrough, though, came last week. When it was confirmed that your blood is infectious." Frowning, he looks her in the eye. "Did they tell you this part? That every blood sample put into contact with yours showed the same signs of alteration? Namely, the blood type altered, and an extra chromosomal pair was added. An XY pair for female blood, and an XX pair for male blood."

Pat gasps. "That's *incredible!*"

Sam snorts. "You could say that."

Which explains why they hauled her off to the hospital yesterday and wouldn't let her out of their sight.

"But of course the next mystery – beyond etiology and the like," Sam resumes, "is how the thing was transmitted to you. According to your file, when questioned yesterday you swore up and down that the only needles ever stuck into your body were of legitimate medical provenance. And we know from visual examinations that your hymen is still intact, that you have no vaginal or anal tearing...." Sam clears his throat. "Don't you see, Pat. We need to know if this thing was transmitted sexually. Or if not, just how it *was* transmitted." He presses his lips together. "Your room-mate's blood test has come up negative, so we know it can't be entirely casual, say through aerobic or dermal contact."

Pat thinks of how he put his hand on hers a few minutes ago – he's obviously confident he couldn't catch "it" from her in that way. "I don't understand what you're asking me." Her voice comes out small. And her cheeks, damn them, are burning again.

Sam executes a long elaborate ritual of cracking all the joints on his knuckles one at a time. "You were being fitted for an IUD, presumably because you intended to have sexual intercourse." He frowns fiercely as he finishes the knuckles on the right hand and starts on the left. "You know, Pat, I feel compelled to interject here that if you're going to be having sexual intercourse you should be using a condom. Since there's more than simply contraception at stake."

"I told them all already," Pat snaps (wanting to ask him whether *he* uses condoms every time he has sex). "I was only seeing one man, Joshua. And I decided to get fitted just in case we did decide to... have sex. It wasn't that we were necessarily going to. But that I wanted to be prepared in case we did."

"Your room-mate says you were out most nights over the last five months."

Pat swallows. It drives her nuts that Ulrike has been dragged in. Testing her. Asking her questions. And telling her what? That she, Pat, is carrying some new plague virus no one has ever seen before? The thought enrages her. "Yes," she seethes, "yes I slept with him. As I already told the others, with pajama bottoms." She glares at him. "Pretty damned funny, isn't it. That a man and woman who aren't married would sleep with one another without screwing. A real pair of freaks, right?"

Sam rises and plants his bare foot on the concrete bench, just at the edge of her skirt. "Why do you say that?" he wonders. Pat stares out at the ocean. The waves, it seems to her, are getting smaller. "What I'm really asking is, was there anything sexual? Did you, for instance, *kiss?*"

Pat's eyes fill with tears. "Yes," she answers. "Yes, we kissed. A lot."

"And petted?"

Her throat chokes with emotion. "Yes, if that's what you want to call it." Even though she's so furious she wants to destroy something, tears overflow her eyes.

"Genital petting?"

She stands up and crosses her arms over her chest. "I don't want to talk about it anymore," she announces.

"Pat. You know how sexually transmitted diseases are passed. You have to know what I'm asking and why. Don't you?"

She turns her back on him and the ocean. For a few seconds she listens to the surf beating on the sand and distant rocks. When she closes her eyes she can almost imagine she is on Torrey Pines beach. She can almost imagine Joshua is nearby, his fingers ready to touch hers, his arms ready to enfold her when she presses herself close.

But Joshua is gone. And she is here, on this private beach, with an "investigator" wanting to know the details of her sex life with him. She hates them, all of them, for picking at her, for prying into her private self, for frightening Joshua away. A month ago everything was beautiful and life was a constant high.

She opens her eyes to the glare and turns and faces him. "His semen never touched my lips," she spits out. "I never even *saw* his penis. Okay? But he... we had... cunnilingus." Her tongue trips over the word, so technical, so nothing to do with the real thing. She stares out at the water. "And I had no cuts or sores in the pubic area at any time. Is that what you wanted to know?"

The world is silent, except for the surf and the cry of a gull circling overhead. Then, "Yes, Pat. And I thank you. You can be sure now that no one's going to ask you any more questions about sex."

Pat hefts her bag to her shoulder and they head back for the Institute. Sam tells her about how backwards he was, compared to her, doing his required premed courses as an undergraduate (Princeton, '72). As they walk Pat watches the waves rip crookedly to shore. Never has she missed Joshua as much as she does now.

The four of them pile into the shiny gray Mercedes parked in the circle drive just outside the front entrance. Pat and Sam sit in the back. Wagner drives. And Shelley, introduced as "support" (the designation given on the Institute photo-badge pinned to her dress), rides shotgun with a laptop in her lap and a radio clipped to one shoulder. (Overkill, Pat thinks, noting the cellular phone in the dash.) It is Sam's idea that Pat would feel more "comfortable" with a woman present during meetings that are not "one-on-one." At lunch he told the story of how he had had his "consciousness raised" a couple of years back, when, dining out, he had overheard a group of women talking at a nearby table. One of them had told how she had been in an elevator that morning with six men, the lone woman for a twenty-floor ascent, and of how creeped-out she had been. The others had then chimed in with similar tales. The conversation, Sam said, had "struck" him. He said that before then he had always assumed women felt unsafe with single men rather than a crowd, since by his logic a woman could always count on at least one man to come to her rescue against the depredations of another.... Wagner and Johns had rolled their eyes, but agreed to assign Shelley to "chaperone duty" (as they keep calling it). Shelley looks and acts so Vanna White, though, that Pat has so far taken little "comfort" in her presence.

The car is comfortable and she knows she should be glad for the chance to get out, but Pat is in such an aftermath of confusion that all she can think is that a) it is weird to be going out driving when she is really basically a prisoner, and b) her parents would not approve of the car. As they pass through the outer set of gates she fantasizes flinging open the door and running, and yelling that she's being held prisoner against her will. But at once the idea strikes her as crazy. She imagines that anyone who happened to be around to hear (and there are only cars in this neighborhood, certainly no pedestrians that she's yet spotted) would assume her to be a paranoid schizophrenic and simply ignore her claims. She thinks that is how she herself would likely react were she in their shoes.

They drive south down La Jolla Boulevard. Pat snatches glimpses of the water as it repeatedly enters and leaves their line of vision. They are going to Hillcrest, they told her. Supposedly to look for Joshua.

She has the feeling that what just happened on the top deck was important. Certainly it upset Wagner. If only she could have some time to herself to *think*. But the wine at lunch and all these *people* constantly surrounding her make it just about impossible.

Lying on the chaise lounge, headphones feeding her a much-needed hit of Sinead's power passion, she fell asleep. Stuck in that hospital isolation unit she hadn't slept much during the night. And she wasn't used to drinking wine at lunch. The Big Boys were all inside, having a meeting. (She could just guess about what.) Shelley, nearby, sat at a white metal table, under an umbrella, tapping a keyboard – presumably keeping her under surveillance. Still, closing her eyes and listening to Sinead she could almost believe she was lying in the sun at Torrey Pines beach. The wind felt the same on her skin, and the air smelled of the same salt sea. It was, therefore, *natural* that she fall asleep and dream... about Joshua.

In the dream they were on Torrey Pines Beach after dark, lying on Joshua's old chenille bedspread. The remains of a wood fire smoldered nearby. The pounding rhythm of the surf engulfed them, the way it sometimes did. And Joshua's hands were caressing her balls and penis, and his tongue was sliding between her labia, making her close to crazy with sensation. She pressed her hands against the side of his head, tight. And then slipped her index fingers into his ears. She thought she might be making a lot of noise, but Sinead kept belting out *Nothing compares, nothing compares to you*, again and again and again.

"Pat!" a voice – not Joshua's – dragged her out of the dream.

"Jesus God it's gross! It makes me sick to my stomach, kind of like that creepy feeling I got in sophomore English class, having to look at Mrs. Anderson's flat-as-a-washboard no-titness from two to three o'clock every fucking afternoon. Only this, man, this is really, really *sick!*"

That was Wagner talking, Pat discovered when she opened her eyes. He was staring at her, shaking his head, staring staring staring as if she were the Gorgon and he couldn't take his eyes away though the sight of her was killing him. Really foul stuff kept coming out of his mouth, Major Misogyny – until Sam, after telling him to "Cool it, man," went over to him, grabbed him by the lapels, and warned that if he didn't "chill out" he'd be "yanked from the case."

Pat had no idea what had set Wagner off. But then Dr. Johns said: "Don't you believe in wearing underwear, young lady?" Pat gaped at him, and first wondered how he knew, and then grew suspicious that they had somehow peeked under her skirt while she was sleeping. "If modesty doesn't concern you, perhaps you might be interested to know you're just asking for a bladder infection," he went on. "And if there's one thing women are always getting besides yeast infections, it's bladder infections." And he tsked-tsked at her in that you're-so-disgusting way all adults, no matter their ideological persuasion, have.

"How do you know I'm not wearing underwear?" Pat demanded of him.

Sam came over to her and bent to whisper in her ear. "Your erection is showing."

Astonished, she looked down at her lap and saw her skirt flare up into a point, then as suddenly drop flat. The movement, she noticed, coincided with one of those delicious new genital sensations that had been introduced in the dream. Preoccupied with this revelation, she said (somewhat absently), "It's just that none of my underwear fits right, and larger sizes don't work because then they're too big everywhere else and just slide off."

Pat understands what happened up to this point. Gazing out the window, observing that they are accessing the San Diego Freeway, she can't help but smile at the memory of her having created such a humorous sight, *viz.*, her penis popping up and down, basically out of control. (How much easier, she thinks, not having to worry about the signs of one's sexual arousal showing. This new experience is a little like the kind of practical and psychological hassle you go through when you first start menstruating, or when your breasts are growing and you have to worry about bras, cup-sizes, straps, and the embarrassment of bouncing and all that...)

No, it's what happened next that she doesn't understand. Actually, it was perfectly *natural* for her to put her hand over it – to hide it from view (and to keep it under control). Maybe it was the greasy white look on Wagner's face, or the pursed lips on Baldie's and the echo of Sinead's voice endlessly repeating *Nothing compares, nothing compares to you...* (*not* from her tape-player, which had long since shut off). But when she put her hand on it, it reminded her of putting her hand on Joshua's – maybe because it was through cloth, as she'd always felt his? But also, the pressure of her hand had caused a wonderful, shimmering sensation that ran through her entire body.... And so, smiling (she remembers that she was, because her whole being had in that moment been illuminated with joy), not thinking, she just started rubbing it, gently, with one finger....

Except, of course, that Wagner had then gone *berserk*. And Sam said, "Pat, hey, *cool* that – if you'll just think for a second how you'd feel if *we* did that in front of *you*!"

Which had made her *giggle* (she still doesn't know why) – and say to Baldie off the top of her head, "I guess Freud was wrong, hunh? When he said that little boys feel threatened with castration when they discover that a woman or a girl doesn't have a penis. Because if that were true, wouldn't men feel less threatened when they saw that a woman did have a penis?" At which Wagner, cursing, screaming at her to "shut [her] mouth," charged her. And then suddenly Sam and Shelley were pulling her out of the chaise longue and hustling her off to the bathroom, Sam all the while lecturing her about "behaving" herself and threatening her with "57 different kinds of hell to pay" if she didn't.

What stymies her is that the whole thing makes her want to laugh – and masturbate (both sets of genitals). Never has she in front of another person touched herself in a sexual way. Previously the idea would have horrified her. So why isn't she mortified at having been caught in the act by four people?

When they pass the exit to Interstate 8, Pat speaks for the first time since getting into the car. "Hey, I thought we were going to Hillcrest?"

"We are," Sam says, "but we're going to stop at your place first." He stretches his arm along the back of the seat. "So, tell me something, Pat."

Pat makes a face and turns almost sideways to stare out the window, to put her back to him. She hates it when men use their arms and legs to mark territory in that fake-casual way.

"I've been wondering, given what you said earlier about your reasons for not going to Berkeley or Santa Cruz," Sam plows on anyway, "whether you've told your parents about what's happening to you."

Pat freezes. Most of the time she lay awake in the hospital bed last night had been spent debating whether or not to tell them. Her first thought had been that they would make a big deal about it, would get lawyers, possibly the ACLU, maybe even involve the press. Which would turn her into a freak. And her parents and their collective would probably get hassled, her father's record dragged out. (SEX FREAK'S FATHER SHOT OFF TWO TOES OUTSIDE ARMY INDUCTION CENTER DURING VIETNAM WAR! HISTORY OF FAMILY INSANITY! WAS IT IN THE GENES ALL ALONG?) The winery could get blacklisted, or people might come to associate it with a mysterious virus, thereby washing twenty years of hard work down the tubes....

"Did you even tell them you were seeing Joshua?" Sam presses. "Or are you so estranged from them that – "

Pat rockets back in her seat. "My relationship with my parents is none of your fucking business!" she blazes at him. All that seemingly *casual* conversation on the beach, about college choices, about how *weird* it was that someone who'd taken UC summer courses at Santa Cruz during her last two years in high school, someone with test scores

220 L. TIMMEL DUCHAMP

as exceptional as hers, would go to a place like UCSD when Berkeley would obviously be glad to have her: all that had been simply a fishing expedition.

Sam leans slightly forward and puts his hand on Shelley's headrest. "Could you take down a note for me, Shelley?"

Shelley flicks on the laptop (which Pat hadn't thought could be used literally in one's lap), flips the screen upright and makes several keystrokes. "All right, Dr. Hardwick, I'm all ready to go. Shoot."

Sam checks his Casio. "Two-twelve p.m. Subject continues to display signs of escalating aggression. Take blood sample immediately on return to Institute to have testosterone levels checked. Speculation that t-production has surged since lunch. End note, Shelley." Sam settles back. "And thanks."

"Hah, hah, hah, that's really really cute," Pat jeers, just barely holding onto her temper. But that scene in the bathroom... She supposes that's what he means by aggression. Well if he thinks he can bamboozle her into believing such raging-hormone shit...

"I'm serious," Sam says.

Wagner swings the car off the freeway onto Fifth Avenue. "The sooner she has her operation, the better," he rumbles – then hits the horn in irritation at another driver's braking before giving a turn-signal.

A lump rises in Pat's throat. Without thinking she touches her hand to her lap. Though she was eager enough to get rid of it all only a few hours ago, the thought of losing these new sensations stuns her. They can't *make* her have it all removed, can they?

Whether they can or not, she vows that they won't. And it comes to her, for the first time, that it is all she has left of Joshua.

Ulrike had left a letter in the usual place. Acutely aware of Sam's gaze, Pat pounces on it. The entire crew has swarmed into the cottage, like locusts ready for a good chomp. "What are you doing?" Pat shouts at Wagner when she sees that he's seated himself at her desk and is going through the drawers. Hadn't they seen there was nothing to find when they searched the place last week?

"You let us in yourself, honey," Wagner says, unperturbed. "But don't worry. We won't *take* anything."

Pat rounds on Sam, who's still watching her (probably with designs on the letter). "You tricked me," she accuses.

"Go pack your bag," is all he says.

Shelley follows her into the bedroom, like a shadow. Thinking of how easy it would be to "lose" the letter, Pat stuffs it down the front of her shirt.

When they'd pulled up alongside the "court" of cottages, Sam had told her they were there so that she could pack "a few things" that would make her "stay at the Institute more comfortable." Always thinking of her comfort, that man. What a guy! "For how long are you people holding me?" she nevertheless demanded. "I told you what you wanted to know. *I* kept *my* side of the bargain."

"Bargain?" he repeated, as though incredulous. But then he sidled close and half-whispered, "It'll just be for a couple of days, Pat. So that we can run a few more tests. And make sure the virus doesn't kick anything else up at you. The Institute's more comfortable than the hospital, isn't it? Anyway, I've no doubt you'll be returning to classes on Monday. So if I were you I'd just relax, and enjoy the beach and the food and whatever else we can do for you." And then he leaned past her and opened the door.

Instead of getting out, she said, as though the idea had just occurred to her, "This is crazy, Sam. You know? It's not like this virus is *deadly*. You don't even treat people infected with HIV like this!"

"We don't *know* that it's not deadly," he said very gently. "And more importantly," he went on, his eyes agleam with sudden excitement, "you're the only one known to have it. Imagine if we'd gotten hold of the first case of HIV before it had been trans – " But there he stopped, as though realizing he was giving away more than he'd intended.

Pat throws a few things into a suitcase and heads for the bathroom. The door's got a bolt, and this she at once slides home. Relieved to be alone at last, she settles on the floor against the door and pulls out the letter.

MONDAY EVENING

Pat –

There's so much I have to tell you. (Though I don't know if you'll even get this – that's how little idea I have of what the eff is going on.) First, regret to say I'm off to l.a. as planned. Feel bad about leaving town, even for three days when god knows what your situation really is. But I don't think there's anything here I can do straight off, and then of course my parents have paid a lot for the workshop... Suspect I'll be too worried to get much out of it. If so, I'll exit prematurely.

Hope you won't be pissed at me when I say I did a stupid thing, namely blabbed out some stuff about Joshua before I realized I shouldn't. (Me and my big mouth.) I said, for one thing, that you'd been staying over with him regularly. I also told how you met him at the Quel. (It was their great interest in that that made me wake up, sorry to say.)

I really feel rotten about this. I mean, I don't even know what it is you have. they seemed to think it was ultra-dangerous. Why didn't you tell me, Pat O'Pat? Don't you know I care too much to be scared off? If you had aids I'd be sad, sure, but not phobic for christsake. ('Course, I suppose I could still turn out to have this thing – otherwise why would they have taken a blood sample. And then we'd be in the same boat together, right?)

Nevermind, as you-know-who always said...

Now. The Second Big Thing. God, Pat, I agonized like mad over this one. But I finally decided to do it. I called your parents, and told them about the men who questioned me and took my blood. I mean, it sounds like somebody should know where you are. Since they wouldn't tell me, or let me talk to you on the phone much less visit, how the hell do I know if you're all right? To my nose, the whole thing stinks like rotten fish. And anyway, if you're seriously ill, they need to know. I mean hell, Pat, you may not like them being so political and all, but you're close, still, in spite of the differences. Considering how my folks are – busy in their respective remarried lives, not all that interested in the detritus of divorce... Anyway. The bad thing is, I knew only your gynecologist's name. Couldn't tell them anything else. But they're flying down here tomorrow. Probably they'll find you before you find this letter.

Anyway. If I don't hear from you by the time I'm back, I'll join forces with your parents and tear this damned county apart looking for you. (And that's a promise.) If only, though, I had your address... (But then I might as well wish we were both telepathic, right?)

Hang in there kid –

– U.

Knuckles hit the door, making it rattle against Pat's back. "Pat?" Shelley calls. "Are you all right? You've been in there a long time."

Feeling sick to lose this small scrap of not-aloneness, Pat rips the letter into shreds, drops the shreds into the bowl and flushes. Ulrike hadn't known when she wrote the letter that she tested out negative. What the hell could she be thinking and feeling? And if she knew? What would she think *then?* Sharing a cottage with *that?*

Pat opens the medicine chest and pulls out the toiletries she wants to pack. Seeing the tube of Chapstick makes her think of lipstick and the old trick of writing messages on mirrors. But neither she nor Ulrike wears lipstick. Or uses eyebrow pencil or mascara. Her eyes rove the shelves....

This time a fist lays into the door. "Pat?" Sam shouts. "I want some voice contact, woman. And now! Or we'll come in through the window!"

Pat unscrews the cap on the tube of toothpaste. "You wouldn't fit!" she yells back. And then she quite carefully dabs GLEASON INST. OFF LA JOL BLVD, BEACHFRONT on the plain metal surface lining the inside of the cabinet door.

"What the hell are you doing in there, taking a bath?"

"No, of course not. I'm too horny for that!" Pat shouts back – but then spoils it by dissolving into giggles.

"Shit, man, she's *masturbating!*" It's Wagner's voice, right beside the door. Pat imagines the three of them crowded against it, competing for a place to lay their ears.

Very very gently Pat clicks the cabinet door shut. Then she checks the bowl to make sure the paper all flushed, gathers up the toiletries, slides the bolt back, and flings open the door. She's disappointed when only Wagner falls into the room.

Sam hustles her out to the car. "Surely you must have some memory of how you got from your house to his?" he says when Wagner asks for instructions.

Pat sighs; she studies her nails; she puts her hand to her throat. "Really, I don't. It was always dark. And we were on a motorcycle. From a motorcycle everything looks the same, nothing looks familiar. As I said before, it was one of those residential sections, somewhere in the vicinity of the zoo."

Sam leans his head back against the seat. "Liar," he mutters. But instead of trying to strike another bargain with her, he simply tells

Wagner to drive to the other side of the park, near the zoo. They will "pick up the trail there," he says.

All the time he's watching, waiting, for something to show in her face. A facial twitch or a verbal slip are their only chances of finding Joshua. Which is why she's going to keep her nose glued to the window, out of sight, and her mouth shut whenever Joshua is mentioned.

Joshua's kisses on her neck, and the soft stroking of his hand on her belly, wake her, and his special smell fills her with recognition and joy. For a few seconds, in the dark, she's confused. Her senses tell her she's in Joshua's bed, and that Joshua himself is lying beside her, his hands and lips caressing and kissing her. But as she comes fully awake she knows that cannot be. She has a very clear and distinct memory of going to sleep in the room they'd given her in the Gleason Institute, of lying in a proper bed made with starched hospital sheets. Yet the sheet now covering her body is soft, unstarched cotton, and reaching out over the edge of the bed she can knock the wood floor with her knuckles. And when she strains to hear the ocean, she hears instead a car passing, as she had not done either while sitting up in bed reading or lying flat with the lights out, trying to go to sleep.

But she's so happy to have Joshua back she gives herself over to the delight of feeling, smelling, tasting, and touching him, without trying to decide whether she's dreaming, hallucinating, or somehow really with him. She murmurs his name between kisses, and it becomes an incantation she chants again and again and again in honor of the dream, hallucination or miracle she wants the incantation to preserve.

It's when he's pulling the nightgown over her head that she realizes he's completely naked. No underwear, no pajama bottoms, no sweat pants keep her now from touching him. And how strange and delicious it is, taking in through her fingers such riches, warm and mysterious and slippery to the touch, folds and bulges and odd textures to stroke and penetrate. "Do you like it? Are you glad?" Joshua whispers, bringing the first words (other than names) into the night.

"It's beautiful," Pat whispers back. "But will you let me see?"

Joshua switches on the reading lamp he keeps on the floor next to his mattress and focuses the light on the wall. They stare for a long time into one another's eyes. "I'm sorry I had to leave for a while," he says finally. And then he lies back and spreads his legs wide.

Pat examines him with amazement. (Is this what *she* looks like?) She's aware that she has no live experience of male genitalia with which to compare it, but she knows this is the way it's *supposed* to be. At last, she thinks, she knows what is wrong with human beings. Sexual dimorphism, it is obvious, has been nothing but a disaster!

"I just couldn't stand it any longer, being around you while I was waiting," Joshua says. The smooth full lips under his mustache are curved into a smile, in amusement at the intentness of her examination, she thinks. "I guess I should have told you in advance, so that you wouldn't have exposed yourself to that doctor. But I was afraid you'd be horrified if you knew. And so I just couldn't." Joshua takes her hand. "I hope you're not mad at me for not asking you first?"

Pat imagines herself drowning in his dark liquid eyes. "I'm so happy to see you," she says. She ignores the hard knot forming in her stomach, she keeps herself from thinking much about his admission that it is he who's caused her to change. "And I love it, the way I am now. Though at first I hated it and felt like a freak, now I wouldn't give it up for anything." She frowns. "Except, maybe my freedom."

Joshua gestures at the room around her. "You don't need to worry about that," he says. "Haven't you noticed, I've sprung you?"

She glances around at the dimly lit walls, at the window exactly where it is supposed to be, at the dust bunnies dancing in the slight draft coming in through the window, at the cracks in the ceiling and even the cobweb in the corner where it has been allowed to remain for months, undisturbed (since Joshua does not believe in killing spiders that aren't poisonous). She *knows* she's not at the Gleason Institute, she *knows* she's not dreaming. She peers at Joshua speculatively. If he could induce her body to grow a second set of genitals, perhaps "springing" her while she's asleep isn't such an impossible feat to have pulled off. He does look beautiful lying there, staring up at her. And his body is so... *there.*

She takes his hand and brings it to her mouth. "They're just dying to remove everything they think doesn't belong there," she remarks between kisses to his palm. "But I won't let them, Joshua. Just as I wouldn't let them find you." Almost breathless, she turns his hand over and kisses the back of it knuckle by knuckle, and then licks and sucks his index finger.

For the next couple of hours they don't stop to talk. It's all so fantastic Pat wants to do it again and again in every combination she can think of. Later, though, when they are lying quietly, drifting almost into sleep, her mind resumes work. "What a shame we can't both screw one another simultaneously," she says, sighing. "Don't you think that would be *neat*?"

"In most things human, precise complementarity is disastrous," Joshua observes, as though stating a universally acknowledged truth. "Hadn't you noticed? Also, though in theory it would be nice, geometrically it would be a little like trisecting the angle." Pat giggles at the image, and Joshua joins her. "But we call *this* symmetrical equivalence. Given this sexual arrangement, we can all get pregnant, can all impregnate, can all even do it solo, through artificial insemination. Though of course since it wouldn't be too good for the collective gene pool, self-impregnation is virtually taboo."

"Like incest," Pat says, then thinks that "doing it solo" would really mean that the same genes would be reproduced, rather than a possible slew of recessives. So the analogy doesn't quite hold up. But this *we* that Joshua refers to, as though a whole community of persons are as he is himself and has made her to be... It is time, she thinks, to pin him down. "Who *is* this 'we' you're referring to?" she asks him. "Are you saying there are others like you?" She has, since he admitted he had changed her, been thinking that his chromosomes must have mutated, and have mysteriously developed the power to cause hers to mutate, too. But then there's the mystery of how he got her from the Institute to his room (and without waking her, yet)...

Joshua props himself on an elbow and gazes down into her face. "If I told you any of it, you'd think I was handing you a *National Enquirer* special."

That cracks Pat up. And so she has to tell him the conversation she overheard, in which Sam said that when he started reading the file Lewis had faxed him, he'd thought it was a hoax, *National Enquirer* style. "So," she concludes, "I don't think you have to worry about my dismissing it out of hand – considering how improbable *this* – " she gestures at his and her own genitals – "is."

"First, there aren't many of us left here." Joshua's face grows sober. "Which is why I broke the rules and got involved with you. I was born here – on this planet, I mean – but this is not where my people come from. Before I was born, a subset of our constellation – this is hard to explain, I'm not sure what the best English equivalences are. By constellation I mean something remotely like a guild, or association – but no. The thing is, it's more like a tribe, to which a certain kind of work has been allotted...." Joshua frowns. "But 'tribe' must sound primitive to your ears, and it's not that...." He fidgets with the top hem of the sheet. "Well, a number of us, from the group that is meant to do comparative sorts of studies – sort of a combination of your disciplines of anthropology, sociology, psychology, history, and philosophy with quite a lot of the sciences thrown in – anyway, a group of us arrived here about 100 years ago. Humans are especially interesting to us because they're physiologically very similar – except that they're sexually dimorphic." He smiles, almost shyly, and blinks his so sweet brown eyes slowly at her. "You can't imagine how weird my people find it that most of the large animals on your planet are sexually dimorphic. Though actually, I probably can't imagine how weird it is to them, either, since I was raised here, and so have been used to it all my life."

It's all coming so fast. It's fantastic, but one part of her, the part coldly watching, doesn't feel all that surprised. Still, she knows she should be astounded and disbelieving (even after all that has happened to her). "You're saying you – your family or whatever – are from *another planet!*" she exclaims. And the watcher inside her thinks of how he told her nothing about this before, of how he did not warn her that her body would be changing (much less ask her permission to change it)....

He half-laughs; his eyes meeting hers get even shyer. "You see, I told you. Anyway, the problem is that most of us have died. Which we weren't supposed to do. I mean, ordinarily our lifespan is several of your centuries. But disease and all sorts of accidents have been a problem." He shrugs. "I suppose if my constellation had realized that before the window-for-transit next opened humans would develop the capacity for destroying the planet any number of ways, we probably wouldn't have come. Anyway, we're stuck here. And those few of us born here who have survived are in need of mates. But of those available to my age-cohort all are forbidden me, because they are too closely affinial. And so I knew that if I wanted to have a child I'd have to mate with a human to do so. And though it's forbidden to mate with humans..."

It wildly elates her to think that not only did he choose *her*, but that he went against his own people in doing so. She grabs his free wrist. "You're saying you broke your people's laws when you got involved with me?"

His smile is so warm it touches even the watcher. She wonders how he rates with his own people, and whether they will accept what he has done. "Well, yes. But I think it will be all right. Because, you see, there are so few of us left here. And the travel window won't open until after I've passed the age at which I can bear children."

Pat flops onto her back and stares up at the dimly lit ceiling. "I can't handle this. You're saying *you* want to get pregnant by *me*?"

Joshua nods. "I suppose that sounds strange to you – because you think of me as a male. But remember, I'm no more a male than you are."

She turns her head and gestures. "But your mustache and beard. And you don't have developed breasts."

"All secondary characteristics, Pat. I chose them when I elected to present myself as a male. Since one must choose one or another on this world. And we've learned the hard way it's too risky to present as females. Too many times those of us presenting as females have been sexually attacked – and discovered. In addition to being less vulnerable to rape, men have greater mobility and access than women. It's simply safer for us to look like men."

"Does that mean I'm going to be growing out a beard, too?"

Joshua laughs. "Only if you want to."

She shakes her head. "I don't see how. Controlling hormones and all that..."

"It's easy. I'll show you." He leans over and kisses her lips very lightly. "Well, what do you think? Am I a liar or a lunatic?"

Pat throws her arms around him. "A charmer," she retorts. "I'm completely taken in." Or almost, the watcher murmurs. Because how can you really trust someone who has lied so massively, who chooses manipulation over honest discussion and decision-making? Half-smiling, she strokes his flat furry stomach and tries to imagine it swelling under her hands with the persistent fullness of pregnancy. (With *her* child.) She kisses his shoulder. "There's just one thing...."

He withdraws a little to look into her face. "What's that?"

"Will you please just say the words, 'I want to have your baby'?"

Joshua's eyes gleam. "Pat, darling, I want to have your baby," he repeats with utter gravity.

Pat laughs hysterically. Now *that*, she thinks, is true *National Enquirer*. But when she finishes laughing, she sits up so as to be more serious. "Another thing," she says, "that I absolutely have to know.

How can we be here in your room? When I first woke I thought I must be dreaming, or maybe hallucinating. How *could* we be *here*?"

Joshua sits up, too. "I can't tell you. The strictures against showing our technology to humans are even more serious than those forbidding me to mate with you." He frowns. "Which reminds me. Pat, you must not ever have sexual intercourse with another human, or give others your blood." He gestures at her genitals. "It would spread, you know."

"I know." She bites her lip. More decisions he's making for her, about what to do with *her* body? I'm not sure I like your deciding for me that I'm going to be permanently monogamous." She frowns. "But wait a minute, that's not how you changed me, is it. Because we never did have intercourse. So how *did* you do it?"

Joshua hesitates a few seconds before answering. "You remember that time you cut yourself chopping onions?"

Pat shakes her head. "No, not really..."

"Well you did. It was, I think, in January. And I kissed and licked the cut." His lips pressed tightly together. "Because I forgot. It completely slipped my mind that I could change you that way – though all the while I was being so excruciatingly careful in our sexual relations...."

Pat's stomach drops. After maybe half a minute she asks in a very small voice: "You mean you didn't *mean* to?" So he *didn't* 'specially choose her?

Joshua sighs. "I'm afraid not." His eyes meet hers. "But I'm glad I did. My people are scattered all over the world – mostly in Asia. A person gets lonely. And, as I said, now I'll be able to bear a child."

Pat nods slowly. So it was an accident. But he came back for her anyway, didn't he. And surely that counts for a lot....

Dawn is breaking when they finally settle down with the intention to sleep. In the morning, she thinks (even as she's watching the walls lighten), she'll call the collective, and they'll tell her where her parents are staying. They'll raise hell for her, and the bastards won't be able to touch her. All of her genitals will be left intact, of that she is determined. And they will not re-incarcerate her. Next Monday she'll start classes, right on schedule. They don't *know* it's a virus. And whether it should be considered harmful or not is in any case a social, not a medical, issue.

Lying with her head on Joshua's chest, drifting off to sleep, she thinks how easy it would be to spread the virus. His people are here to study humans' innate perversity. It seems only fair to take advantage of her privilege, to spread the wealth around to others. She would be a traitor to her own kind if she didn't. So what if she spoils Joshua's and his people's research project? Humans did not ask to be studied. And what could be a more massive violation of privacy than to treat an entire sentient species as research subjects without their knowing consent?

Drifting to the edge of sleep, Pat imagines Wagner pregnant. Would it change even his kind? But how could it not?

A little fear scrapes up that cold pit in her stomach again. Joshua won't approve when he finds out. And Sam will know who's responsible. But she struck no "bargains" with either of them. And Joshua did not even ask her first. And besides, the privilege Joshua's bestowed on her confers its obligations. She may not choose to bear a child in her womb like Joshua, but she can be another kind of mother, mother to an age, mother to the Age of the Hermaphrodite....

At nineteen, yet.

When Pat drops off to sleep she's smiling. It's a big job, changing the world. But she's ready for it.

R. GARCIA Y ROBERTSON
The Other Magpie

■■■
■□■
■■■

A true description of the aboriginal American Indian dare not be put in print. Novelists of the future will give him a new character; like the Spanish Cid Campeador, the Indians will be knighted and put on horseback after his death. But as the Buddha says, "Amid the brambles a lily may bloom."

  – Capt. E.F. Ware, 7th Iowa Cavalry

MEDICINE WHEEL

The Other Magpie knelt on a dusty knoll, sharpening her knife against a flat rock, her heart beating like a rabbit's. Spring starvation stretched her dark skin taut. Ribs and hips poked at her doeskin dress; cheekbones stood out beneath eyes hollow from crying. She mourned her only brother – scalped and killed by the Sioux.

Spread around her were the contents of her weasel-skin Medicine bag: an antelope's tooth, a breath feather, two stone shells from the days when the prairie was a sea, the bright body of a stuffed woodpecker – all the power she had gathered in her fifteen winters. It seemed small and pitiful, pitted against the Faceless Destroyer. Dead eyes on the little woodpecker watched as she sharpened the knife – the slick scrape of iron on stone hid every other sound. Above her rose the black-white tops of the Big Horns; below the knoll stood the tall hourglass tipis of the Kicks Belly Crow.

She stopped. The shining blade was silent. From out of the woods came the drumming of a live woodpecker – the bird's fearless pounding shouted out to her, "Be brave before the world!"

Listening to the living bird, she told herself, "I will cry no more. I will not fear pain, or give in to death." Reaching up, she hacked at her black braids. Feeling the rough fringe of hair brush her shoulders, she promised, "I will mourn my brother as long as my hair is short."

She pressed her left hand hard against the flat rock, splaying her fingers. The butcher knife had been her great grandmother's; decades of women's sharpening had worn the blade down to a steel sliver. Laying the bright edge against the little finger of her left hand, just below the first joint, she struggled to control her fear, trying to feel only grief for her dead brother. Belly muscles tightened as she tasted coldness in the air. There would be more snow before Sundance time.

She pulled the blade back in a single convulsive stroke. Her grandmother's knife sliced skin, then bone, as easily as it carved grizzly meat. Shock shuddered down her spine. Half a finger lay next to the severed braids. She told herself, "As long as I have a left hand, I will remember him – if I grow old and gray, grandchildren will know I lost a brother."

Horrified by what she had done to her guiltless hand, the Other Magpie thought how weak she was – "But with my brother beside me, I was strong. I was everything, brother and sister, man and woman, the two halves to the hoop of life." Now the hoop was cut, like her finger.

Using teeth and her right hand, she tore a thong from her half-sleeve, tying it around her finger to stop the bleeding. Working one-handed was awkward, but that too reminded her of her lost brother. Refilling her Medicine bag, she placed the braids and fingertip in with her antelope tooth, breath feather, stone shells, and dead woodpecker. Lightheaded with grief and loss of blood, she got up to look for Finds-and-Kills, the only person in the Kick-Belly camp likely to help her. Her hurting hand left red stains on everything it touched.

Afternoon shadows stretched out from the tipis. She found Finds-and-Kills at the edge of camp, sitting on a cutbank by Rotten Grass Creels, humming a Medicine song as she mended a moccasin with a long steel needle. Finds-and-Kills had big hands, big feet, and other body peculiarities that separated her from most women. This separateness was why the Other Magpie sought her out; the Magpie needed a woman who had men's Medicine in her, who knew the Sundance and understood death in battle. Finds-and-Kills had the Medicine to open the Way Between the Worlds, the trail that led to the Camp of the Dead.

Sitting down next to her friend, the Magpie trailed her hand in the tumbling water, cleaning and numbing her aching finger. "My brother is dead," she declared, "killed and scalped by Sioux."

'This is so." Finds-and-Kills used a high piping voice. Her coarse features were hardly even feminine, but she had done her damnedest to improve them, tattooing circles on her forehead and a line from lips to chin – painfully determined to look more womanly. "That is why they call them Sioux" – she made the slash across the throat that means "Sioux" in sign talk.

"I must do something for him."

Finds-and-Kills looked up, shocked by the sense of urgency that went beyond mourning. She nodded toward the Other Magpie's cropped hair and cut finger. "You have done what a sister should."

"I must do more." The Magpie meant to have her brother back, even though Death stood between them.

"You cannot be more than a sister," Finds-and-Kills reminded her. The brother-sister taboo was not strong among the Crows, but everyone had a horror of sexes reared in the same tipi becoming too close. "The dead are dead. We tell them, 'Go, do not come back.'" Crows were convinced that death could be catching – no one, not even the Magpie, dared use her brother's name now that he was dead.

"I miss him," the Magpie insisted. "I do not care if he is dead. I must see him again, if only to say goodbye." Coming from a Crow, this was dangerous blasphemy – like a drunk Baptist damning salvation.

"Nah, nah, nah, nah." Now Finds-and-Kills sounded like an old woman. "The Other Magpie cares for nothing but herself and her brother. She is the girl who closed the smoke flaps on the council lodge, who chased a buffalo cow into camp. She is the young woman for whom no man is good enough. The dead go to the Land Beyond. We do not ask them back."

The Other Magpie made the "no" sign. "You have the power to help me. You have the Sundance Medicine. Last spring the men dragged you out to cut the Sundance tree. I have cut off my hair, and cut off my finger – but I cannot cut off my *brother*." She could not stand to think of him lying scalped and naked on the prairie, feeding the coyotes – she could not let their life together end like that.

Finds-and-Kills asked politely if she had gone insane, telling her, "You are far too extravagant, even in grief."

The Magpie smiled, "I am far too extravagant in everything – that is my charm." She had a wild beauty that the big woman both loved and envied, the beauty of a strong brown foal with dainty feet. If it were in Finds-and-Kills to love another woman, she would have loved the Other Magpie, and the Magpie counted on that attraction. She could be merciless in love. Dozens of men had brought ponies to her tipi, only to be turned away: chiefs' sons with round arms, seasoned warriors with many wives – all had been sent home with their horses.

Finds-and-Kills sighed, "Your skin smells of pine and sage. If I were a man, I would be outside your tipi, waiting with a blanket whenever you went for wood or water. But one day this wildness will kill you."

"Better to die young and wild, than old and sick in a winter lodge."

No Crow could argue with that. Finds-and-Kills got up and put on her moccasins. "Wait here. I will help you." Watching the big woman walk off toward camp, the Magpie noticed that one moccasin was still unmended – Finds-and-Kills left two different prints in the dust, one torn and the other whole. Sitting, waiting, soaking her finger, the Magpie knew that she was pressing her Medicine. But what else could she do? She would not give in, even to Death, the Faceless Destroyer, the striding terror whose war club is raised over all our heads.

As the sun set behind the Big Horns, Finds-and-Kills came back, carrying what a man would take to search for power: a bone pipe, a plug of short tobacco, and a buffalo robe tanned with the hair on. Wrapped in the robe was her rifle, a Sharps Sporter chambered for half-inch shells – her shooting bag held two dozen .50-70 centerfire cartridges, stamped out at the Frankford Arsenal.

The Magple cut her brother's trail ponies from the herds, two sorrels and a gray. They had always shared horses, and he had been an only son, indulged in everything. His ponies were all fast and strong, but not fast enough – now his favorite war pony was picketed beside some Sioux lodge. In bright twilight, the two women rode up the Big Horn River, past the ghostly remains of Fort C.T. Smith, burned by the Sioux under Red Cloud and Crazy Horse. Chorus frogs sang by the water, trilling like a thumbnail run over the teeth of a comb. Owls hooted, filling the burnt timbers with the cries of lost souls. Mournful hoots meant that the Magpie was on the path to the Beyond, the way she wanted to go.

Dawn found them deep in the canyon of the Big Horn. Here, half-mile cliffs towered over the river like giant painted lodges, striped with sandstone. For a time, four ravens flew behind them. The Magpie could tell by their calls that the birds hoped that the women were buffalo hunters.

The land tilted up under their ponies' hooves. By the time they reached the timbered slopes of Medicine Mountain, atop Porcupine Creek, even the ravens had turned back. Blue peaks rose one above the other, like the backs of giant buffalo. Now the Magpie could hear the Beyond calling in the cries of eagles and in the wind whistling off black pine tops, between the mountains and the sky.

Near the treeline, they hobbled their ponies, walking the rest of the way. On the rocky shoulder of Medicine Mountain, the Magpie saw the gateway to the Spirit World. The spokes of a great stone Medicine Wheel poked up through the windblown snow – twenty-eight spokes; the number of nights in a moon, the number of days in a woman's cycle, the number of poles in a Sundance Lodge. A stone hub stood in the center. Six cairns marked the midsummer sunrise and sunset, and the risings of Sirius, Rigel, and Aldebaran

Finds-and-Kills gave her the pipe and tobacco, telling her in a low deep voice, "This is as far as I will go. Stay here. Seek a vision, mourn your brother, but remember that you are letting go. Do not say his name. Do not call him back." The Magpie did not answer, already observing a holy silence. She wrapped her buffalo robe about her, hair side in, planting herself beside the Medicine Wheel, feeling the sacredness of the place. Her brother would come for her here if she waited long enough. Finds-and-Kills lit a fire and then left.

Darkness crept out of the earth, swallowing the light. Watching the first and brightest stars come out, the Magpie felt her frailty. She smoked to greet the stars, lighting Finds-and-Kills' pipe, holding it aloft, letting the winds fan the flames, sharing her smoke with the sky. Between puffs, she stared at the Medicine Wheel, waiting for a vision. Her fire was fixed up Crow fashion, logs laid with only their ends touching; every so often she pushed a little more of one log into the fire – making the wood burn longer, giving her something to do.

Stars wheeled overhead. Sirius and the Seven Sisters set. The Hanging Road shone like a band of frost in the sky. She could see how the world moved in circles, with the great stone wheel matching the spinning heavens overhead. Her mind rolled with the night, but her brother did not come. Finally, a great square of four stars rose in the east; behind it came the light, blotting out the night.

At noon, the sun beat down on the snow. Finds-and-Kills came with fresh wood for the fire, and gave the Other Magpie a sip from her water bag. The Magpie was thankful, but said nothing that might break the Medicine. The next nights were worse. Her fire went out.

No stars kept her company – the Magpie was blinded from staring all day at the gleaming white blanket covering the Medicine Wheel. Numb to the cold, she could only hear the night birds and smell the mountain scent of pine pitch and bear grass. Her stomach felt small and empty. Her body was lighter than a breath feather, but the barrier between here and the Beyond is not easily broken.

Strength ebbed. In the cavernous darkness, she lost track of days and nights, no longer knowing how long she had gone without sleeping and eating. Dreams invaded her blindness, bright flashes and moving shadows. Defeat closed in. "I have lost," she thought bitterly, but she did not have the strength to leave. Death had claimed her brother – now she felt the Faceless Destroyer coming for her. Tears fell from snow-blind eyes. Unwilling to die alone, the Other Magpie whispered her brother's name, the name that no one had dared speak since the day he died – calling on him to come for her.

A spirit wind swept over the Medicine Wheel, opening her sightless eyes. She saw neither night nor day, but a strange in-between where the snow was black and the sky was white. Raven's-wing clouds hung overhead, and the Medicine Wheel was a great gray web, stretched over black snow. Out of the center of that web staggered a wraith in worn moccasins and ragged leggings. Death came for her wearing her brother's stricken face – ash-white skin stopped above his eyebrows, black naked bone shown through the circle made by a Sioux scalping knife.

"*Sister,*" he moaned, opening his hands, showing the ragged wound in his chalk-white chest. "*why have you called me?*"

She reached out. Their hands met but did not touch. "I could not say goodbye without seeing you again."

"*You called me back. I am lost. I cannot enter the Camp of the Dead. Do you like what you see?*"

The Magpie hated what she saw. She wanted to look away, ashamed to have called him back, but you cannot shut your eyes to a vision. "I did not do this to you."

"*You called me back. Now I wander, without a robe against the cold, without hair to cover my head.*" Her brother's voice rose, filling her with the shrill force of his suffering. "*I cannot enter the Beyond without some token of honor.*"

"What do you need?" She was ready to give anything – her hair and fingertip seemed trivial compared to his loss. "What token of honor?"

"I must have a Sioux scalp."

The Magpie wanted to tell him how impossible that was, but her tongue was twisted from thirst. She was trapped by her own Medicine – having called him back, how could she dare deny him?

He started to shrink and recede, saying, *"Help me, sister. Help me go whole into the Beyond."* She tried to rise, to go to him. Tottering, she stumbled and fell.

At noon on the fourth day, Finds-and-Kills found her stretched out beside the high Medicine Wheel.

> Men won't tell about the woman who rode with Three Stars to the Rosebud battle, because she was a wild one, with no man; bad and brave. People called her the Other Magpie.
> – Pretty Shield, Crow Medicine Woman

THE ROSEBUD

By starving her body and staying awake, the Magpie had pushed her spirit into the Shadow World. She recovered slowly, lying in a wickiup Finds-and-Kills had made out of bent boughs. The wickiup fire made her limbs burn. The least light sent sparks flying into her eyes. She heard Finds-and-Kills shuffle about in the blackness like a mother bear, and felt her friend's thick fingers flick snow into her eyes, moistening and soothing.

When the Magpie had eaten and slept, and her eyes could stand the burning daylight, the two women rode back down the Big Horn. Chickadees called out to them, saying, "Summer's near."

At the Kick-Belly camp, the Magpie's parents saw her shorn hair and missing finger joint, and assumed that she had been in the hills mourning her brother. As their daughter grew older and wilder, they'd learned to put the best interpretation on her wanderings – what could be worse than having a grown daughter hanging around the tipi, refusing to marry and behaving like a boy? Asking no questions, her father collected his son's ponies and gave them away, to show the family's grief and to give his ghost no reason to return.

It was already too late. The Magpie had ridden his horses to the Medicine Wheel and called his name. Her family's cut-down tipi, short hair, and deliberate poverty were constant reminders of her brother's wretched condition. Unless she avenged him, he would never be the strong handsome man she remembered from life.

But freeing him was a crushing obligation. How was she to get her hands on a Sioux scalp? Wife Stealing Time was over, and the first war parties had gone out. The Yellow-eye soldier chief, No-Hip-Bone, had come upriver in a Fire Boat, asking for Crow wolves to help the Long Knives find the Sioux. Two boys barely older than her, named Curly and Grandmother's Knife, had gone with No-Hip-Bone, to meet Son of the Morning Star on the Yellowstone. They had no brothers to avenge, but they went because they were boys. The Magpie complained at the unfairness of this.

Finds-and-Kills had no sympathy, "You have done too much already. Stay in camp. Mourn your brother. You have no gun, and no horse. You are no Woman Chief, to slip into Sioux Country with a skinning knife and come back with a scalp."

To prove her point, Curly and Grandmother's Knife came trudging back into camp a few days later, saying that the Crow who went with No-Hip-Bone had lost all their horses – "Sioux swam the Yellowstone and came right into camp. The Long Knives could not tell Sioux from Crow, and let them have our ponies." The horseless Crows had been cold and miserable, with no women to cook or pitch tipis, lining up every morning to be counted by the Long Knives. The Magpie could see that there was no profit in joining No-Hip-Bone's Long Knives – but at night she still heard her brother's cries in the hoots of owls and in the wind howling between the tipi ears.

In the Moon When Leaves are Full, at Sundance time, a strange Snake rode into camp. She knew at once that he was a Snake, because Snake men are short and shabby but make a tremendous show. Soon the Magpie heard a Caller going around. Rattler, the Great Snake himself, had invited the Kick-Bellies to join a war party against the Sioux. Rattler's invitation was bound to be accepted. Unlike the Long Knives, Rattler did not dither about, or do things backward. If Rattler said that he would fight the Sioux, he would fight the Sioux. He would not waste mornings lining up and counting his warriors. And if Rattler's Snakes went alone against the Sioux, the Crows would never be able to forget it. Snakes would see to that.

Late that night, the Other Magpie sat in the family lodge, listening to her parents sleep, and watching sparks fly up from the fire, following the spiraling lodge poles into the Beyond. The moon was nearly full – perfect for pulling smoke poles out of tipi ears – but she was not that sort of wild girl anymore.

Her wildness must now have a purpose, even if it meant joining Rattler's war party with just a skinning knife. Lifting the lodge cover, she slipped out to where Finds-and-Kills picketed her ponies. Taking two trail ponies, a black mare and a paint, she left a bloody braid tied to a picket pin, so her friend would know who had the horses.

Men had gathered near the ruins of Fort Smith, stripped for war. Their muscles stood out in the half light like the humps on a buffalo herd. The Snake was not with them, but a half-breed named Grabber told them that Long Knives were waiting for Rattler south of the Tongue. The Magpie went with them, crossing the headwaters of the Little Big Horn by moonlight.

Day dawned hot and dry. Men looked her over. She hoped that her shorn hair and cut finger spoke for her – telling them that she was not just tired of being a virgin, looking for education and excitement. By dawn light, she saw how few they were.

There were famous warriors among them, like Flathead Woman and Alligator-Stands-Up. Plenty Coups had brought his Burnt Mouth Crazy Dogs, and Bull Snake was leading some Lumpwoods Without Sweethearts, but she saw only three chiefs – Old Crow, Medicine Crow, and Good Heart. Up ahead, the Sioux would be gathering in their thousands – Sitting Bull, Crazy Horse, Crow King, Red Top, Lame Deer, Big Road, and Runs-the-Enemy would be waiting with their bands, along with hundreds of Cheyenne.

Bull Snake dropped back to ride beside her – his broad forehead painted white with clay. He was as near perfect as a man could be, tough as teak, not too short, not too tall, with a straight nose and smooth face. His hands and feet were small as a woman's, smaller than Finds-and-Kills's He was everything a woman could want – with four wives to prove it; his gaze charmed females as easily as a snake charms a chickadee.

He gave her a cool glance. "We need no nervous virgins. This is Sundance time. The grass is thick in the bottoms, and the Sioux come together like buffalo in rut." He was half boasting, half hoping to scare her.

She made the sign that means, "I know that."

"Go back," Bull Snake advised. When your brother was alive, no man's horses were good enough to win you. He turned aside every offer. But now he is dead, and you know nothing about battle or scalp taking."

"I can learn," she retorted, twisting her drag rope around her hands, refusing to be turned aside.

Bull Snake snorted and kicked his pony, going back to be with his Lumpwoods. It was unseemly for a handsome war chief to argue with a silly virgin.

Crossing over a series of ridges, they descended the bluffs and forded the Tongue. There were no Long Knives on the south bank. Men spread out to look for sign. Near the mouth of Prairie Dog Creek, they found iron-shod prints and mounds of firewood – showing that the Yellow-eyes had camped there – and also several arrows fletched with turkey feathers. Long wavy lines snaked down their shafts, and they were not poorly notched like Sioux arrows – the men all agreed that they were Cheyenne. Hostile Cheyenne had met the Long Knives on the Tongue, warning them away, or challenging them to come over – either way, the Long Knives had turned and headed back in the direction of their forts along the Platte Road.

For most of the men, this meant that the war party was over. Old Crow said he would go south with Grabber and look for the Long Knives. Men agreed that this was fine for Old Crow, who did not have many moons left and was clearly senile to trust a guide like Grabber – a half-breed who promised much and delivered nothing.

The Other Magpie sat on her borrowed horse, watching the war party melt in the morning sun. She was torn between duty to her brother and fear of being left alone in incredibly dangerous country.

Bull Snake declared that Crazy Dogs and scared virgins could run away – "I will do some hunting." He made a nonchalant show of crossing the Tongue to look for breakfast.

That decided her. Death could not be worse than coming home shame-faced and hearing the Lumpwoods sing about her. She dismounted and watered her ponies, rubbing them down with bunches of bluestem.

The war party dwindled to a dozen nervous young Lumpwoods Without Sweethearts, sitting in a circle, playing cards, and laying bets on who would return first: Bull Snake, Old Crow, and Grabber, or the Cheyenne and Sioux. None supposed they would see any Long Knives.

They kept looking at her and laughing, then one got up and walked over. He wore pink body paint with silver zig-zags, and she could smell the sweat on his limbs.

Loosening the blanket about his waist, he dropped it at her feet, nodding toward the low willows by the river – "Virgin, come into the bushes. You can keep the blanket when we are done." He told her that he had the virility of a rutting bull, and that any girl could count herself lucky to begin with him.

She replied politely that she would not even defecate under the same bush with him. Raising her voice so that the others could hear, she held up her shorn finger, "I do not want your blankets, or what is beneath your breechcloths – I want one of you ready-to-die Lumpwoods to avenge my brother! The man who gets me a Sioux scalp may bring ponies to my parents' lodge." She doubted that a dozen Lumpwoods could come up with even a lock of Sioux hair, but it was worth a try.

The Lumpwoods laughed, making the pinwheel motion beside their heads to show that she was crazy – the Other Magpie was a wellknown man hater. The smiling brave picked up his blanket and went back to the card game.

From the bluff above came a Coyote call that meant that a rider was approaching. Lumpwoods scrambled up to see who had won – but the arriving rider was not Cheyenne or Sioux, and not Bull Snake or Old Crow. It was Finds-and-Kills, riding down from the north with her Sharps Sporter across her lap.

She dismounted, thanking the Magpie for taking care of her horses, then saying, "It was silly of you to slip off on the vague hope of meeting the Long Knives." She reminded the Magpie how poorly things had gone for the Crows who went with No-Hip-Bone.

"This war party is with Rattler's Snakes," the Magpie insisted. "It will be different."

"Different does not always mean better – with Snakes, it may mean a whole lot worse. Besides, I see no war party" – Finds-and-Kills nodded toward the card player – "just a handful of Lumpwoods Without Sweethearts playing Red Dog for pony stakes."

Before the Magpie could reply, the Coyote call sounded again. Bull Snake came splashing back across the river, a dead buck slung over his horse's withers. Without a word he dropped the deer between the arguing women, then dismounted to smoke with the Lumpwoods. The effect on Finds-and-Kills was magical. She stopped haranguing the Other Magpie, drew her hatchet, and began to cut kindling for a cooktire.

The Magpie was disgusted. She told Finds-and-Kills that she would rather be yelled at than see a friend so eager to be used. "He treats us like we are his, here to clean his kill and fix his breakfast."

Finds-and-Kills was unashamed. "Of course, what woman can resist him?" The big woman took a percussion cap from her shooting bag, twisting it in a rag with some black powder. She laid the rag atop the kindling, hitting it with a hatchet until the cap burst and the rag caught fire. "They say he has an elk-bone whistle, and when he blows it, you just have to go with him into the brush – to find out why he is called Bull Snake."

"I have heard his whistle, and I would not go with him if his name was Pole-in-the-Crotch." The missing part of her finger hurt, and she could not scratch it.

"Nah, nah, nah – no man is good enough for you."

"Not true. Remember Kills Good, the wife of Chief Long Horse – the woman who had such long lovely hair?"

"Who could forget her hair." Finds-and-Kills sounded wistful.

"Every morning, Long Horse brushed and braided her hair so that the whole camp would know how much he loved her. *That* is the kind of man I want. Not the kind that takes me in the bushes so that he may sing my name to the Lumpwoods."

"I wish Bull Snake would just hum *my* name." Finds-and-Kills looked up at her. "You can be free and virtuous, with your straight face and small feet. Is it a wonder people talk? You menstruate, but you are not married."

"You talk like my mother." The Magpie knelt down to help gut the buck. "Besides, it will be a long time before I am married. I told the Lumpwoods I would only go with a warrior who avenged my brother – if I even look at another man, think what they will sing about me."

A pair of Coyote calls came from the bluff. Two Yellow-eyes came splashing across the Tongue and into camp. The lead rider whistled through a gap in his teeth, letting the Crows know he was coming. He was a bear of a man with long filthy hair, wearing a battered felt hat, woolen leggings, and a raffish scalp shirt shining with grease. Worn moccasins were thrust through huge wooden Mexican stirrups. Across his saddle horn lay a Springfield .45–75 "Long Tom" infantry rifle a bone-handled Bowie knife and two dead rabbits dangled from his belt. Beneath the wild hair and whiskers, the Magpie recognized the squaw-man Crows called Plenty Good.

Behind Plenty Good came a completely different sort of Yellow-eye: a young Long Knife dressed in blue, clean-faced as a Crow, wearing a neatly creased white hat. Not too tall, not too short, he did not have the blue watery eyes that made many Yellow-eyes look like spirit persons. Long stripes ran down his pant seams. Army rank was a mystery to the Magpie, but leg stripes meant a Long Knife chief, a "Captain," to use a word the Crows borrowed from Spanish.

Plenty Good's rabbits landed right beside Bull Snake's dead buck. The trapper swung out of the saddle, pulled a pipe from his hatband, and asked the Lumpwoods if they wanted to smoke – every movement was lethargic, meant to put the Crows at ease. The Long Knife with him moved quicker, brimming with barely contained energy, dark eyes flicking back and forth as he dismounted. Even squatting on his heels, he seemed half in action, holding in his Medicine. The Magpie guessed that this handsome Yellow-eye could not speak Crow. Every so often, the trapper had to turn to him to translate. By listening closely, she caught some of what the captain said. He called Plenty Good "*Très Bon*," or sometimes "T-Bone."

Suddenly the Long Knife leaped up, hitting his gloved hands together, saying, "Jesus!" She knew that he was praying. Jesus was a Yellow-eye name for the Great Mystery.

He started kicking the dirt, like a Mandan doing the Buffalo Dance, saying, "My God, *Très Bon*, all Grabber got was a dozen warriors, an old man, and two women?" God was another name for the Great Mystery – but the rest was meaningless to the Magpie. Still, she was pleased to find him so pious. She liked his voice, and the funny-serious face he made when he prayed. There was something far-off yet appealing about him.

Plenty Good cocked his head to indicate the Lumpwoods. "Those bucks claim *beaucoup* Crow were here not long ago."

"But what in Heaven are we going to do *now?*" He swung his arm, taking in the camp, the stream, and half the Big Horns in a single sweep. Heaven was a name for the Beyond.

"Nothin' much," Plenty Good shrugged, "not till the breed gets back with the ole chief." He gestured toward Finds-and-Kills, bent over the buck, tearing back the skin, scooping out steaming entrails. "I'm gonna get myself some rabbit 'n' venison, an' maybe some Crow for dessert."

The officer glanced at Finds-and-Kills, then at Plenty Good, giving both of them a queer look that the Other Magpie could not interpret. She got up to find more firewood, watching as she worked.

Plenty Good took her place, tossing his saddle down to use as a back rest, giving Finds-and-Kills a gap-toothed grin. "Howdy, pretty," he addressed her in pidgin Crow. The big woman laughed at Plenty Good's insolence, but the Magpie could see that her friend was pleased to be getting male attention, even from a Yellow-eye.

The Magpie had gotten about a dozen sticks when the Long Knife captain bounded up without warning. She stood stock-still, unable to guess what he would do next. The man smiled, bent down, and began *to gather wood!!* She could barely believe it, but there he was, working like a woodchuck, grinning all the time, gathering up one load, dumping it by the fire, then starting on another. Crows say, "Yellow-eyes keep warm by gathering firewood" – and soon the captain had stacked enough wood for a week. She could hear the Lumpwoods laughing. To hide her confusion, the Magpie sat down, drawing her knife to skin and gut the rabbits.

"What's so funny, T-Bone?" asked the captain, standing beside Plenty Good, breathing hard, looking about for something else to do.

"Yew'r the show," drawled the squaw man. "No Crow gathers wood for a woman unless he's got the itch to lift her skirt."

The captain looked flustered. "I only wanted to help." Plenty Good gave him a leathery grin, "Hell, help yerself. *This* hoss has got his own hindsights set on the big 'un."

"Surely one is too young and the other married." The Magpie heard irritation in her captain's voice. She wished she could thank him for his flattering attention, but explain that she could hardly copulate until her brother had been avenged.

Plenty Good shook his head. "Ain't any such thing as too young among the Crow. If a girl is ready, she is ready. An' I saw no husband sign. This hoss guesses these women are here to avenge a killing – an' maybe see a little man-action on the side."

The captain stood with his mouth hanging open. "Well, I mean, I merely...."

Plenty Good laughed, "Sir, say what yew please. It's a free country an' these coons don't hear American." He gave Finds-and-Kills a friendly grin, saying in English, "As good as deaf, ain't yew, sister?"

Finds-and-Kills blushed, bending down, hiding her face in her work. The captain shrugged, "I thought it terrible to see a girl working while men loafed – I certainly had no designs on her."

"That's good." Plenty Good studied the Magpie, "cause *this girl* is one of yer high-toned, high-strung, Crow virgins. Pretty to look at, but wild as a peck o' panthers. See her shorn hair and short finger? Probably lost a father, or a brother, and she is out to get some of her own back from the Sioux." Magpie recognized the word *Sioux,* and guessed that Plenty Good was talking about her.

"No, the older doe's fur *this* coon," Plenty Good concluded. "She's a big 'un, but I wager I can wrassle with her. Two falls in three anyway. That young 'un's pretty, but lookit her handle her knife. If yew don't come onto her just right, she'll feed you yer pecker on a plate."

"I'll remember that," replied the captain dryly, seeing the Magpie strip the bloody skin off the second rabbit, then drape their pink bodies over the flames. She was secretly happy to have him watching. Despite being a Yellow-eye, he had shown his desire to copulate in a refined but energetic way – not like the insolent Lumpwood who had thrown his blanket at her feet.

While the men breakfasted on venison, the women shared Plenty Good's rabbits. Finds-and-Kills leaned over, whispering to the Magpie. "The big hairy one likes me." The Magpie agreed that Plenty Good had done everything short of dragging Finds-and-Kills into the brush.

Her friend hastened to add, "The one who wants to copulate with you is handsome.

"Yes," the Magpie eyed her captain carefully, "he moves like a man with much Medicine." Her own Medicine felt shaky. The handsome Long Knife had shown his interest at the worst possible time. She was duty bound to avenge her brother, and likely to be dead and scalped when the Sioux were done with her – in poor condition to attract a man.

"But he cannot speak." Finds-and-Kills spit out a pair of small rabbit bones. "I could not love a man I could not talk with afterward."

"True," admitted the Magpie. "He does not talk, but he has a strong friendly voice, and he carried wood for me." No man needed words to show his desire.

Plenty Good entertained the women by telling them how the Long Knives had gotten lost, mistaking Prairie Dog Creek for Little Goose Creek. "They stumbled onto the Tongue, bumped into some Cheyenne, rebounded, an' came to rest by the Forks of the Goose, where they had meant to be in the first place."

The Magpie could not understand how hundreds of men and horses could lose themselves, mistaking one stream for another.

"Weren't hard," replied Plenty Good, half in Crow, half in English. "Army's a lot of ex-clerks and unemployed gandy dancers, led by coons that wouldn't know a goose from a prairie dog if it flew over-head an' shat on 'em." His explanation made no sense to the Magpie.

He treated them to cups of Black Medicine and handfuls of white sap. Yellow-eyes food is not like real food – the Black Medicine was bitter and bracing, and the white sap looked like sand but tasted sweeter than honey. Plenty Good shrugged off their thanks, saying something nonsensical about "catching more flies with sugar." Licking sweet grains off her fingers, the Magpie wondered why the Yellow-eyes caught flies – perhaps they ate them, too.

When the sun had moved the width of a small pine, Grabber and Old Crow returned, saying that the Long Knives were indeed camped at the Forks of the Goose. Everyone mounted up to gallop after the retreating war party. Collecting stragglers as they went, they caught the main body loafing through the fat country above the Greasy Grass and got them turned around. The Other Magpie rode back beside her captain, who looked splendid on his big American horse. He smiled at her, gesturing at the landscape and making meaningless comments. Around them rode a barbaric retinue of tall Crow braves on painted ponies, carrying guns, bull-hide shields, and sharp-bladed war clubs – the Magpie understood now why men so loved the warpath.

At the Forks of the Goose, they found the Long Knives lined up to greet them, neat and straight on their huge mounts, sitting stirrup to stirrup for nearly a mile. Behind them was their huge square canton-ment. A Crow went to war with weapons, blanket, breechcloth, and a pair of ponies, but Yellow-eyes would not even take a piss that poorly equipped. Their camp was stocked with wagons, tents, bedrolls, cots, kegs, barrels, cookstoves, packs, mules, horses, cattle, pigs, and pets – it was as big as the Main Band's camp at the Crow Agency, and overflowed with Yellow-eyes – sleeping, cleaning, cooking, running footlraces, cursing and hectoring each other with no sense of privacy or restraint. Everything was done by men, which worried the Magpie as much as the Sioux ever had.

Plenty Good and the captain took them to see the only woman in the cantonment. She sat under guard, wearing a man's shirt and a makeshift skirt fashioned from a striped Mackinaw blanket. Plenty Good introduced her as Calamity Jane. She was plainly bored with being a prisoner, saying "How" and smiling at the captain. The Magpie was not jealous – a man like her captain must have many sweethearts; besides, she could see that the Calamity's attention embarrassed him tremendously. He tipped his hat to hide his blushing face.

The Magpie asked why Jane was not allowed to cook or gather wood. Plenty Good grinned, "Calamity was caught posing as a teamster. She did a man's work, but acted overfriendly to the mules – didn't cuss 'em enough. Now she's suspected of being overfriendly with the men, too." When Finds-and-Kills understood that Calamity's crimes were wearing pants, helping with the packing, and wanting to copulate, she was horrified – and insisted on leaving. The Magpie tried to comfort her, pointing out, "They are Yellow-eyes. We are Crow." Finds-and-Kills did not feel safe until they were back in the Crow camp, working on a wickiup.

The Magpie kept looking back toward the cantonment, hoping to see her captain. Bugles blew. The Long Knives lined up to count themselves. Then Rattler arrived. His Snakes galloped up to the line of Long Knives, waving glittering lances, neatly turning left-front into line. Rattler employed Texans, former Confederate officers, to teach his warriors how to parade, but he had brought even fewer braves than the Crows.

She did not see her captain again until evening council. There she spotted him sitting among the Long Knife chiefs by a huge bonfire of crackling boughs. She realized that his restless Medicine was natural – all the Long Knife chiefs were staring about, wide-eyed and inquisitive, unable to sit still like warriors. The only movement among the Crows was the slow circulation of pipes. Even the Snakes managed to look dignified and attentive.

Half-breeds and squawmen had to repeat each word in three languages, so that the Magpie had plenty of time to dwell on what was happening. She saw death all around her, in the ghostly white of the wagon covers, in the intense blackness of the night. Crows and Snakes were horribly few, less than three hundred, and the night hid thousands of Sioux warriors. Out beyond the firelight was Sitting Bull with his deadly visions, and Crazy Horse with his never-miss Medicine gun. She imagined the avalanche of arrows, and the hideous cry, "Hwoon,

hwoon," as Sioux war clubs thudded into flesh. The thousand-odd Long Knives in the cantonment were scant comfort, considering how easily they got lost or confused. Determined to meet her fears head-on, she got up, walking away from the circle of men, straight into the darkness. Either powerful Medicine protected her, or she was going to die; there was no middle way. No one seemed to notice her going.

The night was covered by clouds. The only light came from the huge campfires lit by the Yellow-eyes – the dark plain burned in a hundred places, as if all the stars in the sky had fallen between the Forks of the Goose. Turning her back to the fires, she called out into inky void, saying to her brother, "Come, guide me, protect me, or I can never do as you ask."

Buffalo grass brushed her ankles, nodding in the night wind. She heard the hoarse chirp of a Mormon cricket, followed by the yips and laughter of Old Man Coyote. Then from far off came a low eerie call.

Whooo! Whooo!

She pictured the huge shadowy bird of death, with his speckled body, powerful wings, and heart-shaped face, his round eyes looking almost human. From out of that ghostly face, the call grew louder, coming closer.

Whooo! Whooo!

The last mournful note broke into harsh screeching directly overhead. Darkness parted behind the bird of death, and her brother strode toward her. He lacked color and substance, but stood upright, with a proud look on his hideously mutilated head. In his hand, he held a long coup stick, wrapped in buffalo hide and trimmed with hair. A single breath feather fluttered at the base of the shaft.

His mouth split in a skeletal grin. *"Sister, take this coup stick against the Sioux. Take it and count coup for me."*

Shaking, she reached into the Beyond, taking the coup stick. Wind howled. Rain started to fall. Her brother shrank back, vanishing into the night. She found herself holding an ordinary length of cherrywood – cold, hard, familiar. It had no hide, hair, or feather.

Drumming rose up from the Crow camp. Men's hands beaten taut parfleche, pushing back the night. She followed the drumming back to camp. The council was over. Flickering light came from the cracks in the wickiups. Yellow-eyes wandered about looking amazed, including Plenty Good and her captain. Plenty Good nudged the officer, "Take a peek into one of those lodges. It's a peephole into Hell."

The Magpie watched her captain lean over, looking through a crack in the covering of a men's wickiup. She pictured the men huddled inside, half-naked, crouched around a small fire, moaning and chanting, making Medicine for the coming fight. He straightened up, shaking his head. "I thought they would be resting after riding all night and half a day."

"Resting?" Plenty Good chuckled. "They figure they'll sleep enough when they're dead."

Unable to understand what they were saying, the Magpie sat down before her own wickiup and began to wrap the cherrywood staff in buffalo hide. Rain pattered down. Winding the hide as tight as she could, she trimmed the staff with tufts of hair, fixing her breath feather to the bottom, making it match the stick in her vision. As she worked, she stole glances at the captain's boots, shining in the firelight.

Plenty Good stood over her, saying, "Bet she lost a brother. Now she's making herself a coup stick."

"She'll be going into battle with only that?" The Magpie heard incredulity in her captain's voice.

"Damn straight," declared the squawman, "and you are gonna need to be one eager beaver to stay ahead of her."

The officer shook his head, saying she looked young and helpless.

"Sure she is. But that's how the Crows make war – the cussedest mix of cruelty, calculated idiocy, and raw courage you are ever likely to see."

At dawn, the Long Knives put on a ridiculous display, mounting two hundred soldiers on pack mules – they had not brought enough horses. Neither mules nor riders liked the idea. All morning, the Magpie saw mules bucking off riders and breaking saddles, or charging about with cursing Long Knives clinging to their backs. Yellow-eyes never lost their ability to amaze. The mule rodeo made them a day late leaving the camps at the Forks of the Goose. Without her handsome captain beside her, there was nothing romantic about the ride. Rattlers snaked through the buffalo grass, emerging from their winter holes to rejoin society.

Shots made her sit up, staring wildly about, but it was only some Lumpwoods shooting buffalo for the thrill of seeing them fall over. The men's antics angered her. So did her own fear – here she was, trying to part a warrior from his hair, but frightened by men shooting buffalo. She told herself bitterly, "Silly fool, you better get used to guns going off." Riding a strange pony, surrounded by armed and nervous men, the Magpie realized that she might never live to see the Sioux. Already, a Long Knife had managed to shoot himself dead while chopping wood.

At sundown, they pitched camp near the headwaters of the Rosebud. Horses, happy to be free of their saddles, rolled down grassy slopes strewn with blue phlox and prairie clover. Bull Snake strode over to their fire, bringing some tripe and tongue. Finds-and-Kills made the meat into sausage, threading it on a ramrod and rolling it on the coals until it was cooked.

Neither woman got to taste it. Bull Snake took the sausage back to his fire, where Lumpwoods, Fox Warriors, and Crazy Dogs were "Naming Married Women." This naming was something the Other Magpie had heard of but never seen, because it only happened on the warpath in enemy country. Men passed the buffalo sausage like a pipe, each man biting off a bit, saying what he would do in battle and then naming a married woman he had copulated with. Bull Snake started off, "I will take a pony for my sweetheart Pretty Bottom." The Crazy Dogs laughed, and each named several women. Crazy Dogs are so wild and reckless most husbands let them have their way.

The Other Magpie studied the husbands' faces. Each tried to show no emotion, but she could tell by their eyes which were expecting their wives' names, and which did not see it coming. The sausage came to Pretty Bottom's husband. He bit off a big piece, saying he would count coup, calmly naming Bull Snake's youngest wife. Foxes snickered. Crazy Dogs howled. A man who swore by buffalo meat staked his life on his words – Pretty Bottom's husband was either telling the truth, or risking death just to take Bull Snake down a notch.

Having no one to name, she wrapped herself in a buffalo robe and lay staring at the starless sky. As she fell asleep, it began to rain again.

At half-light, she was awakened by a hand on her shoulder. Rain had stopped. Finds-and-Kills' huge silhouette knelt over her. "Our wolves found a Sioux campfire in the hills." Men at the next fire were admiring a blanket brought back by the scouts, made of rubber, useful for keeping the rain off. Who knew the Sioux had such luxuries?

"I am afraid," whispered Finds-and-Kills.

"So am I," the Magpie admitted – she only hoped that her coming death would be creditable enough to set her brother free.

'I am worried by more than death." Finds-and-Kills' voice was low and hoarse.

The Magpie told her that death was enough of a worry.

'I am afraid of disgrace as well."

She found this hard to imagine; Finds-and-Kills was as straight and stalwart as anyone she knew.

'I am afraid of what will happen if the Sioux kill me, and then strip my body. I know how they will laugh when they see me naked."

The Magpie was not looking forward to that either. She did not expect to cut much of a figure sprawled naked and bloody on the prairie. Her friend produced a bundle of men's clothes wrapped in a blanket, saying, "Help me change. Hold up this blanket so the men will not see."

The Magpie got up and covered the big woman as best she could. By dawnlight, she could see what Finds-and-Kills was hiding. Her friend's body was not like other women's bodies – no breasts, just a broad chest, and men's private parts hanging down between hairy thighs. Finds-and-Kills was not a woman by birth, but by choice. When she stepped out from behind the blanket, she did not look like a woman at all, except for her tattoos. The blanket shirt, leggings, and breechcloth fit naturally – and must have belonged to Finds-and-Kills before she became a woman.

"If I am killed in my dress, the Sioux will laugh, saying, 'This Crow was hiding in a dress.' Now they will merely think I am a man."

The Magpie stood glumly holding the blanket. "If I am killed, there will be no surprises, nothing for the Sioux to even smile at."

"Yes," her friend agreed, "you are lucky."

The Magpie did not feel lucky. Preparing her Medicine as best she could, she painted her forehead yellow and took the stuffed woodpecker from her Medicine bag to tie in her hair. Everyone mounted up. Setting off over sodden ground, following the south fork of the Rosebud, the war party was amused by the "new man" among them. The Magpie did not find her friend's transformation funny. The new man next to her seemed half a stranger – and her captain rode with the Long Knives. She felt abandoned, going into battle very alone.

The south fork of the Rosebud corkscrewed through thickets of wild roses and sweet briar. At the big double bend where the forks came together, the ground rose up – benches by the river blended into low bluffs topped by conical hills, forming a natural amphitheater, alive with menace. Her brother whispered to her on the wind, *"This is the place."*

Yellow-eyes straggled along the bottom in a line stretched all the way back to last night's camp. Their leaders called a halt for the rear to catch up, before plunging into the wooded defile where the bluffs came within a long bowshot of the river. The Magpie saw Medicine Crow in his buffalo headdress making signs, saying that the Long Knives should stay mounted while scouts swept the hills for Sioux. The Yellow-eyes ignored him, dismounting to smoke, talk, and play cards, moving like men in a dream.

Finds-and-Kills looked grim in a man's clothes and a man's paint, saying, "Sitting Bull has made Medicine over the Long Knives. They cannot see the bluffs. They see only what the Sioux want them to see."

Morning turned to noontime. Hot air shimmered like water. The Magpie scanned the hills, too scared to speak or spit. She had not seen a single Sioux or heard a shot in anger, but the way the land rolled up toward the bluffs was enough to set her heart racing. Fear crawled down her spine and dug a pit in her stomach.

Shots rang out, followed by a wild ululation. Crow wolves poured down from the bluffs, whipping their ponies into a run. Shock made each detail impossibly sharp. A wounded wolf rode past the Magpie, swaying in his saddle and holding his side. His eyes were glazed. Flecks of spittle flew from his lips – red blood welled up between his fingers, like in a Medicine man's trick.

Strange riders spilled out of the draws, demons springing straight from Grandmother Earth, wearing war bonnets or half-masks with the faces of animals, waving lances and eight-foot tomahawks. For all her fear and anticipation, she did not understand who they were, until men cried out, "Sioux, Sioux!"

Mesmerized, she sat helpless on her borrowed mare. Long Knives darted about like blue butterflies drunk on locoweed, chasing their horses and mules, trying to mount. Others stood stock-still, wanting someone to tell them what to do. Crows and Snakes charged straight up the benches to meet the oncoming Sioux, waving their weapons and making horrid noises in their throats. It seemed that they must be swallowed up by so many enemy. Masses of men and ponies met with a sickening crash – a terrible amalgam of shots, yells, and screaming mounts. The Magpie saw Long Knives scramble up onto the benches in the wake of the Crows and Snakes; mostly on foot, shooting as they went. She hoped they were firing high. Yellow-eyes could never tell one warrior from another.

Not happy to be targets for both sides, Crows turned and galloped back. As they returned, she expected to see empty saddles and slopes littered with the fallen, but the Crows came back carrying no dead and leaving no bodies behind. It amazed the Magpie that hundreds could meet thousands – fighting hand to hand – without losing anyone. Sioux came pounding down from the bluffs on either side of the Crows, whooping and shouting, "Hoka hey." Again she expected a massacre, but they turned about as soon as the Long Knives formed a firing line. The fight dissolved into private shows by single braves attempting to draw the troopers forward with feigned retreats and feats of daring. An enemy rider would break from cover, hanging behind his mount with only a leg showing, firing from under the pony's neck or trying to touch the troopers. As that warrior dashed off, another would emerge to put on his own display of devil-may-care riding at breakneck speed. The cavalry's continuous firing deafened the Magpie, but did not seem to disturb the Sioux.

Shaken and weak, terrified almost to tears, she had done nothing to avenge her brother. She had not gone up the bluffs. Her coup stick had not touched the enemy. She could not even claim to have been close to death, since there had been so little killing.

A band of Long Knives rode up, with chief's stripes on their pant legs. Among them was a tall old man with a funny braided beard who wore plain pants and a battered slouch hat – the Magpie thought the silly man in the shabby coat was a mule skinner, until men said this was Three Stars, the Long Knife big chief. A squawman rode over to tell the Crows it was time to turn their backs on the Sioux, to continue downriver into the canyon where the bluffs came closest to the stream. Warriors made the pinwheel motion beside their heads – the Long Knife leader was mad or crazy drunk. If the firing line opened up, thousands of angry Sioux would swarm down from the bluffs like hornets from a broken hive. The Crows and Long Knives could never negotiate the thickly timbered canyon with Crazy Horse hanging on their heels. This was the worst possible moment for Three Stars to get lost in the woods.

Crows flatly refused to move. A Snake boy who had been holding the horses ran up to Rattler, begging to be allowed to fight. Rattler agreed, and the boy ran off to paint himself. There would be no safety anywhere if the Long Knives opened the line. The Magpie realized that she too was going to be thrust into battle, brave or not.

Long Knives mounted up, pulling out of line, heading downriver, leaving a yawning gap. If Sitting Bull himself had commanded the Long Knives, he could not have done more to wreck their line. With a whoop and holler, Sioux streamed toward the opening, blowing their eagle bone whistles and firing from the saddle. Crows braced themselves. Men around the Magpie sang their death songs. As she resigned herself to death, she saw her captain ride up with Plenty Good at his side. The captain was wild-eyed, waving his arms like he had a wasp in his pants, yelling orders in English. From his excitement, the Magpie guessed that he too was disobeying Three Stars. She was proud to see him act like a thinking man.

Plenty Good had the sense to speak Crow, "Come on, you Crazy Dogs, an' ready-to-die Lumpwoods, don't let Rattler get ahead of you!" He pointed to the Snakes, already catapulting themselves at the onrushing Sioux.

The Magpie kicked her pony and rode over to her captain. Nothing could stop the Sioux from coming through, and she wanted to die beside him. He smiled at her, saying, "Howdy, Ma'am," looking shocked and shy, oddly formal given the havoc around them. "That's a girl," yelled Plenty Good. He had lost the pipe he carried in his hatband. "Get moving! No Sioux can hit nothin' smaller than a buffalo from horseback. Crazy Horse hisself jumps off to shoot." The squawman turned in his saddle to shout at the Crows, "Let's go, Lumpwoods! Gonna let girls an' Snakes get ahead of you?"

Sioux were swarming out of the draws, gaining momentum, singing their own death songs. Her captain led the Crows right at them, firing his revolver, shouting more meaningless commands. The Magpie was shouting too, but she did not know what. Every word, every thought, was swallowed by the inferno of buzzing bullets, rearing ponies, blinding dust, and multicolored horsemen. Sioux slammed into the Crows, screaming "Hwoon, hwoon," swinging tomahawks round their heads, trying to beat them from the saddle.

Somehow they broke through to the Snakes. The Magpie saw Rattler stripped to the waist, wearing a feathered bonnet that swept all the way to the ground. The Great Snake had seen seventy winters, but fought like a warrior in his prime. Long Knives were with the Snakes, fighting in isolated groups against terrible odds. She reined in her black mare, breathing dust, her heart beating like a bird in a snare. She had lost her captain. Was he hurt? Killed? Her coup stick had still not touched the enemy, and she certainly did not have a scalp. Sioux were all about her, shooting and showing off their trick riding. None were offering up their hair.

A Long Knife leader rode back and forth, trying to re-form the firing line. Suddenly he reeled in the saddle, shot through the face. His jaw dropped against his chest, blood gushed out of his mouth. For a moment he stayed mounted, then he toppled. Long Knives around him broke and ran.

She rode anxiously up to him, but the wounded man was not her captain.

Bull Snake burst past her, painted black and yellow like a real bull snake. He jerked instantly backward, somersaulting off his mount in an absurd display of horsemanship – not until he hit the ground did she realize that he'd been shot. The Lumpwood chief flopped like a fish on land, his handsome features twisted. Sioux came storming up to count coup and take scalps from the fallen. She felt helpless to stop them.

A big figure dashed forward, dismounting beside Bull Snake. It took a moment for the Magpie to recognize Finds-and-Kills, still disguised as a man. Standing over the fallen warrior, she fired her Sharps Sporter as s fast as she could work the breech.

The Magpie had to decide. She could run with the Long Knives, or die beside her friend – there were no other choices. Kicking her pony, she felt a sudden surge of courage. The Sioux could do no worse than kill her, and they had already done that to her brother. For the first time that day, her mouth ran wet with saliva. Having no weapon, she spit at the charging Sioux, showing how she did not fear them. Circling in front of Finds-and-Kills, she shouted, "Spit is my arrow. I dare you to face it."

The lead Sioux took her up, nocking a wicked war arrow – its barbed head fixed flat to slide between her ribs. He dropped down on the far side of his horse where Finds-and-Kills could not hit him, showing nothing but his left foot.

The Magpie charged forward, putting all her fear into her lungs, screaming as she swung the coup stick around her head. Her yell startled the man's pony, a beautiful bay with dainty white stockings.

The bay turned sharply, not willing to play toss-the-pony with a wild-eyed woman.

Hanging by his left foot, holding both bow and arrow, the Sioux struggled to stay with his horse. His foot slipped and he fell. The white-stockinged bay bounded off.

Scrambling upright, the man took aim at the Magpie – she saw the big barbed point, and behind it the man's eye, sighting on her breast.

Finds-and-Kills' buffalo gun boomed. The Sioux flipped over, bow and arrow flying in different directions. Finds-and-Kills was a formidable shot, who could place a bullet as carefully as a stitch – her shells were painted yellow and blue to add to their Medicine. The Sioux did not so much as twitch.

The Other Magpie dismounted and gingerly whacked the man with her coup stick. He was sure-enough dead. She drew the steel sliver that had taken off her finger. Bending down, she made a neat cut along the man's hairline, running across his forehead and above his ears. She grabbed the man's hair and pulled back. There was a gruesome ripping. A lifetime of skinning animals made the task easy, if not pleasant. She slashed through the last flap of skin, and the scalp came off in her hand.

She stood up with the man's bloody skin and hair in her hand. He was her enemy, who had tried to kill her, but her hate evaporated into vast emptiness. A warrior would be taking his bow as well, but she could not even look at the corpse. She swung back onto her mount.

Finds-and-Kills was still firing, keeping the Sioux back. Two tall Snakes, one wearing a jaguar-skin headdress, stood over the fallen Long Knife chief, a pair of panthers holding the buzzards at bay. Lumpwoods were hauling Bull Snake away by the heels. Her captain came up, rallying the Long Knives, forming a new firing line.

She had the hair her brother needed. *Her* fight was over – but the battle was still on. Sitting on her horse, chest heaving, she saw two dismounted Long Knives running in terror for the safety of the riormed firing line. A pair of Cheyenne split off from the Sioux, tearing after the two men.

Crows mustered for a coun025charge. The Magpie braved herself to go with them. But then a squawman came riding up, yelling in Crow – Three Stars wanted everyone to fall back. Anxious as she was to leave, the Magpie was disgusted. She saw the two Cheyenne catch up with the running soldiers. The frightened men raised their hands in surrender, offering their guns to the Cheyenne – who took them eagerly, turning them on the terrified soldiers, shooting them down with their own weapons. Then they leaped off their horses and began to prune body parts in typical Cheyenne fashion.

The Magpie felt mortified. Glittering piles of cartridges marked the line they were leaving. Soldiers had spilled the shells from their pouches to have bullets ready at hand. Now they were abandoning the ammunition, to be scooped up by the Sioux and someday fired at the Crows. Long Knives seemed to care for nothing, leaving their bullets and weapons, their comrades dead and living.

Three Stars himself came up, looking more than ever like a load of old clothes flung on a post. He signed that the Crows should get ready to ride downriver into the wooded defile – not satisfied with his original blunder, he was hell-bent to repeat it. White Feather swept Three Stars's suggestion aside, signing, "What is the use of going farther, if you will not fight here?" Completely obsessed, Three Stars acted like an old man with only one idea left in his head, pointing at the canyon, claiming Crazy Horse's camp was somewhere downstream.

White Feather laughed. He turned his chin toward the Sioux swarming on the heights, practically encircling them – "Here is a petty war party, a thousand, two thousand; I had no time to count. Go downriver to their camps; you will find more Sioux than there are leaves of grass." He rubbed his palms together imitating a woman grinding seeds between two stones. "They will rub you out." After the silly show Three Stars had put on, no Crow was about to ride into a blind canyon looking for Crazy Horse.

Ashamed for her captain, the Magpie rode slowly back to the little stream where they had left the led horses. They were gone. The Snake boy who had been watching the ponies lay by the brook, his face half painted, his bare skull white and bloody. When Three Stars opened the line, Sioux had ridden through, shot the boy, and scalped him.

Three Stars kept threatening to ride into the canyon, looking for Crazy Horse. But when he counted his men, he found that he had scores of wounded whom he could not take into battle, or leave behind for the Sioux. So he changed his mind, and everyone trooped back to the Forks of the Goose – not a moment too quick for the Crows. The next day they rode off up the Tongue. Sioux country was no place to blunder aimlessly about. The Magpie had avenged her brother, taken a scalp, and fought beside her captain, but it all tasted of ashes.

> The little soldier chief (Maj. Reno) ran away, knowing how the fight would end. My man, Goes Ahead, rode down Medicine Tail Coulee with Son of the Morning Star. He heard the Sioux shout, "Go back, go back. You are dead men."
> – Pretty Shield

LITTLE BIG HORN

Dawn sky on midsummer's day was the color of a newly cast skillet. Snow lay in the shadows between the trees, but the great Medicine Wheel was blown completely clear. The Other Magpie sat by the northwest cairn, watching the sun rise over the stone hub, her face painted black to show that the fires of revenge had burnt down to embers. She laid her last hank of Sioux hair on the flames of a small fire – the rest of the scalp had been cut up so important members of the war party could all have a piece to dance with. Bull Snake was shot through both hips, in no shape to scalp dance or strut before the women, but even Old Crow, shot in the knee cap, managed to hobble about with the dancers.

The smell of singed hair and burning flesh filled the air, and her brother's spirit appeared, striding purposefully out of the hub of the Wheel with the dawn behind him. For the first time she saw his ghost in daylight, fully fleshed out, hair restored, no longer a wraith. Each time she saw him, he seemed to take on substance, becoming the strong young man she remembered.

"Sister. see what you have done for me."

The Magpie felt whole as well, able to look straight at him, sure she had earned forgiveness. "Brother," she told him, "I must ask something of you." Crows considered ghosts troublesome, but able to be helpful – if they wished.

"Ask, sister."

"I want my brother's permission to marry."

"You have my permission, even if he is too poor to give ponies." Her brother was not near as proprietary as when he was alive no longer needing horses to ride, or women to tend his tipi. *"Just so long as he has not shamed himself in battle, or taken back a runaway wife."*

"He is the Yellow-eye captain who rode beside me at the Rosebud. We know he is brave in battle, and he must have ponies since all Yellow-eyes are rich. I do not know how many wives he has, or if any have run off."

The ghost looked grim. *"Sister, you must choose another."*

"Why? I have earned the right to pick my man." Would no one let her have her way?

"You have," her brother agreed, *"but this Long Knife captain will soon be dead."*

"Dead?"

"Already they are making a feast for him in the Camp of the Dead." Her brother turned his chin toward the rising sun. *"The Long Knives have lost themselves again. Right now this captain and Plenty Good are in the Wolf Mountains, trying to slink past Crazy Horse's village which they think is on the Rosebud. Three Stars has sent them to find No-Hip-Bone and Son of the Morning Star – but the Sioux have left the Valley of the Rosebud and crossed the Wolf Mountains to camp along the Little Big Horn. It is Son of the Morning Star and his Long Knives who are headed down the Rosebud."* Three Stars's confusion was complete – Son of the Morning Star was where he thought Crazy Horse was; the most foolish Lumpwood Without a Sweetheart knew more of war. And her captain was on an idiot's errand, going the wrong way around the Sioux camps.

"We must help him." The Magpie had no faith that the two Yellow-eyes could find their way through Sioux Country on their own.

"We must?"

"Yes, you owe me that."

Her brother's smile turned benevolent. *"Yes, you have earned this. Before I go into the Beyond, I will unite you with your captain and help him find Son of the Morning Star."*

Finds-and-Kills waited below the shoulder of Medicine Mountain, wearing women's clothes again. When the Magpie walked into camp with her brother, the big woman said nothing and did not seem shocked – the Magpie guessed that her friend could not see the ghost. Just as well. She explained what had happened on the Medicine Wheel, and how she had to find her captain.

Finds-and-Kills listened, then sighed, seeing yet another insane venture ahead – "You have a brave and foolish nature that leads you into mischief. But you stood by me when I fought as a man. If you must do this, I will do it with you." The Magpie added that Plenty Good was with her captain, so they both had a man to look forward to if they were so lucky as to get through Sioux Country alive.

Even though they were guided by her brother's spirit, it still took them days to track Plenty Good and the captain through deep ravines crisscrossed by Sioux trails. They finally found the two men holed up in a cottonwood draw, afraid to travel by day or make a fire, drinking cold coffee with their guns in their laps. Plenty Good saw them first, slapping her captain on the knee. "Hot damn, sir, it's our honeys!"

The captain responded with one of his short vehement prayers. "Jesus, what are *they* doing here? How'd they ever find us?"

Finds-and-Kills was suddenly shy in the squawman's presence – so the Magpie spoke for both of them, telling Plenty Good as much as she considered safe. She did not want to scare him by mentioning her brother's spirit, though the ghost was standing a few feet away, studying her captain. A spirit person could stare all he wanted without seeming impolite.

Plenty Good turned to the captain, shaking his head. "Got any of that bacca left? This needs a smoke."

The captain fished out a pouch of pipe tobacco.

"Appears these women have come to lead us to Custer." Custer was what the Yellow-eyes called Son of the Morning Star.

"Did General Crook send them?" The Magpie could hear disbelief in her captain's voice – Crook was their name for Three Stars.

"No." Plenty Good took the pouch. "Crook's still sittin' by Goose Creek, his head up his arse, fishing for trout an' wonderin' where Terry and Custer might be. But these women say Custer has cut hisself loose and is coming down the Rosebud alone."

"Do you believe that, T-Bone?"

Plenty Good got out a bit of paper and rolled a *cigarrillo* from the pipe tobacco. "Yew askin' me if I believe General George A. Custer would cut loose from Gibbon and Terry an' go riding off on his own, to take on half the Sioux Nation with nothing but the 7th Cavalry and a pair of bulldog revolvers?"

"I suppose it was a silly question," the captain grimaced. "Custer will kill his horses to be in at the death."

Plenty Good licked the *cigarrillo,* taking a long look toward the Rosebud. "But yew can bet your pants bottoms ol' Son of the Morning Gun don't know Crook ain't comin' north to meet him."

"Then it's our duty to tell him."

The trapper tapped the white tube against his thumbnail. "Suppose that's what we're paid our four-bits-a-day for."

"Do you think these women can find Custer?" The captain gave the Magpie and Finds-and-Kills an uneasy look. "I hate to drag them into danger."

"They found *us* easy enough, and I thought we were damn well cached.

"Besides, they are already *in* danger. We all are. I'll tell you plain, I don't take to traipsing after Custer. That man has killed more cavalry than the cholera. If we pitch into *beaucoup* Sioux, I'll figure I've earned my fifty cents, an' Son of the Morning Star can look out for hisself." He stared down at the *cigarrillo* in his hand, "Got a locofoco to light this?" The captain handed him a match, and they passed the burning paper like a pipe.

Plenty Good was dead against moving during daylight, saying there was way too much "sign" around, so they rested until the sun went down, leaving a red streak of war paint above the western hills. Mounting up, the Magpie managed a private conference with her brother. *"Do not worry,"* the spirit assured her, *"I see with the eyes of an owl. I can guide you as well in the dark as in daylight."*

"We will not miss Son of the Morning Star?" The Magpie knew how easy it was for Long Knives to get lost.

"I will lead you right to him."

But about midnight, descending a plum-choked canyon, the Magpie heard Plenty Good mutter, "I smell woodsmoke." All four froze atop their horses. The Magpie strained to see over the plum bushes.

Tipi ears showed against the sky. Shots rattled from the thicket. She realized they had ridden right into a Sioux camp. The trapper yelled, "Cache yourselves," grabbing Finds-and-Kills's bridle, leading her up a bank, crashing through the brambles and plum brush. The Magpie tried to follow, but Plenty Good soon outdistanced both her and the Sioux. She "cached" herself and her captain in the dense thicket, waiting for dawn, no longer trusting her brother's owl eyes.

"How could you have missed those Sioux?" she whispered. Spirits are supposed to be superhuman, above stupid mistakes.

"I did not miss them; they missed us," her brother chuckled. *"It was like when we chased the buffalo through camp."* It was hard to get a ghost to take life seriously.

"But now we have lost Finds-and-Kills and Plenty Good."

"No harm will come to them."

The Magpie stopped arguing, afraid her whispers would wake her captain, making him think she was crazy. How could she explain her spirit brother to a Long Knife who did not know Crow? Instead she curled up and slept, saving her strength for the long morning.

In the Moon of Midsummer, there is hardly any night. First light edged over the rim of the world. The Magpie fed her captain pounded meat, mixed with berries and kidney fat, along with a rather tasteless root that grows in the Big Horns. Etiquette called for them to eat apart, but the Magpie decided that was absurd. Her man was properly thankful, nodding his head, smacking his lips, saying, "Not Delmonico's, but it beats hardtack and uncooked bacon." Tipping his white hat back, he looked right at her, the way a Yellow-eye will. "You know Delmonico's, don't you? Steak house in New York?"

She could see by his smile that he thought they were alone and enjoyed being forward. She returned the smile, though it was hardly the time to copulate – not when the mosquitoes were up and half the Sioux Nation might be watching.

A little encouragement went a long way. The captain's idiot grin grew wider, "No, I guess you don't know Delmonico's." He shook his head, saying a short morning prayer. "God, how do I get myself into these things – all alone with a girl I can't talk to, and a few thousand Sioux!"

Her brother stepped between them, acting as ghostly chaperon *"Son of the Morning Star is stirring; by midday he will be moving."*

The Magpie made the sign for Morning Star, holding her hand up toward the star itself, still visible in the predawn.

"Venus?" Her captain nodded vigorously. "Sure, the Morning Star, that means Custer, right?"

She crooked her finger to show him the sign for agreement. Then they mounted up and headed for the Valley of the Rosebud, with her brother riding her led horse, the black mare she had ridden at the Rosebud. It was strange to have the two men she cared most about riding beside her – only one of them able to see the other. The valley was silent, smelling of roses and crab apples. No smoke hovered in the morning air. Her brother led them across to the west bank, where the wind blew the mosquitoes away. Then he turned south. Her captain's impulse was to collect the straying mare and head downstream, where

No-Hip-Bone would be waiting. The Magpie had to dismount in the half-light and show him the ironshod hoofprints headed upstream. Hundreds of American horses had passed not long ago, going south.

"Son of the Morning Star?" asked her captain, making the sign she had shown him: holding up his hand, thumb and forefinger forming a circle, tapping the two fingers together to indicate twinkling.

She smiled, turning his arm about until it pointed to where the dawn had been. Then she crooked her finger.

"Have to say I'm learning quickly," her captain smiled, plainly enjoying the finger play and physical contact. They headed up the Rosebud, following the ghost-ridden pony. Where the valley widened, the Magpie saw the remains of tipi rings, surrounded by skeletal wickiup frames. Grass was cropped to the roots and covered with pony droppings. She made the cutthroat sign, saying "Sioux," opening and closing her hands many times so the captain could know there were more than could be counted.

The captain turned in his saddle, looking around, "Right, *beaucoup* Sioux. But where is *Custer?*"

Upstream, they found a giant twenty-eight-pole Sundance lodge, laid out like the Medicine Wheel. Everywhere were signs that the Sundance had been cut short, with rituals half-completed. Axheads and cooking pots lay hastily abandoned. A scalp hung from the Sundance Lodge. If that were not enough of a warning, some Sioux had drawn a row of men head down in the sand, ringed by horseshoe prints to show that they were Long Knives.

"Primitive art." Her captain smiled at the sand drawing. "The guy wasn't Rembrandt. He got it upside down."

Head down meant dead. The Sioux were supremely confident – with good reason, so far as the Magpie could see. Where the trail mounted the divide, headed for the Little Big Horn, the ironshod tracks were surrounded by thousands of pony prints and travois ruts. So many lodgepoles had been dragged over the divide that in places it looked like a plowed field.

They followed the trail west, into the direction of death and sunset. By late morning, they found the first body, facedown in a dusty alkali draw, circled by turkey vultures. Her captain dismounted, turning the dead person over. He was a Sioux boy, shot through both lungs; buzzards and magpies had already been at him. Her captain remounted, showing her something he had found under the body. "It's hardtack."

He crumbled the slab in his hand. The Magpie did not want to touch either the dead boy or the Long Knife bread – both looked to be very bad luck.

He paused, pointing his thumb back down the creek. "That boy back there. Is he Sioux?"

"Hunkpapa Sioux," replied the Magpie, signing as she spoke. "Maybe Sitting Bull's band."

"I suppose all that means yes. He is not long dead."

A rising sun baked the trail. Near to noon, they reached the watershed and climbed a tall spire called the Crow's Nest, to get a good look over the dry arroyos and grassy mesas. A thin haze from hundreds of cooltires hung over the Valley of the Little Big Horn. Through the haze, the Magpie saw pony herds blanketing the prairie, wriggling like brown worms in the sun. From the size of the herds, the village had to be immense.

Her captain saw nothing but haze, so she pointed to dust trails moving through the badlands closer at hand, signing, "Son of the Morning Star."

"Custer? Really?" The captain shaded his eyes, "Great, I'll get the horses." He clambered eagerly down the spire. When he was gone, she asked her brother if there were Crows with Son of the Morning Star, not trusting Yellow-eyes to see how many Sioux lay ahead.

"*Oh, yes,*" he assured her, "*Half-Yellow Face is with him. Also White Swan, Hairy Moccasin, Goes Ahead, White-Man-Runs-Him, and the boy Curly.*"

Farther off, she saw the white flash of pronghorns fleeing from smaller dust devils, little whirlwinds moving north and south of the Long Knife columns. She asked what his spirit vision made of them.

"*Sioux,*" he pointed with his chin, "*and Little Wolf's Cheyenne.*"

"You can get us through them?" She looked back at the huge pony herds crawling over the benches along the Little Big Horn. They had to move fast, before the Sioux got angry.

"*I will get you to Son of the Morning Star,*" the ghost promised.

"In daylight? No more owl eyes nonsense?" She was not forgetting the fright he had given her.

"*By midafternoon, before he reaches the big village by the Little Big Horn.*"

Descending the spire, she found her captain in an agitated state, trying to make coffee over a tiny fire, anxious to press on. She explained with words and signs about the hostiles around them, but assured him she would get them through to Son of the Morning Star.

"Right," he nodded, *"beaucoup* Sioux, but we can get through to Custer." He took a sip of his half-brewed coffee, and spit it out.

"Bad water," signed the Magpie, cupping her hand to drink, then making a throw-away motion – streams trickling down the divide were shallow and alkali.

"Bitter as a mule's behind," her captain agreed. He poured the coffee into the ground, and they mounted up.

The bleak sameness of the badlands hid sharp turnings and sudden folds in the earth. The Magpie watched the winding trails of ironshod hooves diverge, a smaller trickle of horseshoe prints turning southward, but her brother led them straight on, following the greater stream. Sage and buffalo grass gave way to ash and cottonwood as they entered a shallow canyon. The bottom was mostly dry, with a few swampy mud holes surrounded by red-tipped paintbrush. Smoke drifted up the canyon.

At each turning, the Magpie tensed, expecting to see Sioux. Instead they came upon a second scene as ghastly as the dead boy in the draw. In the middle of the wash was a burning tipi, a burial lodge with its hide cover consumed by flames. Tongues of fire climbed the burial scaffold, which was collapsing under the weight of the body wrapped in buffalo skins.

The Magpie looked quickly away. Here the tracks of the Long Knives split again. And again her brother followed the larger path, but the stream of hoofprints had shrunk almost by half. She told her captain, "Son of the Morning Star scatters his men like sparrows before a storm."

"Custer?" He looked puzzled. "But where is he?"

She nodded toward the empty slopes ahead, where shortgrass bluffs ran parallel to the river, like the spines of long dead animals. Dust hung in the air, and summer flowers were trampled by the passage of hundreds of horses.

As they mounted the bluffs, the Magpie heard firing coming from the Valley of the Little Big Horn. She turned her horse to get a look.

Her brother tried to stop her, *"Do not turn aside, sister. We can get to Son of the Morning Star before he reaches the village."*

"I must see for myself," she shouted.

"The trail goes straight ahead."

"There is fighting in the valley," she insisted. The firing grew, sounding like a ripping blanket.

The captain looked surprised by her burst of loud one-sided conversation, but he turned his horse to follow. Climbing the back of the bluffs, she saw her first Long Knife, standing over his fallen horse, hitting the tired beast, trying to get his mount to rise. Man and horse seemed half-asleep until her captain stopped to shout, "Where's Custer?" The man waved toward the head of Medicine Tail Coulee.

Reaching the ridge, the Magpie looked down into the Valley of the Little Big Horn. Slopes dotted with bunch grass danced in the heat. Blackbirds with bright red-wing flashes flitted between wild sunflowers and patches of buffalo beans. Beyond the red-wing blackbirds, a white sea of tipis stretched downriver, camp circle following camp circle, until the lodge tops were lost in the haze of cook fires – each circle had hundreds of lodges: Hunkpapas, Minniconjous, No Bows, Oglalas, plus the Cheyenne, Santee Dakota, and smaller bands. At the near end of the village, she saw a small knot of Long Knives fleeing for their lives, trying to reach the bluffs. Warriors rode in and around them, whooping and killing.

Shaken, she turned to her brother. "Is Son of the Morning Star down there?"

"No, he is ahead, descending Medicine Tail Coulee." Both their horses dripped sweat, nipping grass tops in the windless heat.

"But he will be rubbed out!" A handful of Crows, a few hundred Long Knives, facing thousands of Sioux and Cheyenne what other result was possible?

Her brother looked grave. "Yes, he will be rubbed out."

"Then why are you taking us to him?"

"Sister, I must go into the Beyond; so must Son of the Morning Star. Now you and your captain can come with us."

The Magpie stared at her brother, hardly believing. One look back into the valley took the mist from her eyes. She saw where he had been leading her. No ghost can ever be trusted – they are of the dead. "Go," she told him, "you are dead. We don't want you."

Her brother looked hurt and anguished. "I love you, sister. I do not want to go into the Beyond without you."

She saw stems of wheatgrass appear behind him, showing through his body. "Go," she repeated, "You belong in the Beyond. We do not want you back."

"Sister, I fear to go alone." He faded, his smoky image reaching out to her, imploring. A gust of ghost wind wrapped him up and whipped him away.

Sadness replaced anger. She whispered, "Someday I'll join you." But not now – she leaped onto the black mare, who had carried only a ghost all day, dashing down the hill.

The captain pointed to where Medicine Tail Coulee split the bluffs. "That trooper claimed Custer went that way." Whatever he was saying was utterly unimportant. The Magpie did not pretend to listen. Grabbing his reins, she dug her heels into her mare's flanks, making the signs for many Sioux, turning him toward the pine ridges to the east. They pounded down the bluffs and up a snake-headed draw.

"Well, yes," her captain gasped, "there are many Sioux, but Custer's command is right here." He waved toward Medicine Tail Coulee. From the top of the draw they could see a line of troopers waiting on big bay horses. She had no time to pay polite attention and tugged harder on his reins, dragging him toward a line of pines. He kept turning his head, trying to see what was happening on the bluffs above the Little Big Horn.

The column waiting by the coulee advanced along the crest, becoming enveloped by dust and gun smoke. Soon the only riders they could see were Cheyenne and Hunkpapas whirling around the cloud of dust, darting in and out like swallows. "Well damn," he complained, "We'll never get to Custer *now!*"

Pines closed around them. For a time, they could still hear the gunfire – it lasted for as long as it would take a leisurely man to load and smoke a pipe.

In the dry bluffs above Tulloch's Fork, a lone Crow in war paint came over the crest, riding with deliberate haste, his tired pony taking the slope in slow motion. Seeing the oncoming brave, the captain clawed at his holster. The Magpie stopped him before he got his pistol out. The rider was Curly, the boy who had gone with Grandmother's Knife to scout for No-Hip-Bone.

Curly was exhausted. His face, sharp and handsome as a hatchet, looked pale and drawn. His pony's flanks heaved.

"You are tired," the Magpie told him.

The boy gave her weary agreement, "We rode for half the night and most of the day behind Son of the Morning Star. No-Hip-Bone sent us to guide him, but he would not be guided."

"So where's Custer?" Her captain inserted English into the conversation.

Curly did not understand, but the Magpie knew what her captain was asking. "Where is Son of the Morning Star now?"

Curly ground his hands together, like a woman crushing seeds. "Rubbed out. He would not listen. He called us women. He was like a breath feather, blown to his fate. They are all dead men now."

Magpie had no signs to express the magnitude of what had happened, so she signed to her captain, "Come, No-Hip-Bone will have someone who speaks." He seemed to understand, and they headed downstream toward the Big Horn, with Curly lagging behind on his tired horse. Dusk settled, and they lost the boy in the darkness.

By dawn the next day, they had reached the Big Horn. Finding a cold stream, she drank, inviting her captain to do the same. "Thin your blood," she told him. "Our bodies are water." He drank, then turned politely away while she washed, showing that he was a man of feeling.

When she was done, she handed him her porcupine-tail brush, showing him with hand motions that she wanted him to brush her hair. Smiling, he sat behind her, using long even strokes on her wet hair. It was wonderful to sit, hips against his knees, feeling him stroke her hair, watching morning light shine on the water. Yellow butterflies sat on black-eyed Susans by the bank, opening and closing their wings, warming themselves in the sun. Every woman's day should begin this way.

By the time her hair was shining, she saw a Fire Boat churning its way upstream beneath a pillar of smoke, and she knew that her delightful morning would end here. The captain stood up when he saw the boat, handing her back her brush, looking embarrassed. She turned to face him, having important things to say. If he could not understand her words, he might at least see her feelings. "I am sorry that we will not copulate. You are a good man, you gathered wood with energy and you brushed my hair beautifully, but it is hard to be a Crow – being pretty, brave, and helpful is not enough. Each year the Yellow-eyes crowd closer, and the buffalo go away. I cannot live my life looking out for you, keeping you out of danger, finding you when you get lost. It is better for us if that Fire Boat takes you to your own people."

Her captain stared at her, seeming dumbfounded by the speech.

From the brush above came the "Yak, yak, yak," of someone imitating a magpie. Finds-and-Kills and Plenty Good descending the draw, leading their horses. They too had seen the smoke from the Fire Boat. After an enthusiastic reunion, the Magpie turned her chin toward the Fire Boat, saying, "They will take you to No-Hip-Bone. You do not need us anymore." Plenty Good reckoned that was so, slapping Finds-and-Kills on the back, and offering his hand to the Magpie. She shook it. Then both women took their horses and headed west.

On the far bank of the Big Horn, they turned to take a last look at the Fire Boat – fine and impressive with its white woodwork, black-belching stacks, and its huge wheel whacking the water. The Magpie felt wistful, But Finds-and-Kills looked happy. Seeing her friend's smile, the Magpie asked, "Did you have a good time?"

"Oh yes," replied Finds-and-Kills. "Plenty Good is as good as his name."

On the deck of the steamer *Far West*, moored to a cottonwood at the mouth of the Little Big Horn, the captain told his story to Plenty Good. "She led me almost to Custer – then, when we got to the bluffs by the Little Big Horn, she started acting crazy, talking to herself, holding loud conversations with the air. She got angry, turned around, and brought me straight here. It was almighty strange, even for an Indian."

Plenty Good agreed that you could never tell what a Crow would do.

"Then she had me brush her hair. I thought I did a damned good job, too – but when I was done, she gives me a long lecture in Crow, and rides off. Can't figure out why. I thought she liked me."

"That's yer high-toned Crow virgin," Plenty Good laughed. "Yew were lucky to come away with both balls."

The captain raised an eyebrow, "Well, how did you do, T-Bone?"

The squawman smiled, "Well enuff. Hell, I knew right off me an' that big 'un had itches in common. When I got her in the brush, this hoss was almighty surprised to see just how *much* we had in common. But I'd say our itches are well-scratched."

The captain called Plenty Good a sly bastard, clapping him on the back, saying that he wished he handled women half so well. The steamboat's tall stacks continued to draw stragglers – a sleepy Crow rode up on a tired horse. The captain pointed him out to Plenty Good, "Hey, here's that boy we met."

The trapper took a look. "Damned if it ain't *Curly*, Gibbon's scout."

"Well, good, call to him. Find out where in the Hell Custer's gone to."

Hell, of course, is a Yellow-eye name for the Beyond.

LISA TUTTLE

Food Man

DINNER WAS the real problem.

Mornings, it was easy to rush out of the house without eating, but when it wasn't, when her mother made an issue of it, she could eat an orange or half a grapefruit. At lunchtime she was usually either at school or out so there was no one to pressure her into eating anything she didn't want. But dinner was a problem. She had to sit there, surrounded by her family, and eat whatever her mother had prepared, and no matter how she pushed it around her plate it was obvious how little she was eating. She experimented with dropping bits on the floor and secreting other bits up her sleeves or in her pockets, but it wasn't easy, her mother's eyes were so sharp, and she'd rather eat than suffer through a big embarrassing scene.

Her brother, the creep, provided the solution. He was always looking at her, staring at her, mimicking her, teasing, and while she didn't like it at any time, at meal-times it was truly unbearable. She honestly could not bear to put a bite in her mouth with him staring at her in that disgusting way. Her parents warned him to leave her alone, and shifted their places so they weren't directly facing each other, but still it wasn't enough. He said she was paranoid. She knew that even paranoids have enemies. Even if he wasn't staring at her right now he had stared before and the prospect that he might stare again clogged her throat with fear. How could she be expected to eat under such circumstances? How could anyone? If she could have dinner on a tray in her room alone, she would be fine.

Her mother, relieved by the prospect of solving two family problems at once, agreed to this suggestion. "But only for as long as you eat. If I don't see a clean plate coming out of your room you'll have to come back and sit with the rest of us."

It was easy to send clean plates out of her room. After she'd eaten what she could stomach she simply shoved the rest of the food under her bed. Suspecting that the sound of a toilet flushing immediately after a meal would arouse her mother's suspicions, she planned to get rid of the food in the morning. Only by morning she'd forgotten, and by the time she remembered it was dinnertime again.

It went on like that. Of course the food began to smell, rotting away down there under her bed, but no one else was allowed into her bedroom, and she knew the smell didn't carry beyond her closed door. It was kind of disgusting, when she was lying in bed, because then there was no avoiding it, the odor simply rose up, pushed its way through the mattress and forced itself upon her. Yet even that had its good side; she thought of it as her penance for being so fat, and was grateful for the bad smell because it made her even more adamantly opposed to the whole idea of food. How could other people bear the constant, living stink of it? The cooking, the eating, the excreting, the rotting?

When she could no longer bear the enforced, nightly intimacy with the food she refused to eat, she decided it was time to get rid of it. Before looking at it, she decided she'd better arm herself with some heavy-duty cleaning tools, paper towels, rubber gloves, maybe even a small shovel. But when she opened the door of her room to go out, there was her mother, looking as if she'd been waiting awhile.

"Where are you going?"

"What is this, a police state?" Hastily, afraid the smell would get out, she pulled her door shut behind her. "I want a glass of water."

"From the bathroom?"

"No, I thought I'd go down to the kitchen and get a glass. Why, aren't I allowed to go to the bathroom?"

"Of course you are. I was just worried – Oh, darling, you're so thin!"

"Thin is good."

"Within limits. But you're too thin, and you're getting thinner. It's not healthy. If you really are eating – "

"Of course I'm eating. You've seen my plates. I thought they'd be clean enough even for you."

"If you've been flushing your good dinners down the toilet – "

"Oh, Mother, honestly! Of course I haven't! Is that why you were lurking around up here? Trying to catch me in the act?" She realized, with considerable irritation at herself, that she could have been flushing her dinner neatly and odorlessly away for a couple of weeks before arousing suspicion, but that it had now become impossible.

"Or throwing up after you eat – "

"Oh, yuck, you'll make me sick if you talk about it! Yuck! I hate vomiting; I'm not some weirdo who likes to do it! Really!"

"I'm sorry. But I'm worried about you. If you can eat regular meals and still lose weight there must be something wrong. I think you should see a doctor."

She sighed wearily. "All right. If it will make you happy, I'll see a doctor."

She was just beginning to feel good about her body again. She didn't care what the doctor said, and when he insisted she look at herself in a full-length mirror, wearing only her underwear – something she had not dared to do for months – she was not grossed-out. The pendulous breasts, the thunder-thighs, all the fat, all the jiggling flesh, had gone, leaving someone lean, clean, and pristine. She felt proud of herself. The way the doctor looked at her was just right, too: with a certain distance, with respect. Not a trace of that horrible, furtive greed she'd seen in the eyes of her brother's friends just six months ago. The look of lust mixed with disgust which men had started giving her after her body had swelled into womanhood was something she hoped she'd never see again.

"How long since you had a period?" the doctor wanted to know.

"About four months." She was pleased about that, too. You weren't supposed to be able to turn the clock back and reject the nasty parts of growing up, but she had done it. She was in control of herself.

In reality, of course, the control was in the hands of others. As a minor, she was totally dominated by adults, chief among them her parents. After the doctor's diagnosis that she was deliberately starving herself, she was forced to return to the dinner table.

Resentful and humiliated, she pushed food around on her plate and refused to eat it. Threats of punishment only strengthened her resolve.

"That's right," she snarled. "Make me a prisoner. Let everybody know. Keep me locked up, away from my friends, with no phone and no fun – that's really going to make me psychologically healthy. That's really going to make me eat!"

Bribes were more successful, but her parents either weren't willing or could not afford to come up with a decent bribe at every single mealtime, and she simply laughed to scorn the notion that she'd let someone else control every bit of food that passed her lips for an entire week just for a pair of shoes or the use of the car on Saturday. She didn't need new clothes, CDs, the car, or anything her parents could give her, and she wanted them to know it.

Now that the battlezone was marked out and war had been openly declared, food was a constant, oppressive preoccupation. She was reminded of food by everything she saw, by everything around her. Hunger, which had once been the pleasurably sharp edge that told her she was achieving something was now a constant, miserable state. She no longer even controlled the amounts she ate; she ate even less than she wanted because she couldn't bear to let her mother feel that she was winning, that anything she put in her mouth was a concession to her. She couldn't back down now, she couldn't even appear to be backing down. If she did, she would never recover; her whole life would be lived out meekly under her mother's heavy thumb.

Lying in bed one night, trying to get her mind away from food, she realized that the smell which permeated her mattress and pillow and all her bedclothes had changed. A subtle change, yet distinctive. What had been a foul stench was now... not so foul. There was something interesting about it. She sniffed a little harder, savoring it. It was still far from being something you could describe as a good smell – it was a nasty smell, not something she'd want anyone else to suspect she could like, and yet there was something about it which made her want more. It was both deeply unpleasant and curiously exciting. She couldn't explain even to herself why the bad smell had become so pleasurable to her. It made her think of sex, which sounded so awful when it was described. No matter how they tried to make it glamorous in the movies, the act itself was clearly awkward and nasty. And yet it was obvious that the participants found that embarrassing, awkward nastiness deeply wonderful and were desperate for a chance to do it again. It was one of the great mysteries of life.

She wondered what the food under her bed looked like now. All the different foods, cooked and uncooked, pushed together into one great mass, breaking down, rotting, flowing together... Had it undergone a change into something rich and strange? Or would the sight of it make her puke? She had decided she was never going to clean under her bed – her refusal, although unknown by her mother, was another blow against her – but now, all of a sudden, she wished she could see it.

There was a movement under her bed.

Was it her imagination? She held very still, even holding her breath, and it came again, stronger and more certain. This time she felt as well as heard it. The bed was rocked by something moving underneath. Whatever was moving under there was coming out.

Although she'd turned out her lamp before going to bed, her room was not totally dark; it never was. The curtains were unlined and let in light from the street, so there was always a pale, yellowish glow. By this dim, constant light she saw the man who emerged from under her bed.

Her heart beat harder at the sight of him, but she was not frightened. There might not be light enough to read by, but there was enough to show her this man was no ordinary serial killer, burglar, or rapist from off the street. For one thing, he wore no clothes. For another, he was clearly not a normal human being. The smell of him was indescribable. It was the smell of rotting food; it was the smell of her own bed. And, she did not forget, she had wished to see what her food had become.

He made no menacing or seductive or self-willed motions but simply stood there, showing himself to her. When she had looked her fill she invited him into her bed, and he gave himself to her just as she wanted.

What took place in her bed thereafter was indescribable. She could not herself remember it very clearly the next day – certainly not the details of who did what to whom with what when and where. What she would never forget was the intense, sensory experience of it all: his smell, that dreadful stench with its subtle, enticing undercurrent, that addictive, arousing odor which he exuded in great gusts with every motion, and which, ultimately, seemed to wrap around her and absorb her like the great cloak of sleep; the exciting pressure of his body on hers, intimate and demanding and satisfying in a way she could never have imagined; and her own orgasms, more powerful than anything she'd previously experienced on her own.

She understood about sex now. To an outsider it looked ridiculous or even horrible, but it wasn't for looking at, and certainly not by outsiders – it was for feeling. It was about nothing but feeling, feeling things you'd never felt before, having feelings you couldn't have by yourself, being felt. It was wonderful.

In the morning she woke to daylight, alone in her deliciously smelly bed, and she felt transformed. She suspected she had not, in the technical sense, lost her virginity; far from losing anything, she had gained something indescribable. She felt different; she felt expanded and enriched; she felt powerful; she felt hungry. She went downstairs and, ignoring as usual her mother's pitiful breakfast offering, went to the counter and put two slices of bread in the toaster.

Wisely, her mother did not comment. Her brother did, when she sat down at the table with two slices of toast thickly spread with peanut butter. "What's this, your new diet?"

"Shut up, pig-face," she said calmly, and, yes, her mother let her get away with that, too. Oh, she was untouchable today; she had her secret, a new source of power.

At lunchtime the apple she'd intended to eat wasn't enough, and she consumed the cheese sandwich her mother had made for her, and the carrot sticks, a bag of potato chips, and a pot of strawberry yoghurt. Sex, she realized, took a lot of energy, burned a lot of calories. She had to replace them, and she had to build herself up. Now that she had a reason for wanting to be fit and strong she recognized how weak she had become by not eating. She wouldn't have to worry about getting fat, not for a long time, not as long as the nightly exercise continued.

It did continue, and grew more strenuous as her strength, her curiosity, her imagination, all her appetites increased. She no longer feared getting fat; on the contrary, she was eager to gain weight. She wanted to be stronger, and she needed more weight for muscle. More flesh was not to be sneered at, now that she knew how flesh could be caressed and aroused. She ate the meals that were prepared for her, and more. She no longer had to be obsessive about controlling her intake of food because it was no longer the one area of her life she felt she had some control over. Now she controlled the creature under her bed, and their passionate nights together were the secret which made the daytime rule of parents, teachers, and rules bearable.

Her nights were much more important than her days, and during the night she was in complete control. Or so she thought, until the night her creature did something she didn't like.

It was no big deal, really; he just happened to trap her in an uncomfortable position when he got on top of her, and he didn't immediately respond to her attempts to get him to move. It was something anyone might have done, inadvertently, unaware of her feelings – but he was not "anyone" and he'd never been less than totally aware of her every sensation and slightest desire. Either he'd been aware that he was hurting her because he'd intended it, or he'd been unaware because he was no longer so much hers as he'd been in the beginning, because he was becoming someone else. She wasn't sure which prospect she found the more frightening.

The rot had started in their relationship, and although each incremental change was tiny – hardly noticeable to someone less sensitive than she – they soon demolished her notion of being in control.

She was not in control. She had no power. She lived for her nights with him; she needed him. But what if he didn't need her? What if one night he no longer wanted her?

It could happen. He'd started to criticize, his fingers pinching the excess flesh which had grown back, with her greed, on her stomach and thighs, and she could tell by the gingerly way he handled her newly expanded breasts and ass that he didn't like the way they jiggled. When he broke off a kiss too quickly she knew it was because he didn't like the garlic or the onions on her breath. The unspoken threat was always there: one night he might not kiss her at all. One night he might just stay under the bed.

She didn't think she could bear that. Having known sex, she was now just like all those people she'd found so incomprehensible in books and movies: she had to keep on having it. And she knew no other partner would satisfy her. She'd been spoiled by her food man for anyone else.

She began to diet. But it was different this time. Once not-eating had been pleasurable and easy; now it was impossibly difficult. She no longer liked being hungry; it made her feel weak and cranky, not powerful at all, not at all the way she'd used to feel. This time she wasn't starving to please herself and spite the world, but to please someone else. She went on doing it only because she decided she preferred sex to food; she could give up one if allowed to keep the other. And by promising herself sex, rewarding herself with explicit, graphic, sensual memories every time she said no to something to eat, she managed to continue starving herself back to desirability.

This suffering wouldn't be forever. Once she'd reached her – or his – ideal weight, she hoped to maintain it with sufficient exercise and ordinary meals.

But the sex that she was starving herself for was no longer all that great. She was so hungry it was hard to concentrate. His smell kept reminding her of food instead of the sex they were engaged in. Except when she was on the very brink of orgasm, she just couldn't seem to stop thinking about food.

And as time went on, and she still wasn't quite thin enough to please him, not quite thin enough to stop her killing diet, she began to wonder why she was doing it. What was so great about sex, anyway? She could give herself an orgasm any time she wanted, all by herself. Maybe they weren't so intense, maybe they were over quicker, but so what? When they were over she used to fall asleep contented, like someone with a full stomach, instead of lying awake, sated in one sense but just beginning to remember how hungry she still was for food. As for arousal – what was so great about arousal? It was too much like hunger. It was fine in retrospect, when it had been satisfied, but while it was going on it was just like hunger, an endless need, going on and painfully on.

She didn't know how much longer she could bear it. And then, one night, she went from not knowing to not being able. When her lover climbed into bed with her, swinging one leg across her, holding her down as he so often did now, keeping her in her place, the smell of him made her feel quite giddy with desire, and her mouth filled with saliva.

As his soft, warm, odorous face descended to hers she bit into it, and it was just like a dinner roll freshly baked. She even, as her teeth sank into his nose, tasted the salty tang of butter.

He did not cry out – he never had made a sound in all the nights she had known him – nor did he try to escape or fight back as she bit and tore away a great chunk of his face and greedily chewed and swallowed it. She felt a tension in him, a general stiffening, and then, as, unable to resist, she took a second bite, she recognized what he was feeling. It was sexual excitement. It was desire. He wanted to be eaten. This was what he had wanted from the very first night, when he had pressed himself, first his face and then all the other parts of his body in turn, against her mouth – only she had misunderstood. But this was what he was for.

She ate him.

It was the best ever, better by far than their first night together, which had seemed to her at that time so wonderful. That had been only sex. This was food and sex together, life and death.

When she had finished she felt enormous. Sprawling on the bed, she took up the whole of it and her arms and legs dangled off the sides. She was sure she must be at least twice her usual size. And the curious thing was that although she felt satisfied, she did not feel at all full. She was still hungry.

Well, maybe hungry wasn't exactly the right word. Of course she wasn't hungry. But she still had space for something more. She still wanted something more.

The springs groaned as she sat up, and her feet hit the floor much sooner than she'd expected. She was bigger than usual; not only fatter, but taller, too. She had to duck to get through her own bedroom door.

She stood for a moment in the hall, enjoying her enormous new size and the sense of power it gave her. This, not starving herself and not having secret sex, was true power. Food and eating and strength and size. She knew she wanted to eat something more, maybe a lot of something more before the night was over. There was a smell in the air which had her moist and salivating with desire. She licked her lips and looked around, her fingers flexing, but there wasn't much of interest in the hallway. A framed, studio portrait of the family hung above the only piece of furniture, a small table with a wobbly leg. On the table was a telephone, a pad of yellow post-it notes, and a gnawed wooden pencil. The taste of the pencil was as immediately familiar to her as the salty tang of her own dandruff and sloughed skin cells beneath a nibbled fingernail, and did about as much to satisfy her hunger. The shiny, dark chocolate-colored telephone wasn't as easy to eat as the pencil had been, but she persevered, and had crunched her way through more than half of it before the unpleasant lack of taste, and the discomfort of eating shards of plastic, really registered. She finished it anyway – it was all fuel – and then sniffed the air.

From the bedrooms where her brother and her parents slept drifted the rich, strong, disturbing smells of sex and food. Aroused and ravenous, she followed the scent of her next meal.

DELIA SHERMAN
Young Woman in a Garden

▚▚

BEAUVOISIN (1839 – 1898)

Edouard Beauvoisin was expected to follow in the footsteps of his father, a provincial doctor. However, when he demonstrated a talent for drawing, his mother saw to it that he was provided with formal training. In 1856, Beauvoisin went to Paris, where he worked at the Académie Suisse and associated with the young artists disputing romanticism and classicism at the Brasserie des Martyres. In 1868, he married the artist Céleste Rohan. He exhibited in the Salon des Refusés in 1863, and was a member of the 1874 Salon of Impressionists. In 1876 he moved to Brittany where he lived and painted until his death in 1898. He is best known for the figure-studies *Young Woman in a Garden* and *Reclining Nude*.

  Impressions of the Impressionists
    Oxford University Press, 1970

M. Henri Tanguy
Director
Musée La Roseraie
Portrieux, Brittany
France
January 6, 1990

Monsieur:

  I write to you at the suggestion of M. Rouart of the Musée d'Orsay to request permission to visit the house of M. Edouard Beauvoisin and to consult those of his personal papers that are kept there.

  In pursuit of a Ph.D. degree in the History of Art, I am preparing a thesis on the life and work of M. Beauvoisin, who, in my opinion, has been unfairly neglected in the history of Impressionism.

Enclosed is a letter of introduction from my adviser, Professor Boodman of the Department of Art History at the University of Massachusetts. She has advised me to tell you that I also have a personal interest in M. Beauvoisin's life, for his brother was my great-great-grandfather.

I expect to be in France from May 1 of this year, and to stay for at least two months. My visit to La Roseraie may be scheduled according to your convenience. Awaiting your answer, I have the honor to be

– Your servant, Theresa Stanton

When Theresa finally found La Roseraie at the end of an unpaved, narrow road, she was tired and dusty and on the verge of being annoyed. Edouard Beauvoisin had been an Impressionist, even if only a minor Impressionist, and his house was a museum, open by appointment to the public. At home in Massachusetts, that would mean signs, postcards in the nearest village, certainly a brochure in the local tourist office with color pictures of the garden and the master's studio and a good clear map showing how to get there.

France wasn't Massachusetts, not by a long shot.

M. Tanguy hadn't met her at the Portrieux station as he had promised, the local tourist office had been sketchy in its directions, and the driver of the local bus had been depressingly uncertain about where to let her off. Her feet were sore, her backpack heavy, and even after asking at the last two farmhouses she'd passed, Theresa still wasn't sure she'd found the right place. The house didn't look like a museum: gray stone, low-browed and secretive, its front door unequivocally barred, its low windows blinded with heavy white lace curtains. The gate was stiff and loud with rust. Still, there was a neat stone path leading around to the back of the house and a white sign with the word "*jardin*" printed on it and a faded black hand pointing down the path. Under the scent of dust and greenery, there was a clean, sharp scent of salt water. Theresa hitched up her backpack, heaved open the gate, and followed the hand's gesture.

"Monet," was her first thought when she saw the garden, and then, more accurately, "Beauvoisin." Impressionist, certainly – an incandescent, carefully balanced dazzle of yellow light, clear green grass, and carmine flowers against a celestial background. Enchanted, Theresa unslung her camera and captured a couple of faintly familiar views of flower beds and sequined water before turning to the house itself.

The back door was marginally more welcoming than the front, for at least it boasted a visible bell-pull and an aged, hand-lettered sign directing the visitor to "*sonnez*," which Theresa did, once hopefully, once impatiently, and once again for luck. She was just thinking that she'd have to walk back to Portrieux and call M. Tanguy when the heavy door opened inward, revealing a Goya-esque old woman. Against the flat shadows of a stone passage, she was a study in black and white: long wool skirt and linen blouse, sharp eyes and finely crinkled skin.

The woman looked Theresa up and down, then made as if to shut the door in her face.

"Wait," cried Theresa, putting her hand on the warm planks. "*Arretez. S'il vous plait. Un moment.* Please!"

The woman's gaze travelled to Theresa's face. Theresa smiled charmingly.

"*Eh, bien?*" asked the woman impatiently.

Pulling her French around her, Theresa explained that she was making researches into the life and work of the famous M. Beauvoisin, that she had written in the winter for permission to see the museum, that seeing it was of the first importance to completing her work. She had received a letter from M. le Directeur, setting an appointment for today.

The woman raised her chin suspiciously. Her smile growing rigid, Theresa juggled camera and bag, dug out the letter, and handed it over. The woman examined it front and back, then returned it with an eloquent gesture of shoulders, head, and neck that conveyed her utter indifference to Theresa's work, her interest in Edouard Beauvoisin, and her charm.

"*Ferme,*" she said, and suited the action to the word.

"*Parent,*" said Theresa rather desperately. "*Je suis de la famille de M. Beauvoisin.*"

From the far end of the shadowy passage, a soft, deep voice spoke in accented English. "Of course you are, my dear. A great-grand-niece, I believe. Luna," she shifted to French, "surely you remember the letter from M. le Directeur about our little American relative?" And in English again. "Please to come through. I am Mme. Beauvoisin."

In 1874, Céleste's mother died, leaving La Roseraie to her only child. There was some talk of selling the house to satisfy the couple's immediate financial embarrassments, but the elder Mme. Beauvoisin came to the rescue once again with a gift of 20,000 francs. After paying off his debts, Beauvoisin decided that Paris was just too expensive, and moved with Céleste to Portrieux in the spring of 1875.

"I have taken some of my mother's gift and put it towards transforming the ancient dairy of La Roseraie into a studio," he wrote Manet. "Ah, solitude! You cannot imagine how I crave it, after the constant sociability of Paris. I realize now that the cafés affected me like absinthe: stimulating and full of visions, but death to the body and damnation to the soul."

In the early years of what his letters to Manet humorously refer to as his "exile," Beauvoisin travelled often to Paris, and begged his old friends to come and stay with him. After 1879, however, he became something of a recluse, terminating his trips to Paris and discouraging visits, even from the Manets. He spent the last twenty years of his life a virtual hermit, painting the subjects that were dearest to him: the sea, his garden, the fleets of fishing-boats that sailed daily out and back from the harbor of Portrieux.

The argument has been made that Beauvoisin had never been as clannish as others among the Impressionists – Renoir and Monet, for example, who regularly set up their easels and painted the same scene side by side. Certainly Beauvoisin seemed unusually reluctant to paint his friends and family. His single portrait of his wife, executed not long after their marriage, is one of his poorest canvases: stiff, awkwardly posed, and uncharacteristically muddy in color. "Mme. Beauvoisin takes exception to my treatment of her dress," he complained in a letter to Manet, "or the shadow of the chair, or the balance of the composition. God save me from the notions of women who think themselves artists!"

In 1877, the Beauvoisins took a holiday in Spain, and there met a young woman named Luz Gascó, who became Edouard's favorite – indeed his only – model. The several nude studies of her, together with the affectionate intimacy of Young Woman in a Garden leaves little doubt as to the nature of their relationship, even in the absence of documentary evidence. Luz came to live with the Beauvoisins at La Roseraie in 1878, and remained there even after Beauvoisin's death in 1898. She inherited the house and land from Mme. Beauvoisin and died in 1914, just after the outbreak of the First World War.

    – Lydia Chopin. "Lives Lived in Shadow: Edouard and Céleste
    Beauvoisin." *Apollo*. Winter, 1989.

The garden of La Roseraie extended through a series of terraced beds down to the water's edge and up into the house itself by way of a bank of uncurtained French doors in the parlor. When Theresa first followed her hostess into the room, her impression was of blinding light and color and of flowers everywhere – scattered on the chairs and sofas, strewn underfoot, heaped on every flat surface, vining across the walls. The air was somnolent with peonies and roses and bee-song.

"A lovely room."

"It has been kept just as it was in the time of Beauvoisin, though I fear the fabrics have faded sadly. You may recognize the sofa from *Young Woman Reading* and *Reclining Nude,* also the view down the terrace."

The flowers on the sofa were pillows, printed or needlepointed with huge, blowsy, ambiguous blooms. Those pillows had formed a textural contrast to the model's flat black gown in *Young Woman Reading* and sounded a sensual, almost erotic note in *Reclining Nude.* As Theresa touched one almost reverently – it had supported the model's head – the unquiet colors of the room settled in place around it, and she saw that there were indeed flowers everywhere. Real petals had blown in from the terrace to brighten the faded woven flowers of the carpet, and the walls and chairs were covered in competing chintzes to provide a background for the plain burgundy velvet sofa, the wooden easel, and the portrait over the mantel of a child dressed in white.

"Céleste," said Mme. Beauvoisin. "Céleste Yvonne Léna Rohan, painted at the age of six by some Academician – I cannot at the moment recollect his name, although M. Rohan was as proud of securing his services as if he'd been Ingres himself. She hated it."

"How could you possibly…" Theresa's question trailed off at the amusement in Mme. Beauvoisin's face.

"Family legend. The portrait is certainly very stiff and finished, and Céleste grew to be a disciple of Morisot and Manet. Taste in aesthetic matters develops very young, do you not agree?"

"I do," said Theresa. "At any rate, I've loved the Impressionists since I was a child. I wouldn't blame her for hating the portrait. It's technically accomplished, yes, but it says nothing about its subject except that she was blonde and played the violin."

"That violin!" Mme. Beauvoisin shook her head, ruefully amused. "Mme. Rohan's castle in Spain. The very sight of it was a torture to

Céleste. And her hair darkened as she grew older, so you see the portrait tells you nothing. This, on the other hand, tells all."

She led Theresa to a small painting hung by the door. "Luz Gascó," she said. "Painted in 1879."

Liquid, animal eyes gleamed at Theresa from the canvas, their gaze at once inviting and promising, intimate as a kiss. Theresa glanced aside at Mme. Beauvoisin, who was studying the portrait, her head tilted to one side, her wrinkled lips smoothed by a slight smile. Feeling unaccountably embarrassed, Theresa frowned at the painting with self-conscious professionalism. It was, she thought, an oil study of the model's head for Beauvoisin's most famous painting, *Young Woman in a Garden*. The face was tilted up to the observer and partially shadowed. The brushwork was loose and free, the boundaries between the model's hair and the background blurred, the molding of her features suggested rather than represented.

"A remarkable portrait," Theresa said. "She seems very... alive."

"Indeed," said Mme. Beauvoisin. "And very beautiful." She turned abruptly and, gesturing Theresa to a chair, arranged herself on the sofa opposite. The afternoon light fell across her shoulder, highlighting her white hair, the pale rose pinned in the bosom of her high-necked dress, her hands folded on her lap. Her fingers were knotted and swollen with arthritis. Theresa wondered how old she was and why M. Tanguy had said nothing of a caretaker in his letter to her.

"Your work?" prompted Mme. Beauvoisin gently.

Theresa pulled herself up and launched into what she thought of as her dissertation spiel: neglected artist, brilliant technique, relatively small oeuvre, social isolation, mysterious ménage. "What I keep coming back to," she said, "is his isolation. He hardly ever went to Paris after 1879, and even before that he didn't go on those group painting trips the other Impressionists loved so much. He never shared a studio even though he was so short of money, or let anyone watch him paint. And yet his letters to Manet suggest that he wasn't a natural recluse – anything but."

"Thus Luz Gascó?" asked Mme. Beauvoisin.

"I'm sorry?"

"Luz Gascó. Perhaps you think she was the cause of Beauvoisin's – how shall I say? – Beauvoisin's retreat from society?"

Theresa gave a little bounce in her chair. "That's just it, you see. No one really knows. There are a lot of assumptions, especially by *male* historians, but no one really knows. What I'm looking for is evidence one way or the other. At first I thought she couldn't have been..." She hesitated, suddenly self-conscious.

"Yes?" The low voice was blandly polite, yet Theresa felt herself teased, or perhaps tested. It annoyed her, and her answer came a little more sharply than necessary.

"Beauvoisin's mistress." Mme. Beauvoisin raised her brows and Theresa shrugged apologetically. "There's not much known about Céleste, but nothing suggests that she was particularly meek or down-trodden. I don't think she'd have allowed Luz to live here all those years, much less left the house to her, if she knew she was... involved with her husband."

"Perhaps she knew and did not concern herself." Mme. Beauvoisin offered this consideringly.

"I hadn't thought of that," said Theresa. "I'd need proof, though. I'm not interested in speculation, theory, or even in a juicy story. I'm interested in the truth."

Mme. Beauvoisin's smile said that she found Theresa very young, very charming. "Yes," she said slowly. "I believe you are." Her voice grew brisker. "Beauvoisin's papers are in some disorder, you understand. Your search may take you some weeks, and Portrieux is far to travel twice a day. It would please me if you would accept the hospitality of La Roseraie."

Theresa closed her eyes. It was a graduate student's dream come true, to be invited into her subject's home, to touch and use his things, to live his life. Mme. Beauvoisin, misinterpreting the gesture, said, "Please stay. This project – Beauvoisin's papers – it is of great importance to us, to Luna and to me. We feel that you are well suited to the task."

To emphasize her words, she laid her twisted hand on Theresa's arm. The gesture brought her face into the sun, which leached her eyes and skin to transparency and made a glory of her silvered hair. Theresa stared at her, entranced.

"Thank you," she said. "I would be honored."

YOUNG WOMAN IN A GARDEN (LUZ AT LA ROSERAIE) 1879
Edouard Beauvoisin's artistic reputation rests on this portrait of his
Spanish mistress, Luz Gascó, seated in the garden of La Roseraie. As in
Reclining Nude, the composition is arranged around a figure that seems
to be the painting's source of light as well as its visual focus. Luz sits
with her face and body in shade and her feet and hands in bright sunlight. Yet the precision with which her shadowy figure is rendered, the
delicate modeling of the face, and the suggestion of light shining down
through the leaves onto the dark hair draw the viewer's eye up and
away from the brightly-lit foreground. The brushwork of the white
blouse is especially masterly, the coarse texture of the linen suggested
with a scumble of pale pink, violet, and gray.
   – Exhibition Catalogue, "The Unknown Impressionists,"
     Museum of Fine Arts, Boston, MA

"This is the studio."

Mme. Beauvoisin laid her hand on the blue-painted door, hesitated,
then stepped aside. "Please," she said, and gave Theresa a courteous
nod.

Heart tripping over itself with excitement, Theresa pushed open the
door and stepped into Beauvoisin's studio. The room was shuttered,
black as midnight; she knocked over a chair, which fell with an echo-
ing clatter.

"I fear the trustees have hardly troubled themselves to unlock the
door since they came into possession of the property," said Mme.
Beauvoisin apologetically. "And Luna and I have little occasion to
come here." Theresa heard her shoe-heels tapping across the flagstone
floor. A creak, a bang, and weak sunlight struggled over a clutter of
easels, canvases, trunks and boxes, chairs, stools, and small tables dis-
posed around a round stove and a shabby sofa. *The French sure are
peculiar*, Theresa thought. *What a way to run a museum!*

Mme. Beauvoisin had taken up a brush and was standing before
one of the easels in the attitude of a painter interrupted at work. For a
moment, Theresa thought she saw a canvas on the easel, an oil sketch
of a seated figure. An unknown Beauvoisin? As she stepped forward to
look, an ancient swag of cobweb broke and showered her head with
flies and powdery dust. She sneezed convulsively.

"God bless you," said Mme. Beauvoisin, laying the brush on the empty easel. "Luna brings a broom. Pah! What filth! Beauvoisin must quiver in his tomb, such an orderly man as he was!"

Soon, the old woman arrived with the promised broom, a pail of water, and a settled expression of grim disapproval. She poked at the cobwebs with the broom, glared at Theresa, then began to sweep with concentrated ferocity, raising little puffs of dust as she went and muttering to herself, witch-like.

"So young," she said. "Too young. Too full of ideas. Too much like Edouard, *enfin.*"

Theresa bit her lip, caught between curiosity and irritation. Curiosity won. "How am I like him, Luna?" she asked. "And how can you know? He's been dead almost a hundred years."

The old woman straightened and turned, her face creased deep with fury. "Luna!" she snarled. "Who has given you the right to call me Luna? I am not a servant, to be addressed without respect."

"You're not? I mean, of course not. I beg your pardon, Mlle...?" And Theresa looked a wild appeal to Mme. Beauvoisin, who said, "The fault is entirely mine, Mlle. Stanton, for not introducing you sooner. Mlle. Gascó is my companion."

Theresa laughed nervously, as at an incomprehensible joke. "You're kidding," she said. "Mlle. Gascó? But that was the model's name, Luz's name. I don't understand. Who are you, anyway?"

Mme. Beauvoisin shrugged dismissively. "There is nothing to understand. We are Beauvoisin's heirs. And the contents of this studio are our inheritance, which is yours also. Come and look." With a theatrical flourish, she indicated a cabinet built along the back wall. "Open it," she said. "The doors are beyond my strength."

Theresa looked from Mme. Beauvoisin to Mlle. Gascó and back again. Every scholar knows that coincidences happen, that people leave things to their relatives, that reality is sometimes unbelievably strange. And this was what she had come for, after all, to open the cabinet, to recover all the mysteries and illuminate the shadows of Beauvoisin's life. Perhaps this Mlle. Gascó was his illegitimate granddaughter or something. Perhaps both women were playing some elaborate and obscure game with her. In any case, it wasn't any of her business. Her business was with the cabinet and its contents.

The door was warped, and Theresa had to struggle with it for a good while before it creaked stiffly open on a cold stench of mildew and the shadowy forms of dispatch boxes neatly arranged on long shelves. Theresa sighed happily. Here they were, Beauvoisin's papers, a scholar's treasure-trove, her ticket to a degree, a career, a profession. And they were all hers. She reached out both hands and gathered in the nearest box. As the damp cardboard yielded to her fingers, she felt a sudden panic that the papers would be mildewed into illegibility. But the papers were wrapped in oilcloth and perfectly dry.

Reverently, Theresa lifted out a packet of letters, tied with black tape. The top one was folded so that some of the text showed. Having just spent a month working with Beauvoisin's letters to Manet at the Bibliothéque National, she immediately recognized his hand, tiny and angular and blessedly legible. Theresa slipped the letter free from the packet and opened it. *I have met*, she read, *a dozen other young artists in the identical state of fearful ecstasy as I, feeling great things about Art and Beauty which we are half-shy of expressing, yet must express or die.*

"Thérèse." Mme. Beauvoisin sounded amused. "First we must clean this place. Then you may read Beauvoisin's words with more comfort and less danger of covering them with smuts."

Theresa became aware that she was holding the precious letter in an unforgivably dirty hand. "Oh," she said, chagrined. "I'm so sorry. I *know* better than this."

"It is the excitement of discovery." Mme. Beauvoisin took the letter from her and rubbed lightly at the corner with her apron. "See, it comes clean, all save a little shadow that may easily be overlooked." She folded the letter, slipped it back into the packet, returned it to the box, and tucked the oilcloth over it.

"Today, the preparation of the canvas," she said. "Tomorrow, you may begin the sketch."

Edouard Beauvoisin had indeed been an orderly man. The letters were parcelled up by year, in order of receipt, and labelled. Turning over Manet's half of their long correspondence, Theresa briefly regretted her choice of research topic. Manet's was a magic name, a name to conjure up publishers and job offers, fame and what passed for fortune among art historians. But Manet, who had been documented, described, and analyzed by every art historian worth a pince-nez, could never be hers as Beauvoisin was hers.

Theresa sorted out all the business papers, the bills for paint and canvas, the notes from obscure friends. What was left was what she gleefully called the good stuff: a handful of love-notes written by Céleste Rohan over the two years Beauvoisin had courted her, three boxes of letters from his mother, and two boxes of his answers, which must have been returned to him at her death.

It took Theresa a week to work through the letters, a week of long hours reading in the studio and short, awkward meals eaten in the kitchen with Mme. Beauvoisin and Luna. It was odd. In the house and garden, they were everywhere, present as the sea-smell, forever on the way to some domestic task or other, yet never too busy to inquire politely and extensively after her progress. Or at least Mme. Beauvoisin was never too busy. Luna mostly glared at her, hoped she wasn't wasting her time, warned her not to go picking the flowers or walking on the grass. It didn't take long for Theresa to decide that she didn't like Luna.

She did, however, discover that she liked Edouard Beauvoisin. In the studio, Theresa could lose herself in Beauvoisin's world of artists and models. The letters to his mother from his early years in Paris painted an intriguing portrait of an intelligent, passionate, and above all, naive young man whose most profound desire was to capture and define Beauty in charcoal and oils. He wrote of poses and technical problems and what his teacher M. Couture had said about his life studies, reaffirming in each letter his intention *to draw and draw and draw until every line breathes the essence of the thing itself*. A little over a year later, he was speaking less of line and more of color; the name Couture disappeared from his letters, to be replaced by Manet, Degas, Duranty, and the brothers Goncourt. By 1860, he had quit the Ecole des Beaux Arts and registered to copy the Old Masters at the Louvre. A year later, he met Céleste Rohan at the house of Berthe Morisot's sister Edma Pontillon:

She is like a Raphael Madonna, tall and slender and pale, and divinely unconscious of her own beauty. She said very little at dinner, but afterwards in the garden with Morisot conversed with me an hour or more. I learned then that she is thoughtful and full of spirit, loves Art and Nature, and is herself something of an artist, with a number of watercolors and oil sketches to her credit that, according to Morisot, show considerable promise.

Three months later, he announced to his mother that Mlle. Rohan had accepted his offer of hand and heart. Mme. Beauvoisin the elder said everything that was proper, although a note of worry did creep through in her final lines:

> I am a little concerned about her painting. To be sure, painting is an amiable accomplishment in a young girl, but you must be careful, in your joy at finding a soul-mate, not to foster useless ambitions in her breast. I'm sure you both agree that a wife must have no other profession than seeing to the comfort of her husband, particularly when her husband is an artist and entirely unable to see to his own.

When she read this, Theresa snorted. Perhaps her mother-in-law was why Céleste, like Edma Morisot and dozens of other lady artists, had laid down her brush when she married. Judging from her few surviving canvases, she'd been a talented painter, if too indebted to the style of Berthe Morisot. Now, if Céleste had just written to her future husband about painting or ambition or women's role in marriage, Theresa would have an easy chapter on the repression of women artists in nineteenth-century France.

It was with high hope, therefore, that Theresa opened the small bundle of Céleste's correspondence. She soon discovered that however full of wit and spirit Céleste may have been in conversation, on paper she was terse and dull. Her letters were limited to a few scrawled lines of family news, expressions of gratitude for books her fiancé had recommended, and a few, shy declarations of maidenly affection. The only signs of her personality were the occasional vivid sketches with which she illustrated her notes: a seal pup sunning itself on the rocks at the mouth of the bay; a cow peering thoughtfully in through the dairy window.

Theresa folded Céleste's letters away, tied the tape neatly around them, and sighed. She was beginning to feel discouraged. No wonder there'd been so little written on Edouard Beauvoisin. No wonder his studio was neglected, his museum unmarked, his only curators an eccentric pair of elderly women. There had been dozens of competent but uninspired followers of the Impressionists who once or twice in the course of their lives had managed to paint great pictures. The only thing that set Edouard Beauvoisin apart from them was the mystery of Luz Gascó, and as Theresa read his dutiful letters to his mother, she found that she just could not believe that the man who had written them could bring his mistress to live with his wife. More importantly, found herself disbelieving that he could ever have painted *Young Woman in a Garden*. Yet there it incontrovertibly was, hanging in the Museum of Fine Arts, signed "Edouard Beauvoisin, 1879," clear as print and authenticated five ways from Sunday.

A breeze stirred the papers scattered across the work-table. Under the ever-present tang of the sea, Theresa smelled lilies of the valley. She propped her hands on her chin and looked out into the garden. A pretty day, she thought, and a pretty view. It might make a picture, were there anything to balance the window-frame and the green shade of the linden tree in the left foreground. Oh, there was the rose-bed, but it wasn't enough. Then a figure stepped into the scene, bent to the roses, clipped a bloom, laid it in the basket dangling from her elbow: Gascó, a red shawl tied Spaniard-wise across her white morning gown, her wild hair escaping from its pins and springing around her face as she stooped. Her presence focussed the composition, turned it into an interesting statement of light and tension.

Don't move, Theresa thought. For God's sake, Gascó, don't move. Squinting at the scene, she opened a drawer with a practiced jerk and felt for the sketchbook, which was not on top, where it should be, where it always was. Irritated, she tore her eyes from Gascó to look for it. Lying in the drawer was a child's *cahier*, marbled black-and-white, with a plain white label pasted on its cover and marked "May–June 1898" in a tiny, angular, blessedly legible hand.

"Out of place," she murmured angrily, then, "This is *it*," without any clear idea of what she meant by either statement.

Theresa swallowed, aware that something unimaginably significant had happened, was happening, that she was trembling and sweating with painful excitement. Carefully, she wiped her hands on her jeans, lifted the *cahier* from its wooden tomb, opened it to its last entry: June 5, 1898. The hand was scratchier, more sprawled than in his letters, the effect, perhaps, of the wasting disease that would kill him in July.

The Arrangement. A pity my death must void it. How well it has served us over the years, and how happily! At least, C. has seemed happy; for L.'s discontents, there has never been any answer, except to leave and make other arrangements of her own. Twenty years of flying into rages, sinking into sulks, refusing to stand thus and so or to hold a pose not to her liking, hating Brittany, the cold, the damp, the gray sea. And still she stays. Is it the Arrangement that binds her, or her beloved garden? *Young Woman in a Garden: Luz at La Roseraie*. If I have a fear of dying, it is that I must be remembered for that painting. God's judgment on our Arrangement, Maman would have said, had she known of it. When I come to make my last Confession, soon, oh, very soon now, I will beg forgiveness for deceiving her. It is my only regret.

By dusk, Theresa had read the notebook through and begun to search for its fellows. That there had to be more notebooks was as clear as Monet's palette: the first entry began in mid-sentence, for one thing, and no man talks to himself so fluently without years of practice. They wouldn't be hidden; Beauvoisin hadn't been a secretive man. Tidy-minded. Self-contained. Conservative. He stored them somewhere, Theresa thought. Somewhere here. She looked around the darkening studio. Maybe it would be clearer to her in the morning. It would certainly be lighter.

Out in the garden, Theresa felt the depression of the past weeks release her, like a hand opening. *A discovery! A real discovery!* What difference did it make whether Beauvoisin had painted two good paintings or a dozen? There was a mystery about him, and she, Theresa Stanton, was on the verge of uncovering it. She wanted to babble and sing and go out drinking to celebrate. But her friends were three thousand miles away, and all she had was Mme. Beauvoisin. And Luna. Always Luna.

Theresa's quick steps slowed. What was her hurry, after all? Her news would keep, and the garden was so lovely in the failing light, with the white pebble path luminous under her feet, the evening air blue and warm and scented with lilies.

In the parlor, an oil lamp laid its golden hand upon the two women sitting companionably together on the velvet sofa, their heads bent to their invisible tasks. The soft play of light and shadow varnished their hair and skin with youth. Theresa struggled with a momentary and inexplicable sense of déjà vu, then, suddenly embarrassed, cleared her throat. "I found a notebook today," she announced into the silence. "Beauvoisin's private journal."

Luna's head came up, startled and alert. Theresa caught a liquid flash as she glanced at her, then at Mme. Beauvoisin.

"A journal?" asked Mme. Beauvoisin blandly. "Ah. I might have guessed he would have kept a journal. You must be very pleased – such documents are important to scholars. Come. Pour yourself a brandy to celebrate – the bottle is on the sideboard – and sit and tell us of your great discovery."

As Theresa obediently crossed the room and unstopped the decanter, she heard a furious whisper. "*Mierda!*"

"Hush, Luna." Mme. Beauvoisin's tone was happy, almost gleeful. "We agreed. Whatever she finds, she may use. It is her right."

"I withdraw my agreement. I know nothing of these journals. Who can tell what he may have written?"

A deep and affectionate sigh. "Oh, Luna. Still so suspicious?"

"Not suspicious. Wise. The little American, she is of Edouard's blood and also Edouard's soul. I have seen him in her eyes."

Theresa set down the decanter and came back into the lamplight. "Wait a minute. I don't understand. Of course I have the right to use the journals. M. Tanguy promised me full access to all Beauvoisin's papers. And he didn't say anything about you. Where is he anyway?"

Mme. Beauvoisin's dark, faded eyes held hers for a moment. "Please, do not discommode yourself," she said. "Sit and tell us what you have found."

Hesitant under Luna's hot and disapproving gaze, Theresa perched herself on the edge of a chair and did as she was told.

"I'd no idea he was so passionate," she said at last. "In his letters, although he speaks of passion, he's always so moderate about expressing it."

"Moderate!" Luna's laugh was a scornful snort. "Hear the girl! *Madre de Dios!*"

"Hush, Luna. Please continue."

"That's all. I didn't really learn much, except that he knew in June that he was dying. One interesting thing was his references to an Arrangement – that's with a capital *A* – and how he'd never told his *maman* about it." Excitement rose in her again. "I have to find the rest of the journals!"

Mme. Beauvoisin smiled at her. "Tomorrow. You will find them, I'm sure of it."

"Céleste," said Luna warningly.

"Hush, my dear."

Theresa retired, as always, before her elderly companions. As polite as Mme. Beauvoisin was, she always felt uncomfortable in the parlor, as if her presence there were an intrusion, a threat, a necessary evil. Which, she told herself firmly, in a way, it was. The two women had been living here alone for Heaven only knew how long. It was only natural that they'd feel put out by her being there. It was silly of her to resent her exclusion from their charmed circle. And yet, tonight especially, she did.

Theresa curled up in a chair by the window, tucked the duvet around her legs, and considered the problem of Edouard's notebooks. A full moon washed the pale roses and the white paths with silver. In her mind, Theresa followed Edouard down one of those luminous paths to the studio, sitting at his desk, pulling his current notebook from the right-hand drawer and re-read his last entry only to discover that he'd barely one page left. He shook his head, rose, went to the cabinet, opened one of the long drawers where he kept his paints and pigments neatly arranged in shallow wooden trays. Carefully, he lifted one tray, slipped a new marbled *cahier* from under it, returned to his desk, and began to write.

When Teresa opened her eyes, the garden was cool in a pale golden dawn. Her neck was in agony, her legs were hopelessly cramped, but she was elated. The notebooks were in the cabinet under the paint trays – they just had to be!

Twenty minutes later, she was in the studio herself, with the paint trays stacked on the floor, gloating over layers of black-and-white marbled *cahiers*.

There were more than a hundred of them, she discovered, distributed over four drawers and forty-two years, from Beauvoisin's first trip to Paris in 1856 to his death in 1898. Theresa took out five or six of them at random and paged through them as she had paged through books as a child, stopping to read passages that caught her eye. Not entirely professional, perhaps. But thoroughly satisfying.

APRIL 20, 1875

Paris is so full of bad paintings, I can't begin to describe them. I know C.'s would enjoy some modest success, but she will not agree. One of Mlle. Morisot's canvases has sold for a thousand francs – a seascape not so half as pretty as the one C. painted at La Roseraie last month. I compliment her often on her work, and am somewhat distressed that she

does not return the courtesy, from love of the artist if not from admiration of his work. But then C. has never understood my theory of light
and evanescence, and will not agree with my principles of composition.

Theresa closed the notebook with a snap, unreasonably disappointed with Beauvoisin for his blindness to the structures of his society. Surely he must have known, as Céleste obviously knew, that men
were professionals and women were amateurs, unless they were honorary men like Berthe Morisot and Mary Cassatt? Poor Céleste,
Theresa thought, and poor Edouard. What had they seen in one another?

Over the next few days, Theresa chased the answer to that question
through the pages of Edouard's journals, skipping from one capital
"C." to the next, composing a sketch-portrait of a very strange marriage. That Beauvoisin had loved Céleste was clear. That he had loved
her as a wife was less so. He spoke of her as a travelling-companion, a
hostess, a house-keeper. A sister, Theresa thought suddenly, reading
how Céleste had arranged the details of their trip to Spain in the winter of 1877. She's like the maiden sister keeping house for her brilliant
brother. And Edouard, he was a man who saved all his passion for his
art, at any rate until he went to Spain and met Luz Gascó.

I have made some sketches of a woman we met in the Prado – a respect-
able woman and tolerably educated, although fallen on evil times. She
has quite the most beautiful skin I have seen – white as new cream and
so fine that she seems to glow of her own light, like a lamp draped with
heavy silk. Such bones! And her hair and eyes, like black marble polished and by some miracle brought to life and made supple. C. saw her
first, and effected an introduction. She is a joy to paint, and not expensive.

Eagerly, Theresa skimmed through the next months for further references to the beautiful señorita. Had Edouard fallen in love at last?
He certainly wrote as if he had – long, poetic descriptions of her skin,
her hair, her form, her luminous, living presence. At the same time, he
spoke fearfully of her temper, her unaccountable moods, her uncontrollable "gypsy nature." In the end, however, simple painterly covet-
ousness won out and he invited Gascó to spend the summer at La
Roseraie.

MAY 6, 1878

Luz Gascó expected tomorrow. C., having vacated the blue chamber for her, complains of having nowhere to paint. Perhaps I'll build an extension to my studio. Gascó is a great deal to ask of a wife, after all, even though C. knows better than any other how unlikely my admiration is to overstep propriety. As a model, Gascó is perfection. As a woman, she is like a wild cat, ready to hiss and scratch for no reason. Yet that skin! Those eyes! I despair of capturing them and ache to make the attempt.

Fishing Boats not going well. The boats are wooden and the water also. I shall try Gascó in the foreground to unbalance the composition....

How violently the presence of Luz Gascó had unbalanced the nicely calculated composition of Edouard Beauvoisin's life became clearer to Theresa the more she read. She hardly felt excluded now from her hostesses' circle, eager as she was to get back to the studio and to Edouard, for whom she was feeling more and more sympathy. Pre-Gascó, his days had unfolded methodically: work, walks with Céleste, drives to the village, letter-writing, notebook-keeping, sketching – each allotted its proper time and space, regular as mealtimes. G. rises at noon, he mourned a week into her visit. She breaks pose because she has seen a bird in the garden or wants to smell a flower. She is utterly impossible. Yet she transforms the world around her.

Imperceptibly, the summer visit extended into autumn and the autumn into winter as Beauvoisin planned and painted canvas after canvas, experimenting with composition, technique, pigment. By the spring of 1879, there was talk of Gascó's staying. By summer, she was a fixture, and Beauvoisin was beside himself with huge, indefinite emotions and ambitions, all of them arranged, like his canvases, around the dynamic figure of Luz Gascó. Then came July, and a page blank save for one line:

JULY 6, 1879

Luz in the parlor. Ah, Céleste!

A puzzling entry, marked as if for easy reference with a scrap of cheap paper folded in four. Theresa picked it up and carefully smoothed it open – not carefully enough, however, to keep the brittle paper from tearing along its creases. She saw dark lines – a charcoal sketch – and her heart went cold in panic. What have I done? she thought. What have I destroyed?

With a trembling hand, she arranged the four pieces on the table. The image was a reclining woman, her face turned away under an upflung arm, her bodice unbuttoned to the waist and her chemise loosened and folded open. A scarf of dark curls draped her throat and breast, veiling and exposing her nakedness. The sketch was intimate, more tender than erotic, a lover's mirror.

Theresa put her hands over her eyes. She'd torn the sketch; she didn't need to cry over it too. Spilt milk, she told herself severely. M. Rouart would know how to restore it. And she should be happy she'd found it, overjoyed to have such dramatic proof of Beauvoisin's carnal passion for his Spanish model. So why did she feel regretful, sad, disappointed, and so terribly, overwhelmingly angry?

A shadow fell across the page. A gnarled, nail-bitten forefinger traced the charcoaled line of the subject's hair.

"Ah," said Luna softly. "I wondered what had become of this."

Theresa clenched her own hands in her lap, appalled by the emotion that rose in her at the sound of that hoarse, slightly lisping voice. Luna was certainly irritating. But this was not irritation Theresa felt. It was rage.

"A beautiful piece, is it not?" The four torn pieces were not perfectly aligned: the woman seemed broken at the waist; her left arm, lying across her hips, was dismembered at the elbow. Luna coaxed her back together with delicate touches. "A pity that my own beauty may not be so easily repaired."

Surprised, Theresa looked up at Luna's aged turtle face. She'd never imagined Luna young, let alone beautiful. Yet now she saw that her bones were finely turned under her leathery skin and her eyes were unfaded and bright black as a mouse's. A vaguely familiar face, and an interesting one, now that Theresa came to study it. Something might be made of it, against a background of flowers, or the garden wall.

Luna straightened, regarding Theresa with profound disgust. "You're his to the bone," she said. "You see what you need to see, not what is there. I told her a stranger would have been better."

Theresa's fury had subsided, leaving only bewilderment behind. She rubbed her eyes wearily. "I'm sorry," she said. "I don't understand. Do you know something about this sketch?"

The old woman's mouth quirked angrily. "What I know of this sketch," she spat, "is that it was not meant for your eyes." And with a haughty lift of her chin, she turned and left the studio.

Was Mlle. Gascó crazy, or senile, or just incredibly mean? Theresa wondered, watching her hobble across the bright prospect of the garden like an arthritic crow. Surely she couldn't actually know anything about that sketch – why, it had been hidden for over a hundred years. For a moment, the garden dimmed, as though a cloud had come over the sun, and then Theresa's eyes strayed to the notebook open before her. A sunbeam dazzled the single sentence to blankness. She moved the notebook out of the glare and turned the page.

The next entry was dated the 14th of July and spoke of Bastille Day celebrations in Lorient and a family outing with Céleste and Gascó, all very ordinary except that Beauvoisin's prose was less colorful than usual. Something was going on. But Theresa had already known that. Beauvoisin had grown immensely as a painter over the summer of 1879, and had also cut himself off from the men who had been his closest friends. She was already familiar with the sharp note he'd written Manet denying that he had grown reclusive, only very hard at work and somewhat distracted, he hinted, by domestic tension: "For two women to reside under one roof is far from restful," he had written, and "Céleste and I have both begun paintings of Gascó – not, alas, the same pose."

Theresa flipped back to July 6. *Luz in the parlor. Ah, Céleste!* Such melodrama was not like Beauvoisin, nor was a week's silence, nor the brief, lifeless chronicles of daily events that occupied him during the month of August. Theresa sighed. Real life is often melodramatic, and extreme emotion mute. Something had happened on July 6, something that had changed Beauvoisin's life and art. Perhaps he had declared himself to Gascó, or fought with Céleste over her.

In any case, late in 1879 Beauvoisin had begun to develop a new style, a lighter, more brilliant palette, a more painterly technique that broke definitively from the line-obsessed training of his youth. Reading the entries for the fall of '79 and the winter of '80, Theresa learned that he had developed his prose style as well, in long disquisitions on light and composition, life and art. He gave up all accounts of ordinary events in favor of long essays on the beauty of the ephemeral: a young girl, a budding flower, a spring morning, a perfect understanding between man and woman. He became obsessed with a need to capture even the most abstract of emotions on canvas: betrayal, joy, contentment, estrangement.

> I have set G. a pose I flatter myself expresses most perfectly that moment of suspension between betrayal and remorse. She is to the left of the central plane, a little higher than is comfortable, crowded into a box defined by the straight back of her chair and the arm of the sofa. Her body twists left, her face is without expression, her eyes are fixed on the viewer. The conceit pleases G. more than C., of course, G. being the greater cynic. But C. agrees that the composition is out of the ordinary way and we all have great hopes of it at the next Salon. Our Arrangement will answer very well, I think.

Reading such entries – which often ran to ten or fifteen closely-written pages – Theresa began to wonder when Beauvoisin found time to paint the pictures he had so lovingly and thoughtfully planned. It was no wonder, she thought, that *Interior* and *Woman at a Window* seemed so theoretical, so contrived. She was not surprised to read that they had not brought as much as *Young Woman in a Garden* or *Reclining Nude*, painted two years later and described briefly as *a figure study of G. on the parlor sofa, oddly lighted. Pure whim, and not an idea anywhere in it. C. likes it, though, and so does G.; have allowed myself to be overborne.*

June had laid out its palette in days of Prussian blue, clear green, and yellow. In the early part of the month, when Theresa had been reading the letters, the clouds flooded the sky with a gray and white wash that suppressed shadow and compressed perspective like a Japanese print. After she found the notebooks, however, all the days seemed saturated with light and static as a still-life.

Theresa spent her time reading Beauvoisin's journals, leaving the studio only to eat a silent meal alone in the kitchen, to wander through the garden or, in the evenings, to go down to the sea-wall where she would watch the sun set in Turneresque glories of carmine and gold. Once, seeing the light, like Danae's shower, spilling its golden seed into the sea, Theresa felt her hand twitch with the desire to paint the scene, to capture the evanescent moment in oil and make it immortal.

What am I thinking of? she wondered briefly. I can't paint. It must be Edouard rubbing off on me. Or the isolation. I need to get out of here for a couple days, go back to Paris, see M. Rouart about the sketch, maybe let him take me out to dinner, talk to someone real for a change. But the next day found her in the studio and the next evening by the sea-wall, weeping with the beauty of the light and her own inadequate abilities.

As June shaded into July, Theresa abandoned the notebooks and began to sketch the pictures she saw around her in the studio and garden. Insensible of sacrilege, she took up Beauvoisin's pastel chalks and charcoal pencils and applied herself to the problem of reproducing her impressions of the way the flowers shimmered under the noon-day sun and how the filtered light reflected from the studio's whitewashed walls.

At first, she'd look at the untrained scrawls and blotches she'd produced and tear them to confetti in an ecstasy of disgust. But as the clear still days unfolded, she paid less and less attention to what she'd done, focussing only on the need of the moment, to balance mass and shape, light and shade. She hardly saw Mme. Beauvoisin and Luna, though she was dimly aware that they were about – in the parlor, in the garden, walking arm in arm across her field of vision: figures in the landscape, motifs in the composition. Day bled into day with scarcely a signpost to mark the end of one or the beginning of the next, so that she sketched and read in a timeless, seamless present, without past, without future, without real purpose.

So it was with no clear sense of time or place that Theresa walked into the studio one day and realized that she had left her sketchbook in the parlor. Tiresome, she thought to herself. But there was that study she'd been working on, the one of the stone wall. She'd just have to go back to the house and get it.

The transition from hall to parlor was always blinding, particularly in the afternoon, when the sun slanted through the French doors straight into entering eyes. That is perhaps why Theresa thought at first that the room was empty, and then that someone had left a large canvas propped against the sofa, a painting of two women in an interior.

It was an interesting composition, the details blurred by the bright back-light, the white dress of the figure on the sofa glimmering against the deep burgundy cushions, the full black skirts of the figure curled on the floor beside her like a pool of ink spilled on the flowery carpet.

Both figures were intent on a paper the woman on the sofa held on her up-drawn knees. Her companion's torso was turned into the sofa, her arms wreathed loosely around her waist.

What a lovely picture they make together, Theresa thought. I wonder I never thought of posing them so. It's a pity Céleste will not let me paint her.

Céleste laid the sketch aside, took Gascó's hand, and carried it to her lips. Her gaze met Theresa's.

"Edouard," she said.

Theresa's cheeks heated; her heart began a slow, deep, painful beating that turned her dizzy. She put her hand on the doorframe to steady herself just as Gascó surged up from floor and turned, magnificent in her rage and beauty, to confront the intruder. Her face shone from the thundercloud of her hair, its graceful planes sharpened and defined by the contemptuous curve of her red mouth, and the wide, proud defiance of her onyx eyes. Edouard released the doorframe and helplessly reached out his hand to her.

"Be a man, Edouard!" Gascó all but spat. "Don't look like that. I knew this must come. It would have come sooner had you been less blind. No," as Edouard winced, "I beg your pardon. It was not necessary to say that. Or the other. But you must not weep."

Céleste had swung her legs to the floor and laid the sketch on the sofa-back on top of the piled cushions. She looked composed, if a little pale, and her voice was even when she said, "Sit down, Luna. He has no intention of weeping. No, get us some brandy. We must talk, and we'd all be the better for something to steady us."

"Talk?" said Edouard. "What is there for us to say to one another?"

Gascó swept to the sideboard, poured brandy into three snifters, and handed them around, meeting Edouard's eyes defiantly when she put his into his hand.

"Drink, Edouard," said Céleste gently. "And why don't you sit down?"

He shook his head, but took a careful sip of his brandy. The liquor burned his throat.

"Doubtless you want us to leave La Roseraie," said Céleste into a long silence.

"Oh, no, my heart," said Gascó. "I'll not run away like some criminal. This house is yours. If anyone is to leave, it must be Beauvoisin."

"In law," said Edouard mildly, "the house is mine. I will not leave it. Nor will you, Céleste. You are my wife." His voice faltered. "I don't want you to leave. I want things as they were before."

"With your model your wife's lover, and you as blind as a mole?"

Edouard set down his half-finished brandy and pinched the bridge of his nose. "That was not kind, Gascó. But then, I have always known that you are not kind."

"No. I am honest. And I see what is there to be seen. It is you who must leave, Edouard."

"And ruin us all?" Céleste sounded both annoyed and amused. "You cannot be thinking, my love. We may find some compromise, some way of saving Edouard's face and our reputations, some way of living together."

"Never!" said Gascó. "I will not. You cannot ask it of me."

"My Claire de Lune. My Luna." Céleste reached for Gascó's hand and pulled her down on the sofa. "You do love me, do you not? Then you will help me. Edouard loves me too: we all love one another, do we not? Edouard. Come sit with us."

Edouard set down his brandy snifter. Céleste was holding her hand to him, smiling affectionately. He stepped forward, took the hand, allowed it and the smile to draw him down beside her. At the edge of his vision, he saw the paper slide behind the cushions and turned to retrieve it. Céleste's grip tightened on his hand.

"Never mind, my dear," she said. "Now. Surely we can come to some agreement, some arrangement that will satisfy all of us?"

The taste in Theresa's mouth said she'd been asleep. The tickle in her throat said the sofa was terribly dusty, and her nose said there had been mice in it, perhaps still were. The cushions were threadbare, the needlework pillows motheaten into woolen lace.

Without thinking what she was doing, Theresa scattered them broadcast and burrowed her hand down between sofa-back and seat, grimacing a bit as she thought of the mice, grinning triumphantly as she touched a piece of paper. Carefully, she drew it out, creased and mildewed as it was, and smoothed it on her knees.

A few scrawled lines of text with a sketch beneath them. The hand was not Edouard's. Nor was the sketch, though a dozen art historians would have staked their government grants that the style was his. The image was an early version of *Young Woman in a Garden*, a sketch of Gascó sitting against a tree with her hands around her knees, her pointed chin raised to display the long curve of her neck. Her hair was loose on her shoulders. Her blouse was open at the throat. She was laughing.

Trembling, Theresa read the note:

My Claire de Lune:

How wicked I feel, how abandoned, writing you like this, where any-one could read how I love you, my *maja*. I want to write about your neck and breasts and hair – oh, your hair like black silk across my body. But the only words that come to my mind are stale when they are not comic, and I'd not have you laugh at me. So here is my memory of yes-terday afternoon, and your place in it, and in my heart always.

– Céleste

Theresa closed her eyes, opened them again. The room she sat in was gloomy, musty, and falling into ruin, very different from the bright, comfortably shabby parlor she remembered. One of the French doors was ajar; afternoon sun spilled through it, reflecting from a thousand swirling dust-motes, raising the ghosts of flowers from the faded carpet. Out in the garden, a bird whistled. Theresa went to the door, looked out over a wilderness of weedy paths and rose-bushes grown into a thorny, woody tangle.

Céleste's letter to Luz Gascó crackled in her hand, reassuringly solid. There was clearly a lot of work to be done.

IAN R. MACLEOD

Grownups

Bobby finally got around to asking Mum where babies came from on the evening of his seventh birthday. It had been hot all day and the grownups and a few of the older children who had come to his party were still outside on the lawn. He could hear their talk and evening birdsong through his open window as Mum closed the curtains. She leaned down to kiss his forehead. She'd been drinking since the first guests arrived before lunch and her breath smelt like windfall apples. Now seemed as good a time as any. As she turned towards the door, he asked his question. It came out as a whisper, but she heard, and frowned for a moment before she smiled.

"You children always want to know too soon," she said. "I was the same, believe me, Bobby. But you must be patient. You really must."

Bobby knew enough about grownups to realise that it was unwise to push too hard. So he forced himself to yawn and blink slowly so she would think he was truly sleepy. She patted his hand.

After his door had clicked shut, after her footsteps had padded down the stairs, Bobby slid out of bed. Ignoring the presents piled in the corner by the wardrobe – robots with sparking eyes, doll soldiers, and submarines – he peered from the window. They lived at the edge of town, where rooftops dwindled to green hills and the silver curl of the river. He watched Mum emerge from the french windows onto the wide lawn below. She stooped to say something to Dad as he sat lazing in a deckchair with the other men, a beercan propped against his crotch. Then she took a taper from the urn beside the barbecue and touched it to the coals. She proceeded to light the lanterns hanging from the boughs of the cherry trees.

The whole garden filled with stars. After she had lit the last lantern, Mum put the taper to her mouth and extinguished it with her tongue. Then she rejoined the women gossiping on the white wrought iron chairs. The remaining children were all leaving for home. Cars were starting up, turning out from the shaded drive. Bobby heard his brother Tony call goodnight to the grownups and thunder up the stairs. He tensed in case Tony should decide to look in on him before he went to bed, but relaxed after the toilet had flushed and his bedroom door had slammed. It was almost night. Bobby knew that his window would show as no more than a darker square against the wall of the house. He widened the parting in the curtain.

He loved to watch the grownups when they thought they were alone. It was a different world. One day, Mum had told him often enough, one day sweet little Bobby you'll understand it all, touching his skin as she spoke with papery fingers. But give it time my darling one, give it time. Being a grownup is more wonderful than you children could ever imagine. More wonderful. Yes, my darling. Kissing him on the forehead and each eye and then his mouth the way she did when she got especially tender.

Bobby gazed down at the grownups. They had that loose look that came when the wine and the beer had gone down well and there was more to come, when the night was warm and the stars mirrored the lanterns. Dad raised his can from his crotch to his lips. One of the men beside him made a joke and the beer spluttered down Dad's chin, gleaming for a moment before he wiped it away. The men always talked like this, loud between bursts of silence, whilst the women's voices – laughing serious sad – brushed soft against the night. Over by the trellis archway that led by the bins to the front, half a dozen uncles sat in the specially wide deckchairs that Dad kept for them behind the mower in the shed.

Bobby couldn't help staring at the uncles. They were all grossly fat. There was Uncle Stan, Uncle Harold, and of course his own Uncle Lew. Bobby saw with a certain pride that Lew was the biggest. His tie was loose and his best shirt strained like a full sail across his belly. Like all the uncles, Lew lived alone, but Dad or the father of one of the other families he was uncle to was always ready to take the car down on a Saturday morning, paint the windows of his house or see to the lawn. In many ways, Bobby thought it was an ideal life. People respected uncles. Even more than their girth required, they stepped aside from them in the street. But at the same time, his parents were often edgy when Lew was around, uncharacteristically eager to please. Sometimes late in the night, Bobby had heard the unmistakable clatter of his van on the gravel out front, Mum and Dad's voices whispering softly excited in the hall. Gazing at Lew seated with the other uncles, Bobby remembered how he had dragged him to the moist folds of his belly, rumbling Won't You Just Look At This Sweet Kid? His yeasty aroma came back like the aftertaste of bad cooking.

Someone turned the record player on in the lounge. Sibilant music drifted like smoke. Some of the grownups began to dance. Women in white dresses blossomed as they turned, and the men were darkly quick. The music and the sigh of their movement brushed against the humid night, coaxed the glow of the lanterns, silvered the rooftops and the stars.

The dancing quickened, seeking a faster rhythm inside the slow beat. Bobby's eyes fizzed with sleep. He thought he saw grownups floating heartbeat on heartbeat above the lawn. Soon, they were leaping over the lanterned cherry trees, flying, pressing close to his window with smiles and waves, beckoning him to join them. Come out and play, Bobby, out here amid the stars. The men darted like eels, the women did high kicks across the rooftop, their dresses billowing coral frills over their heads. The uncles bobbed around the chimney like huge balloons.

When Bobby awoke, the lanterns were out. There was only darkness, summer chill.

As he crawled back to bed, a sudden sound made him freeze. Deep and feral, some kind of agony that was neither pain nor grief, it started loud then came down by notches to a stuttering sob. Bobby unfroze when it ended and hauled the blankets up to his chin. Through the bedroom wall, he could hear the faint mutter of Dad's voice, Mum's half-questioning reply. Then Uncle Lew saying goodnight. Slow footsteps down the stairs. The front door slam. Clatter of an engine coming to life.

Sigh of gravel.

Silence.

Bobby stood at the far bank of the river. His hands clenched and unclenched. Three years had passed. He was now ten; his brother Tony was sixteen.

Tony was out on the river, atop the oildrum raft that he and the other kids of his age had been building all summer. The wide sweep that cut between the fields and the gasometers into town had narrowed in the drought heat. Tony was angling a pole through the sucking silt to get to the deeper current. He was absorbed, alone; he hadn't noticed Bobby standing on the fissured mud of the bank. Earlier in the summer, there would have been a crowd of Tony's friends out there, shouting and diving, sitting with their heels clutched in brown hands, chasing Bobby away with shouts or grabbing him with terrible threats that usually ended in a simple ducking or just laughter, some in cutoff shorts, their backs freckled pink from peeling sunburn, some sleekly naked, those odd dark patches of hair showing under their arms and bellies. Maggie Brown with a barking voice you could hear half a mile off, Pete Thorn who kept pigeons and always seemed to watch, never said anything, maybe Johnnie Redhead and his sidekicks, even Trev Lee if his hay fever, asthma, and psoriasis hadn't kept him inside, the twin McDonald sisters whom no one could tell apart.

Now Tony was alone.

"Hey!" Bobby yelled, not wanting to break into his brother's isolation, knowing he had to. "Hey, Tony!"

Tony poled once more towards the current. The drums shook, tensed against their bindings, then inched towards the main sweep of the river.

"Hey Tony, Mum says you've got to come home right now."

"Alright, *alright.*"

Tony let go of the pole, jumped down into the water. It came just below his naked waist. He waded out clumsily, falling on hands and knees. He crouched to wash himself clean in a cool eddy where the water met the shore, then shook like a dog. He grabbed his shorts from the branch of a dead willow and hauled them on.

"Why didn't you just come?" Bobby asked. "You must have known it was time. The doc's waiting at home to give you your tests."

Tony slicked back his hair. They both stared at the ground. The river still dripped from Tony's chin, made tiny craters in the sand. Bobby noticed that Tony hadn't shaved, which was a bad sign in itself. Out on the river, the raft suddenly bobbed free, floating high on the quick current.

Tony shook his head. "Never did that when I was on it. Seemed like a great idea, you know? Then you spend the whole summer trying to pole out of the mud."

Around them, the bank was littered with the spoor of summer habitation. The blackened ruin of a bonfire, stones laid out in the shape of a skull, crisp packets, an old flap of canvas propped up like a tent, ringpull cans and cigarette butts, a solitary shoe. Bobby had his own friends – his own special places – and he came to this spot rarely and on sufferance. But still, he loved his brother and was old enough to have some idea of how it must feel to leave childhood behind. But he told himself that most of it had gone already. Tony was the last; Pete and Maggie and the McDonald twins had grown up. Almost all the others too. That left just Trev Lee who had locked himself in the bathroom and swallowed a bottle of bleach whilst his parents hammered at the door.

Tony made a movement that looked as though it might end in a hug. But he slapped Bobby's head instead, almost hard enough to hurt. They always acted with each other as though they were tough; it was too late now to start changing the rules.

They followed the path through the still heat of the woods to the main road. It was midday. The shimmering tarmac cut between yellow fields towards town. Occasionally, a car or truck would appear in the distance, floating silent on heat ghosts before the roar and the smell suddenly broke past them, whipping dust into their faces. Bobby gazed at stalking pylons, ragged fences, the litter-strewn edges of the countryside; it was the map of his own childhood. It was Tony's too – but Tony only stared at the verge. It was plain that he was tired of living on the cliffedge of growing up.

Tony looked half a grownup already, graceful, clumsy, self absorbed. He hadn't been his true self through all this later part of the summer, or at least not since Joan Trackett had grown up. Joan had a fierce crop of hair and protruding eyes; she had come to the area with her parents about six years before. Bobby knew that she and Tony had been having sex since at least last winter and maybe before. He'd actually stumbled across them one day in spring lying on a dumped mattress in the east fields up beyond the waste tip, hidden amid the bracken in a corner that the farmer hadn't bothered to plough. Tony had chased him away, alternately gripping the open waistband of his jeans and waving his fists. But that evening Tony had let Bobby play with his collection of model cars, which was a big concession even though Bobby knew that Tony had mostly lost interest in them already. They had sat together in Tony's bedroom that smelled of peppermint and socks. I guess you know what Joan and I were doing, he had said. Bobby nodded, circling a black v8 limo with a missing tire around the whorls and dustballs of the carpet. It's no big deal, Tony said, picking at a scab on his chin. But his eyes had gone blank with puzzlement, as though he couldn't remember something important.

Bobby looked up at Tony as they walked along the road. He was going to miss his big brother. He even wanted to say it, although he knew he wouldn't find the words. Maybe he'd catch up with him again when he turned grownup himself, but that seemed a long way off. At least five summers.

The fields ended. The road led into Avenues, Drives, and Crofts that meandered a hundred different ways towards home.

The doctor's red estate car was parked under the shade of the poplar in their drive.

"You *don't* make people wait," Mum said, her breath short with impatience, shooing them both quickly down the hallway into the kitchen. "I'm disappointed in you Tony. You too, Bobby. You're both old enough to know better." She opened the fridge and took out a tumbler of bitter milk. "And Tony, you didn't drink this at breakfast."

"Mum, does it matter? I'll be a grownup soon anyway."

Mum placed it on the scrubbed table. "Just drink it."

Tony drank. He wiped his chin and banged down the glass.

"Well, off you go," Mum said.

He headed up the stairs.

Doctor Halstead was waiting for Tony up in the spare room. He'd been coming around to test him every Thursday since Mum and Dad received the brown envelope from school, arriving punctually at twelve thirty, taking best china coffee with Mum in the lounge afterwards. There was no mystery about the tests. Once or twice, Bobby had seen the syringes and the blood analysis equipment spread out on the candlewick bedspread through the open door. Tony had told him what it was like, how the doc stuck a big needle in your arm to take some blood. It hurt some, but not much. He had shown Bobby the sunset bruises on his arm with that perverse pride that kids display over any wound.

Doctor Halstead came down half an hour later looking stern and non-committal. Tony followed in his wake. He shushed Bobby and tried to listen to Mum's conversation with the doc over coffee in the lounge by standing by the door in the hall. But grownups had a way of talking that was difficult to follow, lowering their voices at the crucial moment, clinking their cups. Bobby imagined them stifling their laugh-

ter behind the closed door, deliberately uttering meaningless fragments they knew the kids would hear. He found the thought oddly reassuring.

Tony grew up on the Thursday of that same week. He and Bobby
had spent the afternoon together down at Monument Park. They had
climbed the whispering boughs of one of the big elm trees along the
avenue and sat with their legs dangling, trying to spit on the heads of
the grownups passing below.

"Will you tell me what it's like?" Bobby had asked when his mouth
finally went dry.

"What?" Tony looked vague. He picked up a spider that crawled
onto his wrist and rolled it between finger and thumb.

"About being a grownup. You will talk to me afterwards. I
want... I want to know."

"Yeah, yeah. We're still brothers, right."

"You've got it. And – "

"– Hey, shush!"

Three young grownups were heading their way, a man, a woman
and an uncle. Bobby supposed they were courting – they had their
arms around each other in that vaguely passionless way that grownups
had, their faces absent, staring at the sky and the trees without seeing.
He began to salivate.

"Bombs away."

Bobby missed with his lob, but Tony hawked up a green one and
scored a gleaming hit on the crown of the woman's head. The
grownups walked on, stupidly oblivious.

It was a fine afternoon. They climbed higher still, skinning their
palms and knees on the greenish bark, feeling the tree sway beneath
them like a dancer. From up here, the park shimmered, you could see
everything; the lake, the glittering greenhouses, grownups lazing on
the grass, two fat kids from Tony's year lobbing stones at a convoy of
ducks. Bobby grinned and threw back his head. Here, you could feel
the hot sky around you, taste the clouds like white candy.

"You will tell me what it's like to be a grownup?" he asked again.

But Tony suddenly looked pale and afraid, holding onto the trembling boughs. "Let's climb down," he said.

When Bobby thought back, he guessed that that was the beginning.

Mum took one look at Tony when they got home and called Doctor

Halstead. He was quick in coming. On Mum's instructions, Bobby also phoned Dad at the office, feeling terribly grownup and responsible as he asked to be put through in the middle of a meeting.

Tony was sitting on the sofa in the lounge, rocking to and fro, starting to moan. Dad and the doc carried him to the spare bedroom. Mum followed them up the stairs, then pulled the door tightly shut. Bobby waited downstairs in the kitchen and watched the shadows creep across the scrubbed table. Occasionally, there were footsteps upstairs, the rumble of voices, the hiss of a tap.

He had to fix his own tea from leftovers in the fridge. Later, somehow all the house lights got turned on. Everything was hard and bright like a fierce lantern, shapes burned through to the filaments beneath. Bobby's head was swimming. He was someone else, thinking, this is my house, my brother, knowing at the same time that it couldn't be true. Upstairs, he could someone's voice screaming, saying My God No.

Mum came down after ten. She was wearing some kind of plastic apron that was wet where she'd wiped it clean.

"Bobby, you've got to go to bed." She reached to grab his arm and pull him from the settee.

Bobby held back for a moment. "What's happening to Tony, Mum? Is he okay?"

"Of course he's *okay*. It's nothing to get excited about. It happens to us all, it..." Anger came into her face. "Will you just get upstairs to bed, Bobby? You shouldn't be up this late anyway. Not tonight, not any night."

Mum followed Bobby up the stairs. She waited to open the door of the spare room until he'd gone into the bathroom. Bobby found there was no hot water, no towels; he had to dry his hand on squares of toilet paper and the flush was slow to clear, as though something was blocking it.

He sprinted across the dangerous space of the landing and into bed. He tried to sleep.

In the morning there was the smell of toast. Bobby came down the stairs slowly, testing each step.

"So you're up," Mum said, lifting the kettle from the hob as it began to boil.

It was eight thirty by the clock over the fridge; a little late, but everything was brisk and sleepy as any other morning. Dad stared at the sports pages, eating his cornflakes. Bobby sat down opposite him at the table, lifted the big cereal packet that promised a scale model if you collected enough coupons. That used to drive Tony wild, how the offer always changed before you had enough. Bobby shook some flakes into a bowl.

"How's Tony?" he asked, tipping out milk.

"Tony's fine," Dad said. Then he swallowed and looked up from the paper – a rare event in itself. "He's just resting, son. Upstairs in his own room, his own bed."

"Yes, darling." Mum's voice came from behind. Bobby felt her hands on his shoulders, kneading softly. "It's such a happy day for your Dad and me. Tony's a grownup now. Isn't that wonderful?" The fingers tightened, released.

"That doesn't mean you don't go to school," Dad added. He gave his paper a shake, rearranged it across the teapot and the marmalade jar.

"But be sure to tell Miss Gibson what's happened." Mum's voice faded to the back of the kitchen. The fridge door smacked open. "She'll want to know why you're late for register." Bottles jingled. Mum wafted close again. She came around to the side of the table and placed a tumbler filled with white fluid beside him. The bitter milk. "We know you're still young," she said. "But there's no harm and now seems as good a time as any." Her fingers turned a loose button on her blouse. "Try it darling, it's not so bad."

What happens if I don't... Bobby glanced quickly at Mum, at Dad. What happens if... Through the kitchen window, the sky was summer grey, the clouds casting the soft warm light that he loved more than sunlight, that brought out the green in the trees and made everything seem closer and more real. What happens... Bobby picked up the tumbler in both hands, drank in down in breathless gulps the way he'd seen Tony do so often in the past.

"Good lad," Mum sighed after he'd finished. She was behind him again, her fingers trailing his neck. Bobby took a breath, suppressed a shudder. This bitter milk tasted just as Tony always said it did; disgusting.

"Can I see Tony now, before I go to school?"

Mum hesitated. Dad looked up again from his newspaper. Bobby knew what it would be like later, the cards, the flowers, the house lost in strangers. This was his best chance to speak to his brother.

"Okay," Mum said. "But not for long."

Tony was sitting up in bed, the TV Mum and Dad usually kept his their own bedroom propped on the dressing table. Having the TV was a special sign of illness; Bobby had had it twice himself, once with chicken pox, and then with mumps. The feeling of luxury had almost made the discomfort worthwhile.

"I just thought I'd see how you were," Bobby said.

"What?" Tony lifted the remote control from the bedspread, pressed the red button to kill the sound. It was a reluctant gesture Bobby recognized from Dad.

"How are you feeling?"

"I'm fine, Bobby."

"Did it hurt?"

"Yes... Not really." Tony shrugged. "What do you want me to say? You'll find out soon enough, Bobby."

"Don't you remember yesterday? You said you'd tell me everything."

"Of course I remember, but I'm just here in bed... watching the TV. You can see what it's like." He spread his arms. "Come here, Bobby."

Bobby stepped forward.

Tony grinned. "Come on, little brother."

Bobby leaned forward over the bed, let Tony clasp him in his arms. It was odd to feel his brother this way, the soft plates of muscle, the ridges of chest and arm. They'd held each other often enough before, but only in the wrestling bouts that Bobby launched into when he nothing better to do, certain that he'd end up bruised and kicking, pinned down and forced to submit. But now the big hands were patting his back. Tony was talking over his shoulder.

"I'll sort through all the toys in the next day or so. You can keep all the best stuff to play with. Like we said yesterday, we're still brothers, right?" He leaned Bobby back, looked into his eyes. "Right?"

Bobby had had enough of grownup promises to know what they meant. Grownups were always going to get this and fix that, build wendy houses on the lawn, take you to the zoo, staple the broken strap on your satchel, favors that never happened, things they got angry about if you ever mentioned them.

"All the best toys. Right?"

"Right," Bobby said. He turned for the door, then hesitated. "Will you tell me one thing?"

"What?"

"Where babies come from."

Tony hesitated, but not unduly; grownups always thought before they spoke. "They come from the bellies of uncles, Bobby. A big slit opens and they tumble out. It's no secret, it's a natural fact."

Bobby nodded, wondering why he'd been so afraid to ask. "I thought so... thanks."

"Any time," Tony said, and turned up the TV.

"Thanks again." Bobby closed the door behind him.

Tony finished school officially at the end of that term. But there were no awards, no speeches, no bunting over the school gates. Like the other new grownups, he just stopped attending, went in one evening when it was quiet to clear his locker as though the whole thing embarrassed him. Bobby told himself that that was one thing he'd do differently when his time came. He'd spent most of his life at school, and he wasn't going to pass it by that easily. Grownups just seemed to let things go. It had been the same with Dad when he moved from the factory to the admin offices in town, suddenly ignoring men he'd shared every lunchtime with and talked about for years as though they were friends.

Tony sold his bicycle through the classified pages to a kid from across town who would have perhaps a year's use of it before he too grew up. He found a temporary job at the local supermarket. He and Dad came home at about the same time each evening, the same bitter work smell coming off their bodies. Over dinner, Mum would ask them how everything had gone and the talk would lie flat between them, drowned by the weak distractions of the food.

For Tony, as for everyone, the early years of being a grownup were a busy time socially. He went out almost every night, dressed in his new grownup clothes and smelling of soap and aftershave. Mum said he looked swell. Bobby knew the places in town he went to by reputation. He had passed them regularly and caught the smell of cigarettes and booze, the drift of breathless air and sudden laughter. There were strict rules against children entering. If he was with Mum, she would snatch his hand and hurry him on. But she and Dad were happy for Tony to spend his nights in these places now that he was a grownup, indulging in the ritual dance that led to courtship, marriage, and a fresh uncle in the family. On the few occasions that Tony wasn't out late, Dad took him for driving lessons, performing endless three-point turns on the tree-lined estate roads.

Bobby would sit with his homework spread on the dining room

table as Mum saw to things that didn't need seeing to. There was a distracting stiffness about her actions that was difficult to watch, difficult not to. Bobby guessed that although Tony was still living at home and she was pleased that he'd taken to grownup life, she was also missing him, missing the kid he used to be. It didn't require a great leap of imagination for Bobby to see things that way; he missed Tony himself. The arguments, the fights, the sharing and the not-sharing, all lost with the unspoken secret of being children together, of finding everything frightening, funny, and new.

In the spring, Tony passed his driving test and got a proper job at the supermarket as trainee manager. There was a girl called Marion who worked at the checkout. She had skin trouble like permanent sunburn and never looked at you when she spoke. Bobby already knew that Tony was seeing her in the bars at night. He sometimes answered the phone by mistake when she rang, her slow voice saying Is Your Brother About as Tony came down the stairs from his room looking annoyed. The whole thing was supposed to be a secret until suddenly Tony started bringing Marion home in the second-hand coupe he'd purchased from the dealers on the high street.

Tony and Marion spent the evenings of their courtship sitting in the lounge with Mum and Dad, watching the TV. When Bobby asked why, Tony said that they had to stay in on account of their saving for a little house. He said it with the strange fatality of grownups. They often talked about the future as though it was already there.

Sometimes a strange uncle would come around. Dad always turned the TV off as soon as he heard the bell. The uncles were generally fresh-faced and young, their voices high and uneasy. If they came a second time, they usually brought Bobby an unsuitable present, making a big show of hiding it behind their wide backs.

Then Uncle Lew began to visit more often. Bobby overheard Mum and Dad talking about how good it would be, keeping the same uncle in the family even if Lew was a little old for our Tony.

Looking down at him over his cheeks, Lew would ruffle Bobby's hair with his soft fingers.

"And how are you, young man?"

Bobby said he was fine.

"And what is it you're going to be this week?" This was Lew's standard question, a joke of sorts that stemmed from some occasion when

Bobby had reputedly changed his mind about his grownup career three or four times in a day.

Bobby paused. He felt an obligation to be original.

"Maybe an archaeologist," He said.

Lew chuckled. Tony and Marion moved off the settee to make room for him, sitting on the floor with Bobby.

After a year and half of courtship, the local paper that Tony had used to sell his bicycle finally announced that he, Marion, and Uncle Lew were marrying. Everyone said it was a happy match. Marion showed Bobby the ring. It looked big and bright from a distance, but close to, he saw that the diamond was tiny, centered in a much larger stub of metal that was cut to make it glitter.

Some evenings, Dad would fetch some beers for himself, Tony, and Uncle Lew, and let Bobby sip the end of a can to try the flat dark taste. Like most other grownup things, it was a disappointment.

So Tony married Marion. And he never did get around to telling Bobby how it felt to be a grownup. The priest in the church beside the crematorium spoke of the bringing together of families and of how having Uncle Lew for a new generation was a strengthened commitment. Dad swayed in the front pew from nerves and the three whiskeys he'd sunk beforehand. Uncle Lew wore the suit he always wore at weddings, battered victim of too much strain on the buttons, too many spilled buffets. There were photos of the families, photos of the bridesmaids, photos of Lew smiling with his arms around the shoulders of the two newlyweds. Photograph the whole bloody lot, Dad said, I want to see where the money went.

The reception took place at home on the lawn. Having decided to find out what it was like to get drunk, Bobby lost his taste for the warm white wine after one glass. He hovered at the border of the garden. It was an undeniably pretty scene, the awnings, the dresses, the flowers. For once, the boundaries between grownups and children seemed to dissolve. Only Bobby remained outside. People raised their glasses and smiled, drunken uncles swayed awkwardly between the trestle tables. Darkness carried the smell of the car exhaust and the dry fields beyond the houses. Bobby remembered the time when he had watched from his window and the music had beaten smoky wings, when the grownups had flown over the cherry trees that now seemed so small.

The headlights of the rented limousine swept out of the darkness. Everyone ran to the drive to see Tony and Marion duck into the leather interior. Uncle Lew squeezed in behind them, off with the newlyweds to some secret place. Neighbors who hadn't been invited came out onto their drives to watch, arms folded against the non-existent chill, smiling. Marion threw her bouquet. It tumbled high over the trees and the rooftops, up through the stars. Grownups oohed and ahhed. The petals bled into the darkness. It dropped back down as a dead thing of grey and plastic. Bobby caught it without thinking; a better, cleaner catch than anything he'd ever managed in the playing fields at school. Everyone laughed – that a kid should do that! – and he blushed furiously. Then the car pulled away, low at the back from the weight of the three passengers and their luggage. The tail-lights dwindled, were cut out by the bend in the road. Dad swayed and shouted something, his breath reeking. People went inside and the party lingered on, drawing to its stale conclusion.

Uncle Lew had Tony and Marion's first child a year later. Mum took Bobby to see the baby at his house when he came out of hospital few days after the birth. Uncle Lew lived in town up on the hill on the far side of the river. Mum was nervous about gradient parking and always used the big pay and display down by the library. From there, you had to cut through the terraced houses, then up the narrowly winding streets that formed the oldest part of town. The houses were mostly grey pebbledash with deepset windows, yellowed lace curtains, and steps leading though steep gardens. The hill always seemed steeper than it probably was to Bobby; he hated visiting.

Uncle Lew was grinning, sitting in his usual big chair by the bay window. The baby was a mewing thing. It smelled of soap and sick. Marion was taking the drugs to make her lactate and everything was apparently going well. Bobby peered at the baby lying cradled in her arms. He tried to offer her the red plastic rattle Mum had made him buy. Everyone smiled at that. Then there was tea and rock cakes that Bobby managed to avoid. Uncle Lew's house was always dustlessly neat, but it had a smell of neglect that seemed to emanate from behind the old-fashioned green cupboards in the kitchen. Bobby guessed that the house was simply too big for him; too many rooms.

"Are you still going to be an archaeologist?" Uncle Lew asked, leaning forward from his big chair to take both of Bobby's hands. He was wearing a dressing gown with neatly pressed pyjamas underneath but for a moment the buttons parted and Bobby glimpsed wounded flesh.

The room went smilingly silent; he was obviously expected to say more than simply no or yes. "I'd like to grow up," he said, "before I decide."

The grownups all laughed. Then the baby stared to cry. Grateful for the distraction, Bobby went out through the kitchen and into the grey garden where someone's father had left a fork and spade on the crazy paving, the job of lifting out the weeds half-done. Bobby was still young enough to pretend that he wanted to play.

Then adolescence came. It was a perplexing time for Bobby, a grimy anteroom leading to the sudden glories of growing up. He watched the hair grow on his body, felt his face inflame with spots, heard his voice change to an improbable whine before finally settling on an octave that left him sounding forever like someone else. The grownups themselves always kept their bodies covered, their personal actions impenetrably discreet. Even in the lessons and the chats, the slide-illuminated talks in the nudging darkness of the school assembly hall, Bobby sensed that the teachers were disgusted by what happened to children's bodies, and by the openness with which it did so. The things older children got up to, messy tricks that nature made them perform. Periods. Masturbation. Sex. The teachers mouthed the words like an improbable disease. Mum and Dad both said Yes they remembered, they knew exactly how it was, but they didn't want to touch him any longer, acted awkwardly when he was in the room, did and said things that reminded him of how they were with Tony in his later childhood years.

Bobby's first experience of sex was with May Barton one afternoon when a crowd of school friends had cycled out to the meadows beyond town. The other children had headed back down to the road whilst Bobby was fixing a broken spoke on his back wheel. When he turned around, May was there alone. It was, he realized afterwards, a situation she'd deliberately engineered. She said Let's do it Bobby. Squinting, her head on one side. You haven't done it before have you? Not waiting for an answer, she knelt down in the high clover and pulled her dress up over her head. Her red hair tumbled over her freckled shoulders. She asked Bobby to touch her breasts. Go on, you must have seen other boys doing this. Which he had. But still he was curious to touch her body, to find her nipples hardening in his palms. For a moment she seemed different in the wide space of the meadow, stranger almost than a grownup, even though she was just a girl. Here, she said, Bobby, and Here. Down on the curving river, a big barge with faded awnings seemed not to be moving. A tractor was slicing a field from green to brown, the chatter of its engine lost on the warm wind. The town shimmered. Rooftops reached along the road. His hand travelled down her belly, explored the slippery heat of her arousal as her own fingers began to part the buttons of his shirt and jeans, did things that only his own hands had done before. He remembered the slide shows at school, the teacher's bored, disgusted voice, the fat kids sniggering more than anyone at the back, as though the whole thing was nothing to do with them.

May Barton lay down. Bobby had seen the drawings and slides, watched the mice and rabbits in the room at the back of the biology class. He knew what to do. The clover felt cool and green on his elbows and knees. She felt cool too, strangely uncomfortable, like wrestling with someone who didn't want to fight. A beetle was climbing a blade of grass at her shoulder. When she began to shudder, it flicked its wings and vanished.

After that, Bobby tried sex with several of the other girls in the neighborhood, although he tended to return most often to May. They experimented with the variations you were supposed to be able to do, found that most of them were uncomfortable and improbable, but generally not impossible.

Mum caught Bobby and May having sex one afternoon in the fourth year summer holidays when a cancelled committee meeting brought her home early. Peeling off her long white cotton gloves as she entered the lounge, she found them naked in the curtained twilight, curled together like two spoons. She just clicked her tongue, turned, and walked back out into the hall, her eyes blank, as if she'd just realized she'd left something in the car. She never mentioned the incident afterwards – which was tactful, but to Bobby also seemed unreal, as though the act of sex had made him and May Barton momentarily invisible.

There was a sequel to this incident when Bobby returned home one evening without his key. He went through the gate round the back to find the french windows open. He'd expected lights on in the kitchen, the murmur of the TV in the lounge. But everything was quiet. He climbed the stairs. Up on the landing where the heat of the day still lingered, mewing sounds came from his parents bedroom. The door was ajar. He pushed it wide – one of those things you do without ever being able to explain why – and walked in. It was difficult to make out the partnership of the knotted limbs. Dad seemed to be astride Uncle Lew, Mum half underneath. The sounds they made were another language. Somehow, they sensed his presence. Legs and arms untwined like dropped coils of rope.

It all happened very quickly. Mum got up and snatched her dressing gown from the bedside table. On the bed, Dad scratched at his groin and Uncle Lew made a wide cross with his forearms to cover his womanly breasts.

"It's okay," Bobby said, taking a step back towards the door, taking another. The room reeked of mushrooms. Mum still hadn't done up her dressing gown and Bobby could see her breasts swaying as she walked, the dark triangle beneath her belly. She looked little different from all the girls Bobby had seen. Through the hot waves of his embarrassment he felt a twinge of sadness and familiarity.

"It's okay," he said again, and closed the door.

He never mentioned the incident. But it helped him understand Mum's reasons for not saying anything about finding him in the lounge with May. There were plenty of words for sex, ornate words and soft words and words that came out angry, words for what the kids got up to and special words too for the complex congress that grownups indulged in. But you couldn't use any of them as you used other words; a space of silence surrounded, walled them into a dark place that was all their own.

Bobby grew. He found to his surprise that he was one of the older kids at school, towering over the chirping first years with their new blazers, having sex with May and the other girls, taking three-hour exams at the ends of term, worrying about growing up. He remembered that this had seemed a strange undersea world when Tony had inhabited it; now that he had reached it himself, this last outpost of childhood, it hardly seemed less so.

The strangeness was shared by all the children of his age. It served to bring them together. Bobby remembered that it had been the same for Tony's generation. Older kids tended to forget who had dumped on whom in the second form, the betrayals and the fights behind the bicycle sheds. Now, every experience had a sell-by date, even if the date itself wasn't clear.

In the winter term when Bobby was fifteen the children all experienced a kind of growing up in reverse, an intensification of childhood. There was never any hurry to get home after school. A crowd of them would head into the bare dripping woods or sit on the steps of the monument in the park. Sometimes they would gather at Albee's Quick Restaurant and Take Away along from the bridge. It was like another world outside beyond the steamed windows, grownups drifting past in cars or on foot, greying the air with breath and motor exhaust. Inside, lights gleamed on red seats and cheap wood panelling, the air smelled of wet shoes and coffee, thinned occasionally by a cold draft and the broken tinkle of the bell as a new arrival joined the throng.

"I won't go through with it," May Barton said one afternoon when the pavements outside were thick with slush that was forecasted to freeze to razored puddles overnight.

No one needed to ask what she meant.

"Jesus, it was disgusting."

May stared into her coffee. That afternoon in biology they had seen the last in a series of films entitled The Miracle Of Life. Half way through, the pink and black cartoons had switched over to scenes that purported to come from real life. They had watched a baby tumble wet onto the green sheet from an uncle's open belly, discreet angles of grownups making love. That had been bad enough – I mean we didn't *ask* to see these things – but the last five minutes had included shots of a boy and a girl in the process of growing up. The soundtrack had been discreet, but every child in the classroom had felt the screams.

The voice over told them things they had read a hundred times in the school biology textbooks that automatically fell open at the relevant pages. Chapter thirteen – unlucky for some, as many a schoolroom wit had quipped. How the male's testicles and scrotal sac contracted back inside the body, hauled up on some fleshy block and tackle. How the female's ovaries made their peristaltic voyage along the fallopian tubes to nestle down in the useless womb, close to the equally useless cervix. A messy story that had visited them all in their dreams.

"Where the hell am I supposed to be when all this is going on?" someone asked. "I'm certainly not going to be there."

Silence fell around the corner table in Albee's. Every kid had their own bad memory. An older brother or sister who had had a hard time growing up, bloodied sheets in the laundry bin, a door left open at the wrong moment. The espresso machine puttered. Albee sighed and wiped the counter. His beer belly strained at a grey singlet – he was almost fat enough to be an uncle. Almost, but not quite. Every kid could tell the difference. It was in the way they smelled, the way they moved. Albee was just turning to fat, some ordinary guy with a wife and kids back at home, and an uncle with a lawn that needed mowing and crazy paving with the weeds growing through. He was just getting through life, earning a living of sorts behind his counter, putting up with Bobby and the rest of the kids from school as long as they had enough money to buy coffee.

Harry, who was a fat kid, suggested they all go down to the bowling rink. But no one else was keen. Harry was managing to keep up a jollity that the other children had lost. They all assumed that he and his friend Jonathan were the most likely candidates in the year to grow into uncles. The complicated hormonal triggers threw the dice in their favor. And it was a well known fact that uncles had it easy, that growing up for them was a slow process, like putting on weight. But for everyone, even for Harry, the facts of life were closing in. After Christmas at the start of the new term their parents would all receive the brown envelopes telling them that the doctor would be around once a week.

The café door opened and closed, letting in the raw evening air as the kids began to drift away. A bus halted at the newsagents opposite, grownup faces framed at the windows, top deck and bottom, ordinary and absorbed. When it pulled away, streetlight and shadow filled the space behind. Underneath everything, Bobby thought, lies pain, uncertainty, and blood. He took a pull at the coffee he'd be nursing the last half hour. It had grown a skin and tasted cold, almost as bitter as the milk Mum made him drink every morning.

He and May were the last to leave Albee's. The shop windows were filled with promises of Christmas. Colors and lights streamed over the slushy pavement. The cars were inching headlight to brakelight down the high street, out of town. Bobby and May leaned on the parapet of the bridge. The lights of the houses on the hill where Uncle Lew lived were mirrored in the sliding water. May was wearing mittens, a scarf, a beret, her red hair tucked out of sight, just her nose and eyes showing.

"When I was eight or nine," she said, "Mum and Dad took me on holiday to the coast. It was windy and sunny. I had a big brother then.

His name was Tom. We were both kids and he used to give me piggy backs, sometimes tickle me till I almost peed. We loved to explore the dunes. Had a whole world there to ourselves. One morning we were sliding down this big slope of sand, laughing and climbing all the way up again. Then Tom doubled up at the bottom and I thought he must have caught himself on a hidden rock or something. I shouted Are You Okay but all he did was groan."

"He was growing up?"

May nodded. "The doc at home had said it was fine to go away, but I realized what was happening. I said You Stay There which was stupid really and I shot off to get someone. The sand kept sliding under my sandals. It was a nightmare, running through treacle. I ran right into Dad's arms. He'd gone looking for us. I don't know why, perhaps it's something grownups can sense. He found someone else to ring the ambulance and we went back down the beach to see Tom. The tide was coming in and I was worried it might reach him...."

She paused. Darkness was flowing beneath the river arches. "When we got back he was twisted and I knew he couldn't be alive, no one could hold themselves that way. The blood was in the sand, sticking to his legs. Those black flies you always get on a beach were swarming."

Bobby began, "That doesn't..." but he pulled the rest of the chilly sentence back into his lungs.

May turned to him. She pulled the scarf down to her chin. Looking at her lips, the glint of her teeth inside, Bobby remembered the sweet hot things they had done together. He wondered at how close you could get to someone and still feel alone.

"We're always early developers in our family," May said. "Tom was the first in his class. I suppose I'll be the same."

"Maybe it's better... get it over with."

"I suppose everyone thinks that it'll happen first to some kid in another form, someone you hardly know. Then a few others. Perhaps a friend, someone you can visit afterwards and find out you've got nothing to say but that's it's no big deal after all. Everything will always be fine."

"There's still a long – "

"– How long? What difference is a month more or less?" She was angry, close to tears. But beneath, her face was closed off from him. "You had an elder brother who survived, Bobby. Was he ever the same?"

Bobby shrugged. The answer was obvious, all around them. Grownups were grownups. They drove cars, fought wars, dressed in boring and uncomfortable clothes, built roads, bought newspapers every morning that told them the same thing, drank alcohol without getting merry from it, pulled hard on the toilet door to make sure it was shut before they did their business.

"Tony was alright," he said. "He's still alright. We were never that great together anyway – just brothers. I don't think it's the physical changes that count... or even that that's at the heart of it...." He didn't know what the hell else to say.

"I'm happy as I am," May said. "I'm a kid. I feel like a kid. If I change, I'll cease to be me. Who wants that?" She took off her mitten, wiped her nose on the back of her hand. "So I'm not going through with it."

Bobby stared at her. It was like saying you weren't going through with death because you didn't like the sound of it. "It can't be that bad, May. Most kids get through alright. Think of all the grownups.... Jesus, think of your own parents."

"Look, Bobby. I know growing up hurts. I know it's dangerous. I should know, shouldn't I? That's not that I care about. What I care about is losing *me*, the person I am and want to be.... You just don't believe me do you? I'm not going through with it, I'll stay a kid. I don't care who I say it to because they'll just think I'm acting funny, but Bobby I thought you might believe me. There has to be a way out."

"You can't..." Bobby said. But already she was walking away.

The envelopes were handed out at school. A doctor started to call at Bobby's house, and at the houses of all his friends. Next day there was always a show of bravado as they compared the bruises on their arms. The first child to grow up was a boy named Arthur Mumford whose sole previous claim to fame was the ability to play popular tunes by squelching his armpits. In that way that the inevitable always has, it happened suddenly and without warning. One Tuesday in February, just five weeks after the doctor had started to call at their houses, Arthur didn't turn up for registration. A girl two years below had spotted the doctor's car outside his house on her paper round the evening before. Word was around the whole school by lunchtime.

There was an unmistakable air of disappointment. When he wasn't performing his party piece, Arthur was a quiet boy: he was tall and stooped from embarrassment at his height. He seldom spoke. But it wasn't just that it should happen first to someone as ordinary as Arthur – I mean, it has to be all of us sooner or later, right? But none of the children felt as excited – or even as afraid – as they had expected. When it had happened to kids in the senior years, it had seemed like something big, seeing a kid they'd known suddenly walking the high street in grownup clothes with the dazed expression that always came to new grownups, ignoring old school friends, looking for work, ducking into bars. They had speculated excitedly about who would go next, prayed that it would be one of the school bullies. But now that it was their turn, the whole thing felt like a joke that had been played too many times. Arthur Mumford was just an empty desk, a few belongings that needed picking up.

In the spring, at least half a dozen of the children in Bobby's year had grown up. The hot weather seemed to speed things up. Sitting by the dry fountain outside the Municipal Offices one afternoon, watching the litter and the grownups scurry by, a friend of Bobby's named Michele suddenly dropped her can of drink and coiled up in a screaming ball. The children and the passing grownups all fluttered uselessly as she rolled around on the paving until a doctor who happened to be walking by forced her to sit up on the rim of the fountain and take deep slow breaths. Yes, she's growing up, he snapped, glowering at the onlookers, then down at his watch. I suggest someone rings her parents or gets a car. Michele was gasping through tears and obviously in agony, but the doctor's manner suggested that she was making far too much of the whole thing. A car arrived soon enough and Michele was bundled into the back. Bobby never saw her again.

He had similar although less dramatic partings with other friends. One day, you'd be meeting them at the bus stop to go to the skating rink. The next, you would hear that they had grown up. You might see them around town, heading out of a shop as you were going in, but they would simply smile and nod, or make a point of saying Hello Bobby just to show that they remembered your name. Everything was changing. That whole summer was autumnal, filled with a sense of loss. In their own grownup way, even the parents of the remaining children were affected. Although there would inevitably be little time left for their children to enjoy such things, they became suddenly generous with presents, finding the cash that had previously been missing for a new bike, a train set, or even a pony.

May and Bobby still spent afternoons together, but more often now they would just sit in the kitchen at May's house, May by turns gloomy and animated, Bobby laughing with her or – increasingly against his feelings – trying to act reassuring and grownup. They usually had the house to themselves. In recognition of the dwindling classes, the teachers were allowing any number of so-called study periods, and both of May's parents worked days and overtime in the evenings to keep up with the mortgage on their clumsy mock-Tudor house.

One afternoon when they were drinking orange juice mixed with sweet sherry filched from the drinks cabinet and wondering if they dared to get drunk, May got up and went to the fridge. Bobby thought she was getting more orange, but instead she produced the plastic flask that contained her bitter milk. She laughed at his expression as she unscrewed the childproof cap and put the flask to her lips, gulping it down as though it tasted good. Abstractly, Bobby noticed that her parents used a branded product. His own parents always bought the supermarket's own.

"Try it," she said.

"What?"

"Go on."

Bobby took the flask and sipped. He was vaguely curious to find out whether May's bitter milk was any less unpleasant than the cheaper stuff he was used to. It wasn't. Just different, thicker. He forced himself to swallow.

"You don't just drink this, do you?" he asked, wondering for the first time whether her attitude wasn't becoming something more than simply odd.

"Of course I don't," she said. "But I could if I liked. You see, it's not bitter milk."

Bobby stared at her.

"Look."

May opened the fridge again, took out a carton of ordinary pasteurized milk. She put it on the worktop, then reached high inside a kitchen cabinet, her blouse briefly raising at the back to show the ridges of her lower spine that Bobby so enjoyed touching. She took down a tin of flour, a plastic lemon dispenser and a bottle of white wine vinegar.

"The flour stops it from curdling," she said, "and ordinary vinegar doesn't work. It took me days to get it right." She tipped some milk into a tumbler, stirred in the other ingredients. "I used to measure everything out, but now I can do it just anyhow."

She handed him the tumbler. "Go on."

Bobby tasted. It was quite revolting, almost as bad as the branded bitter milk.

"You see."

Bobby put the glass down, swallowing back a welcome flood of saliva to weaken the aftertaste. Yes, he saw, or at least he was beginning to see.

"I haven't been drinking bitter milk for a month now. Mum buys it, I tip it down the sink when she's not here and do my bit of chemistry. It's that simple…" she was smiling, then suddenly blinking back tears "…that easy…. Of course, it doesn't taste exactly the same, but when was the last time your parents tried tasting bitter milk?"

"Look, May… don't you think this is dangerous?"

"Why?" She tilted her head, wiped a stray trickle from her cheek. "What exactly is going to happen to me? You tell me that."

Bobby was forced to shrug. Bitter milk was for children, like cod liver oil and rusks. Grownups avoided the stuff, but it was good for you, it *helped*.

"I'm not going to grow up, Bobby," she said. "I told you I wasn't joking."

"Do you really think that's going to make any difference?"

"Who knows?" she said. She gave him a sudden hug, her lips wet and close to his ear. "Now let's go upstairs."

Weeks later, Bobby got a phone call from May one evening at home. Mum called him down from his bedroom, holding the receiver as though it might bite.

He took it.

"It's me, Bobby."

"Yeah." He waited for the lounge door to close. "What is it?"

"Jesus, I think it's started. Mum and Dad are out at a steak bar and I'm getting these terrible pains."

The fake bitter milk. The receiver went slick in his hand.

"It can't be. You can't be sure."

"If I was sure I wouldn't be… Look, Bobby, can you come around." She gave a gasp. "There it is again. You really must. I can't do this alone."

"You gotta ring the hospital."

"No."

"You – "

"No!"

Bobby gazed at the telephone directories that Mum stacked on a shelf beneath the phone as though they were proper books. He remembered that night with Tony, the lights on everywhere, burning though everything as though it wasn't real. He swallowed. The TV was still loud in the lounge.

"Okay," he said. "God knows what I'm supposed to tell Mum and Dad. Give me half an hour."

His excuse was a poor one, but his parents took it anyway. He didn't care what they believed; he'd never felt as shaky in his life.

He cycled through the estate. The air rushed against his face, drowning him in that special feeling that came from warm nights. May must have been watching for him from a window. She was at the door when he scooted down the drive.

"Jesus, Bobby, I'm bleeding."

"I can't see anything."

She pushed her hand beneath the waistband of her dress, then held it out. "Look. Do you believe me now?"

Bobby swallowed, then nodded.

She was alone in the house. Her parents were out. Bobby helped her up the stairs. He found an old plastic mac to spread across the bed, and helped her to get clean. The blood was clotted and fibrous, then watery thin. It didn't seem like an ordinary wound.

When the first panic was over, he pushed her jumbled clothes off the bedside chair and slumped down. May's cheeks were flushed and rosy. For all her talk about not wanting to grow up, he reckoned that he probably looked worse than she did at that moment. What was all this about? Had she ever had a brother named Tom? One who died? She'd lived in another estate then. Other than asking, there was no way of knowing.

"I think I'd better go and ring – "

"– Don't!" She forced a smile and reached out a hand towards him. "Don't."

Bobby hesitated, then took her hand.

"Look, it's stopped now anyway. Perhaps it was a false alarm."

"Yeah," Bobby said, "False alarm," although he was virtually sure there was no such thing. You either grew up or you didn't.

"I feel okay now," she said. "Really, I do."

"That's good," Bobby said.

May was still smiling. She seemed genuinely relieved. "Kiss me, Bobby," she said.

Her eyes were strange. She smelled strange. Like the river, like the rain. He kissed her, softly on the warmth of her cheek; the way you might kiss a grownup. He leaned back from the bed and kept hold of her hand.

They talked.

Bobby got back home close to midnight. His parents had gone up to bed, but as he crossed the darkened landing he sensed that they were both awake and listening beyond bedroom door. Next morning, nothing was said, and May was at school with the rest of what remained of their class. The teachers had mostly given up with formal lessons, getting the children instead to clear out stockrooms or tape the spines of elderly textbooks. He watched May as she drifted through the chalk-clouded air, the sunlight from the tall windows blazing her hair. Neither grownup nor yet quite a kid, she moved between the desks with unconscious grace.

That lunchtime, she told Bobby that she was fine. But Yes, she was still bleeding a bit. I have to keep going to the little girl's room. I've got through two pairs of knickers, flushed them away. It's a real nuisance, Bobby, she added above the clatter in the dining hall, as though it was nothing, like hay fever or a cold sore. Her face was clear and bright, glowing through the freckles and the smell of communal cooking. He nodded, finding that it was easier to believe than to question. May smiled. And you will come see me tonight, won't you, Bobby? We'll be on our own. Again, Bobby found himself nodding.

He announced to Mum and Dad after dinner that evening that he was going out again. He told them he was working on a school play that was bound to take up a lot of his time.

Mum and Dad nodded. Bobby tried not to study them too closely, although he was curious to gauge their reaction.

"Okay," Mum said. "But make sure you change the batteries on your lamps if you're going to cycle anywhere after dark." She glanced at Dad, who nodded and returned to his paper.

"You know I'm careful like that." Bobby tried to keep the wariness out of his voice. He suspected that they saw straight through him and knew that he was lying. He'd been in this kind of situation before.

That was an odd thing about grownups: you could tell them the truth and they'd fly into a rage. Other times such as this when you had to lie, they said nothing at all.

May was waiting at the door again that evening. As she had promised, her parents were out. He kissed her briefly in the warm light of the hall. Her lips were soft against his, responding with a pressure that he knew would open at the slightest sign from him. She smelled even more rainy than before. There was something else too, something that was both new and familiar. Just as her arms started to encircle his back, he stepped back, his heart suddenly pounding.

He looked at her. "Christ, May what are you wearing?"

"This." She gave a twirl. The whole effect was odd, yet hard to place for a moment. A tartanish pleated dress. A white blouse. A dull necklace. Her hair pulled back in a tight bun. And her eyes, her mouth, her whole face... looked like it had been sketched on, the outlines emphasized, the details ignored. Then he licked his lips and knew what it was; the same smell and taste that came from Mum on nights when she leaned over his bed and said, you will be good while we're out won't you my darling, jewelry glimmering like starlight around her neck and at the lobes of her ears. May was wearing make-up. She was dressed like a grownup.

For a second, the thought that May had somehow managed to get through the whole messy process of growing up since leaving school that afternoon came to him. Then he saw the laughter in her eyes and he knew it couldn't be true.

"What do you think, Bobby?"

"I don't know why grownups wear that stuff. It isn't comfortable, it doesn't even look good. What does it feel like?"

"Strange," May said. "It changes you inside. Come upstairs. I'll show you."

May led him up the stairs and beyond a door he had never been through before. Even though they were out, her parents' bedroom smelled strongly of grownup, especially the wardrobe where the dark lines of suits swung gently on their hangers. Bobby was reasonably tall for his age, as tall as many grownups, May's father included.

The suit trousers itched his legs and the waist was loose, but not so loose as to fall down. He knotted a tie over a white shirt, pulled on the jacket. May got some oily stuff from the dresser, worked it into his hair and combed it smooth. Then she stood beside him as he studied himself in the mirror. Dark and purposeful, two strange grownups gazed back. He glanced down at himself, hardly believing it was true. He pulled a serious face back at the mirror, the sort you might see behind the counter at a bank. Then he started to chuckle. And May began to laugh. It was so inconceivably easy. They were doubled over, their bellies aching. They held each other tight. They just couldn't stop.

An hour later, May closed the front door and turned the deadlock. Heels clipping the pavement, they walked to the bus stop. Perhaps in deference to their new status as grownups, the next service into town came exactly when it was due. They travelled on the top deck, which was almost empty apart from a gaggle of cleaning ladies at the back. They were busy talking, and the driver hadn't even bothered to look up when he gave them two straight adult fares (don't say please, May had whispered as the tall lights of the 175 had pulled into the stop, grownups don't do that kind of thing). Dressed in his strange grownup clothes, his back spreading huge inside the jacket shoulder pads, Bobby felt confident anyway. Like May said, the grownup clothes changed you inside.

They got off outside Albee's Quick Restaurant and Take Away. For some reason, May wanted to try visiting a place where they were actually known. Bobby was too far gone with excitement to argue about taking an unnecessary extra risk. Her manner was smooth; he doubted if anyone else would have noticed the wildness in her eyes beneath the clothes, the make-up. Rather than dodge the cars across the road, they waited for a big gap and walked slowly, sedately. The lights of Albee's glowed out to greet them. They opened the door to grownup laughter, the smell of smoke and grownup sweat. People nodded and smiled, they moved to let them through. Albee grinned at them from the bar, eager to please the way the teachers were at school when the headmaster came unexpectedly into class. He said Good evening Sir and What'll it be. Bobby heard his own voice say something calm and easy in reply. He raked a stool back for May and she sat down, tucking her dress neatly under her thighs. He glanced around as drinks were served, half expecting the other grownups to float up from their chairs, to begin to fly. They'd been here after school a hundred times, but this was a different world.

It was the same on a dozen other nights, whenever they hit on an excuse that they had the nerve to use on their unquestioning parents.

Albee's, they found, was much further from the true heart of the grownup world than they'd imagined. They found hotel bars where real fountains tinkled and the drinks were served chilled on paper coasters that stuck to the bottom of the glass. There were loud pubs where you could hardly stand for the yellow-lit crush and getting served was an evening's endeavor. There were restaurants where you were offered bowls brimming with crackers and salted nuts just to sit and read the crisply printed menus and say Well Thanks, But It Doesn't Look As Though Our Friends Are Coming And The Baby Sitter You Know... Places they had seen day in and day out through their whole lives were changed by the darkness, the hot charge of car fumes, buzzing street lights, glittering smiles, the smell of perfume, changed beyond recognition to whispering palaces of crystal and velvet.

After changing at May's house back into his sweatshirt and sneakers, Bobby would come home late, creeping down the hall in the bizarre ritual of pretending not to disturb his parents, whom he was certain would be listening open-eyed in the darkness from the first unavoidable creak of the front door. In the kitchen, he checked for new bottles of bitter milk. By the light of the open fridge door, he tipped the fluid down the sink, chased it away with a quick turn of the hot tap – which was quieter than the cold – and replaced it with a fresh mixture of spirit vinegar, lemon juice, milk, and flour.

The summer holidays came. Bobby and May spent all their time together, evenings and days. Lying naked in the woods on the soft prickle of dry leaves, looking up at the green latticed sky. Bobby reached again towards May. He ran his hand down the curve of her belly. It was soft and sweet and hard, like an apple. Her breath quickened. He rolled onto his side, lowered his head to lick at her breasts. More than ever before, her nipples swelled amazingly to his tongue. But after a moment her back stiffened.

"Just kiss me here," she said, "my mouth," gently cupping his head in her hands and drawing it up. "Don't suck at me today Bobby. I feel too tender."

Bobby acquiesced to the wonderful sense of her around him, filling the sky and the woods. She'd been sensitive about some of the things he did before, often complaining about tenderness and pain a few days before she started her bleeding. But the bleeding hadn't happened for weeks, months.

They still went out some nights, visiting the grownup places, living their unbelievable lie. Sometimes as he left the house, or coming back late with his head spinning from the drink and the things they'd done, Bobby would look up and see Mum's face pale at the bedroom window. But he said nothing. And nothing was ever said. It was an elaborate dance, back to back, Mum and Dad displaying no knowledge or denial, each moment at the kitchen table and the rare occasions when he shared the lounge passing without question. A deception without deceit.

The places they went to changed. From the smart rooms lapped with deep carpets and chrome they glided on a downward flight path through urine-reeking doorways. This was where the young grownups went, people they recognized as kids from assembly at school just a few years before. Bars where the fermented light only deepened the darkness, where the fat uncles sat alone as evening began, looking at the men and the women as the crowds thickened, looking away.

Bobby and May made friends, people who either didn't notice what they were or didn't care. Hands raised and waving through the chaos and empty glasses. Hey Bobby, May, over here, sit yourselves right down here. Place for the old butt. Jokes to be told, lips licked, lewd eyes rolled, skirt hems pulled firmly down then allowed to roll far up again. Glimpses of things that shouldn't be seen. They were good at pretending to be grownups by now, almost better than the grownups themselves. For the purposes of the night, Bobby was out of town from a university in the city, studying whatever came into his head. May was deadly serious or laughing, saying my God you wouldn't believe the crap I have to put up with at the office, the factory, the shop. Playing it to a tee. And I'm truly glad to be here and now with you all before it starts again in the morning.

Time broke in beery waves. The account at the Post Office that Bobby had been nurturing for some unspecified grownup need sunk to an all-time low. But it could have been worse – they were a popular couple, almost as much in demand as the unattached fat uncles when a few drinks had gone down. They hardly ever had to put in for a round.

The best part was when they came close to discovery. A neighbor who probably shouldn't have been there in the first place, a family friend, a teacher. Then once it was Bobby's brother Tony. Late, and he had his arms around a fat uncle, his face sheened with sweat. He was grinning and whispering wet lips close to his ear. There was a woman with them too, her hands straying quick and hard over both of their bodies. It wasn't Marion.

"Let's go," Bobby said. There was a limit to how far you could take a risk. But May would have none of it. She stared straight at Tony through the swaying bodies, challenging him to notice.

For a moment his eyes were on them, his expression drifting back from lust. Bobby covered his hand with his mouth, feeling the grownup clothes and confidence dissolve around him, the schoolkid inside screaming to get out. Tony made to speak, but there was no chance of hearing. In another moment he vanished into the mass of the crowd.

Now the danger had passed, it was the best time of all; catching Tony out in a way that he could never explain. Laughter bursting inside them, they ran out into the sudden cool of the night. May held onto him and her lips were over his face, breathless and trembling from the sudden heightening of the risk. He held tight to her, swaying, not caring about the cars, the grownups stumbling by, pulling her close, feeling the taut rounded swell of her full breasts and belly that excited him so.

"Do you want to be like them?" she whispered. "Want to be a fool and a grownup?"

"Never." He leaned back and shouted it at the stars. "Never!"

Arm in arm, they swayed down the pavement towards the bus stop. Incredibly, Tuesday was coming around again tomorrow; Doc Halstead would be pulling up the drive at home at about eleven, washing his hands one more time and saying How Are You My Man before taking best china coffee with Mum in the lounge, whispering things he could never quite hear. May's eyes were eager, gleaming with the town lights, drinking it all in. More than him, she hated this world and loved it. Sometimes, when things were swirling, she reminded him of a true grownup. It all seemed far away from that evening in town after biology, leaning on the bridge alone after leaving Albee's and gazing down at the river, May saying I won't go through with it Bobby, I'm not just some kid acting funny. As though something as easy as fooling around with the bitter milk could make that much of a difference.

Doctor Halstead arrived next morning only minutes after Bobby had finished breakfast and dressed. In the spare bedroom, he spread out his rubber and steel. He dried his hands and held the big syringe up to the light before leaning down.

Bobby smeared the fresh bead of blood over the bruises on his forearm, then licked the salt off his fingertips.

Doctor Halstead was watching the readouts. The paper feed gave a burp and chattered out a thin strip like a supermarket receipt. The doc tore it off, looked at it for a moment and tutted before screwing it into a ball. He pressed a button that flattened the dials, pressed another to make them drift up again.

"Is everything okay?"

"Everything's fine."

The printer chattered again. He tore it off. "You've still got some way to go."

"How many weeks?"

"If I had a pound for every time I've been asked that question."

"Don't you know?"

He handed Bobby the printout. Faint figures and percentages. The machine needed a new ribbon.

"Us grownups don't know everything. I know it seems that way."

"Most of my friends have gone." He didn't want to mention May, although he guessed Mum had told him anyway. "How long can it go on for?"

"As long as it takes."

"What if nothing happens?"

"Something always happens."

He gave Bobby a smile.

Bobby and May went out again that night. A place they'd never tried before a few stops out of town with a spluttering neon sign, a shack motel at the back and a dusty parking area for the big container rigs. Inside was huge with bare boards and patches of lino, games machines lining the walls, too big to fill with anything but smoke and patches of yellowed silence on even the busiest of nights. Being a Wednesday, and the grownups' pay packets being thin until the weekend, it was quiet. They sat alone in the smoggy space for most of the evening. They didn't know anyone and for once it seemed that no one wanted to know them. Bobby kept thinking of the way Doctor Halstead had checked the readouts, checked them again. And he knew May had her own weekly test the following afternoon. It wasn't going to be one of their better nights. May looked pale. She went out to the Ladies room far more often than their slow consumption of the cheap bottled beer would explain. Once, when she came back and leaned forward to tell him something, he realized that the rain had gone from her breath. He smelled vomit.

At about ten, a fat uncle crossed the room, taking a drunken detour around the chairs.

"Haven't seen you two here before," he said, his belly swaying above the table, close to their faces. "I've got a contract delivering groceries from here to the city and back. Every other day, I'm here."

"We must have missed you."

He squinted down at them, still swaying but now seeming less than drunk. For places like here, Bobby and May wore casual clothes. Bobby dressed the way Dad did for evenings at home in an open collared striped shirt and trousers that looked as though they had started out as part of a work suit. May hadn't put on much make-up, which she said she hated anyway. Bobby wondered if they were growing complacent, if this fat uncle hadn't seen what all the other grownups had apparently failed to notice.

"Mind if I..." The uncle reached for a chair and turned it around, sat down with his legs wide and his arms and belly propped against the backrest. "Where are you from anyway?"

Bobby and May exchanged secret smiles. Now they were in their element, back in the territory of the university in the city, the office, the shop, the grownup places that had developed a life of their own through frequent re-telling.

It was pleasant to talk to an uncle on equal terms for a change, away from the pawings and twitterings of other grownups which usually surrounded them. Bobby felt he had a lot of questions to ask, but the biggest one was answered immediately by this uncle's cautious but friendly manner, by the way he spoke of his job and the problems he was having trying to find a flat. In all the obvious ways, he was just like any other young grownup. He bought them a drink. It seemed polite to buy him one in return, then – what the hell – a chaser. Soon, they were laughing. People were watching, smiling but keeping their distance across the ranks of empty tables.

Bobby knew what was happening, but he was curious to see how far it would go. He saw a plump hand stray to May's arm – still covered by a long sleeved shirt to hide the bruises – then up to her shoulder. He saw the way she reacted by not doing anything.

"You don't know how lonely it gets," the uncle said, leaning forward, his arm around Bobby's back too, his hand reaching down. "Always on the road. I stay here, you know. Most Wednesdays. A lot of them sleep out in the cab. But they pay you for it and I like to lie on something soft. Just out the back." He nodded. "Through that door, the way you came in, left past the kitchens."

"Will you show us?" May asked, looking at Bobby. "I think we'd like to see."

The motel room was small. Someone had tried to do it up years before but the print had rubbed off the wallpaper by the door and above the green bed. The curtains had shrunk and Bobby could still see the car park and the lights of the road. A sliding door led to a toilet and the sound of a dripping tap.

The fat uncle sat down. The bed squealed. Bobby and May remained standing, but if the uncle saw their nervousness he didn't comment. He seemed more relaxed now, easy with the drink and the certainty of what they were going to do. He unlaced his boots and peeled off his socks, twiddling his toes with a sigh that reminded Bobby of Dad at the end of a hard day. He was wearing a sweatshirt that had once said something. He pulled it off over his head with his hands on the waistband, the way a girl might do, threw it onto the rug beside his feet. He had a singlet on underneath. The hems were unraveling but he and it looked clean enough, and he smelt a lot better than Uncle Lew did at close quarters, like unbaked dough. He pulled the singlet off too. His breasts were much bigger than May's. There was hardly any hair under his arms. Bobby stared at the bruised scar that began under his ribcage and vanished beneath the wide band of his jeans, slightly moist where it threatened to part.

"You're going to stay dressed, are you?" he said with a grin. He scratched himself and the springs squealed some more. "This Goddamn bed's a problem."

"We'd like to watch," May said. "For now, if that's okay with you."

"That's great by me. I'm not fussy... I mean..." He stood up and stepped out of his trousers and underpants in one movement. "Well, you know what I mean."

Under the huge flap of his belly, Bobby couldn't see much of what lay beneath. Just darkness and hair. Every night, he thought, a million times throughout the world, this is going on. Yet he couldn't believe it, couldn't even believe it about his parents with Uncle Lew although he'd seen them once on that hot afternoon.

"Tell you what," the uncle said. "It's been a long day. I think you'd both appreciate it if yours truly freshened up a bit." He went over to Bobby, brushed the fine hairs at the back of his neck with soft fingers. "I won't be a mo. You two sort yourselves out, eh?"

He waddled off into the toilet, slid the door shut behind him. They heard the toilet seat bang down, a sigh and the whisper of moving flesh. Then a prolonged fart. A pause. A splash. Then another.

May looked at Bobby. Her face reddened. She covered her mouth to block the laughter. Bobby's chest heaved. He covered his mouth too. He couldn't help it: the joke was incredibly strong. Signalling to Bobby, tears brimming in her eyes, May stooped to pick up the sweatshirt, the shoes, the singlet. Bobby gathered the jeans. There were more clothes heaped in a corner. They took those too, easing the door open as quietly as they could before the laughter rolled them over like a high wind.

They sprinted madly across the car park, down the road, into the night.

Next morning, the sky was drab. It seemed to Bobby like the start of the end of summer, the first of the grey veils that would eventually thicken to autumn. Downstairs, Mum was humming. He went first into the kitchen, not that he wanted to see her, but he needed to re-establish the charade of ignoring his nights away from the house. One day, he was sure it would break, she'd have a letter from the police, the doctor, the owner of some bar, a fact that couldn't be ignored.

"It's you," she said. Uncharacteristically, she kissed him. He'd been taller than she for a year or two, she didn't need to bend down but it still felt that way. "Do you want anything from the supermarket? I'm off in a few minutes."

Bobby glanced at the list she kept on the wipe-clean plastic board above the cooker. Wash powd, loo pap, marg, lemon jce, wne vigr. He looked at her face, but it was clear and innocent.

"Aren't you going to go into the dining room? See what's waiting?"

"Waiting?"

"Your birthday, Bobby." She gave him a laugh and a quick, stiff hug. "I asked you what you wanted weeks ago and you never said. So I hope you like it. I've kept the receipt – you boys are so difficult."

"Yeah." He hadn't exactly forgotten, he'd simply been pushing the thing back in his mind, the way you do with exams and visits from the doctor, hoping that if you make yourself forget, then time the rest of the world will forget too.

He was seventeen and still a kid. It was at least one birthday too many. He opened the cards first, shaking each envelope carefully to see if there was any money. Some of them had pictures of archaic country-side and inappropriate verses, the sort that grownups gave to each other. One or two people had made the effort to find a child's card, but there wasn't much of a market for seventeen year olds. The most en-terprising had combined stick-ons for 1 and 7. Bobby moved to the presents, using his toast knife to slit the tape, trying not to damage any of the wrapping paper, which Mum liked to iron and re-use. Although she hadn't spoken, he was conscious that she was standing watching at the door. Fighting the sinking feeling of discovering books on subjects that didn't interest him, accessories for hobbies he didn't pursue, model cars for a collection he'd given up years ago, he tried to display excitement and surprise.

Mum and Dad's present was a pair of binoculars, something he'd coveted when he was thirteen for reasons he couldn't now remember. He gazed at the marmalade jar in close up, through the window at the individual leaves of the nearest cherry tree in the garden.

"We thought you'd find them useful when you grew up too," Mum said, putting her arms around him.

"It's great," he said. In truth, he liked the smell of the case – leather, oil and glass – more than the binoculars themselves. But he knew that wasn't the point. And then he remembered why he'd so wanted a pair of binoculars, how he'd used to love looking up at the stars.

"Actually, I've lots of stuff to get at the supermarket, Bobby. Dad's taking a half day and we're going to have a party for you. Everyone's coming. Isn't that great?"

Bobby went with Mum to the supermarket. They drove into town past places he and May had visited at night. Even though the sky was clearing to sun, they looked flat and grey. Wandering the supermarket aisles, Mum insisted that Bobby choose whatever he want. He settled at random for iced fancies, paté, green-veined cheese. Tony came out from his office behind a window of silvered glass, a name badge on his lapel and his hair starting to recede. He clapped Bobby's shoulder with a biro-stained hand and said he'd never have believed it, Seventeen, my own little brother. They chatted awkwardly for a while in the chill drift of the frozen meats. Even though there was a longer queue, they chose Marion's checkout. She was back working at the supermarket part time now that their kid had started infants. It wasn't until Bobby saw her blandly cheerless face that he remembered that night with Tony and the other uncle in the bar. He wondered if she knew, if she cared.

There were cars in the drive at home and spilling along the cul de sac three that afternoon, little kids with names he couldn't remember running on the lawn. The weather had turned bright and hot. Dad had fished out all the deckchairs as soon as he got home, the ordinary ones and the specials he kept for uncles. People kept coming up to Bobby and then running out of things to say. He couldn't remember whether they'd given him cards or presents, what to thank them for. Uncle Lew was in a good mood, the facets of one of the best wine glasses trembling sparks across his rounded face.

"Well, Bobby," he said, easing himself down in his special deckchair. He was starting to look old, ugly. Too many years, too many happy events. He was nothing like the fresh fat uncle at the motel. "And what are you going to be when you grow up?"

Bobby shrugged. He grown sick of thinking up lies to please people. The canvas of Lew's deckchair was wheezing and slightly torn. Bobby hoped that he'd stay a kid long enough to see him fall through.

"Well get yourself a nice girlfriend," he said. "It means a lot to me that I'm uncle to your Momma and Poppa and to Tony and Marion too." He sucked at his wine. "But that's all down to you."

Looking back up the lawn towards the house, Bobby saw May and her parents emerging into the sunlight from the open french widows. May looked drab and tired. Her belly was big, her ankles swollen.

She waddled over to them, sweat gleaming on her cheeks.

"Hello, Bobby." She leaned over to let Uncle Lew give her a hug. He put his lips to her ear. She wriggled and smiled before she pulled away.

"Hello, May."

She was wearing a cheap print, something that fell in folds like a tent.

"This whole party is a surprise, isn't it? Your Mum insisted that I didn't say anything when she told me last week. Here. Happy birthday."

She gave him a package. He opened it. Five minutes later, he couldn't remember what it contained.

Dad banged the trestle table and people gathered around on the lawn as he made a speech about how he could hardly believe the way the years had flown, saying the usual things that grownups always said about themselves when it was a child's birthday. He raised his glass. A toast. Bobby. Everyone intoned his name. Bobby. The sun retreated towards the rooftops and the trees, filling the estate with evening, the weary smell of cooking. Those grownups who hadn't been able to skip work arrived in their work clothes. Neighbors drifted in.

May came over to Bobby again, her face flushed with the drink and the sun.

"Did the doc come over to see you today?" he asked for want of anything better. The hilarious intimacy of the things they had done in the night suddenly belonged to a world even more distant than that of the grownups.

"Nothing happened," she said, spearing a herring mop on the paper plate she carried with a plastic fork. "Nothing ever happens." She took a bite at the gleaming vinegared scale, then pulled a face. "Disgusting. God knows how the grownups enjoy this shit."

Bobby grinned, recognizing the May he knew. "Let's go somewhere. No one will notice."

She shrugged Yes and propped her plate on the concrete bird bath. They went through the back gate, squeezed between the bumpers on the drive and out along the road.

"Do you still think you'll never grow up?" Bobby asked.

May shook her head. "What about you?"

"I suppose it's got to happen. We're not fooling anyone, are we, going out, not drinking the milk? I'm sure Mum and Dad know. They just don't seem to care. I mean, we can't be the first kids in the history of the world to have stumbled on this secret. Well, it can't be a secret, can it?"

"How about we climb up to the meadows?" May said. "The town looks good from up there."

"Have you ever read *Peter Pan*?" Bobby asked as they walked up the dirt road between the allotments and the saw mill. "He never grew up. Lived in a wonderful land and learnt how to fly." He held open the kissing gate that led into the fields. May had to squeeze through. The grass was high and slivered with seed, whispering under a deepening sky. "When I was young," he said, "on evenings like this, I used to look out of my bedroom window and watch the grownups. I thought that they could fly."

"Who do you think can fly now?"

"No one. We're all the same."

They stopped to catch their breath and look down at the haze below. Hills, trees, and houses, the wind carrying the chime of an ice-cream van, the river stealing silver from the sky. He felt pain spread though him, then dissolve without finding focus.

May took his hand. "Remember when we were up here alone that time years ago." She drew it towards her breast, then down. "You touched me here, and here. We had sex. You'd never done it before." She let his hand fall. Bobby felt no interest. May no longer smelled of rain, and he was relieved he didn't have to turn her down.

The pain came again, more strongly this time. He swayed. The shimmering air cleared and for one moment there was a barge on the river, a tractor slicing a field from green to brown, a hawk circling high overhead, May smiling, sweet and young as she said Let's Do It Bobby, pulling her dress up over her head. He blinked.

"Are you okay?"

"I'm fine," he said, leaning briefly against her, feeling the thickness of her arms.

"I think we'd better go back."

Down the hill, the pain began to localize. First circling in his spine, then gradually shifting orbit towards his belly. It came and went. When it was there it was so unbelievable that he put it aside in the moments of recession. Had to be a bad dream. The trees swayed with the rush of twilight, pulling him forward, drawing him back.

Progress was slow. Night came somewhere along the way. Helped by May, he staggered from lamp-post to lamp-post, dreading the darkness between. People stared or asked if everything was okay before hurrying on. He tasted rust in his mouth. He spat on the pavement, wiped his hand. It came away black.

"Nearly there," May said, half-holding him around his searing belly.

He looked up and saw houses he recognized, the postbox that was the nearest one to home. His belly was crawling. He remembered how that postbox had been a marker of his suffering one day years before when he'd been desperate to get home and pee, and another time walking back from school when his shoes were new and tight. Then the pain rocked him, blocking his sight. True pain, hard as flint, soft as drowning. He tried to laugh. That made it worse and better. Bobby knew that this was just the start, an early phase of the contractions.

He couldn't remember how they reached home. There were hands and voices, furious diallings of the phone. Bobby couldn't get upstairs and didn't want to mess the settee by lying on it. But the grownups insisted, pushed him down, and then someone found a plastic sheet and tucked it under him in between the worst of the waves. He thrashed around, seeing the TV, the mantelpiece, the fibers of the carpet, the light burning at his eyes. I'm not here, he told himself, this isn't real. Then the biggest, darkest wave yet began to reach him.

Wings of pain settled over him. For a moment without time, Bobby dreamed that he was flying.

Bobby awoke in a chilly white room. There was a door, dim figures moving beyond the frosted glass. He was still floating, hardly conscious of his own body. The whiteness of the room hurt his eyes. He closed them, opened them again. Now it was night. Yellow light spilled through the glass. The figures moving beyond had globular heads, no necks, tapering bodies.

One of the figures paused. The door opened. The silence cracked like a broken seal. He could suddenly hear voices, the clatter of trolleys. He was conscious of the hard flatness of the bed against his back, coils of tubing descending into his arm from steel racks. His throat hurt. His mouth tasted faintly of licorice. The air smelled the way the bathroom cabinet did at home. Of soap and aspirins.

"Your eyes are open. Bobby, can you see?"

The shape at the door blocked the light. It was hard to make it out. Then it stepped forward, and he saw the soft curve of May's cheek, the glimmer of her eye.

"Can you speak?"

"No," he said.

May turned on a light over the bed and sat down with a heavy sigh. He tried to track her by moving his eyes, but after the brief glimpse of her face all he could see was the dimpled curve of her elbow.

"This is hospital?"

"Yes. You've grown up"

Hospital. Growing up. They must have taken him here from home. Which meant that it had been a difficult change.

May said, "You're lucky to be alive."

Alive. Yes. Alive. He waited for a rush of some feeling or other – relief, gratitude, achievement, pride. There was nothing, just this white room, the fact of his existence.

"What happens now?" he asked.

"Your parents will want to see you."

"Where are they?"

"At home. It's been *days*, Bobby."

"Then why..." the taste of licorice went gritty in his mouth. He swallowed it back. "Why are you here May?"

"I'm having tests, Bobby. I just thought I'd look in."

"Thanks."

"There's no need to thank me. I won't forget the times we had."

Times. We. Had. Bobby put the words together, then let them fall apart.

"Yes," he said.

"Well." May stood up.

Now he could see her. Her hair was cut short, sitting oddly where her fat cheeks met her ears. Her breasts hung loose inside a tee shirt. Along with everything else about her they seemed to have grown, but the nipples had gone flat and she'd given up wearing a bra. She shrugged and spread her arms. He caught a waft of her scent: she needed a wash. It was sickly but somehow appealing, like the old cheese that you found at the back of the fridge and needed to eat right away.

"Sometimes it happens," she said.

"Yes," Bobby said. "The bitter milk."

"No one knows really, do they? Life's a mystery."

Is it? Bobby couldn't be bothered to argue.

"Will you change your name?" he asked. "Move to another town?"

"Maybe. It's a slow process. I'm really not an uncle yet, you know."

Still a child. Bobby gazed at her uncomfortably, trying to see it in her eyes, finding with relief that the child wasn't there.

"What's it like?" May asked.

"What?"

"Being a grownup."

"Does anyone ask a child what it's like to be a child?"

"I suppose not."

His head ached, his voice was fading. He blinked slowly. He didn't want to say more. What else was there to say? He remembered waiting stupidly as his brother Tony sat up in bed watching TV that first morning after he'd grown up. Waiting as though there was an answer. But growing up was just part of the process of living, which he realized now was mostly about dying.

May reached out to touch his face. The fingers lingered for a moment, bringing a strange warmth. Their odor was incredibly strong to Bobby. But it was sweet now, like the waft from the open door of a bakery. It hit the back of his palate and then ricocheted down his spine. He wondered vaguely if he was going to get an erection and killed the thought as best he could; he hated the idea of appearing vulnerable to May. After all, she was still half a child.

"You'd better be going," he said.

May backed away. "You're right." She reached for the handle of the door, clumsily, without looking.

"Goodbye, May," Bobby said.

She stood for a moment in the open doorway. For a moment the light fell kindly on her face and she was beautiful. Then she stepped back and all her youth was gone.

"Goodbye, Bobby," she said, and glanced down at her wristwatch. "I've got things to do. I really must fly."

URSULA K. LE GUIN
The Matter of Seggri

The first recorded contact with Seggri was in year 242 of Hain-ish Cycle 93. A Wandership six generations out from Iao (4-Taurus) came down on the planet, and the captain entered this report in his ship's log.

CAPTAIN AOLAO-OLAO'S REPORT

We have spent near forty days on this world they call Se-ri or Ye-ha-ri, well entertained, and leave with as good an estimation of the natives as is consonant with their unregenerate state. They live in fine great buildings they call castles, with large parks all about. Outside the walls of the parks lie well-tilled fields and abundant orchards, reclaimed by diligence from the parched and arid desert of stone that makes up the greatest part of the land. Their women live in villages and towns huddled outside the walls. All the common work of farm and mill is performed by the women, of whom there is a vast superabundance. They are ordinary drudges, living in towns which belong to the lords of the castle. They live amongst the cattle and brute animals of all kinds, who are permitted into the houses, some of which are of fair size. These women go about drably clothed, always in groups and bands. They are never allowed within the walls of the park, leaving the food and necessaries with which they provide the men at the outer gate of the castle. The women evinced great fear and distrust of us, and our hosts advised us that it were best for us to keep away from their towns, which we did.

The men go freely about their great parks, playing at one sport or another. At night they go to certain houses which they own in the town, where they may have their pick among the women and satisfy their lust upon them as they will. The women pay them, we were told, in their money, which is copper, for a night of pleasure, and pay them

347

yet more if they get a child on them. Their nights thus are spent in carnal satisfaction as often as they desire, and their days in a diversity of sports and games, notably a kind of wrestling, in which they throw each other through the air so that we marvelled that they seemed never to take hurt, but rose up and returned to the combat with marvelous dexterity of hand and foot. Also they fence with blunt swords, and combat with long light sticks. Also they play a game with balls on a great field, using the arms to catch or throw the ball and the legs to kick the ball and trip or catch or kick the men of the other team, so that many are bruised and lamed in the passion of the sport, which was very fine to see, the teams in their contrasted garments of bright colors much gauded out with gold and finery seething now this way, now that, up and down the field in a mass, from which the balls were flung up and caught by runners breaking free of the struggling crowd and fleeting towards the one or the other goal with all the rest in hot pursuit. There is a "battlefield" as they call it of this game lying without the walls of the castle park, near to the town, so that the women may come watch and cheer, which they do heartily, calling out the names of favorite players and urging them with many uncouth cries to victory.

Boys are taken from the women at the age of eleven and brought to the castle to be educated as befits a man. We saw such a child brought into the castle with much ceremony and rejoicing. It is said that the women find it difficult to bring a pregnancy of a boy child to term, and that of those born many die in infancy despite the care lavished upon them, so that there are far more women than men. In this we see the curse of god laid upon this race as upon all those who acknowledge him not, unrepentant heathens whose ears are stopped to true discourse and blind to the light.

These men know little of art, only a kind of leaping dance, and their science is little beyond that of savages. One great man of a castle to whom I talked, who was dressed out in cloth of gold and crimson and whom all called Prince and Grandsire with much respect and deference, yet was so ignorant he believed the stars to be worlds full of people and beasts, asking us from which star we descended. They have only vessels driven by steam along the surface of the land and water, and no notion of flight either in the air or in space, nor any curiosity about such things, saying with disdain, "That is all women's work," and indeed I found that if I asked these great men about matters of common knowledge such as the working of machinery, the weaving of cloth, the transmission of holovision, they would soon chide me for taking interest in womanish things as they called them, desiring me to talk as befit a man.

In the breeding of their fierce cattle within the parks they are very knowledgeable, as in the sewing up of their clothing, which they make from cloth the women weave in their factories. The men vie in the ornamentation and magnificence of their costumes to an extent which we might indeed have thought scarcely manly, were they not withal such proper men, strong and ready for any game or sport, and full of pride and a most delicate and fiery honor.

The log including Captain Aolao-olao's entries was (after a 12-generation journey) returned to the Sacred Archives of The Universe on Iao, which were dispersed during the period called The Tumult, and eventually preserved in fragmentary form on Hain. There is no record of further contact with Seggri until the First Observers were sent by the Ekumen in 93/1333: an Alterran man and a Hainish woman, Kaza Agad and Merriment. After a year in orbit mapping, photographing, recording and studying broadcasts, and analyzing and learning a major regional language, the Observers landed. Acting upon a strong persuasion of the vulnerability of the planetary culture, they presented themselves as survivors of the wreck of a fishing boat, blown far off course, from a remote island. They were, as they had anticipated, separated at once, Kaza Agad being taken to the Castle and Merriment into the town. Kaza kept his name, which was plausible in the native context; Merriment called herself Yude. We have only her report, from which three excerpts follow.

FROM MOBILE GERINDU'UTTAHAYUDETWE'MENRADE
MERRIMENT'S NOTES FOR A REPORT TO THE EKUMEN, 93/1334.
34/223. Their network of trade and information, hence their awareness of what goes on elsewhere in their world, is too sophisticated for me to maintain my Stupid Foreign Castaway act any longer. Ekhaw called me in today and said, "If we had a sire here who was worth buying or if our teams were winning their games, I'd think you were a spy. Who are you, anyhow?"

I said, "Would you let me go to the College at Hagka?"

She said, "Why?"

"There are scientists there, I think? I need to talk with them."

This made sense to her; she made their "Mh" noise of assent.

"Could my friend go there with me?"

"Shask, you mean?"

We were both puzzled for a moment. She didn't expect a woman to call a man 'friend,' and I hadn't thought of Shask as a friend. She's very young, and I haven't taken her very seriously.

"I mean Kaza, the man I came with."

"A man – to the college?" she said, incredulous. She looked at me and said, "Where do you come from?"

It was a fair question, not asked in enmity or challenge. I wish I could have answered it, but I am increasingly convinced that we can do great damage to these people; we are facing Resehavanar's Choice here, I fear.

Ekhaw paid for my journey to Hagka, and Shask came along with me. As I thought about it I saw that of course Shask was my friend. It was she who brought me into the motherhouse, persuading Ekhaw and Azman of their duty to be hospitable; it was she who had looked out for me all along. Only she was so conventional in everything she did and said that I hadn't realized how radical her compassion was. When I tried to thank her, as our little jitney-bus purred along the road to Hagka, she said things like she always says – "Oh, we're all family," and "People have to help each other" and "Nobody can live alone."

"Don't women ever live alone?" I asked her, for all the ones I've met belong to a motherhouse or a daughterhouse, whether a couple or a big family like Ekhaw's, which is three generations: five older women, three of their daughters living at home, and four children – the boy they all coddle and spoil so, and three girls.

"Oh yes," Shask said. "If they don't want wives, they can be singlewomen. And old women, when their wives die, sometimes they just live alone till they die. Usually they go live at a daughterhouse. In the colleges, the vev always have a place to be alone." Conventional she may be, but Shask always tries to answer a question seriously and completely; she thinks about her answer. She has been an invaluable informant. She has also made life easy for me by not asking questions about where I come from. I took this for the incuriosity of a person securely embedded in an unquestioned way of life, and for the self-centeredness of the young. Now I see it as delicacy.

"A vev is a teacher?"

"Mh."

"And the teachers at the college are very respected?"

"That's what vev means. That's why we call Eckaw's mother Vev Kakaw. She didn't go to college, but she's a thoughtful person, she's learned from life, she has a lot to teach us."

So respect and teaching are the same thing, and the only term of respect I've heard women use for women means teacher. And so in teaching me, young Shask respects herself? And/or earns my respect? This casts a different light on what I've been seeing as a society in which wealth is the important thing. Zadedr, the current mayor of Reha, is certainly admired for her very ostentatious display of possessions; but they don't call her Vev.

I said to Shask, "You have taught me so much, may I call you Vev Shask?"

She was equally embarrassed and pleased, and squirmed and said, "Oh no no no no." Then she said, "If you ever come back to Reha I would like very much to have love with you, Yude."

"I thought you were in love with Sire Zadr!" I blurted out.

"Oh, I am," she said, with that eye-roll and melted look they have when they speak of the Sires. "Aren't you? Just think of him fucking you, oh! Oh, I get all wet thinking about it!" She smiled and wriggled. I felt embarrassed in my turn and probably showed it. "Don't you like him?" she inquired with a naiveté I found hard to bear. She was acting like a silly adolescent, and I know she's not a silly adolescent. "But I'll never be able to afford him," she said, and sighed.

So you want to make do with me, I thought, nastily.

"I'm going to save my money," she announced after a minute. "I think I want to have a baby next year. Of course I can't afford Sire Zadr, he's a Great Champion, but if I don't go to the Games at Kadaki this year I can save up enough for a really good sire at our fuckery, maybe Master Rosra. I wish, I know this is silly, I'm going to say it anyway, I kept wishing you could be its lovemother. I know you can't, you have to go to the college. I just wanted to tell you. I love you." She took my hands, drew them to her face, pressed my palms on her eyes for a moment, and then released me. She was smiling, but her tears were on my hands.

"Oh, Shask," I said, floored.

"It's all right!" she said. "I have to cry a minute." And she did. She wept openly, bending over, wringing her hands, and wailing softly. I patted her arm and felt unutterably ashamed of myself. Other passengers looked round and made little sympathetic grunting noises. One old woman said, "That's it, that's right, lovey!" In a few minutes Shask stopped crying, wiped her nose and face on her sleeve, drew a long, deep breath, and said, "All right." She smiled at me. "Driver," she called, "I have to piss, can we stop?"

The driver, a tense-looking woman, growled something, but stopped the bus on the wide, weedy roadside; and Shask and another woman got off and pissed in the weeds. There is an enviable simplicity to many acts in a society which has, in all its daily life, only one gender. And which, perhaps – I don't know this but it occurred to me then, while I was ashamed of myself – has no shame?

34/245. (Dictated) Still nothing from Kaza. I think I was right to give him the ansible. I hope he's in touch with somebody. I wish it was me. I need to know what goes on in the Castles.

Anyhow I understand better now what I was seeing at the Games in Reha. There are sixteen adult women for every adult man. One conception in six or so is male, but a lot of nonviable male fetuses and defective male births bring it down to one in sixteen by puberty. My ancestors must have really had fun playing with these people's chromosomes. I feel guilty, even if it was a million years ago. I have to learn to do without shame but had better not forget the one good use of guilt. Anyhow. A fairly small town like Reha shares its Castle with other towns. That confusing spectacle I was taken to on my tenth day down was Awaga Castle trying to keep its place in the Maingame against a castle from up north, and losing. Which means Awaga's team can't play in the big game this year in Fadrga, the city south of here, from which the winners go on to compete in the big big game at Zask, where people come from all over the continent – hundreds of contestants and thousands of spectators. I saw some holos of last year's Maingame at Zask. There were 1280 players, the comment said, and forty balls in play. It looked to me like a total mess, my idea of a battle between two unarmed armies, but I gather that great skill and strategy is involved. All the members of the winning team get a special title for the year, and another one for life, and bring glory back to their various Castles and the towns that support them.

I can now get some sense of how this works, see the system from outside it, because the college doesn't support a Castle. People here aren't obsessed with sports and athletes and sexy sires the way the young women in Reha were, and some of the older ones. It's a kind of obligatory obsession. Cheer your team, support your brave men, adore your local hero. It makes sense. Given their situation, they need strong, healthy men at their fuckery; it's social selection reinforcing natural selection. But I'm glad to get away from the rah-rah and the swooning and the posters of fellows with swelling muscles and huge penises and bedroom eyes.

I have made Resehavanar's Choice. I chose the option: Less than the truth. Shoggrad and Skodr and the other teachers, professors we'd call them, are intelligent, enlightened people, perfectly capable of understanding the concept of space travel, etc., making decisions about technological innovation, etc. I limit my answers to their questions to technology. I let them assume, as most people naturally assume, particularly people from a monoculture, that our society is pretty much like theirs. When they find how it differs, the effect will be revolutionary, and I have no mandate, reason, or wish to cause such a revolution on Seggri.

Their gender imbalance has produced a society in which, as far as I can tell, the men have all the privilege and the women have all the power. It's obviously a stable arrangement. According to their histories, it's lasted at least two millennia, and probably in some form or another much longer than that. But it could be quickly and disastrously destabilized by contact with us, by their experiencing the human norm. I don't know if the men would cling to their privileged status or demand freedom, but surely the women would resist giving up their power, and their sexual system and affectional relationships would break down. Even if they learned to undo the genetic program that was inflicted on them, it would take several generations to restore normal gender distribution. I can't be the whisper that starts that avalanche.

34/266. (DICTATED) Skodr got nowhere with the men of Awaga Castle. She had to make her inquiries very cautiously, since it would endanger Kaza if she told them he was an alien or in any way unique. They'd take it as a claim of superiority, which he'd have to defend in trials of strength and skill. I gather that the hierarchies within the Castles are a rigid framework, within which a man moves up or down issuing challenges and winning or losing obligatory and optional trials. The sports and games the women watch are only the showpieces of an endless series of competitions going on inside the Castles. As an untrained, grown man Kaza would be at a total disadvantage in such trials. The only way he might get out of them, she said, would be by feigning illness or idiocy. She thinks he must have done so, since he is at least alive; but that's all she could find out – "The man who was cast away at Taha-Reha is alive."

Although the women feed, house, clothe, and support the Lords of the Castle, they evidently take their noncooperation for granted. She seemed glad to get even that scrap of information. As I am.

But we have to get Kaza out of there. The more I hear about it from Skodr the more dangerous it sounds. I keep thinking "spoiled brats!" but actually these men must be more like soldiers in the training camps that militarists have. Only the training never ends. As they win trials they gain all kinds of titles and ranks you could translate as "generals" and the other names militarists have for all their power-grades. Some of the "generals," the Lords and Masters and so on, are the sports idols, the darlings of the fuckeries, like the one poor Shask adored; but as they get older apparently they often trade glory among the women for power among the men, and become tyrants within their Castle, bossing the "lesser" men around, until they're overthrown, kicked out. Old sires often live alone, it seems, in little houses away from the main Castle, and are considered crazy and dangerous – rogue males.

It sounds like a miserable life. All they're allowed to do after age eleven is compete at games and sports inside the Castle, and compete in the fuckeries, after they're fifteen or so, for money and number of fucks and so on. Nothing else. No options. No trades. No skills of making. No travel unless they play in the big games. They aren't allowed into the colleges to gain any kind of freedom of mind. I asked Skodr why an intelligent man couldn't at least come study in the college, and she told me that learning was very bad for men: it weakens a man's sense of honor, makes his muscles flabby, and leaves him impotent. "'What goes to the brain takes from the testicles,'" she said. "Men have to be sheltered from education for their own good."

I tried to "be water," as I was taught, but I was disgusted. Probably she felt it, because after a while she told me about "the secret college." Some women in colleges do smuggle information to men in Castles. The poor things meet secretly and teach each other. In the Castles, homosexual relationships are encouraged among boys under fifteen, but not officially tolerated among grown men; she says the "secret colleges" often are run by the homosexual men. They have to be secret because if they're caught reading or talking about ideas they may be punished by their Lords and Masters. There have been some interesting works from the "secret colleges," Skodr said, but she had to think to come up with examples. One was a man who had smuggled out an interesting mathematical theorem, and one was a painter whose landscapes, though primitive in technique, were admired by professionals of the art. She couldn't remember his name.

Arts, sciences, all learning, all professional techniques, are *haggyad*, skilled work. They're all taught at the colleges, and there are no divisions and few specialists. Teachers and students cross and mix fields all the time, and being a famous scholar in one field doesn't keep you from being a student in another. Skodr is a vev of physiology, writes plays, and is currently studying history with one of the history vevs. Her thinking is informed and lively and fearless. My School on Hain could learn from this college. It's a wonderful place, full of free minds. But only minds of one gender. A hedged freedom.

I hope Kaza has found a secret college or something, some way to fit in at the Castle. He's very fit, but these men have trained for years for the games they play. And a lot of the games are violent. The women say don't worry, we don't let the men kill each other, we protect them, they're our treasures. But I've seen men carried off with concussions on the holos of their martial-art fights, where they throw each other around spectacularly. "Only inexperienced fighters get hurt." Very reassuring. And they wrestle bulls. And in that melee they call the Maingame they break each other's legs and ankles deliberately. "What's a hero without a limp?" the women say. Maybe that's the safe thing to do, get your leg broken so you don't have to prove you're a hero any more. But what else might Kaza have to prove?

I asked Shask to let me know if she ever heard of him being at the Reha fuckery. But Awaga Castle services (that's their word, the same word they use for their bulls) four towns, so he might get sent to one of the others. But probably not, because men who don't win at things aren't allowed to go to the fuckeries. Only the champions. And boys between fifteen and nineteen, the ones the older women call *dippida*, baby animals, like puppies or kitties or lambies. They like to use the dippida for pleasure, and the champions when they go to the fuckery to get pregnant. But Kaza's thirty-six, he isn't a puppy or a kitten or a lamb. He's a man, and this is a terrible place to be a man.

Kaza Agad had been killed; the Lords of Awaga Castle finally disclosed the fact, but not the circumstances. A year later, Merriment radioed her lander and left Seggri for Hain. Her recommendation was to observe and avoid. The Stabiles, however, decided to send another pair of observers; these were both women, Mobiles Alee Iyoo and Zerin Wu. They lived for eight years on Seggri, after the third year as First Mobiles; Iyoo stayed as Ambassador another fifteen years. They made Resehavanar's Choice as "all the truth slowly." A limit of two hundred visitors from offworld was set. During the next several generations the people of Seggri, becoming accustomed to the alien presence, considered their own options as members of the Ekumen. Proposals for a planetwide referendum on genetic alteration were abandoned, since the men's vote would be insignificant unless the women's vote were handicapped. As of the date of this report the Seggri have not undertaken major genetic alteration, though they have learned and applied various repair techniques, which have resulted in a higher proportion of full-term male infants; the gender balance now stands at about 12:1.

THE FOLLOWING IS A MEMOIR GIVEN TO AMBASSADOR ERITHO TE VES IN 93/1569 BY A WOMAN IN USH ON SEGGRI.
You asked me, dear friend, to tell you anything I might like people on other worlds to know about my life and my world. That's not easy! Do I want anybody anywhere else to know anything about my life? I know how strange we seem to all the others, the half-and-half races; I know they think us backward, provincial, even perverse. Maybe in a few more decades we'll decide that we should remake ourselves. I won't be alive then; I don't think I'd want to be. I like my people. I like our fierce, proud, beautiful men, I don't want them to become like women. I like our trustful, powerful, generous women, I don't want them to become like men. And yet I see that among you each man has his own being and nature, each woman has hers, and I can hardly say what it is I think we would lose.

When I was a child I had a brother a year and a half younger than me. His name was Ittu. My mother had gone to the city and paid five years' savings for my sire, a Master Champion in the Dancing. Ittu's sire was an old fellow at our village fuckery; they called him "Master Fallback." He'd never been a champion at anything, hadn't sired a child for years, and was only too glad to fuck for free. My mother always laughed about it – she was still suckling me, she didn't even use a preventive, and she tipped him two coppers! When she found herself pregnant she was furious. When they tested and found it was a male fetus she was even more disgusted at having, as they say, to wait for the miscarriage. But when Ittu was born sound and healthy, she gave the old sire two hundred coppers, all the cash she had.

He wasn't delicate like so many boy babies, but how can you keep from protecting and cherishing a boy? I don't remember when I wasn't looking after Ittu, with it all very clear in my head what Little Brother should do and shouldn't do and all the perils I must keep him from. I was proud of my responsibility, and vain, too, because I had a brother to look after. Not one other motherhouse in my village had a son still living at home.

Ittu was a lovely child, a star. He had the fleecy soft hair that's common in my part of Ush, and big eyes; his nature was sweet and cheerful, and he was very bright. The other children loved him and always wanted to play with him, but he and I were happiest playing by ourselves, long elaborate games of make-believe. We had a herd of twelve cattle an old woman of the village had carved from gourdshell for Ittu – people always gave him presents – and they were the actors in our dearest game. Our cattle lived in a country called Shush, where they had great adventures, climbing mountains, discovering new lands, sailing on rivers, and so on. Like any herd, like our village herd, the old cows were the leaders; the bull lived apart; the other males were gelded; and the heifers were the adventurers. Our bull would make ceremonial visits to service the cows, and then he might have to go fight with men at Shush Castle. We made the castle of clay and the men of sticks, and the bull always won, knocking the stick-men to pieces. Then sometimes he knocked the castle to pieces too. But the best of our stories were told with two of the heifers. Mine was named Op and my brother's was Utti. Once our hero heifers were having a great adventure on the stream that runs past our village, and their boat got away from us. We found it caught against a log far downstream where the stream was deep and quick. My heifer was still in it. We both dived and dived, but we never found Utti. She had drowned. The Cattle of Shush had a great funeral for her, and Ittu cried very bitterly.

He mourned his brave little toy cow so long that I asked Djerdji the cattleherd if we could work for her, because I thought being with the real cattle might cheer Ittu up. She was glad to get two cowhands for free (when Mother found out we were really working, she made Djerdji pay us a quarter-copper a day). We rode two big, goodnatured old cows, on saddles so big Ittu could lie down on his. We took a herd of two-year-old calves out onto the desert every day to forage for the *edta* that grows best when it's grazed. We were supposed to keep them from wandering off and from trampling streambanks, and when they wanted to settle down and chew the cud we were supposed to gather them in a place where their droppings would nourish useful plants. Our old mounts did most of the work. Mother came out and checked on what we were doing and decided it was all right, and being out in the desert all day was certainly keeping us fit and healthy.

We loved our riding cows, but they were serious-minded and responsible, rather like the grown-ups in our motherhouse. The calves were something else; they were all riding breed, not fine animals of course, just villagebred; but living on edta they were fat and had plenty of spirit. Ittu and I rode them bareback with a rope rein. At first we always ended up on our own backs watching a calf's heels and tail flying off. By the end of a year we were good riders, and took to training our mounts to tricks, trading mounts at a full run, and hornvaulting. Ittu was a marvelous hornvaulter. He trained a big three-year-old roan ox with lyre horns, and the two of them danced like the finest vaulters of the great Castles that we saw on the holos. We couldn't keep our excellence to ourselves out in the desert; we started showing off to the other children, inviting them to come out to Salt Springs to see our Great Trick Riding Show. And so of course the adults got to hear of it.

My mother was a brave woman, but that was too much for even her, and she said to me in cold fury, "I trusted you to look after Ittu. You let me down."

All the others had been going on and on about endangering the precious life of a boy, the Vial of Hope, the Treasurehouse of Life and so on, but it was what my mother said that hurt.

"I do look after Ittu, and he looks after me," I said to her, in that passion of justice that children know, the birthright we seldom honor. "We both know what's dangerous and we don't do stupid things and we know our cattle and we do everything together. When he has to go to the Castle he'll have to do lots more dangerous things, but at least he'll already know how to do one of them. And there he has to do them alone, but we did everything together. And I didn't let you down."

My mother looked at us. I was nearly twelve, Ittu was ten. She burst into tears, she sat down on the dirt and wept aloud. Ittu and I both went to her and hugged her and cried. Ittu said, "I won't go. I won't go to the damned Castle. They can't make me!"

And I believed him. He believed himself. My mother knew better.

Maybe some day it will be possible for a boy to choose his life. Among your peoples a man's body does not shape his fate, does it? Maybe some day that will be so here.

Our Castle, Hidjegga, had of course been keeping their eye on Ittu ever since he was born; once a year Mother would send them the doctor's report on him, and when he was five Mother and her wives took him out there for the ceremony of Confirmation. Ittu had been embarrassed, disgusted, and flattered. He told me in secret, "There were all these old men that smelled funny and they made me take off my clothes and they had these measuring things and they measured my peepee! And they said it was very good. They said it was a good one. What happens when you descend?" It wasn't the first question he had ever asked me that I couldn't answer, and as usual I made up the answer. "Descend means you can have babies," I said, which, in a way, wasn't so far off the mark.

Some Castles, I am told, prepare boys of nine and ten for the Severance, woo them with visits from older boys, tickets to games, tours of the park and the buildings, so that they may be quite eager to go to the Castle when they turn eleven. But we "outyonders," villagers of the edge of the desert, kept to the harsh old-fashioned ways. Aside from Confirmation, a boy had no contact at all with men until his eleventh birthday. On that day everybody he had ever known brought him to the Gate and gave him to the strangers with whom he would live the rest of his life. Men and women alike believed and still believe that this absolute severance makes the man.

Vev Ushiggi, who had borne a son and had a grandson, and had been mayor five or six times, and was held in great esteem even though she'd never had much money, heard Ittu say that he wouldn't go to the damned Castle. She came next day to our motherhouse and asked to talk to him. He told me what she said. She didn't do any wooing or sweetening. She told him that he was born to the service of his people and had one responsibility, to sire children when he got old enough; and one duty, to be a strong, brave man, stronger and braver than other men, so that women would choose him to sire their children. She said he had to live in the Castle because men could not live among women. At this, Ittu asked her, "Why can't they?"

"You did?" I said, awed by his courage, for Vev Ushiggi was a formidable old woman.

"Yes. And she didn't really answer. She took a long time. She looked at me and then she looked off somewhere and then she stared at me for a long time and then finally she said, 'Because we would destroy them.'"

"But that's crazy," I said. "Men are our treasures. What did she say that for?"

Ittu, of course, didn't know. But he thought hard about what she had said, and I think nothing she could have said would have so impressed him.

After discussion, the village elders and my mother and her wives decided that Ittu could go on practicing hornvaulting, because it really would be a useful skill for him in the Castle; but he could not herd cattle any longer, nor go with me when I did, nor join in any of the work children of the village did, nor their games. "You've done everything together with Po," they told him, "but she should be doing things together with the other girls, and you should be doing things by yourself, the way men do."

They were always very kind to Ittu, but they were stern with us girls; if they saw us even talking with Ittu they'd tell us to go on about our work, leave the boy alone. When we disobeyed – when Ittu and I sneaked off and met at Salt Springs to ride together, or just hid out in our old playplace down in the draw by the stream to talk – he got treated with cold silence to shame him, but I got punished. A day locked in the cellar of the old fiber-processing mill, which was what my village used for a jail; next time it was two days; and the third time they caught us alone together, they locked me in that cellar for ten days. A young woman called Fersk brought me food once a day and made sure I had enough water and wasn't sick, but she didn't speak; that's how they always used to punish people in the villages. I could hear the other children going by up on the street in the evening. It would get dark at last and I could sleep. All day I had nothing to do, no work, nothing to think about except the scorn and contempt they held me in for betraying their trust, and the injustice of my getting punished when Ittu didn't.

When I came out, I felt different. I felt like something had closed up inside me while I was closed up in that cellar.

When we ate at the motherhouse they made sure Ittu and I didn't sit near each other. For a while we didn't even talk to each other. I went back to school and work. I didn't know what Ittu was doing all day. I didn't think about it. It was only fifty days to his birthday.

One night I got into bed and found a note under my clay pillow: *in the draw to-nt.* Ittu never could spell; what writing he knew I had taught him in secret. I was frightened and angry, but I waited an hour till everybody was asleep, and got up and crept outside into the windy, starry night, and ran to the draw. It was late in the dry season and the stream was barely running. Ittu was there, hunched up with his arms round his knees, a little lump of shadow on the pale, cracked clay at the waterside.

The first thing I said was, "You want to get me locked up again? They said next time it would be thirty days!"

"They're going to lock me up for fifty years," Ittu said, not looking at me.

"What am I supposed to do about it? It's the way it has to be! You're a man. You have to do what men do. They won't lock you up, anyway, you get to play games and come to town to do service and all that. You don't even know what being locked up is!"

"I want to go to Seradda," Ittu said, talking very fast, his eyes shining as he looked up at me. "We could take the riding cows to the bus station in Redang, I saved my money, I have twenty-three coppers, we could take the bus to Seradda. The cows would come back home if we turned them loose."

"What do you think you'd do in Seradda?" I asked, disdainful but curious. Nobody from our village had ever been to the capital.

"The Ekkamen people are there," he said.

"The Ekumen," I corrected him. "So what?"

"They could take me away," Ittu said.

I felt very strange when he said that. I was still angry and still disdainful but a sorrow was rising in me like dark water. "Why would they do that? What would they talk to some little boy for? How would you find them? Twenty-three coppers isn't enough anyway. Seradda's way far off. That's a really stupid idea. You can't do that."

"I thought you'd come with me," Ittu said. His voice was softer, but didn't shake.

"I wouldn't do a stupid thing like that," I said furiously.

"All right," he said. "But you won't tell. Will you?"

"No, I won't tell!" I said. "But you can't run away, Ittu. You can't. It would be – it would be dishonorable."

This time when he answered his voice shook. "I don't care," he said. "I don't care about honor. I want to be free!"

We were both in tears. I sat down by him and we leaned together the way we used to, and cried a while; not long; we weren't used to crying.

"You can't do it," I whispered to him. "It won't work, Ittu."

He nodded, accepting my wisdom.

"It won't be so bad at the Castle," I said.

After a minute he drew away from me very slightly.

"We'll see each other," I said.

He said only, "When?"

"At games. I can watch you. I bet you'll be the best rider and hornvaulter there. I bet you win all the prizes and get to be a Champion."

He nodded, dutiful. He knew and I knew that I had betrayed our love and our birthright of justice. He knew he had no hope.

That was the last time we talked together alone, and almost the last time we talked together.

Ittu ran away about ten days after that, taking the riding cow and heading for Redang; they tracked him easily and had him back in the village before nightfall. I don't know if he thought I had told them where he would be going. I was so ashamed of not having gone with him that I could not look at him. I kept away from him; they didn't have to keep me away any more. He made no effort to speak to me.

I was beginning my puberty, and my first blood was the night before Ittu's birthday. Menstruating women are not allowed to come near the Gates at conservative Castles like ours, so when Ittu was made a man I stood far back among a few other girls and women, and could not see much of the ceremony. I stood silent while they sang, and looked down at the dirt and my new sandals and my feet in the sandals, and felt the ache and tug of my womb and the secret movement of the blood, and grieved. I knew even then that this grief would be with me all my life.

Ittu went in and the Gates closed.

He became a Young Champion Hornvaulter, and for two years, when he was eighteen and nineteen, came a few times to service in our village, but I never saw him. One of my friends fucked with him and started to tell me about it, how nice he was, thinking I'd like to hear, but I shut her up and walked away in a blind rage which neither of us understood.

He was traded away to a castle on the east coast when he was twenty. When my daughter was born I wrote him, and several times after that, but he never answered my letters.

I don't know what I've told you about my life and my world. I don't know if it's what I want you to know. It is what I had to tell.

The following is a short story written in 93/1586 by a popular writer of the city of Adr, Sem Gridji. The classic literature of Seggri was the narrative poem and the drama. Classical poems and plays were written collaboratively, in the original version and also by re-writers of subsequent generations, usually anonymous. Small value was placed on preserving a "true" text, since the work was seen as an ongoing process. Probably under Ekumenical influence, individual writers in the late sixteenth century began writing short prose narratives, historical and fictional. The genre became popular, particularly in the cities, though it never obtained the immense audience of the great classical epics and plays. Literally everyone knew the plots and many quotations from the epics and plays, from books and holo, and almost every adult woman had seen or participated in a staged performance of several of them. They were one of the principal unifying influences of the Seggrian monoculture. The prose narrative, read in silence, served rather as a device by which the culture might question itself, and a tool for individual moral self-examination. Conservative Seggrian women disapproved of the genre as antagonistic to the intensely cooperative, collaborative structure of their society. Fiction was not included in the curriculum of the literature departments of the colleges, and was often dismissed contemptuously – "fiction is for men."

Sem Gridji published three books of stories. Her bare, blunt style is characteristic of the Seggrian short story.

LOVE OUT OF PLACE
by Sem Gridji

Azak grew up in a motherhouse in the Downriver Quarter, near the textile mills. She was a bright girl, and her family and neighborhood were proud to gather the money to send her to college. She came back to the city as a starting manager at one of the mills. Azak worked well with other people; she prospered. She had a clear idea of what she wanted to do in the next few years: to find two or three partners with whom to found a daughterhouse and a business.

A beautiful woman in the prime of youth, Azak took great pleasure in sex, especially liking intercourse with men. Though she saved money for her plan of founding a business, she also spent a good deal at the fuckery, going there often, sometimes hiring two men at once. She liked to see how they incited each other to prowess beyond what they would have achieved alone, and shamed each other when they failed. She found a flaccid penis very disgusting, and did not hesitate to send away a man who could not penetrate her three or four times an evening.

The Castle of her district bought a Young Champion at the Southeast Castles Dance Tournament, and soon sent him to the fuckery. Having seen him dance in the finals on the holovision and been captivated by his flowing, graceful style and his beauty, Azak was eager to have him service her. His price was twice that of any other man there, but she did not hesitate to pay it. She found him handsome and amiable, eager and gentle, skilful and compliant. In their first evening they came to orgasm together five times. When she left she gave him a large tip. Within the week she was back, asking for Toddra. The pleasure he gave her was exquisite, and soon she was quite obsessed with him.

"I wish I had you all to myself," she said to him one night as they lay still conjoined, languorous and fulfilled.

"That is my heart's desire," he said. "I wish I were your servant. None of the other women that come here arouse me. I don't want them. I want only you."

She wondered if he was telling the truth. The next time she came, she inquired casually of the manager if Toddra were as popular as they had hoped. "No," the manager said. "Everybody else reports that he takes a lot of arousing, and is sullen and careless towards them."

"How strange," Azak said.

"Not at all," said the manager. "He's in love with you."

"A man in love with a woman?" Azak said, and laughed.

"It happens all too often," the manager said.

"I thought only women fell in love," said Azak.

"Women fall in love with a man, sometimes, and that's bad too," said the manager. "May I warn you, Azak? Love should be between women. It's out of place here. It can never come to any good end. I hate to lose the money, but I wish you'd fuck with some of the other men and not always ask for Toddra. You're encouraging him, you see, in something that does harm to him."

"But he and you are making lots of money from me!" said Azak, still taking it as a joke.

"He'd make more from other women if he wasn't in love with you," said the manager. To Azak that seemed a weak argument against the pleasure she had in Toddra, and she said, "Well, he can fuck them all when I've done with him, but for now, I want him."

After their intercourse that evening, she said to Toddra, "The manager here says you're in love with me."

"I told you I was," Toddra said. "I told you I wanted to belong to you, to serve you, you alone. I would die for you, Azak."

"That's foolish," she said.

"Don't you like me? Don't I please you?"

"More than any man I ever knew," she said, kissing him. "You are beautiful and utterly satisfying, my sweet Toddra."

"You don't want any of the other men here, do you?" he asked.

"No. They're all ugly fumblers, compared to my beautiful dancer."

"Listen, then," he said, sitting up and speaking very seriously. He was a slender man of twenty-two, with long, smooth-muscled limbs, wide-set eyes, and a thin-lipped, sensitive mouth. Azak lay stroking his thigh, thinking how lovely and lovable he was. "I have a plan," he said. "When I dance, you know, in the story-dances, I play a woman, of course; I've done it since I was twelve. People always say they can't believe I really am a man, I play a woman so well. If I escaped – from here, from the Castle – as a woman – I could come to your house as a servant – "

"What?" cried Azak, astounded.

"I could live there," he said urgently, bending over her. "With you. I would always be there. You could have me every night. It would cost you nothing, except my food. I would serve you, service you, sweep your house, do anything, anything, Azak, please, my beloved, my mistress, let me be yours!" He saw that she was still incredulous, and hurried on, "You could send me away when you got tired of me – "

"If you tried to go back to the Castle after an escapade like that they'd whip you to death, you idiot!"

"I'm valuable," he said. "They'd punish me, but they wouldn't damage me."

"You're wrong. You haven't been dancing, and your value here has slipped because you don't perform well with anybody but me. The manager told me so."

Tears stood in Toddra's eyes. Azak disliked giving him pain, but she was genuinely shocked at his wild plan. "And if you were discovered, my dear," she said more gently, "I would be utterly disgraced. It is a very childish plan, Toddra: please never dream of such a thing again. But I am truly, truly fond of you, I adore you and want no other man but you. Do you believe that, Toddra?"

He nodded. Restraining his tears, he said, "For now."

"For now and for a long, long, long time! My dear, sweet, beautiful dancer, we have each other as long as we want, years and years! Only do your duty by the other women that come, so that you don't get sold away by your Castle, please! I couldn't bear to lose you, Toddra." And she clasped him passionately in her arms, and arousing him at once, opened to him, and soon both were crying out in the throes of delight.

Though she could not take his love entirely seriously, since what could come of such a misplaced emotion, except such foolish schemes as he had proposed? – still he touched her heart, and she felt a tenderness towards him that greatly enhanced the pleasure of their intercourse. So for more than a year she spent two or three nights a week with him at the fuckery, which was as much as she could afford. The manager, trying still to discourage his love, would not lower Toddra's fee, even though he was unpopular among the other clients of the fuckery; so Azak spent a great deal of money on him, although he would never, after the first night, accept a tip from her.

Then a woman who had not been able to conceive with any of the sires at the fuckery tried Toddra, and at once conceived, and being tested found the fetus to be male. Another woman conceived by him, again a male fetus. At once Toddra was in demand as a sire. Women began coming from all over the city to be serviced by him. This meant, of course, that he must be free during their period of ovulation. There were now many evenings that he could not meet Azak, for the manager was not to be bribed. Toddra disliked his popularity, but Azak soothed and reassured him, telling him how proud she was of him, and how his work would never interfere with their love. In fact, she was not altogether sorry that he was so much in demand, for she had found another person with whom she wanted to spend her evenings.

This was a young woman named Zedr, who worked in the mill as a machine repair specialist. She was tall and handsome; Azak noticed first how freely and strongly she walked and how proudly she stood. She found a pretext to make her acquaintance. It seemed to Azak that Zedr admired her; but for a long time each behaved to the other as a friend only, making no sexual advances. They were much in each other's company, going to games and dances together, and Azak found that she enjoyed this open and sociable life better than always being in the fuckery alone with Toddra. They talked about how they might set up a machine-repair service in partnership. As time went on, Azak found that Zedr's beautiful body was always in her thoughts. At last, one evening in her singlewoman's flat, she told her friend that she loved her, but did not wish to burden their friendship with an unwelcome desire.

Zedr replied, "I have wanted you ever since I first saw you, but I didn't want to embarrass you with my desire. I thought you preferred men."

"Until now I did, but I want to make love with you," Azak said.

She found herself quite timid at first, but Zedr was expert and subtle, and could prolong Azak's orgasms till she found such consummation as she had not dreamed of. She said to Zedr, "You have made me a woman."

"Then let's make each other wives," said Zedr joyfully.

They married, moved to a house in the west of the city, and left the mill, setting up in business together.

All this time, Azak had said nothing of her new love to Toddra, whom she had seen less and less often. A little ashamed of her cowardice, she reassured herself that he was so busy performing as a sire that he would not really miss her. After all, despite his romantic talk of love, he was a man, and to a man fucking is the most important thing, instead of being merely one element of love and life as it is to a woman.

When she married Zedr, she sent Toddra a letter, saying that their lives had drifted apart, and she was now moving away and would not see him again, but would always remember him fondly.

She received an immediate answer from Toddra, a letter begging her to come and talk with him, full of avowals of unchanging love, badly spelled and almost illegible. The letter touched, embarrassed, and shamed her, and she did not answer it.

He wrote again and again, and tried to reach her on the holonet at her new business. Zedr encouraged her not to make any response, saying, "It would be cruel to encourage him."

Their new business went well from the start. They were home one evening busy chopping vegetables for dinner when there was a knock at the door. "Come in," Zedr called, thinking it was Chochi, a friend they were considering as a third partner. A stranger entered, a tall, beautiful woman with a scarf over her hair. The stranger went straight to Azak, saying in a strangled voice, "Azak, Azak, please, please let me stay with you." The scarf fell back from his long hair. Azak recognized Toddra.

She was astonished and a little frightened, but she had known Toddra a long time and been very fond of him, and this habit of affection made her put out her hands to him in greeting. She saw fear and despair in his face, and was sorry for him.

But Zedr, guessing who he was, was both alarmed and angry. She kept the chopping-knife in her hand. She slipped from the room and called the city police.

When she returned she saw the man pleading with Azak to let him stay hidden in their household as a servant. "I will do anything," he said. "Please, Azak, my only love, please! I can't live without you. I can't service those women, those strangers who only want to be impregnated. I can't dance any more. I think only of you, you are my only hope. I will be a woman, no one will know. I'll cut my hair, no one will know!" So he went on, almost threatening in his passion, but pitiful also. Zedr listened coldly, thinking he was mad. Azak listened with pain and shame. "No, no, it is not possible," she said over and over, but he would not hear.

When the police came to the door and he realized who they were, he bolted to the back of the house seeking escape. The policewomen caught him in the bedroom; he fought them desperately, and they subdued him brutally. Azak shouted at them not to hurt him, but they paid no heed, twisting his arms and hitting him about the head till he stopped resisting. They dragged him out. The head of the troop stayed to take evidence. Azak tried to plead for Toddra, but Zedr stated the facts and added that she thought he was insane and dangerous.

After some days, Azak inquired at the police office and was told that Toddra had been returned to his Castle with a warning not to send him to the fuckery again for a year or until the Lords of the Castle found him capable of responsible behavior. She was uneasy thinking of how he might be punished. Zedr said, "They won't hurt him, he's too valuable," just as he himself had said. Azak was glad to believe this. She was, in fact, much relieved to know that he was out of the way.

She and Zedr took Chochi first into their business and then into their household. Chochi was a woman from the dockside quarter, tough and humorous, a hard worker and an undemanding, comfortable lovemaker. They were happy with one another, and prospered.

A year went by, and another year. Azak went to her old quarter to arrange a contract for repair work with two women from the mill where she had first worked. She asked them about Toddra. He was back at the fuckery from time to time, they told her. He had been named the year's Champion Sire of his Castle, and was much in demand, bringing an even higher price, because he impregnated so many women and so many of the conceptions were male. He was not in demand for pleasure, they said, as he had a reputation for roughness and even cruelty. Women asked for him only if they wanted to conceive. Thinking of his gentleness with her, Azak found it hard to imagine him behaving brutally. Harsh punishment at the Castle, she thought, must have altered him. But she could not believe that he had truly changed.

Another year passed. The business was doing very well, and Azak and Chochi both began talking seriously about having children. Zedr was not interested in bearing, though happy to be a mother. Chochi had a favorite man at their local fuckery to whom she went now and then for pleasure; she began going to him at ovulation, for he had a good reputation as a sire.

Azak had never been to a fuckery since she and Zedr married. She honored fidelity highly, and made love with no one but Zedr and Chochi. When she thought of being impregnated, she found that her old interest in fucking with men had quite died out or even turned to distaste. She did not like the idea of self-impregnation from the sperm bank, but the idea of letting a strange man penetrate her was even more repulsive. Thinking what to do, she thought of Toddra, whom she had truly loved and had pleasure with. He was again a Champion Sire, known throughout the city as a reliable impregnator. There was certainly no other man with whom she could take any pleasure. And he had loved her so much he had put his career and even his life in danger, trying to be with her. That irresponsibility was over and done with. He had never written to her again, and the Castle and the managers of the fuckery would never have let him service women if they thought him mad or untrustworthy. After all this time, she thought, she could go back to him and give him the pleasure he had so desired.

She notified the fuckery of the expected period of her next ovulation, requesting Toddra. He was already engaged for that period, and they offered her another sire; but she preferred to wait till the next month.

Chochi had conceived, and was elated. "Hurry up, hurry up!" she said to Azak. "We want twins!"

Azak found herself looking forward to being with Toddra. Regretting the violence of their last encounter and the pain it must have given him, she wrote the following letter to him:

"My dear, I hope our long separation and the distress of our last meeting will be forgotten in the joy of being together again, and that you still love me as I still love you. I shall be very proud to bear your child, and let us hope it may be a son! I am impatient to see you again, my beautiful dancer. Your Azak."

There had not been time for him to answer this letter when her ovulation period began. She dressed in her best clothes. Zedr still distrusted Toddra and had tried to dissuade her from going to him; she bade her "Good luck!" rather sulkily. Chochi hung a mothercharm round her neck, and she went off.

There was a new manager on duty at the fuckery, a coarse-faced young woman who told her, "Call out if he gives you any trouble. He may be a Champion but he's rough, and we don't let him get away with hurting anybody."

"He won't hurt me," Azak said smiling, and went eagerly into the familiar room where she and Toddra had enjoyed each other so often. He was standing waiting at the window just as he had used to stand. When he turned he looked just as she remembered, long-limbed, his silky hair flowing like water down his back, his wide-set eyes gazing at her.

"Toddra!" she said, coming to him with outstretched hands.

He took her hands and said her name.

"Did you get my letter? Are you happy?"

"Yes," he said, smiling.

"And all that unhappiness, all that foolishness about love, is it over? I am so sorry you were hurt, Toddra, I don't want any more of that. Can we just be ourselves and be happy together as we used to be?"

"Yes, all that is over," he said. "And I am happy to see you." He drew her gently to him. Gently he began to undress her and caress her body, just as he had used to, knowing what gave her pleasure, and she remembering what gave him pleasure. They lay down naked together. She was fondling his erect penis, aroused and yet a little reluctant to be penetrated after so long, when he moved his arm as if uncomfortable. Drawing away from him a little, she saw that he had a knife in his hand, which he must have hidden in the bed. He was holding it concealed behind his back.

Her womb went cold, but she continued to fondle his penis and testicles, not daring to say anything and not able to pull away, for he was holding her close with the other hand.

Suddenly he moved onto her and forced his penis into her vagina with a thrust so painful that for an instant she thought it was the knife. He ejaculated instantly. As his body arched she writhed out from under him, scrambled to the door, and ran from the room crying for help.

He pursued her, striking with the knife, stabbing her in the shoulderblade before the manager and other women and men seized him. The men were very angry and treated him with a violence which the manager's protests did not lessen. Naked, bloody, and half-conscious, he was bound and taken away immediately to the Castle.

Everyone now gathered around Azak, and her wound, which was slight, was cleaned and covered. Shaken and confused, she could ask only, "What will they do to him?"

"What do you think they do to a murdering rapist? Give him a prize?" the manager said. "They'll geld him."

"But it was my fault," Azak said.

The manager stared at her and said, "Are you mad? Go home."

She went back into the room and mechanically put on her clothes. She looked at the bed where they had lain. She stood at the window where Toddra had stood. She remembered how she had seen him dance long ago in the contest where he had first been made champion. She thought, "My life is wrong." But she did not know how to make it right.

Alteration in Seggrian social and cultural institutions did not take the disastrous course Merriment feared. It has been slow and its direction is not clear. In 93/1602 Terhada College invited men from two neighboring Castles to apply as students, and three men did so. In the next decades, most colleges opened their doors to men. Once they were graduated, male students had to return to their Castle, unless they left the planet, since native men were not allowed to live anywhere but as students in a college or in a Castle, until the Open Gate Law was passed in 93/1662.

Even after passage of that law, the Castles remained closed to women; and the exodus of men from the Castles was much slower than opponents of the measure feared. Social adjustment to the Open Gate Law has been slow. In several regions programs to train men in basic skills such as farming and construction have met with moderate success; the men work in competitive teams, separate from and managed by the women's companies. A good many Seggri have come to Hain to study in recent years – more men than women, despite the great numerical imbalance that still exists.

The following autobiographical sketch by one of these men is of particular interest, since he was involved in the event which directly precipitated the Open Gate Law.

AUTOBIOGRAPHICAL SKETCH BY MOBILE ARDAR DEZ.

I was born in Ekumenical Cycle 93, Year 1641, in Rakedr on Seggri. Rakedr was a placid, prosperous, conservative town, and I was brought up in the old way, the petted boychild of a big motherhouse. Altogether there were seventeen of us, not counting the kitchen staff – a great-grandmother, two grandmothers, four mothers, nine daughters, and me. We were well off; all the women were or had been managers or skilled workers in the Rakedr Pottery, the principal industry of the town. We kept all the holidays with pomp and energy, decorating the house from roof to foundation with banners for Hillalli, making fantastic costumes for the Harvest Festival, and celebrating somebody's birthday every few weeks with gifts all round. I was petted, as I said, but not, I think, spoiled. My birthday was no grander than my sisters', and I was allowed to run and play with them just as if I were a girl. Yet I was always aware, as were they, that our mothers' eyes rested on me with a different look, brooding, reserved, and sometimes, as I grew older, desolate.

After my Confirmation, my birthmother or her mother took me to Rakedr Castle every spring on Visiting Day. The gates of the Park, which had opened to admit me alone (and terrified) for my Confirmation, remained shut, but rolling stairs were placed against the Park walls. Up these I and a few other little boys from the town climbed, to sit on top of the Park wall in great state, on cushions, under awnings, and watch demonstration dancing, bull-dancing, wrestling, and other sports on the great Gamefield inside the wall. Our mothers waited below, outside, in the bleachers of the public field. Men and youths from the Castle sat with us, explaining the rules of the games and pointing out the fine points of a dancer or wrestler, treating us seriously, making us feel important. I enjoyed that very much, but as soon as I came down off the wall and started home it all fell away like a costume shrugged off, a part played in a play; and I went on with my work and play in the motherhouse with my family, my real life.

When I was ten I went to Boys' Class downtown. The class had been set up forty or fifty years before as a bridge between the motherhouse and the Castle, but the Castle, under increasingly reactionary governance, had recently withdrawn from the project. Lord Fassaw forbade his men to go anywhere outside the walls but directly to the fuckery, in a closed car, returning at first light; and so no men were able to teach the class. The townswomen who tried to tell me what to expect when I went to the Castle did not really know much more than I did. However wellmeaning they were, they mostly frightened and confused me. But fear and confusion were an appropriate preparation.

I cannot describe the ceremony of Severance. I really cannot describe it. Men on Seggri, in those days, had this advantage: they knew what death is. They had all died once before their body's death. They had turned and looked back at their whole life, every place and face they had loved, and turned away from it as the gate closed.

At the time of my Severance, our small Castle was internally divided into "collegials" and "traditionals," a liberal faction left from the regime of Lord Ishog and a younger, highly conservative faction. The split was already disastrously wide when I came to the Castle.

Lord Fassaw's rule had grown increasingly harsh and irrational. He governed by corruption, brutality, and cruelty. All of us who lived there were of course infected, and would have been destroyed if there had not been a strong, constant, moral resistance, centered around Ragaz and Kohadrat, who had been protégés of Lord Ishog. The two men were open partners; their followers were all the homosexuals in the Castle, and a good number of other men and older boys.

My first days and months in the Scrubs' dormitory were a bewildering alternation: terror, hatred, shame, as the boys who had been there a few months or years longer than I were incited to humiliate and abuse the newcomer, in order to make a man of him – and comfort, gratitude, love, as boys who had come under the influence of the collegials offered me secret friendship and protection. They helped me in the games and competitions and took me into their beds at night, not for sex but to keep me from the sexual bullies. Lord Fassaw detested adult homosexuality and would have reinstituted the death penalty if the Town Council had allowed it. Though he did not dare punish Ragaz and Kohadrat, he punished consenting love between older boys with bizarre and appalling physical mutilations – ears cut into fringes, fingers branded with redhot iron rings. Yet he encouraged the older boys to rape the eleven- and twelve-year-olds, as a manly practice. None of us escaped. We particularly dreaded four youths, seventeen or eighteen years old when I came there, who called themselves the Lordsmen. Every few nights they raided the Scrubs' dormitory for a victim, whom they raped as a group. The collegials protected us as best they could by ordering us to their beds, where we wept and protested loudly, while they pretended to abuse us, laughing and jeering. Later, in the dark and silence, they comforted us with candy, and sometimes, as we grew older, with a desired love, gentle and exquisite in its secrecy.

There was no privacy at all in the Castle. I have said that to women who asked me to describe life there, and they thought they understood me. "Well, everybody shares everything in a motherhouse," they would say, "everybody's in and out of the rooms all the time. You're never really alone unless you have a singlewoman's flat." I could not tell them how different the loose, warm commonalty of the motherhouse was from the rigid, deliberate publicity of the forty-bed, brightly-lighted Castle dormitories. Nothing in Rakedr was private: only secret, only silent. We ate our tears.

I grew up; I take some pride in that, along with my profound gratitude to the boys and men who made it possible. I did not kill myself, as several boys did during those years, nor did I kill my mind and soul, as some did so their body could survive. Thanks to the maternal care of the collegials – the resistance, as we came to call ourselves – I grew up.

Why do I say maternal, not paternal? Because there were no fathers in my world. There were only sires. I knew no such word as father or paternal. I thought of Ragaz and Kohadrat as my mothers. I still do.

Fassaw grew quite mad as the years went on, and his hold over the Castle tightened to a deathgrip. The Lordsmen now ruled us all. They were lucky in that we still had a strong Maingame team, the pride of Fassaw's heart, which kept us in the First League, as well as two Champion Sires in steady demand at the town fuckeries. Any protest the resistance tried to bring to the Town Council could be dismissed as typical male whining, or laid to the demoralizing influence of the Aliens. From the outside Rakedr Castle seemed all right. Look at our great team! Look at our champion studs! The women looked no further.

How could they abandon us? – the cry every Seggrian boy must make in his heart. How could she leave me here? Doesn't she know what it's like? Why doesn't she know? Doesn't she want to know?

"Of course not," Ragaz said to me when I came to him in a passion of righteous indignation, the Town Council having denied our petition to be heard. "Of course they don't want to know how we live. Why do they never come into the Castles? Oh, we keep them out, yes; but do you think we could keep them out if they wanted to enter? My dear, we collude with them and they with us in maintaining the great foundation of ignorance and lies on which our civilization rests."

"Our own mothers abandon us," I said.

"Abandon us? Who feeds us, clothes us, houses us, pays us? We're utterly dependent on them. If ever we made ourselves independent, perhaps we could rebuild society on a foundation of truth."

Independence was as far as his vision could reach. Yet I think his mind groped further, towards what he could not see, the body's obscure, inalterable dream of mutuality.

Our effort to make our case heard at the Council had no effect except within the Castle. Lord Fassaw saw his power threatened. Within a few days Ragaz was seized by the Lordsmen and their bully boys, accused of repeated homosexual acts and treasonable plots, arraigned, and sentenced by the Lord of the Castle. Everyone was summoned to the Gamefield to witness the punishment. A man of fifty with a heart ailment – he had been a Maingame racer in his twenties and had over-trained – Ragaz was tied naked across a bench and beaten with 'Lord Long,' a heavy leather tube filled with lead weights. The Lordsman Berhed, who wielded it, struck repeatedly at the head, the kidneys, and the genitals. Ragaz died an hour or two later in the infirmary.

The Rakedr Mutiny took shape that night. Kohadrat, older than Ragaz and devastated by his loss, could not restrain or guide us. His vision had been of a true resistance, longlasting and nonviolent, through which the Lordsmen would in time destroy themselves. We had been following that vision. Now we let it go. We dropped the truth and grabbed weapons. "How you play is what you win," Kohadrat said, but we had heard all those old saws. We would not play the patience game any more. We would win, now, once for all.

And we did. We won. We had our victory. Lord Fassaw, the Lordsmen and their bullies had been slaughtered by the time the police got to the Gate.

I remember how those tough women strode in amongst us, staring at the rooms of the Castle which they had never seen, staring at the mutilated bodies, eviscerated, castrated, headless – at Lordsman Berhed, who had been nailed to the floor with 'Lord Long' stuffed down his throat – at us, the rebels, the victors, with our bloody hands and defiant faces – at Kohadrat, whom we thrust forward as our leader, our spokesman.

He stood silent. He ate his tears.

The women drew closer to one another, clutching their guns, star-ing around. They were appalled, they thought us all insane. Their utter incomprehension drove one of us at last to speak – a young man, Tarsk, who wore the iron ring that had been forced onto his finger when it was red-hot. "They killed Ragaz," he said. "They were all mad. Look." He held out his crippled hand.

The chief of the troop, after a pause, said, "No one will leave here till this is looked into," and marched her women out of the Castle, out of the Park, locking the gate behind them, leaving us with our victory.

The hearings and judgments on the Rakedr Mutiny were all broad-cast, of course, and the event has been studied and discussed ever since. My own part in it was the murder of the Lordsman Tatiddi. Three of us set on him and beat him to death with exercise-clubs in the gymnasium where we had cornered him.

How we played was what we won.

We were not punished. Men were sent from several Castles to form a government over Rakedr Castle. They learned enough of Fassaw's behavior to see the cause of our rebellion, but the contempt of even the most liberal of them for us was absolute. They treated us not as men, but as irrational, irresponsible creatures, untamable cattle. If we spoke they did not answer.

I do not know how long we could have endured that cold regime of shame. It was only two months after the Mutiny that the World Council enacted the Open Gate Law. We told one another that that was our victory, we had made that happen. None of us believed it. We told one another we were free. For the first time in history, any man who wanted to leave his Castle could walk out the gate. We were free!

What happened to the free man outside the gate? Nobody had given it much thought.

I was one who walked out the gate, on the morning of the day the Law came into force. Eleven of us walked into town together.

Several of us, men not from Rakedr, went to one or another of the fuckeries, hoping to be allowed to stay there; they had nowhere else to go. Hotels and inns of course would not accept men. Those of us who had been children in the town went to our motherhouses.

What is it like to return from the dead? Not easy. Not for the one who returns, nor for his people. The place he occupied in their world has closed up, ceased to be, filled with accumulated change, habit, the doings and needs of others. He has been replaced. To return from the dead is to be a ghost: a person for whom there is no room.

Neither I nor my family understood that, at first. I came back to them at twenty-one as trustingly as if I were the eleven-year-old who had left them, and they opened their arms to their child. But he did not exist. Who was I?

For a long time, months, we refugees from the Castle hid in our motherhouses. The men from other towns all made their way home, usually by begging a ride with teams on tour. There were seven or eight of us in Rakedr, but we scarcely ever saw one another. Men had no place on the street; for hundreds of years a man seen alone on the street had been arrested immediately. If we went out, women ran from us, or reported us, or surrounded and threatened us – "Get back into your Castle where you belong! Get back to the fuckery where you belong! Get out of our city!" They called us drones, and in fact we had no work, no function at all in the community. The fuckeries would not accept us for service, because we had no guarantee of health and good behavior from a Castle.

This was our freedom: we were all ghosts, useless, frightened, frightening intruders, shadows in the corners of life. We watched life going on around us – work, love, childbearing, childrearing, getting and spending, making and shaping, governing and adventuring – the women's world, the bright, full, real world – and there was no room in it for us. All we had ever learned to do was play games and destroy one another.

My mothers and sisters racked their brains, I know, to find some place and use for me in their lively, industrious household. Two old live-in cooks had run our kitchen since long before I was born, so cooking, the one practical art I had been taught in the Castle, was superfluous. They found household tasks for me, but they were all makework, and they and I knew it. I was perfectly willing to look after the babies, but one of the grandmothers was very jealous of that privilege, and also some of my sisters' wives were uneasy about a man touching their baby. My sister Pado broached the possibility of an apprenticeship in the clay-works, and I leaped at the chance; but the managers of the Pottery, after long discussion, were unable to agree to accept men as employes. Their hormones would make male workers unreliable, and female workers would be uncomfortable, and so on.

The holonews was full of such proposals and discussions, of course, and orations about the unforeseen consequences of the Open Gate Law, the proper place of men, male capacities and limitations, gender as destiny. Feeling against the Open Gate policy ran very strong, and it seemed that every time I watched the holo there was a woman talking grimly about the inherent violence and irresponsibility of the male, his biological unfitness to participate in social and political decision-making. Often it was a man saying the same things. Opposition to the new law had the fervent support of all the conservatives in the Castles, who pleaded eloquently for the gates to be closed and men to return to their proper station, pursuing the true, masculine glory of the games and the fuckeries.

Glory did not tempt me, after the years at Rakedr Castle; the word itself had come to mean degradation to me. I ranted against the games and competitions, puzzling most of my family, who loved to watch the Maingames and wrestling, and complained only that the level of excellence of most of the teams had declined since the gates were opened. And I ranted against the fuckeries, where, I said, men were used as cattle, stud bulls, not as human beings. I would never go there again.

"But my dear boy," my mother said at last, alone with me one evening, "will you live the rest of your life celibate?"

"I hope not," I said.

"Then…?"

"I want to get married."

Her eyes widened. She brooded a bit, and finally ventured, "To a man."

"No. To a woman. I want a normal, ordinary marriage. I want to have a wife and be a wife."

Shocking as the idea was, she tried to absorb it. She pondered, frowning.

"All it means," I said, for I had had a long time with nothing to do but ponder, "is that we'd live together just like any married pair. We'd set up our own daughterhouse, and be faithful to each other, and if she had a child I'd be its lovemother along with her. There isn't any reason why it wouldn't work!"

"Well, I don't know – I don't know of any," said my mother, gentle and judicious, and never happy at saying no to me. "But you do have to find the woman, you know."

"I know," I said, glumly.

"It's such a problem for you to meet people," she said. "Perhaps if you went to the fuckery…? I don't see why your own motherhouse couldn't guarantee you just as well as a Castle. We could try – ?"

But I passionately refused. Not being one of Fassaw's sycophants, I had seldom been allowed to go to the fuckery; and my few experiences there had been unfortunate. Young, inexperienced, and without recommendation, I had been selected by older women who wanted a plaything. Their practiced skill at arousing me had left me humiliated and enraged. They patted and tipped me as they left. That elaborate, mechanical excitation and their condescending coldness was vile to me, after the tenderness of my lover-protectors in the Castle. Yet women attracted me physically as men never had; the beautiful bodies of my sisters and their wives, all around me constantly now, clothed and naked, innocent and sensual, the wonderful heaviness and strength and softness of women's bodies, kept me continually aroused. Every night I masturbated, fantasizing my sisters in my arms. It was unendurable. Again I was a ghost, a raging, yearning impotence in the midst of untouchable reality.

I began to think I would have to go back to the Castle. I sank into a deep depression, an inertia, a chill darkness of the mind.

My family, anxious, affectionate, busy, had no idea what to do for me or with me. I think most of them thought in their hearts that it would be best if I went back through the gate.

One afternoon my sister Pado, with whom I had been closest as a child, came to my room – they had cleared out a dormer attic for me, so that I had room at least in the literal sense. She found me in my now constant lethargy, lying on the bed doing nothing at all. She breezed in, and with the indifference women often showed to moods and signals, plumped down on the foot of the bed and said, "Hey, what do you know about the man who's here from the Ekumen?"

I shrugged and shut my eyes. I had been having rape fantasies lately. I was afraid of her.

She talked on about the offworlder, who was apparently in Rakedr to study the Mutiny. "He wants to talk to the resistance," she said. "Men like you. The men who opened the gates. He says they won't come forward, as if they were ashamed of being heroes."

"Heroes!" I said. The word in my language is gendered female. It refers to the semi-divine, semi-historic protagonists of the Epics.

"It's what you are," Pado said, intensity breaking through her assumed breeziness. "You took responsibility in a great act. Maybe you did it wrong. Sassume did it wrong in the Founding of Emmo, didn't she, she let Faradr get killed. But she was still a hero. She took the responsibility. So did you. You ought to go talk to this Alien. Tell him what happened. Nobody really knows what happened at the Castle. You owe us the story."

That was a powerful phrase, among my people. "The untold story mothers the lie," was the saying. The doer of any notable act was held literally accountable for it to the community.

"So why should I tell it to an Alien?" I said, defensive of my inertia.

"Because he'll listen," my sister said drily. "We're all too damned busy."

It was profoundly true. Pado had seen a gate for me and opened it; and I went through it, having just enough strength and sanity left to do so.

Mobile Noem was a man in his forties, born some centuries earlier on Terra, trained on Hain, widely travelled; a small, yellowbrown, quick-eyed person, very easy to talk to. He did not seem at all masculine to me, at first; I kept thinking he was a woman, because he acted like one. He got right to business, with none of the maneuvering to assert his authority or jockeying for position that men of my society felt obligatory in any relationship with another man. I was used to men being wary, indirect, and competitive. Noem, like a woman, was direct and receptive. He was also as subtle and powerful as any man or woman I had known, even Ragaz. His authority was in fact immense; but he never stood on it. He sat down on it, comfortably, and invited you to sit down with him.

I was the first of the Rakedr mutineers to come forward and tell our story to him. He recorded it, with my permission, to use in making his report to the Stabiles on the condition of our society, "the matter of Seggri," as he called it. My first description of the Mutiny took less than an hour. I thought I was done. I didn't know, then, the inexhaustible desire to learn, to understand, to hear all the story, that characterizes the Mobiles of the Ekumen. Noem asked questions, I answered; he speculated and extrapolated, I corrected; he wanted details, I furnished them – telling the story of the Mutiny, of the years before it, of the men of the Castle, of the women of the Town, of my people, of my life – little by little, bit by bit, all in fragments, a muddle. I talked to Noem daily for a month. I learned that the story has no beginning, and no story has an end. That the story is all muddle, all middle. That the story is never true, but that the lie is indeed a child of silence.

By the end of the month I had come to love and trust Noem, and of course to depend on him. Talking to him had become my reason for being. I tried to face the fact that he would not stay in Rakedr much longer. I must learn to do without him. Do what? There were things for men to do, ways for men to live, he proved it by his mere existence; but could I find them?

He was keenly aware of my situation, and would not let me withdraw, as I began to do, into the lethargy of fear again; he would not let me be silent. He asked me impossible questions. "What would you be if you could be anything?" he asked me, a question children ask each other.

I answered at once, passionately – "A wife!"

I know now what the flicker that crossed his face was. His quick, kind eyes watched me, looked away, looked back.

"I want my own family," I said. "Not to live in my mothers' house, where I'm always a child. Work. A wife, wives – children – to be a mother. I want life, not games!"

"You can't bear a child," he said gently.

"No, but I can mother one!"

"We gender the word," he said. "I like it better your way.... But tell me, Ardar, what are the chances of your marrying – meeting a woman willing to marry a man? It hasn't happened, here, has it?"

I had to say no, not to my knowledge.

"It will happen, certainly, I think," he said (his certainties were always uncertain). "But the personal cost, at first, is likely to be high. Relationships formed against the negative pressure of a society are under terrible strain; they tend to become defensive, over-intense, unpeaceful. They have no room to grow."

"Room!" I said. And I tried to tell him my feeling of having no room in my world, no air to breathe.

He looked at me, scratching his nose; he laughed. "There's plenty of room in the galaxy, you know," he said.

"Do you mean... I could... that the Ekumen..." I didn't even know what the question I wanted to ask was. Noem did. He began to answer it thoughtfully and in detail. My education so far had been so limited, even as regards the culture of my own people, that I would have to attend a college for at least two or three years, in order to be ready to apply to an offworld institution such as the Ekumenical Schools on Hain. Of course, he went on, where I went and what kind of training I chose would depend on my interests, which I would go to a college to discover, since neither my schooling as a child nor my training at the Castle had really given me any idea of what there was to be interested in. The choices offered me had been unbelievably limited, addressing neither the needs of a normally intelligent person nor the needs of my society. And so the Open Gate Law instead of giving me freedom had left me "with no air to breathe but airless Space," said Noem, quoting some poet from some planet somewhere. My head was spinning, full of stars. "Hagka College is quite near Rakedr," Noem said, "did you never think of applying? If only to escape from your terrible Castle?"

I shook my head. "Lord Fassaw always destroyed the application forms when they were sent to his office. If any of us had tried to apply..."

"You would have been punished. Tortured, I suppose. Yes. Well, from the little I know of your colleges, I think your life there would be better than it is here, but not altogether pleasant. You will have work to do, a place to be; but you will be made to feel marginal, inferior. Even highly educated, enlightened women have difficulty accepting men as their intellectual equals. Believe me, I have experienced it myself! And because you were trained at the Castle to compete, to want to excel, you may find it hard to be among people who either believe you incapable of excellence, or to whom the concept of competition, of winning and defeating, is valueless. But just there, there is where you will find air to breathe."

Noem recommended me to women he knew on the faculty of Hagka College, and I was enrolled on probation. My family were delighted to pay my tuition. I was the first of us to go to college, and they were genuinely proud of me.

As Noem had predicted, it was not always easy, but there were enough other men there that I found friends and was not caught in the paralysing isolation of the motherhouse. And as I took courage, I made friends among the women students, finding many of them unprejudiced and companionable. In my third year, one of them and I managed, tentatively and warily, to fall in love. It did not work very well or last very long, yet it was a great liberation for both of us, our liberation from the belief that the only communication or commonalty possible between us was sexual, that an adult man and woman had nothing to join them but their genitals. Emadr loathed the professionalism of the fuckery as I did, and our lovemaking was always shy and brief. Its true significance was not as a consummation of desire, but as proof that we could trust each other. Where our real passion broke loose was when we lay together talking, telling each other what our lives had been, how we felt about men and women and each other and ourselves, what our nightmares were, what our dreams were. We talked endlessly, in a communion that I will cherish and honor all my life, two young souls finding their wings, flying together, not for long, but high. The first flight is the highest.

Emadr has been dead two hundred years; she stayed on Seggri, married into a motherhouse, bore two children, taught at Hagka, and died in her seventies. I went to Hain, to the Ekumenical Schools, and later to Werel and Yeowe as part of the Mobile's staff; my record is herewith enclosed. I have written this sketch of my life as part of my application to return to Seggri as a Mobile of the Ekumen. I want very

much to live among my people, to learn who they are, now that I
know with at least an uncertain certainty who I am.

About the Authors

ELEANOR ARNASON

Eleanor Arnason has published five novels and over a dozen short stories. Her fourth novel, *A Woman of the Iron People*, co-won the first Tiptree Award. "The Lovers" is one of a series of stories which pretend to be fiction written by an alien species, the *hwarhath*. When complete, this group of stories will form a collection titled *Ten Examples of Contemporary Hwarhath Fiction*. Arnason lives in Minneapolis with her long time companion, Patrick Arden Wood, and their stuffed sheep, Seymour.

L. TIMMEL DUCHAMP

L. Timmel Duchamp's fiction first appeared in the Crossing Press's feminist SF anthology, *Memories and Visions* (ed. Susanna Sturgis, 1989). Since then she's made more than two dozen short fiction sales to a variety of anthologies and magazines, including *Asimov's SF,* the *Magazine of Fantasy and Science Fiction*, and *Dying for It* (ed. Gardner Dozois, HarperPrism, 1997). She has work forthcoming in 1998 in *Bending the Landscape* (ed. Nicola Griffith and Stephen Pagel, Overlook Press), *Leviathan,* and *Asimov's SF.* It is her pleasure to live in Seattle, a city that offers the company of a number of fine feminist writers.

CAROL EMSHWILLER

I guess the important thing is that I have another novel coming out in July. *Leaping Man Hill.* A sequel to *Ledoyt.* Not science fiction or fantasy. Another cowboy story. But I've gone back to "fantasy" now. (I hate that word because it always suggests sword and sorcery.) I wanted to get back to science fictionish stuff for a change, and besides, Ursula Le Guin said do something from the point of view of a horse. I told her – wrote her – no, I couldn't possibly do that, but all of a sudden here I am doing it. And it's gotten to be 90 pages and not even a little bit finished yet.

I'm still teaching at N.Y.U. Continuing Ed. I'm spending every summer in California playing cowboy.

KELLEY ESKRIDGE

Kelley Eskridge's fiction has appeared in *Century*, *The Magazine of Fantasy and Science Fiction* and *Little Deaths*. "Alien Jane" won the Astraea National Lesbian Action Foundation Writer's Award and was a finalist for the Nebula Award. "And Salome Danced" was reprinted in *The 1996 Year's Best Lesbian Erotica*. She recently sold her first novel, *Solitaire*.

PETER HAMILTON

In 1987 wrote my first short story, now shredded, burnt, and spread over my vegetable garden. I did it mainly to escape from bad jobs on the production lines at the local plastics factories, which were interspersed with long periods of unemployment. First novel, *Mindstar Rising* was sold to Macmillan, and published in 1993, followed by *A Quantum Murder* in 1994, *The Nano Flower* in 1995, *The Reality Dysfunction*, 1996, and *The Neutronium Alchemist* in 1997. My collection of short stories and a novella, *A Second Chance at Eden*, is due out summer 1998.

I've collaborated twice with Graham Joyce on short stories, which is always a fun experience. Fortunately our strengths and weaknesses do seem to correspond particularly well. One day, we keep saying to each other, we'll do a novel together.

GRAHAM JOYCE

Three-times winner of the August Derleth Award *Dark Sister* (1992) *Requiem* (1995) *The Tooth Fairy* (1996), these last two published by Tor in the US. Graham Joyce quit an executive job and went to the Greek island of Lesbos to live in a beach shack with a colony of scorpions (setting for *House of Lost Dreams* 1993) to concentrate on writing. Sold first novel *Dreamside* (1991) while still in Greece and travelled in the Middle East on proceeds. Forthcoming novel *The Stormwatcher* scheduled for publication March 1998 by Penguin UK. He has also published a children's SF novel *Spiderbite* (1997). His short stories have appeared in several anthologies and his novels have been widely translated.

He lives in Leicester UK with his wife and daughter.

JAMES PATRICK KELLY
James Patrick Kelly is the author of four novels and more than fifty short stories. His most recent book is *Think Like a Dinosaur and Other Stories* from Golden Gryphon Press. The title story won the Hugo in 1996. He served on the Tiptree Jury in 1997.

URSULA K. LE GUIN
Ursula Kroeber was born in 1929 in Berkeley, California, where she grew up. Her parents were the anthropologist Alfred Kroeber and the author Theodora Kroeber, author of *Ishi*. She married Charles A. Le Guin, a historian, in Paris in 1953; they have lived in Portland, Oregon, since 1958, and have three children and three grandchildren.

Ursula K. Le Guin has written poetry and fiction all her life. Her first publications were poems, and in the 1960s she began to publish short stories and novels. She writes both poetry and prose, and in various modes including realistic fiction, science fiction, fantasy, young children's books, books for young adults, screenplays, essays, verbal texts for musicians, and voicetexts for performance or recording. As of 1997 she has published over a hundred short stories (collected in eight volumes), two collections of essays, ten books for children, five volumes of poetry, two of translation, and sixteen novels. Among the honors her writing has received are a National Book Award, five Hugo and five Nebula Awards, the Kafka Award, a Pushcart Prize, the Howard Vursell Award of the American Academy of Arts and Letters, etc.

Her occupations, she says, are writing, reading, housework, and teaching. She is a feminist, a conservationist, and a Western American, passionately involved with West Coast literature, landscape, and life.

IAN R. MACLEOD
I was born in the West Midlands of England in 1956, and, with one or two short-lived excursions to other parts of the country, have lived most of my life here. My father's family come from the Isle of Lewis, hence the Scottish name, whilst my mother's family are from the Mid-

lands. I made my first sale to *Weird Tales* in 1989 with my story, "1/72nd Scale," which ended up being nominated for the Nebula Award. I've also been nominated for the British Science Fiction Association Award for my story "Returning."

I love music of all kinds, dog-walking, fell-walking, and wish I could fit in more time to get somewhere with photography and painting.

IAN MCDONALD

Born in England to a Irish mother, a Scottish father, I've lived most of my life in Northern Ireland, where these things matter. I used to live in a house built in the back garden of C.S. Lewis's childhood home – checked all the wardrobes, I recently moved into central Belfast to be closer to the action. I sold my first story in 1982, first novel was *Desolation Road* in 1988. I think of myself not so much as a writer as a language sampler and remixer. The most recent is *Kirinya*, a sequel to 1995's *Evolution's Shore*, and I'm now starting a mainstream book.

R GARCIA Y ROBERTSON

Author of *The Spiral Dance* (1991), *The Virgin and the Dinosaur* (1996), *Atlantis Found* (1997), *American Woman* (1998), and *The Moon Maid and Other Fantastic Adventures* (1998) as well as over forty articles and short stories. Born in Oakland, California, he is curently a single father with two children, living in a cabin in the woods in Mt. Vernon, Washington

DELIA SHERMAN

Delia Sherman is a writer and editor living in Boston, MA. She is the author of numerous short stories, of the novels *Through a Brazen Mirror* and *The Porcelain Dove* (which won the Mythopoeic Award), and, with Ellen Kushner, co-author of "The Fall of the Kings" in *Bending the Landscape* and co-editor of *The Horns of Elfland: An Anthology of Music and Magic*.

LISA TUTTLE

Born in Houston, Texas in 1952; lived for awhile in Austin, and then in London; now living on the wild west coast of Scotland with my family. Sold my first short stories in the early 70s and have made my living, such as it is, from writing since 1980. Have had three short story collections published (in the UK, but not in the US) and the novels *Windhaven* (co-written with George R.R. Martin), *Familiar Spirit, Gabriel, Lost Futures,* and *The Pillow Friend* (White Wolf, 1996). I've also written non-fiction works including *Encyclopedia of Feminism* (1984) and *Heroines: Women Inspired by Women* and, for children; a dark fantasy *Panther in Argyll* (1996 – US only).

James Tiptree, Jr Award
Winners & Shortlist

:::

Margaret Atwood, *The Robber Bride*, Bantam Books, 1993
Sybil Claiborne, *In the Garden of Dead Cars,* Cleis Press, 1993
L. Timmel Duchamp, "Motherhood, Etc." in *Full Spectrum* 4, Bantam, 1993
R. Garcia y Robertson, "The Other Magpie," *Asimov's*, 4/1993
James Patrick Kelly, "Chemistry," *Asimov's*, 6/1993
Laurie J. Marks, *Dancing Jack*, DAW, 1993
Ian McDonald, "Some Strange Desire," in *The Best of Omni III*, Omni Publications International Ltd.
Alice Nunn, *Illicit Passage,* Women's Redress Press, 1992
Paul Park, *Coelestis*, Harper Collins, 1993

1994 WINNERS
Ursula K. Le Guin "The Matter of Seggri," *Crank!* #3, 1994
Nancy Springer, *Larque on the Wing*, AvoNova, 1994

1994 SHORTLIST
Eleanor Arnason, "The Lovers," *Asimov's*, 7/1994
Suzy McKee Charnas, *The Furies*, Tor, 1994
L. Warren Douglas, *Cannon's Orb*, Del Rey, 1994
Greg Egan, "Cocoon," *Asimov's*, 5/1994
Ellen Frye, *Amazon Story Bones,* Spinsters Ink, 1994
Gwyneth Jones, *North Wind,* Gollancz, 1994
Graham Joyce & Peter F. Hamilton, "Eat Reecebread," *Interzone*, 8/1994
Ursula K. Le Guin, "Forgiveness Day," *Asimov's*, 11/1994
Ursula K. Le Guin, *A Fisherman of the Inland Sea*, Harper, 1994
Rachel Pollack, *Temporary Agency*, St. Martin's, 1994
Geoff Ryman, *Unconquered Countries*, St. Martin's, 1994
Melissa Scott, *Trouble and Her Friends*, Tor, 1994
Delia Sherman, "Young Woman in a Garden" in *Xanadu* 2, Tor, 1994
George Turner, *Genetic Soldier*, Morrow, 1994

1995 WINNERS
Waking the Moon, by Elizabeth Hand, HarperPrism, 1995
The Memoirs of Elizabeth Frankenstein, by Theodore Roszak, Random House, 1995

1995 SHORTLIST

Kelley Eskridge, "And Salome Danced" in *Little Deaths*, ed. Ellen
Datlow, *Millennium*, 1994; Dell Abyss, 1995

Kit Reed, *Little Sisters of the Apocalypse*, Black Ice Books, 1994

Lisa Tuttle, "Food Man," *Crank!* #4, Fall, 1994

Terri Windling, ed., *The Armless Maiden and Other Stories for
Childhood's Survivors*, Tor, 1995

1996 WINNERS

Ursula K. Le Guin, "Mountain Ways," *Asimov's*, August 1996

Mary Doria Russell, *The Sparrow*, Random House, 1996

1996 SHORTLIST

Fred Chappell, "The Silent Woman" from his novel *Farewell, I'm
Bound to Leave You*, St. Martin's, 1996

Suzy McKee Charnas, "Beauty and the Opera, or The Phantom
Beast," *Asimov's*, March, 1996

L. Timmel Duchamp, "Welcome, Kid, to the Real World," *Tales of
the Unanticipated*, Spring/Summer/Fall, 1996

Alasdair Gray, *A History Maker*, Canongate Press 1994; revised edi-
tion Harcourt Brace, 1996

Jonathan Lethem, "Five Fucks," in his collection *The Wall of the
Sky, The Wall of the Eye*, Harcourt Brace, 1996

Pat Murphy, *Nadya*, Tor, 1996

Rachel Pollack, *Godmother Night*, St. Martin's, 1996

Lisa Tuttle, *The Pillow Friend*, White Wolf, 1996

Tess Williams, "And She Was the Word," *Eidolon*, Winter, 1996

Sue Woolfe, *Leaning Towards Infinity*, Vintage, 1996

1997 WINNERS

Candas Jane Dorsey, *Black Wine*, Tor, 1997

Kelly Link, "Travels With The Snow Queen," *Lady Churchill's Rosebud Wristlet*, Winter, volume 1, Issue 1

1997 SHORT LIST: SHORT FICTION

Storm Constantine, "The Oracle Lips" in *The Fortune Teller*, ed.
Lawrence Schimel & Martin H. Greenberg, Daw Books, 1997

L. Timmel Duchamp, "The Apprenticeship of Isabetta di Pietro Cavazzi" in *Asimov's*, September 1997
Paul Di Filippo, "Alice, Alfie, Ted and the Aliens," *Interzone*, March 1997
Gwyneth Jones, "Balinese Dancer," *Asimov's*, September 1997
Salman Rushdie, "The Firebird's Nest," *New Yorker*, June 23 and 30, 1997

1997 SHORT LIST: NOVELS
Emma Donoghue, *Kissing the Witch: Old Tales in New Skins*, HarperCollins, 1997
Molly Gloss, *The Dazzle of Day*, Tor, 1997
John M. Harrison, *Signs of Life*, St. Martin's Press, 1997
Ian McDonald, *Sacrifice of Fools*, Victor Gonzallencz, 1996.
Vonda N. McIntyre, *The Moon and the Sun* , Pocket Books, 1997
Shani Mootoo, *Cereus Blooms at Night*, Press Gang Publishers, 1996
Paul Witcover, *Waking Beauty*, HarperPrism, 1997

RETROSPECTIVE AWARD WINNERS
Suzy McKee Charnas, *Walk to the End of the World* , 1974
Suzy McKee Charnas, *Motherlines*, 1978
Ursula K. Le Guin, *The Left Hand of Darkness*, 1969
Joanna Russ, *We Who Are About to...*, 1975, 1976, 1977
Joanna Russ, *The Female Man*, 1975

RETROSPECTIVE AWARD SHORT LIST
Margaret Atwood, *The Handmaid's Tale*
Iain Banks, *The Wasp Factory*
Katherine Burdekin, *Swastika Night*
Octavia Butler, *Wild Seed*
Samuel R. Delany, *Babel-17*
Samuel R. Delany, *Triton*
Carol Emshwiller, *Carmen Dog*
Sony Dorman Hess, "When I Was Miss Dow," reprinted in *Women of Wonder: The Classic Years*
Elizabeth Lynn, *Watchtower*

Vonda N. McIntyre, *Dreamsnake*
Naomi Mitchison, *Memoirs of a Spacewoman*
Marge Piercy, *Woman on the Edge of Time*
Joanna Russ, *The Two of Them*
Pamela Sargent, ed., anthologies: *Women of Wonder, More Women of Wonder, New Women of Wonder*
John Varley, *The Barbie Murders*
Kate Wilhelm, *The Clewiston Test*
Monique Wittig, *Les Guérillères,* translated by David Le Vay
Pamela Zoline, "The Heat Death of the Universe," reprinted in *Women of Wonder: The Classic Years*

In some years the jury also chose to identify a "long list" of books considered for the award. These lists and other information about the award can be found on our website at

www.sf3.org/tiptree/index.html

or by sending a stamped, self-addressed envelope to: Jeanne Gomoll, 2825 Union Street, Madison, WI 52704.

THE JAMES TIPTREE JR. AWARD IS ADMINISTERED by the James Tiptree Jr. Literary Award Council, a nonprofit organization dedicated to the exploration and expansion of gender roles in science fiction and fantasy literature. You too can be a member of the Secret Feminist Cabal: for more information about the award, or to send tax-deductible donations, please write to:

The James Tiptree Jr. Literary Award Council
680 66th Street
Oakland, CA 94609

The text type is Sabon, with titles in ITC Stoclet and ITC Rennie Mackintosh. Sabon was designed in 1966 by Jan Tschichold, based on the 16th-century types of Claude Garamond. It was designed to be a functional and elegant text type that could be used simultaneously in hot metal on Monotype and Linotype typesetting machines and for hand-setting in metal foundry type. This is Linotype's digitized version of the typeface. ITC Rennie Mackintosh was designed in 1996 by Phill Grimshaw, based on the hand-lettering on the architectural drawings of Charles Rennie Mackintosh, with ornaments taken from details of Mackintosh's buildings. ITC Stoclet was also designed by Grimshaw, in 1998, based on lettering of the Vienna Sezession.